T0038426

Anthologies edited by Jim Butcher and Kerrie L. Hughes

SHADOWED SOULS
HEROIC HEARTS

PRAISE FOR JIM BUTCHER AND THE DRESDEN FILES

"Butcher is the dean of contemporary urban fantasy." —*Booklist*

"Think *Buffy the Vampire Slayer* starring Philip Marlowe."
—*Entertainment Weekly*

PRAISE FOR PATRICIA BRIGGS

"Patricia Briggs is an incredible writer. . . . I love hanging out with the amazing characters in this series!" —*New York Times* bestselling author Nalini Singh

"[Briggs] spins tales of werewolves, coyote shifters, and magic and, my, does she do it well." —*USA Today*

PRAISE FOR CHARLAINE HARRIS

"[Harris is] the Mark Twain of things that live under your bed." —*Houston Press*

PRAISE FOR KELLEY ARMSTRONG

"Armstrong is a talented and original writer whose inventiveness and sense of the bizarre is arresting." —*The London Free Press*

HEROIC HEARTS

Edited by

JIM BUTCHER
and KERRIE L. HUGHES

ACE
New York

ACE
Published by Berkley
An imprint of Penguin Random House LLC
penguinrandomhouse.com

Library of Congress Cataloging-in-Publication Data

Names: Butcher, Jim, 1971– editor. | Hughes, Kerrie, editor.
Title: Heroic hearts / edited by Jim Butcher and Kerrie L. Hughes.
Description: New York: Ace, 2022.
Identifiers: LCCN 2021034760 (print) | LCCN 2021034761 (ebook) |
ISBN 9780593099186 (trade paperback) | ISBN 9780593099193 (ebook)
Subjects: LCSH: Fantasy fiction, American. | Short stories, American. |
LCGFT: Fantasy fiction. | Paranormal fiction. | Short stories.
Classification: LCC PS648.F3 H47 2022 (print) |
LCC PS648.F3 (ebook) | DDC 813/.0876608—dc23
LC record available at https://lccn.loc.gov/2021034760
LC ebook record available at https://lccn.loc.gov/2021034761

First Edition: May 2022

Printed in the United States of America
2nd Printing

Roxanne Longstreet Conrad, aka Rachel Caine, Roxy to her friends, was supposed to be in this anthology. Sadly, she died November 1, 2020, the Day of the Dead, an appropriate day for the creator of the Morganville Vampires to leave us.

Roxy was careful with all of us who loved her. She made sure we knew about her sarcoma and how she was doing and what her challenges were. She took care of people in that way. Not just her friends, but fellow writers, budding writers, and her readers too.

She was one of those rare people who never put anyone down. She made frequent public appearances at conventions, said yes to people who wanted something signed, and gave good advice to anyone who asked. She made you feel like she was listening and cared, because she did.

She was, and always will be, a hero. We dedicate this collection to her memory.

We miss you, Roxanne.

CONTENTS

INTRODUCTION

Hero, noun
   1. a person who is admired or idealized for courage,
outstanding achievements, or noble qualities
   2. a sandwich

Heroes have fascinated humanity since we started telling stories. They became even more fascinating when we started writing the stories down—and achieved the status previously reserved for pantheons of deities when we started putting them on the big screen. Heroes have become big business.

But heroes, real heroes, aren't titans or icons.

Real heroes are standing behind cash registers, starting cold trucks, getting kids out of bed. They're the everyday humans who happen to be standing there when something bad happens, and when there is a sudden need for skill, courage, or intelligence. They're the regular people in irregular circumstances who find themselves considering others first and standing up to do whatever needs to be done.

Real heroes are created by fate—faced with a challenge that they must rise to overcome, and those who do so become our heroes, our stories, our legends.

It's not complicated to be a hero. It's not easy, but it isn't complicated either. All that's required is that you do the right thing, even when it's difficult. Even when it's hard. Even when it's scary.

Heroes are important because they give us an example of what to do when we find ourselves faced with circumstances that require us to become something more. They're important because we never know when we will be the one faced with the difficult choice, the sudden test, the critical task. Each of us will find ourselves in a position to be a hero in our lives from time to time. Each of us will have to choose whether or not to step up.

The only question is what choice you're going to make.

Enjoy the stories, everyone. I think I'm going to go have a sandwich.

—Jim Butcher

FOREWORD

What makes a hero? Is it a person who goes above and beyond to save someone? Or someone who dedicates their life to a higher purpose? Perhaps it's just an honorific for anyone who does something unselfishly at the right time.

Personally, I've saved a baby from choking, stopped a kid from getting hit by a car, and done volunteer work, counseling work, and a wide range of customer service. I know customer service doesn't sound like a heroic task, but I have never had more people tell me I was their hero than when I was solving their problems with phones, insurance bills, and food stamps. Maybe the time I gave my cat the Heimlich maneuver when she was choking on a chicken bone qualifies. She certainly thought so.

I wanted to assemble a collection of hopeful stories about courage, bravery, codes to live by, and people you can trust. For this volume I got three main themes: animals, monster fighters, and wise hermits. I'm sure this is because the events of the last few years have given us an appreciation of our animal friends, people who fight injustice, and this odd state of lockdown we've been experiencing. I can tell you that producing stories during 2020 was a challenge for every person in this anthology. I'm very happy about how this turned out. I really needed an anthology about heroes with good hearts. We all need to be reminded that they exist.

Enjoy the stories.

—Kerrie L. Hughes

HEROIC HEARTS

LITTLE THINGS

by Jim Butcher

My name is Major General Toot-Toot Minimus, sprite in service to Sir Harry Dresden, Knight of the Winter Court and Wizard of Chicago, and captain of his personal guard. When the skies darken with smoke and ash, when wails of wrong and woe rend the night, when my lord goes to war with titans and unspeakable horrors from Outside of reality, someone must protect him from threats too small to readily discern.

That is my place: not at my lord's side, but at his ankles.

In the days since my lord had defeated a mad goddess in single combat and claimed his Castle as reward, pizza deliveries had been spotty. The troops had begun to express concern. They had, after all, fought for their right to pizza. Castle stores of inferior frozen stuff could only last so long.

There was a dark mortal entity my lord called a conomee. The conomee was very bad, because of all the rubble and the blocked streets after the Battle. Battles make conomees that were once good very bad. Now the bad conomee was preventing pizza from being delivered.

It was a matter of grave concern.

The troops talked in fearful whispers about the conomee all of the time.

"My lord," I said politely. "The troops are worried about the conomee again."

My lord opened one of his eyes and blew out a little breath from between his lips. He had been sitting on a pillow on the floor doing absolutely nothing, which was why I had picked this moment to speak to him. His hair was mussy. There were circles under his eyes. He wore a cast on one arm and had an ankle wrapped so heavily that it was almost as big.

"Toot," he said in a bleary voice. "I am meditating."

He hadn't been doing anything at all when I spoke to him, so he must have meant some other time. "When?" I asked.

He bowed his head forward sharply and sighed. Then he looked up at me and gave me a tired smile. "Shall we go put a couple of pizzas in the oven?"

"That would ease tensions greatly," I told him in my most serious voice. It was good to be very serious when bringing matters to my lord, so that he knew I would not bother him with trivial things.

"Give me a second," he said. I waited for practically forever while he unfolded himself from where he'd been sitting and clambered slowly to his feet.

My lord did not look well. Death had come for his lady during the Battle. At night, he would shut the world away from his chambers, and though he would sleep for hours and hours he never seemed rested. He moved as though the weight of an ocean pressed down on his shoulders.

"Right," he said in a rough voice a moment later. "To the kitchen." There was a rustling sound behind him. A second later, a large, gray, bobtailed tomcat named Mister brushed past his ankles, apparently in an attempt to trip him. My lord absorbed the assault with the reflexes of long practice and started walking. He stumped slowly through the hallways of the Castle, down to the kitchens in the first basement.

I did not like the kitchens. Everything was made of the Bane, which seemed completely unnecessary. Couldn't they have made it out of plastic? My lord assured me that the Bane helped keep mortals safe from illness, but I did not see how. One of the mortal refugees who was residing in the guest quarters of the Castle had left a little cloth catnip mouse out for Mister, who had become the mascot of everyone staying in the Castle. He received all the petting he wished, from which he always seemed smug. The old tomcat pounced upon the mouse happily and began batting it methodically around the large kitchen floor.

My lord tightened the belt of his robe, shivering a little against the Castle's cold as he started the ovens and walked into the freezer to emerge with a pair of frozen pizzas. He hit the switch on a battered, ancient-looking box, and very fancy-sounding human music came out of it, all crackly, like it was on the other side of a large fire.

It is not my place to judge why my lord likes his music crackly. He is a wizard. They're weird.

He waited until the ovens were warm and then slid both pizzas in and twisted a little plastic dial on a plastic box and it started ticking.

Then he put his face in his hands, hunched his shoulders, and was silent.

I wanted to offer him comfort. I think that was the right thing to do. But I'd only been aware of death for a little while. It wasn't a topic I could really discuss with any of my friends among the Little People. Death was not a topic they could really think about, which made conversations about it difficult. Death wasn't a part of the Little People's world.

Just mine.

My lord had lost his lady. And I knew that made him sad. But I didn't think I understood all the reasons why. I didn't know how to comfort a friend who was hurting like he was. I hadn't ever hurt like that, myself. When the other Little People tried to cheer me up, sometimes it hurt on the inside. I didn't want to say or do the wrong thing and hurt my lord's feelings even more by mistake.

Death is really complicated.

There was a soft buzz of wings, and my love Lacuna landed beside me. She was wearing her traveling armor, which was all black leather, and her dark hair was trailing behind her in a braid as long as she was. Her wings looked very pretty. Of the Little People she was one of the few who were as tall as me. She fought ferociously, and I had some scars to prove it.

"Hello, lickspittle of my dreadful captor," Lacuna said in her dreamy monotone. She wasn't shouting, so my lord probably wasn't going to hear her unless he was paying special attention. "Once again, I present myself to you for humiliation."

"You think even pizza is humiliating, my love," I said.

She folded her arms and hunched her shoulders. "The pizza of a captive is little better than death. And it isn't good for your teeth."

"You lost fair and square and got captured!" I told her. "Those were the rules!"

"I am bound to serve your lord, as he defeated my lord," Lacuna replied in a dark tone. "I must serve. I need not like it."

Biggun footsteps came down the hall, and Sir William, who served my lord, poked his head into the kitchen. Sir William was not tall for a human, but looked very square and strong, as if he would be able to hold up the corner of the Castle if that block there failed.

"Harry?" Will called. "Oh, hey."

My lord mopped his hands over his face and looked up. His face was red, especially his nose and eyes. "Will."

"The Velasquezes' little girl is out of the hospital," Will said. "They're bringing her back here tonight."

A faint smile touched my lord's face. "Oh, thank God. Fever broke?"

Sir William nodded, returning the smile. "After Michael Carpenter visited."

Dark creases appeared in the skin at the corner of my lord's eyes for a moment. "Well, obviously." He raised his voice. "Bob?"

For a second, nothing happened. Then a point of blue light appeared and flickered within the stone of the Castle's walls, as if the solid rock had become translucent. A voice emanated from the stone, piping, "Here, boss!"

Mister flew across the kitchen floor, bounded upon a counter with a grace that belied his years, and pounced upon the blue light in the wall, paws flailing.

"Ack!" Bob said. "Harry! This isn't respectful!"

My lord gathered Mister up into his arms, and the big cat purred for a moment before flowing down to the floor again. "Bob, make sure the temperature in the Velasquezes' quarters stays warm and regulated tonight," he said. "Last thing I want is to get her back together with her parents and then have her take a chill and get sick again."

"Will do!" Bob the Castle answered, and the light vanished.

Mister looked about the kitchen for a moment, evidently hoping for the light to return, then flicked his stub of a tail and ambled away in disappointment.

"And actually there's the kitchen budget to go over," Will said. He held up a clipboard covered with the sheets of floppy wood that the humans love so much.

"Hell's bells," my lord said.

"I know, I know," Sir William said, "but there are thirty to fifty people eating here every meal, everything is spotty on deliveries, and prices are getting weird. It's gotta get done."

My lord checked the kitchen timer, nodded, and said, "I have a few minutes. Major General, I'll be back before the pizza is done and we'll take it up to the roof."

I saluted crisply. "Yes, my lord. I will guard the kitchen."

My lord and his castellan walked away on vital business beyond the ken of mere soldiers like me, their huge footsteps and low voices lingering long, long after they had passed.

"And now we wait to poison ourselves with pizza," Lacuna said in her flat, adorable way.

"Nonsense!" I replied. "It is my lord who poisons us!"

Mister batted his catnip mouse across the room and romped after it gamely. Lacuna and I had to flutter out of his way or risk injury. Though we had grown quite large, Mister was yet mighty and fell.

It was only after the buzz of our wings had faded that I heard the villains breach the Castle.

There was a distant, faint, but weirdly piercing hissing sound, a crackling, like bacon on a stove over a fire, and it chewed at the insides of my ears like tiny bugs running around in there. We had only been staying all night in the Castle for two weeks (and my lord said that's why it was called a fortnight!) but I had heard the enchanted stones of the Castle react in anger to invaders before.

Lacuna's head snapped around at the same time as mine—as did Mister's. The big tomcat let out a low, mewling growl, and his gray fur rose.

"We are under attack!" I cried. "The pizza must be guarded!"

Lacuna's blade whispered as it slithered free of its sheath. "Of course, the pizza must be guarded," she snapped affectionately. "I am without armor. You must be the vanguard. I will remain here."

"Aye, my love! Castle Bob!" I thundered.

A blue light that was a whole lot blurrier than when Harry had called it appeared. "Uh, what? Oh, hey, it's, uh . . . what's his name. That little guy that kept getting bigger. What's up, kid?"

"We are under attack!" I cried.

The blue light flickered more brightly for a moment, but then the voice said, "I am sure that's a bunch of hooey."

"Hooey!" I said, shocked. I was a Major General and the captain of the Za-Lord's Guard, after all. "You're hooey!"

"Kid, the defenses on this place are almost as thick as the island's. Nothing can get in here without me knowing it. Are you sure you're not just overly excited? Did you guys get into the Froot Loops again?"

"That was but once only!" I protested. "My lord must be warned!"

"Your lord must not be interrupted," Bob the Castle replied in a very smug and superior voice that I did not like even the smallest little bit. "He has important Wizard of Chicago stuff going on. Budget meetings."

I did not know what manner of monster a budget was, or how it might best be dispatched in order to free my lord's attention, but the hairs on my neck rose and my thumbs prickled until I was almost beside myself—the enemy was nigh.

"The enemy is nigh!" I shouted. "Can you not hear the sound?"

Mister came hurtling across the floor and pounced ferociously upon the blue light.

"Gah!" it said. "I don't have enough to do running this place, with sprites and cats trying to humiliate me every time I turn around!"

"Useless spirit!" I cursed him, drew my sword, and leapt into the air.

I drew the whistle I used to coordinate the movements of my lord's Guard and started piping on it as hard as I could. It would be useless to alert any of the humans, since their ears were just too stupid to hear it, but any of my people would, and would come flying.

The Castle had been built for defense from the ground up. There were no staircases that stretched longer than a single floor. Invaders would have to take one staircase, fight their way the length of the Castle to the next, and so on. I shot down darkened corridors and up close-fit spiral staircases to the passage to the roof—and found it occupied by the enemy.

I had but an instant's warning before a shower of darts slithered through the air I would have been flying in, if I hadn't moved, and something greenish and covered in warty scales flew toward me. I banked and struck with all the power I could put behind my sword and felt the blade bite deep. There was a buzzy shriek, and the creature fell away from me.

"Taste steel, villain!" I howled, dodged more flung darts, and landed on the shoulder of a suit of armor, careful to avoid touching the Bane with my flesh, and took stock of the situation while crouched behind the helmet.

A carpet of creatures the size of sewer rats poured down the staircase from the roof. They were all of the same general caste but varied from one to the next—humanoids, covered in that leathery greenish skin, with flopping ears and oversized hands and feet. The features were exaggerated to various degrees of ridiculousness, but each one of them had the same sharp, vicious teeth, and the same sickly golden reptilian eyes. They wore armor, much as my Guard did, carried weapons and equipment— and I knew them, as they were an ancient foe of my folk.

"Gremlins most foul!" I shouted.

There was a thud as a larger form descended from the roof, this one nearly my size. He stood slowly, a gremlin larger and haler than the others, with but one eye and the other gone in a horrible mass of scars. Scar Eye gripped a human hatchet in both hands, and his cold gaze rose to meet mine.

"Pix," he said, in a voice made of ground asphalt and living beehives. "We have no need to do battle with your ilk. Stand aside."

"Foul gremlin, begone!" I shouted, pointing my sword at him. "You violate the rightfully won lands of my lord Dresden!"

The word rang with Power, and we were within his demesne. The gremlin flinched and snarled at the mention of my lord's name, before staring back at me with slowly growing, gleeful spite. "Then we *do* need to do battle. Ilk."

"*You're* an ilk!" I shouted furiously.

Four very large gremlins plunged down the stairs carrying a bulky package between them. It had rectangles connected to a small jug of liquid connected to spiraling wires connected to a round circle that went *tick tick tick*.

I felt my eyes open very wide.

That was a mortal device. I saw them on televisions and movies. Those were things that went boom.

Scar Eye looked from me to the boom device and back, his teeth showing even more in a slow, evil smile. "Kill the pix."

Gremlins howled like rabid beasts suddenly freed from cages and a cloud of spears flew at me. I dove away from my position on the suit of armor, spears clattering against the Bane behind me. Scar Eye waited for me to move, then seized a spear from one of his lackeys and flung it hard and true at the spot I would have been in if I hadn't been looking for the attack. Instead, I slapped the spear aside with my blade, spread my wings, caught myself just before hitting the floor, and darted down the hall with a small army of gremlins howling on my heels.

"Major General!" shouted a friendly voice.

I looked up to see Bluenose and Wobbleshanks in their dark, oil-slick-colored armor, spears in hand, wings a blur as they flew to my support and fell into formation on my flanks.

"We must slow the enemy and gather the Guard!" I shouted to them.

"Aye-aye, General!" Bluenose shouted. "The tapestry, sir!"

"The tapestry!" I shouted. "Come on!"

One of the humans standing guard during the night walked by in a cross hallway as we zipped toward him. I shouted at him—but like bigguns always do, he didn't notice. Shouting pixies, howling gremlins, death and doom hurtling down the hallways of the Castle—and the big stupid human doesn't even *notice*.

Sometimes it's like we have to hit you people with a rock just to get you to realize we're standing there.

We darted down the hallways toward the Great Hall, where workers had hung tapestries everywhere while they repaired a hole in the ceiling. The tapestries were of terrible quality, as they were simply blank canvas, and I felt that such artisanry was not to the standards of my lord, but for the purposes of the Guard, quantity was a quality all its own.

By then two dozen of the Guard had responded to my whistle, and as we soared into the hall, almost everyone was ready. I gave swift orders. The Guard split into teams of four, each seizing one of the large canvas tapestries, a weight that our wings could just barely manage, and my team led the way as we labored back toward the enemy.

We caught them at the bottom of the stairs from the top floor. "Za-Lord's Guard!" I shouted. "Follow me!"

Down we swept toward the foe, and as we did, we changed grip on the rolled tapestry, let it unfurl—and then dropped it like a massive net upon the gremlins. Down fell the blank tapestry, clunky and flapping, and dropped over a dozen of the enemy.

The other teams dove down as well, canvas falling everywhere, and Scar Eye howled his rage as his troops were bogged down.

"Blades!" I shouted.

Swords sprang from sheaths and spears whirled to couch as a double dozen of my folk shouted their defiance at the enemy.

"Dive!" I screamed, and led the way down toward the foe.

Gremlins are naturally wicked just as my own folk are naturally curious. They're tough, clever, vicious, practical—and relentless. Their armored hide makes them very tough to kill. Dark cousins of breeds like the cobbler gnomes, they shared those folks' cleverness with their hands but continuously turned their talents to mischief and destruction. Crude but sharp and effective blades appeared among them, and the foe began to cut their way free of the tapestries.

We met them with our svartalf-made faemetal blades as they

struggled to free themselves, and their pig iron could not withstand us. The foe outnumbered us three to one—but their three were stuck under big dumb tapestries and our one just started stabbing them right through the cloth.

We couldn't get them all—they were too tough to die fast enough. But we cut the numbers down to something like only two-to-one, just as Scar Eye emerged from beneath the corner of a tapestry and smashed Redcullen out of the air with his mortal hatchet, sending the Guardsman to a broken heap on the floor.

I screamed and threw myself at Scar Eye. He got the hatchet up in time to stop me from changing his name to No-Eyes, but I marked his cheek for him and drew blood from one of his forearms, and if two of his no-good cheating buddies hadn't gotten in the way, I might have finished him before he could recover his balance.

Then two more gremlins joined the first pair, and I was pressed too closely to fly and fighting for my life as gremlin weapons, made of the Bane, hammered at me, their sickly cold aura making my flesh recoil even when my armor stopped the blows, weakening my limbs and making them shake.

For a moment, things looked very bad. Then Bluenose was there, a sprite whose head came most of the way up my shoulder, his spear darting, and bought me a breath. I used it for all it was worth— whipped the flapping ear off one gremlin with my blade, kicked another in its gangly neck, and seized a third by its inordinately long and pointed nose and threw it to the ground, where Bluenose ran his spear through it. Then we turned together and went to the aid of the nearest member of the Guard who was embattled.

"Wait!" I shouted. "Where is Scar Eye and the boom?"

"What?" asked Bluenose, as if we were not standing in a fight with ancient foes.

"The boom!" I shouted. "It's going to boom the Castle!"

Bluenose blinked once. Then he said, "But not the pizza!"

A gremlin blindsided Bluenose and tackled him to the ground, sending Bluenose's spear flying.

"Loo-Tender!" I shouted, and tossed my sword.

Bluenose seized my weapon out of the air, drove it into the gremlin's thigh, and twisted. The creature screamed and rolled away and Bluenose came to his feet fighting.

The battle was desperate. My people were fighting hard, but the odds against them were rising as more gremlins emerged from their temporary prisons. I didn't have time to explain everything to everyone. Right now, Scar Eye and the boom were somewhere I couldn't see, planning to do something bad. I had to stop them.

"Fight them, Loo-Tender!" I shouted. "Their leader fled! I'm after him!"

"Take him, sir!" Bluenose shouted, shattering a Bane-made sword with my blade. He cut down his foe, laughed heartily, and began to sing, and all the Guard nearby began to join him.

I stepped over a fallen gremlin, seized its crude spear, and took to the air, searching for any sign of Scar Eye and the boom. A spark down at the far end of the hallway showed me Scar Eye's swollen-knuckled hand dragging the mortal hatchet along the floor behind him, and I zipped off after them.

Gremlins are ugly, dirty, violent, cruel, mean, and vicious, but also quick and quiet, even for Little Folk. By the time I'd reached the corner, they were already at the bottom of the stairs beyond— and Scar Eye's fangs flashed in a crocodile's smile as he smashed closed the heavy oak door at the stairs' bottom almost perfectly in time to make me break out all my teeth on it.

I swerved and curled into a ball at the last second to take the impact on my shoulders, bounced off the door, and collapsed to the ground. It took me a moment to gather myself and stagger to my feet. My wings were stunned. I had to jump up to grab the doorknob and wrestle the thing open, then start running forward on my slow, stupid legs like some slow, stupid biggun.

I ran anyway, jumping and thrumming my wings as much as I could get them to move, helping me take long steps like in those Hong Kong movies, but it was all I could do to stay on the gremlins' trail, descending through the Castle on the most rapid path to the basement.

I caught up to them in the kitchens, and only as I came through the doors did my wings beat true again, and I zipped up to near the ceiling to observe.

The four large gremlins bearing the boom were rushing toward . . .

Mab's frozen *boogers*.

They were rushing toward the pizza ovens.

Suddenly I saw their plan. The ovens were full of gas that could burn. The boom would go boom and then the Castle would burn, collapsing down into its own guts.

And it would kill everyone inside.

I felt my tummy get cold. Because that wouldn't be a little death, the kind of death that my people hardly noticed. That would be a great big death, the ones I could see now. It would make endings where stories were supposed to be happening.

I gripped my captured spear, clenched my jaw, and prepared to dive on the gremlins with the boom.

"Not so fast, pix!" growled Scar Eye in his horrible buzzing voice.

I whirled to see the gremlin standing on one of the Bane-made tables, grasping the mortal hatchet in one hand.

His other hand was knotted into a fist with Lacuna's dark braid wrapped around it. Even as my eyes widened, he swept the edge of the hatchet toward her throat—stopping only when she flinched back from the touch of the Bane and let out a harsh scream.

"Villain!" I shouted. "You let her go!"

"Here is what happens, pix," Scar Eye said. "You land, drop your weapons, and come with us. Once we're outside, I'll let your man go."

"Oh!" Lacuna said indignantly, her dark eyes flashing as she looked at me. "Oh, did you hear what he said?"

"Do not fear, my love!" I declared. "I will save the day!"

Scar Eye growled and leaned in toward Lacuna a little more. I heard the sizzle as the Bane touched her skin and she let out a thin peal of pain.

I whirled in a circle, searching for options. The four gremlins with the boom slapped it against the side of the pizza ovens and twisted a dial. The boom started making *tick tick tick* noises, which was what booms did on television just before they went boom. Those four were very large and tough-looking warriors, heavy with scars. I mean, as dumb as gremlins are, with that many scars they had to have learned something somewhere.

"Now!" Scar Eye said. "Or I kill him!"

"No!" I said. I dropped the spear and it clattered to the ground. "Wait!" I zipped down to the table, my hands raised. "Don't hurt her."

"Hah," Scar Eye said. "What I thought. Stupid pix." He kicked a coil of leather cord over to me. "Now tie your legs."

I bent over slowly and picked up the cord, trying to think. This situation was bad. The boom kept going *tick tick tick*. The other four big gremlins leapt up onto the table, surrounding me.

Kringle's merry balls, that pizza smelled good. Even the gremlins were noticing that. One of them with extra large rubbery lips eyed the oven and licked them.

"Do it, pix," Scar Eye almost purred. "It's over. You lost."

And then a blue light appeared in the room. It darted erratically across the floor, then up the leg of the Bane-made table.

And thirty pounds of gray tomcat came merrily along behind the light, batting at it excitedly. Mister the cat flung himself up onto the table in pursuit of the blue glowing dot and came to a sudden stop. All seven of the Little Folk standing on the table froze in place. Then the tomcat tilted his head to one side and, with barely more pause than that, pounced on the nearest gremlin.

"Move, kid!" screamed Bob the Castle. "Sixty seconds on the counter!"

The mauled gremlin let out a shriek of terror as Mister's claws began to rake, and I went into action, whirling the coil of leather cord at Scar Eye's face. The leather cord hit him in his only good eye and sent him flinching back and away from Lacuna—who suddenly produced a small, sharp blade from I know not where and struck it cleanly through her own braid, freeing her from Scar Eye's grasp.

I hurtled at Scar Eye and slammed my shoulder into his chest, driving him off the table's edge, across the kitchen, and into the Bane-made doors of the pizza freezer.

Behind me, I caught a glimpse of Mister raking and shaking a second gremlin while Lacuna deflected a thrust spear with a kung-fu hand and flung her little knife at a third.

Scar Eye howled as his back touched the Bane and seized me with terrified strength. His arms fouled my wings and we both crashed to the floor. He bounced to his feet like rubber, took up his hatchet, and smashed it down at me. I rolled clear as he struck thrice more in a single breath, the mortal hatchet raising sparks from the concrete floor and sending chips of poured stone flying.

Tick tick tick went the boom.

I caught the gremlin leader's wrists as he brought the hatchet up for a blow and we struggled for control of the weapon, bodies straining.

"Your lord will fall," the gremlin's buzzing voice murmured. "His house will be laid waste. It is only a matter of time. One night, one day."

"But not *this* night!" I snarled, and then I surged with the full strength of my body and whirled with Scar Eye, driving the mortal hatchet's edge into the thin steel of the refrigerator doors. The hatchet sank into it to the eye and stuck there.

Scar Eye stared at the weapon, his eye wide, then whirled to me.

Lacuna's wings buzzed as she came down beside me, her reclaimed sword dripping with gremlin blood. There was a thump, and a gremlin corpse fell to the floor from the Bane-made table. The form of the big tomcat appeared at the table's edge, bright green eyes on Scar Eye.

The gremlin made a fatal mistake.

He panicked.

Scar Eye darted to one side with the agility of his kind and streaked for the door.

Mister lifted one paw, judged the speed of his target, and made a single lazy bound down from the table.

Which solved the gremlin problem.

"The pizza!" Lacuna hissed.

"Right!" I said. We buzzed over to the boom. The ticking thing went *tick tick tick* and was round and had a lot of little hash lines on it.

The blue light buzzed in and said, "Dresden will be here in forty seconds . . . Oh, crap, only thirty-six left."

The round thing my lord had set out earlier went *bing* and all three of us jumped and let out a little shriek.

"Wait!" Lacuna said. "That's it!" She strode determinedly toward the boom.

"Whoa, there!" Bob the Castle said. "Do you know what you're doin— You know what, thirty seconds, screw it."

Lacuna knelt down by the boom, seized the plastic dial—and turned it mightily. It rotated up until a red hashmark was by a number that said *30*.

"There," Lacuna said firmly. "Now you have thirty minutes to save the pizza."

The blue light wobbled for a second and then said, "Oh. Yeah. Guess this wasn't exactly a Spetsnaz team or anything. Good work, Tiny Tish."

Lacuna narrowed her eyes at the blue light as heavy biggun footsteps plodded closer, and my lord and Sir William came charging into the kitchens. My lord slid to a stop, breathing hard, his dark eyes wide, and surveyed the place.

"Is that a *gremlin*?" he said a second later. "Bob, what the hell did you do with my cat!?"

>≺<

An hour later, we were all on the roof of the Castle, looking at the stars and eating pizza.

"How are the Guard, Major General?" my lord asked.

"Several injuries, one severe, none mortal," I said. "We were fortunate, my lord. We drove the enemy forth."

"Next time try to take one alive," he said. "It'd be nice to know who sent them."

"You'll have to take that up with Mister, my lord."

The big cat, sprawled in my lord's lap, purred contentedly. He apparently had no regrets about leaving none alive to tell tales.

"My lord?" I said after a quiet moment.

Those sad, dark eyes looked down at me. "Yeah, General?"

"I am sorry," I said. "That your heart hurts. She was brave."

He stopped chewing pizza and stared down at me for a long moment. Then he blinked several times and said, "Yes, she was. Thank you, Toot."

I patted his knee awkwardly. He rested a couple of fingertips on my shoulder for a moment in response.

"You did great tonight," he said. "Bob says the Castle's defenses were all calibrated to larger threats. He didn't have them set to see anything as small and sneaky as gremlins. Without you and the Guard, the place might have burned down. People under my protection could have gotten hurt."

I felt my chest stick out a little more. "It was nothing, my lord. All in a night's work." I paused, and said abashedly, "I am sorry about your refrigerator, my lord."

"Necessary action. I try never to second-guess the guy on the ground." He took an entire piece of pizza and offered it to me.

I accepted it gravely.

"My lord," I said. "This battle is done. But what will we do about the conomee?"

He took another piece of pizza of his own and held it forth. We gravely tapped pizza, and then ate. "What we always do, little buddy," he said. "We stick together."

I sat down next to him. A moment later, Lacuna came to sit beside me. I gave her half of my pizza.

"You came for me first," she said. "Not the pizza."

"You," I said, "are more important than pizza."

She stared at me in fond, stony silence for a moment before she said, "You are a great fool."

But she leaned against me while she ate.

THE DARK SHIP

by Anne Bishop

Last night I dreamed about the dark ship.

People say it's bad luck to be on the water when the full moon rises, because that's when the dark ship goes hunting, its tattered black sails catching a fast wind that touches no other ship. People say it is crewed by monstrous beings that capture hardworking fishermen and honest sailors, and its captain drinks the captives' blood before giving the bodies to his crew, who devour the flesh and suck the marrow from the bones.

People say that if your vessel is suddenly becalmed and a fog rolls in without warning, look to the horizon, and if you see those black sails silhouetted against the moon, it is better to die by your own hand than to wait for the monsters to find you. Because they will find you. They always find you.

><

I lived in Pyetra, a small fishing village on the coast of the Mediterran Sea. According to the grandmothers, it had been a prosperous village, and while the buildings near the water had been built out of the gray stone that had given Pyetra its name, the homes of the more affluent residents had been painted in soft pastels— yellow, rose, green, blue—so that, from the water, the village had looked like a bouquet of flowers set against the hills.

Then the Humans First and Last movement declared war on the *terra indigene*, and the Cel-Romano Alliance of Nations was torn apart by the Others' fury and power over the world. Instead of an alliance, nations were separated by veins of wild country, and anything human who stumbled into that land never came out.

Small villages like mine were untouched for the most part because the men who fished in the Mediterran or sailed that water to carry goods from one city to another—or sailed beyond our waters to trade—knew that the sea belonged to the *terra indigene*, and crews that were careful, and respectful, never saw the lethal terror that watched them but let them pass, and those were the men who returned home.

In a world torn apart by war, the vulnerable often fell victim to predators who waited for such opportunities to crack people's sense of right and wrong, using fear as a hammer.

In the end, it wasn't the Others who ruined Pyetra. It was a man called Captain Starr.

>—<

I sense things about ships and the sea. I can't see the future like those prophet girls we'd heard about, but when I walk along the shore and watch the fishing boats heading out for the day, sometimes I know which boats will have a good catch and which ones will come back with an empty hold. Sometimes I can tell when the sea will be unforgiving and it's better not to stray too far from the harbor. I don't tell anyone what I know, except one or two of the canny old grandfathers, and even with them, I am careful. I was a child when it happened, but I remember the last woman in our village who had a feeling about the weather and the sea. She was publicly beaten to death for "ill wishing" because she had warned a captain of a storm on a day when the sea was calm and the sky was clear, and he ignored her. When the storm appeared like screaming fury, she was blamed for the loss of that ship and crew.

I sense things about ships and the sea. It was my misfortune that I had never been able to sense danger to myself.

>―<

I woke up before dawn on the morning that was the beginning of the end. Too restless to go back to sleep and feeling a need I couldn't explain, even to myself, I dressed in my oldest shirt and skirt, put on my half boots, slipped a small folding knife into my skirt pocket, and went down to the water—down to the stretch of sandy beach protected by walls of rock that jutted into the sea. That beach had been turned into a baited trap that Captain Starr's men had set for whatever might leave the water and come ashore. Or for whatever—whoever—might be desperate enough to risk the trap to claim whatever bounty might be found.

That morning I found one of the feral ponies, his front feet caught in the tangles of net. He had a barrel body and chubby legs, but it was his coloring that made me shiver and yet, at the same time, conjured fanciful thoughts. His body was the midnight blue of the sea in the darkest hours of the night, and his mane and tail looked like surf and moonlight.

He was just a feral pony, but I could imagine him being one of the beautiful, deadly steeds that raced over the Mediterran Sea, harbingers of the dark ship's appearance.

I scolded myself as I made my way carefully down the path through the rocks to that stretch of beach. Wasting time imagining things could get both of us killed.

I paused when I reached the last rock and my feet touched sand. I'd have to step into the open in order to reach the pony, and I had a feeling there wasn't much time before Starr's men arrived with knives and clubs. If they found me here . . .

Hilda had been caught trying to free one of the village orphans who begged on the streets and was too hungry to resist the bait. The boy had tried to grab the thick piece of bread smeared with butter and honey—a barely remembered treat from the days before Captain Starr and his crew dropped anchor off our shore and became both terror and law for our village. The child was human, was known to us, had once had a family who lived in Pyetra. None of that had mattered. No one but the captain or his first mate decided the fate of anything caught in the trap, and to free something . . .

Captain Starr made some of us stand on the beach and watch as his men clubbed the boy to death. He made us watch . . .

Hilda wasn't dead after Starr's men finished with her, but she was too broken to save herself when the tide came back in. We watched and listened as she drowned. Then we were allowed to return to our homes or businesses, mute accessories to murder because no one had dared speak out against that cruelty or had taken one step to save Hilda or the boy.

So I knew the risks when I approached the trap. Being here was foolish. Trying to save one feral pony wasn't worth my life. And yet, watching a sea eagle circle above the net before heading out to sea, I *knew* something bad would happen to our village if the pony died.

The wind shifted. The pony snorted, having caught my scent.

"Easy," I said quietly as I scurried toward him. "Easy. I'm here to help you."

The pony neighed and tried to rear, but its efforts to get free tangled its front feet even more.

"Shh!" Now I was sweating. If any of the men heard the pony, they would hurry down to the beach. "If you don't keep quiet, we'll both be clubbed to death!"

He quieted and stood still, allowing me to approach. I took out my folding knife and worked as quickly as I could to cut just enough of the net to free his feet—and tried not to startle and cut myself every time the pony lipped my hair and snuffled to breathe in my scent.

"There." I pushed the net away from his feet before reaching up and pressing a hand to his chest. "Back up. Back."

He backed away from the trap, but he didn't turn and run while I smoothed the sand and arranged the net so that it wouldn't look like someone had messed with it. There would be footprints in the sand—the pony's and mine—but there was nothing I could do about that. The men would know from the size of the print that an adult male hadn't been walking this way, but unless someone saw me, they wouldn't know I had been on this part of the beach.

"Go home now," I said. "Go home."

I ran back to the narrow path in the rocks. I had to get home before Mara noticed I was missing and told my father, who would use his belt on me. I had to get home and wash up and make myself as presentable as possible. But not too presentable.

I used to be pretty. I'm not pretty anymore. Father took care of that. He claimed it was for my own good, but afterward not even his friends believed that.

I ran—and the pony ran with me.

I stopped. He stopped.

"Listen to me."

He pricked his ears.

"You have to go home. If the men see you, they will kill you for the meat, for your hide. You need to go home so that you can stay free." I paused, then added under my breath, "One of us should be free."

He looked at me for a long time, and I could have sworn that something like sympathy filled his dark eyes.

He turned and galloped to the water's edge, running in the surf. A large wave rolled onto the beach, rolled right over him. I stared at the spot, expecting to see him struggling with a broken leg or something just as bad, but when the wave receded, the pony was gone. Just gone. And so were my footprints.

As I turned to climb the path up to the road, I saw a man standing on the nearest rock wall, watching me. He was tall and lean, dressed all in black, and he had black hair and olive skin. More than that I couldn't tell. If he was one of Captain Starr's men . . .

Keeping my face averted, I climbed the path as fast as I could, grabbing the rocks for balance and taking some skin off my palms in my haste. If I could get back to the dockside tavern my father owned, maybe I could get inside and disappear before the man had time to figure out who I was.

Panting, I dared look back when I reached the road.

No man stood on the rock wall. All I saw was smoke drifting toward the sea.

When I was younger, the old grandfathers who hung around the docks and came to the tavern for their midday food and drink would tell me stories about the *terra indigene*, the earth natives who ruled so much of the world and viewed humans much the same way we viewed fish or deer. They told me about islands in the Mediterran—dangerous, secret places where the Others lived and where the dark ship lay anchored when its captain and crew weren't hunting human prey.

In some stories, the ship would appear out of the fog, a marauder that sank the ships of honest merchants who ferried a variety of goods among the Cel-Romano nations. In other stories, the ship was crewed by men the sea had never released. But when the moon was full, beings wearing the skins of those men would come ashore for a reckoning, and woe to those who had somehow escaped the justice of the living.

I heard birds overhead and jerked out of my musing. What was wrong with me? I had to get away from here!

I ran home and slipped up to my attic room unseen. I washed up and plaited my hair, but I didn't wash up enough to smell clean, and I didn't plait my hair to look that neat. I didn't want the men who came to drink in the tavern to see anything pleasing enough to make up for what my father had done to my face after a young man, who was in Pyetra to sell the olive oil produced by his family, wanted to marry me and take me back to his family's villa, depriving my father and his wife Mara of unpaid labor.

I used to be pretty before my father took a knife to one side of my face, before his fist damaged the sight in one eye.

I never saw the young man again. For a long time, I hoped he would come back and take me away, despite the damage to my face. But he never returned. Once I stopped feeling bitter about that, I wondered if something had happened to him and he couldn't return.

My father had wielded the knife, but it says something about my stepmother that the only gift she ever gave me after the bandages were removed was a gilt-edged mirror that my father hung over my dresser.

This is what you are now. As if I could ever forget while I was trapped within these walls, waiting on tables and cleaning up blood and puke after the men had their fun. But when I walked along the shore or stood on one of the rock walls and looked out to sea, I could dream of freedom. I could dream of being someone else, living somewhere else.

I turned toward the bedroom door to go downstairs when I heard a sound at my open window, which reminded me to close it, despite how the heat would build in the attic during the day.

A seashell lay on the windowsill. A perfect, undamaged shell that looked like a white fan with a pearly peach interior.

A raven perched on the neighboring roof, watching me. I don't know how long we stared at each other before it flew away, but I had a feeling the bird was connected to the pony and to the man I had seen on the rock wall.

As I went about my work that day, I thought about the raven, and the gift of a perfect seashell. I thought about a midnight blue pony with a mane and tail the color of surf and moonlight. I thought about the man who had disappeared like smoke. And I wondered if the dark ship would appear in Pyetra's harbor.

But it wasn't the dark ship and its monstrous crew that docked in Pyetra the next day.

It was Captain Starr.

>—<

His name was Jonathan Brogan, but no one who wanted to keep their tongue called him anything but Captain Starr. A big, barrel-chested man with thick, wheat-colored hair, a round face, and big square teeth that you couldn't help but notice since he laughed and smiled a lot. But his blue eyes were cold as a shark's, and what made him smile was often someone else's pain.

Before the war, he'd been a bully with a ship, a thug who strong-armed weaker men into paying protection money if they didn't want their merchant ships to mysteriously disappear or their fishing boats to be found adrift with the hold empty and no sign of the captain and crew. Now he was Pyetra's protector against the Others, Pyetra's hero who could murder a village girl for trying to free an orphan from a baited trap. Anything he or his men wanted, they took in exchange for escorting merchant ships past islands that Starr claimed were inhabited by beings that wanted nothing to do with Cel-Romano except when they came ashore to kill and destroy.

They say he was in a fight when he was young, receiving a terrible blow on the forehead that dented his skull in the shape of a star—a mark still visible and distinctive. They whispered that, perhaps, the damage had gone deeper than his skull and that was what made him such a savage adversary.

Whatever the reason, everyone in Pyetra lived in fear from the moment his sails were sighted to the moment his ship sailed away, its hold carrying precious fuel for the engine that allowed him to maneuver even when there was no wind for the sails, as well as the best foods, ales, and wines from our shops.

That afternoon he walked into my father's tavern—and everyone fell silent. Captain Starr's crew ate and drank here, but Starr and his first mate stayed at an inn far enough from the docks that the rooms didn't stink of fish, and fancy enough that the captain dressed like a gentleman when he met with the village leaders to discuss payments and accommodations.

Captain Starr sat down at a table Mara hurriedly wiped clean and smiled that toothy smile. "Enzo, my good man. A round of drinks for everyone, and your best ale and whiskey for me and my mate."

My father poured the drinks and brought them to the table. No one rushed to the bar to receive their free drink. I hid in the hallway that provided access to the storeroom and the door to the alley, overwhelmed by the feeling that something was going to happen.

Captain Starr sampled the ale and gave a nod of approval. My father relaxed. Everyone else in the tavern was smarter and waited to find out what Starr wanted before they believed they would be allowed to leave unharmed.

"I left two men here to keep an eye on the docks and the fishing boats and to take note of returning merchant ships," Starr said. "And to keep an eye on the baited trap since our enemies often come in by the sea. My men are nowhere to be found, and my first mate tells me the trap's net has been cut in a way that suggests someone freed whatever had been caught. Anyone here know anything about that?" He looked at my father. "Enzo?"

My father shook his head. "I've not been down to the water in days. Neither has my wife. Been too busy with running this place and putting up the supplies that came in the other day."

"What about that daughter of yours?" Starr still sounded friendly, but everyone knew there was nothing friendly about the question or what would happen if he didn't like the answer.

I eased back a little more. A couple of old grandfathers, sitting at the back table, saw me, then pointedly looked away—and said nothing.

"She must be about," my father said, "although she barely does enough work to deserve the food she eats."

"Find out where she was this morning," Starr said. "I don't think she fully appreciates that a daughter should be obedient in all things."

In other words, when he found me, my father would tie my

hands to a spike he'd driven into the wall and beat me until I couldn't stand.

The tavern door opened and something, some change in the air or in the room's silence made me peer around the corner. The man I'd seen on the rock wall that morning walked up to the bar, set a gold coin on the wood, and said, "Whiskey."

The paper money that had been used in Cel-Romano was almost worthless now. Currency in a place like Pyetra was gold or silver or chits of credit that were traded among the residents, becoming a currency exclusive to the village.

After a glance at Starr, my father filled a glass to the brim with whiskey, took the gold coin, and, grudgingly, put two silver coins on the bar as change.

The man pocketed the coins and took a sip of whiskey.

"You're not a villager," Starr said, his blue eyes bright with malice—and suspicion.

"No, I'm not," the man agreed. He had a slight accent, like nothing I'd heard before.

"First time in Pyetra?" Starr asked.

"It is."

"Going to be here long?"

"I'm not sure."

"What's your name?"

"Captain Crow."

Starr's eyes narrowed. "I didn't see an unfamiliar ship moored at the docks or anchored in the harbor. Where is your ship, and what's your business here?"

Crow took another sip of whiskey. "What business is it of yours?"

"I look out for the people in this village. Their protector, you might say. So I'll ask again: Where is your ship, and what's your business?"

"My ship is nearby. As for my business . . ." Crow looked Starr right in the eyes, something no other man would do. "I hunt predators."

Starr's first mate snorted. "Like sharks?"

Crow continued to stare at Starr. "Something less honorable."

Everyone in the tavern held their breath. To call Starr dishonorable was courting death, especially for a man alone. He'd be lucky to get back to his ship without being knifed in an alley.

"There's no fuel for an unregistered ship," Starr said. "Fuel is strictly rationed since the war."

"My ship doesn't require anything but the wind," Crow replied.

A sailing ship without an engine? Fishing vessels relied on engines, but most had been refitted with sails to help the fuel last. And merchant ships ran before the wind with full sails except when coming into or leaving the harbor and docks. A sailing ship without an engine had to be ancient!

I shivered as a thought erased every other, like the incoming tide erases footprints on a beach.

An ancient ship—or an unnatural one.

"If you're here for supplies, spend your coin and be out of Pyetra by sundown," Starr snarled. "And don't come back."

Crow took another sip of whiskey, the level in the glass barely changed. He stepped away from the bar, then stopped. "I go where I please."

"Really? I've never heard of you."

"But I've heard of you, Captain Starr." Crow smiled a tight-lipped smile. "You should be careful about the cargo you carry when you're in Tethys's domain. The salt of tears has a different taste than salt water."

Who was Tethys? I waited for someone to ask the question. No one did.

I glanced at the old grandfathers, saw the way their hands shook.

They knew. And they feared this Tethys more than they feared Starr.

Crow left the tavern. Starr and his first mate walked out a minute later.

Starr and his men searched the docks, the warehouses, the shops, and the taverns, but no one had seen the mysterious man who claimed to be a ship's captain. No one reported sighting an unfamiliar ship near Pyetra.

But that night, when I finally went up to bed, I found Captain Crow sitting on my windowsill.

I stared at him, shocked, before I considered what kind of work Mara would have me doing in the alley behind the tavern if someone spotted him and told her a man had been in my room.

"Get away from there," I whispered fiercely. "You'll be seen!"

He stood, stepped to the side, then leaned against the wall. "Better?"

He sounded amused, and that amusement turned my fear into fury. If Mara came upstairs now . . . Worse, if my father came upstairs to deliver the beating Starr had implied I deserved . . .

"How did you get up here?"

"The window was open."

"It wasn't." I was sure I had closed it.

"Open a crack," he amended. "It was enough. Why did you free the pony?"

"I don't know you." Couldn't trust him is what I meant. "Is Crow your real name?"

"It is when I captain the ship."

"And when you're not captaining the ship?"

"My name is Corvo Sanguinati."

Sanguinati. Blood drinker. One of the *terra indigene.*

It seemed there was some truth in the stories about the dark ship.

"What do you want from me?"

He regarded me calmly. "I want to know why you freed the pony."

"It was caught in the net. Starr's men would have killed it."

"They would have killed you too if they'd seen you." He paused. "'One of us should be free.' That's what you said."

He'd *heard* that?

"What's your name?" he asked.

"Vedette. But everyone calls me Dett." I smiled bitterly. "Mara always says I owe her and my father for letting me live. If she'd been able to have a child of her own, she would have dragged me down to the sea on a moonless night and drowned me years ago."

"If you were free, what would you do? Where would you go?" Corvo asked.

I shrugged and attempted a sassy answer. "I would stow away on a dark ship that was headed anywhere but here."

"Dangerous to be a stowaway on any ship. Especially dangerous to stow away on that one. But paying for your passage? That might be possible."

No, it wasn't. I had no money and nothing to barter except my body, and I doubted Corvo Sanguinati would accept as payment what most other men would take—as long as they could turn one side of my face to the wall while they lifted my skirt.

Corvo rubbed his chin. "How did you know the pony would be on the beach?"

We were back to the pony?

I hesitated. Lying was the safe thing to do, but I had a feeling that Corvo was in my room for a reason, and it wasn't to hide from

Captain Starr. If I lied to him now I would never find out why he had come to see me.

"Sometimes I sense things about ships and the sea. I had a feeling I needed to go down to the beach this morning."

He nodded. "I wondered if you were an Intuit. I was surprised to see one of your kind living in a place like this instead of among your own."

"My kind?" People like me had a name besides ill-wisher?

No one would talk about my mother, and the few things that had been said were vague, but I'd had the impression that she hadn't been a local girl. Had she come here on a visit and stayed because she fell in love with my father? Or had she been forced into that marriage? I would never know about her, but learning there was a place where people like me were accepted was a gift— and a goal.

Corvo studied me. "The world gave humans the land that surrounded the Mediterran Sea as their territory, but the islands within the Mediterran have always belonged to the *terra indigene*. Intuits escaping persecution from other kinds of humans were allowed to settle on those islands, as long as they didn't fight with or interfere with us. They farm and fish—and teach us human skills."

"Like sailing a ship?" I asked.

"Like sailing a ship," he agreed.

He came to some decision. Pushing away from the wall, he reached into a pocket and pulled out two silver coins. Not looking at me, he placed the coins on the windowsill and rested one finger on top of them.

"This will buy one transaction with the *terra indigene*," he said. "You may ask any of us for one thing—including passage on a dark ship heading for an Intuit village."

My head spun with the enormity of what he offered. "But how

can I contact you? The telephones don't work much beyond the neighboring villages anymore."

Another casualty of the war with the *terra indigene*. Humans no longer had quick communication over longer distances because telephone lines had been severed and couldn't be repaired in the veins of wild country that now broke apart the Alliance of Nations. Every attempt to restore the lines had ended in piles of human corpses. We were reduced to communicating as our grandparents had done, with letters sent overland or by ship.

"Set the coins where they can be seen and speak your intention clearly. Someone will hear you and relay the message."

How? I asked a different question. "Who is Tethys?"

Corvo smiled, showing a hint of fang. "She is an Elemental. She is the voice and heart and fury of the Mediterran Sea."

So the Elementals were real.

"Why would you help me?"

"You were willing to help someone who was different from yourself. I felt I should return the favor."

One moment he stood there, looking at me. The next moment, a column of smoke filled the same space before it flowed out the window and Corvo, in his other form, disappeared into the night.

>✕<

The next morning, men checking the baited trap found Captain Starr's missing men. Both had a round mark on their chests bigger than a man's hand—and holes that looked like they had been made by circles of curved teeth latching into flesh while something else had scraped the flesh away to reach the hearts and all that rich blood.

The men's legs had chunks of flesh ripped away, and those bite marks indicated that a large shark had fed on the bodies after death. Maybe after death.

The shark bites disturbed the men who downed rough whiskey before going to work, but the round marks in the dead men's chests terrified all the men whose work brought them into contact with the sea.

As I served drinks and cleared tables, I listened to the grandfathers whisper about giant sea lampreys that were as long as a man is tall—lampreys that had a taste for warm-blooded prey. Human prey. And I heard another word whispered that day to explain a creature that shouldn't exist: *Others*.

><><

Captain Starr's ship set sail a few days later with its hold full of provisions, along with the goods he had wrung from the village's merchants that he would sell for his own profit.

The morning after that, I ran errands for Mara, who claimed to be feeling poorly. I seldom had a chance to visit the shops on the main street, and almost never by myself. Mara didn't like to deprive herself of the enjoyment in seeing people flinch when they looked at my face.

Corvo hadn't flinched. I liked him for that.

That morning, I crossed paths with Lucy, who had been my friend before my father used his fist and a knife. We used to walk on the beach and talk about our hopes and dreams. I wasn't allowed to take those walks after my face healed because Mara decided that Lucy had given me ideas and that was why I'd thought I could get married and work anywhere but the tavern after she and my father had gone through the trouble of raising me.

Lucy came up beside me as I perused a cart of used books,

standing where she could see the undamaged side of my face. She said nothing, just picked up a book and examined it, as if I were a stranger. As if I meant nothing at all and never had.

Then she said in a low voice, "Be careful, Dett. I heard things while Captain Starr was staying at the inn."

Lucy's family owned the inn that catered to ships' captains and well-to-do merchants.

"What things?" I pretended interest in a book that gave me a reason to turn slightly in her direction.

"That some captains are looking for a different kind of cargo these days," Lucy replied. "Apparently there are men in other parts of Cel-Romano who want to buy unspoiled goods." She returned the first book to the cart and picked up another. "Starr asked my father if I was unspoiled goods. He asked if you were. And he wasn't just asking about girls."

My stomach rolled.

"There are cities around the Mediterran that are filled with supplies and hard-to-find goods that can be had just for the asking, but . . . things . . . are hunting in those cities now, so most people who go in to find the goods don't get out alive," Lucy said.

"Nimble orphan boys might be able to get in and out. A couple of times anyway."

She nodded. "That's a possibility. But girls like us . . ." She shuddered.

It wasn't likely that Captain Starr was acting as a marriage broker.

"I'll buy this one so no one thinks to say anything about me standing here so long." Lucy held up the book. "I hope I like it."

She went into the shop to purchase the book. I hurried away and finished the errands for Mara.

That night I sat at the open window clutching the silver coins.

Fear of what might happen the next time Captain Starr's ship was spotted on the horizon filled me, leaving room for nothing else. I tried to convince myself that, at worst, it wasn't any different than Mara wanting to sell me for an alley hump, but it *was* different. What I couldn't sense was how it was different or why it felt dangerous.

I looked at the coins in my hand. One transaction with the *terra indigene*. One chance.

What did I truly want? To get away from Pyetra? Oh, yes, I wanted that. But what about Lucy? What about the orphans the villagers would justify selling to Starr as cargo?

As I sat at my window, the wind brought the smell of the sea— and I had a feeling that it wasn't yet time to ask for the thing I wanted.

>–×–<

A week after Captain Starr's ship left Pyetra, other merchant vessels docked at the wharf or dropped anchor in the harbor. As the crews from those ships came ashore, so did the stories.

The dark ship had been sighted several times. Given that some of the ships had been sailing to Pyetra from the eastern side of the Mediterran while others had sailed from the west, I wondered if there was more than one dark ship. It seemed likely, but I was interested in only one.

Stories spoken quietly, fearfully, of spotting another ship that was suddenly engulfed in an unnatural fog. Seeing the flames as the ship burned. Hearing the screams of the men.

Or seeing a ship sail out of a bank of fog that dissipated in minutes. Finding what was left of the bodies of the crew—some drained of blood, some torn apart by a shark, and some with that queer round hole in their chests that looked similar to the mark a lamprey left on fish but so much bigger and so much worse when that mark was left on a man.

Or a wave rising out of nowhere, topping a ship's masts before the ship rolled, broke apart, and sank.

Or a whirlpool appearing in front of a ship, pulling it down—and men swearing they saw a giant steed galloping round and round the edge of the whirlpool until it, and the whirlpool, vanished.

They whispered about their own ships suddenly becalmed, leaving them helpless as a dark ship, its black sails full with an unnatural wind, caught up to them, drew up alongside—and then sailed past. And how the wind that had disappeared when the dark ship appeared on the horizon suddenly filled the sails again, allowing them to reach the next port.

Stories spoken quietly, fearfully, by men who'd had to sail past slaughter—and who wondered what cargo had provoked that kind of rage.

We found out what kind of cargo when Captain Starr returned to Pyetra.

>-><-<

I'd barely had an hour's sleep when Mara shook me awake.

"Get up," she said in a fierce whisper. "Get dressed and come downstairs. And be quick about it."

"But . . ."

"Be quick or you'll have nothing but your nighty."

The thought of wearing nothing but my nighty and being downstairs with men who had been to sea for a few weeks was enough to wake me up. My fingers shook as I pulled on my underwear and buttoned my shirt and skirt, put on my socks and half boots. I'd made a little pouch from a scrap of cloth in order to hide the silver coins and keep them with me—and hidden from Mara. I pinned the pouch to the back of the skirt's pocket, then slipped my folding knife into the pocket.

As I reached for the shawl I'd folded over the back of my chair, the door opened again.

"You won't need that." Mara grabbed my arm and dragged me down the stairs with such haste we came close to falling.

As she pulled me into the tavern's main room, I saw Captain Starr—and I knew.

"No." I tried to pull away from Mara. "No!"

A rag was stuffed in my mouth and secured with another piece of cloth. My hands were bound with rope.

Starr stared at my face and smiled. "I have a client who will pay well to have you for his new wife." He looked at my father. "You'll receive your portion of the sale price, as agreed."

Two of Starr's men dragged me out of the tavern and down to the dock and his ship. They pulled me up a gangplank. I fought them until they dunked my head in a barrel of water and held me down. When one of them pulled my head out of the water, the other said, "If you keep fighting, we'll hold you down longer next time."

Still struggling to breathe, I didn't resist when they hauled me to the ship's secure hold and left me there, bound and gagged.

But not alone.

There were younger girls, barely more than children, and some of the orphan boys who begged on the streets. None of them were tied up, but there were bruises on their faces, reason enough for them to huddle together now, silent and afraid.

I don't know how long it took them to load their living cargo. No adolescent boys, but several of the village girls who were old enough to be "wives" in a place where there was a shortage of expendable women.

It was still dark when men escorted Lucy into the hold, bound and gagged as I was. She sat next to me, shivering.

Soon after that, I felt the change in the ship's movement and knew Starr had given the order to cast off.

Unspoiled goods being taken to an unknown destination and a mean existence. Most of us wouldn't survive long after arriving at that destination, and those of us who did survive wouldn't want to.

We had one chance—if I could get free.

>—<

I'd started pulling on the gag when one of the boys looked at me and said, "Wait."

I might have resented the sharp command if I hadn't seen him watching the stairs down to the hold. Was he someone like me, who had feelings about things?

I slumped and waited, doing my best to look defeated, which wasn't hard.

A minute later, two men came down the stairs. One dropped a burlap sack on the floor; the other set down a small barrel and a tin cup.

"That's all there is until you're traded," the first one said. "Make it last."

They went up the stairs and secured the door.

The boy waited another minute, watching the stairs. Then he scurried over to Lucy and undid her gag.

"Dett too," Lucy said.

He hesitated, then did what she asked.

"One of Starr's men saw you giving us food," the boy told Lucy. "That's why he took you." He looked at the ropes binding our hands.

"I have a folding knife in my skirt pocket," I said.

I didn't feel his hand, but a moment later he held the knife. He freed Lucy first, then me. Folding the knife, he gave it back—and gave me an odd look, which made me wonder if he'd felt the coins.

Lucy rubbed her wrists while another boy, who looked to be the twin of the first, opened the sack and checked the barrel.

"Some food here," he reported. "Not much if it's meant for all of us. The barrel is half-full of water."

"We won't be here that long," I said, unbuttoning my skirt in order to reach the safety pin and little pouch. Retrieving the pouch, I held it tight.

"Dett . . ." Lucy began.

"We're going to escape."

"How?"

I opened the pouch and showed her the two silver coins. "These will pay for one transaction with the *terra indigene*. The Others will help us get away from Starr and his men."

For a moment it seemed like nobody breathed.

"How?" Lucy asked again.

"You—all of you—need to get to the longboat, get it down to the water. Get into the boat and lower it down or cut the lines so it falls into the sea. It won't capsize. You'll be all right. And you'll be rescued quick enough." That much I sensed.

Lucy stared at me. "You mean *we'll* be rescued quick enough."

"Yes, of course," I lied, "but I need to set up the distraction that will make it possible for you to get away. Then I'll join you." I looked at the hold stairs and sighed. "But you have to get up on deck, and we're locked in."

The second boy smiled, fiddled with a seam in his trousers, and held up a thin piece of metal. "I can pick a lock."

>-><-<

We reviewed the plan and waited. Restless and bored, the children ate most of the food and water while we waited. While I waited. Then . . .

Orders shouted in anger. Responses shouted in fear.

I had a feeling the dark ship had appeared on the horizon and was bearing down on Starr's ship. If the stories had any truth, soon the fog would roll in, hopefully shrouding the deck enough to hide Lucy's and the children's movements as they made their way to the longboat.

The fog would roll in. The ship with its black sails and Sanguinati captain would attack. And the diversion I was about to purchase would ensure freedom for some of us.

I held out my folding knife to the boy who had freed Lucy and me. "It's time."

>-><-<

As soon as the last child slipped out of the hold, I placed the two silver coins in the palm of my hand and held it out. "Corvo Sanguinati said these coins would buy one transaction with the *terra indigene*. I want to make that transaction now—with Fire."

I wasn't sure how this worked. If it took too long for the message to reach the Elemental I'd requested, then Lucy and the children would be caught and this would be for nothing.

One moment I was alone. The next . . .

The female who appeared in front of me would never be mistaken for human, with her long red hair tipped in yellow and blue. She looked around, then looked at me.

"There are children making their way to the longboat to escape from these very bad men," I said. "We need a distraction, something the men will have to pay attention to instead of the children."

She studied me. "What do you want me to do?"

I took a breath and let it out slowly. "Burn this ship. Set the sails on fire and fill the cargo holds. This ship has weapons and supplies that will explode if touched by fire."

"You will not reach the small boat and escape."

"I know." But neither would Captain Starr. I'd make sure of that much.

I took a step forward, set the coins on the floor between us, then stepped back.

Fire pressed her hand against a wooden crate. The wood smoked. Then it began to burn.

She looked at me and said, "Run."

I scrambled out of the hold just as the sails burst into flames, as the masts ignited.

I hadn't paid attention to the location of the longboat. I hoped one of the boys had and could lead the rest to safety.

Fog blinded me. Smoke choked me. I felt a bitter satisfaction at hearing men shouting, scrambling.

The sea calmed. The wind died. Flames consumed the ship.

I reached the railing and clung to it, uncertain what to do. Then I looked toward the stern—and saw Starr and his first mate rushing toward the longboat that the boys were trying to lower into the sea.

I ran toward them, consumed by anger for Starr and men like him.

"No!" I shouted. "The captain goes down with his ship!"

Starr turned toward me. I grabbed his arm and held on, doing everything I could to stop him from getting into that longboat.

I heard the first mate cry out, glimpsed hands made of fire

grabbing the longboat's ropes, burning through them. I heard the children scream as the longboat fell. Heard the splash.

Arms appeared out of two columns of smoke, grabbed the first mate, and threw him overboard.

"You bitch!" Starr roared. His free hand closed around my throat and squeezed.

That was when Fire reached the powder room—and the ship exploded.

I remember flying through the air, surrounded by debris. I remember something grabbing my arms and slowing my plunge into the sea, gently dropping me feet first away from the worst of the debris. I remember seeing the longboat moving swiftly, buoyed by water in the shape of a midnight blue steed with a mane the color of surf.

I remember one of Starr's men swimming toward me—and something large and sinuous swimming past. I remember the nightmarish sight of a round mouth full of curved teeth before the creature latched on to the man's chest.

The last thing I remember was hands closing around my arms again and Corvo Sanguinati saying, "You idiotic female. How did your species survive long enough to become such a nuisance?"

>—×—<

When I came to I was wrapped in a blanket and tucked into a bunk in . . .

"Captain's quarters," a voice said. "Captain Crow isn't pleased with you right now, but he insisted on you staying here while you recover."

I focused on the voice, on the face. A pleasant face that held kindness and humor.

"I'm Alano, ship's medic. Including myself, there are only four humans in the crew, and I take care of stitching them up if someone gets careless." He paused. "We don't usually get careless. And we're not usually reckless. You, however, have more than made up for that and have been the subject of great discussion, with the Others speculating about whether this is typical female behavior in humans or if it's just you."

"I didn't do anything."

Alano's eyebrows rose. "You blew up a ship. Well, you paid Fire to blow up a ship, but it amounts to the same thing."

"Doesn't," I said.

"It does," Corvo Sanguinati said.

I hadn't heard him come in, but I saw the humor wash out of Alano's face to be replaced with caution.

"Captain," Alano began, "she needs—"

"To answer a question," Corvo finished. "Why?"

We'd had this conversation before. Funny thing was, my answer was the same.

"You must have known you wouldn't have time to get off that ship, that *burning* ship," Corvo said. "If we hadn't been pursuing Starr's ship when you called on Fire, you would have died."

"Whether Starr reached port and sold us on or I burned the ship, I didn't expect to survive. At least this way, Lucy and the children will have a chance at a new life, a better life. Besides, I sense things about ships and the sea. I had a feeling you were nearby."

Corvo stared at me. So did Alano.

Then the Sanguinati turned to the medic. "Don't let her die."

When Corvo left the cabin, Alano said, "You won't die. You just need some rest."

As I drifted back to sleep, it occurred to me that Alano, like Corvo, had looked at the ruined side of my face and hadn't flinched.

>×<

The following day I was allowed to join Lucy and the children on deck. The girls were subdued; the boys excited. After all, we were on board the dark ship and headed for its home port.

In whispers, Lucy told me about the crew. There was a Hawk, an Eagle, an Owl, a Raven, a Shark, several Sanguinati, the four Intuits—and two males who could take a human form well enough to have arms and legs and perform tasks around the ship. They looked sinuous, especially when they moved, and the disturbing shape of their faces made me think of round mouths full of curved teeth. All Lucy had been told about them was that they were Elders and their form was ancient.

I didn't want to know more.

Alano and the other Intuit men expressed some concern about the children fitting in. All the towns on the islands in the Mediterran were inhabited by Intuits and Others, and I and the twin boys were the only ones with at least some Intuit blood. But word had traveled to those western islands, and by the time the dark ship dropped anchor and we were rowed ashore, there were families from several towns waiting at the docks to take in the children and give them new homes.

Once I was safely ashore, Corvo wished me well and said he was going home to spend time with his family. I wondered if that was his way of discouraging me from having any foolish romantic notions about him, but Alano confirmed that Captain Crow had a wife and children, and that the Sanguinati part of town was a protected, and private, place.

Lucy found work at an inn near the water and found love with Niklaus, one of the Intuit men who sailed with Corvo.

I went inland for a while and worked for a family who grew

olives—and learned I was meant for water, not land. So I returned to the sea towns and learned to sail, and I studied to be a medic, and on the day Alano didn't return with the dark ship, having chosen a different kind of life on another island, I applied for the position—and was welcomed by Captain Crow.

I sense things about ships and the sea. That had value to a captain who hunted human predators. My face was valuable too, when human leaders were required to come aboard to receive a warning. They looked at the ruined side of my face, and they looked at the table, which contained a silent warning to anyone who thought they could buy and sell humans and transport their cargo through the Others' domain.

The candleholders that were evenly spaced the length of the table were made of human skulls, some yellowed and old and some quite new. All had come from men who had escaped human justice.

I especially liked the skull that had a star-shaped indentation in its forehead.

COMFORT ZONE

by Kelley Armstrong

I was going to be the one who told the stories of heroes. Fictional heroes, characters born in my head and cast out into make-believe worlds where they would, naturally, save the day, rescue the dude-in-distress, bring about world peace, and, if they were really feeling energetic, cure the common cold.

I would tell the stories that would grace a thousand movie screens. Before that, I had to hone my skills, so I joined high school writing clubs, and every time I showed off a new story-board, fellow scribes would point at my protagonist and say, "Is that you?" The answer was always no. For them, stories were wish fulfillment, bringing to life an idealized version of themselves. I could create entire universes in my head, but I could not stretch my imagination far enough to place myself in the role of hero.

I was the quiet girl with the stutter. The poor little rich girl, who lived in a penthouse with a housekeeper while her father traveled for work. To most of my classmates, I was a ghost. An invisible girl who passed without a ripple. Perhaps it's ironic, then, that if they remember me at all, it's as the girl who *saw* ghosts. Who snapped one day and was hustled off to a padded room.

Hey, remember Chloe Saunders? Wasn't she the one who lost it? Started ranting about ghosts? I hear she's still locked up in a psych ward.

Even there, I'm not the hero of my story; I'm the victim of it.

Thankfully, that version isn't the truth, and that ending definitely isn't. My life got a whole lot more interesting after I started seeing ghosts. I became someone else. Someone who is indeed the protagonist of her own story. Hero, though? No. To be a hero, you need to step off your own path to help others in distress, and some of us don't have the luxury of doing that. We have our own safety—and the safety of those we love—to worry about, and we cannot be distracted by altruism. Or that's what we tell ourselves.

I'm twenty-one now, in my last year of university. I haven't lived in the States for four years, and I'm not sure I'll ever go back. It's safer for us in Canada. Also, while I still write, a career in screenwriting feels like the dream of a child. Or, perhaps, the dream of a girl destined to an ordinary life. For me, going to school under an assumed name and suffering twice-weekly check-ins with my parole officers—sorry, *security detail*—is as normal as it gets.

Still, my life is far closer to normal than I'd once imagined possible. I'm going to a regular university, walking from class without a bodyguard trailing behind me, and enjoying a warm October day, gold and scarlet leaves pirouetting around me. I'm heading to the apartment I share with my boyfriend. Tonight we're staying in, studying and making spaghetti, and if we get done with our homework early, we might cut loose and rent a movie. Terribly mundane. *Wonderfully* mundane for a genetically modified necromancer and a genetically modified werewolf. There are days, even weeks, when we are just a regular couple, crazy in love, studying our asses off and enjoying the kind of stability we'd once envied.

Behind our apartment complex, there's a tiny courtyard. As I cut through it, a voice says, "Miss?"

I jump a foot in the air and nearly drop my books, proving that no matter what I've been through, in some ways, I haven't changed at all.

A guy walks toward me, and I curse myself for not noticing him sooner. I'm no longer the girl who can afford to float through life with her head in the clouds. Even at four p.m., in downtown Toronto, I can't step into a quiet spot without being aware of everyone around me. Except, apparently, I just did.

Before I blame myself too much for that, I must acknowledge the possibility that there's a reason I didn't see this guy. Because he made *sure* I didn't until it was too late to flee.

While there are far more valuable subjects from our experiments, Derek and I get our share of unwanted attention from groups hoping to recruit us while we're still young and naive. And they're not above having a guy—my age, blond, cute—waylay me to make their offer. They're also not above kidnapping me so they can deliver a more complete sales pitch.

I should drop my books to free my hands for fighting, but let's be honest, years of martial arts training still hasn't turned my body into a lethal weapon. I'm small and kind of clumsy. I *can* fight. I will. It's just not my primary skill set. As for that primary skill set, well, I'm a necromancer. That limits my choices down to one really unsavory power.

I glance around the park and nod as I spot the remains of a dead squirrel.

When I first came into my abilities, I accidentally raised dead animals. And sometimes dead people. I've learned to control my ability, but as those early accidents prove, my genetic modifications make me a natural at a skill that normal necromancers take decades to perfect.

Even as I take note of the dead squirrel, it twitches, one half-skeletal paw lifting in a grotesque wave. I release the squirrel, and the paw drops, but the connection between us still sizzles like a live wire. One jolt of focused thought, and this guy will have a rotting squirrel going for his throat. Well, more like leaping onto his pant leg, but in my experience, that's enough.

"Miss?" the guy says again, still walking toward me.

I clutch the textbooks to my chest and widen my eyes. "Y-yes," I say. I don't stutter much these days, but faking it can come in handy. It makes me the last person anyone expects to launch a zombified attack squirrel.

As the guy crosses those last steps, I catch . . . I'm never quite sure what I catch in a case like this. It's much easier when the person is dressed in a crinolined gown or a Union soldier uniform. If they look like a regular person, recognizing them as a ghost takes a little more. Some give themselves away by walking through furniture. Or other people ignore them, even dogs not glancing up as they pass. But for the few who give none of the usual "dead people" signals, recognizing them as ghosts has taken years, and I'm still not sure *how* I know.

I cut the connection between myself and the squirrel. Then I do something terrible, something I hate myself for. Something I hate myself for a little *less* each time I do it, and then I feel a little colder, a little further from the person I want to be.

I shake my head and continue walking, and when he jogs up beside me, I say, "No." Just that one word. *No.* A horrible word, in its way, and it doesn't matter how many necromancers tell me this is the right thing to do, the *only* thing to do, I will never lose that initial surge of guilt. And I'm not sure I should.

"Just listen," he says. "Please."

"I can't. I'm sorry."

I *am* sorry. So sorry. I'm the girl who wrote stories about heroes. I'm still the girl who scribbles those stories when she has a spare moment. My heroes are no longer anonymous creations. They're inspired by people I know. At first, by people who made sacrifices to help us. Lately, by two of our friends, Maya and Daniel, who juggle postgrad studies with helping supernaturals.

Maya and Daniel help others, and I don't, and it's killing me a little more each day. I create characters by putting myself in the shoes of others. I can imagine only too well what it's like for ghosts. They wander the world, trapped between dimensions, needing something done before they can cross over. Yet they cannot interact with our world. Cannot speak to anyone . . . until one day, they see a necromancer.

They recognize the faint glow that marks us like an old-fashioned pay phone sign. The shining light in the darkness. At last, here is a way to communicate with the outside world. A way to accomplish what they must accomplish to cross over. They pick up the receiver . . . and there is nothing. The line is severed. The necromancer walks on, heart hardened to their pleas.

"Just two minutes," the guy says. "Two minutes of your time, miss."

Keep walking.

Keep walking.

For ghosts, we're that one pay phone in the desert. For necromancers, though, ghosts are toll booths that spring up in our path everywhere we go, and to pass, we must agree to pay the toll without knowing what it is.

Please tell my wife I love her.

Sure, I can do that. Just pop an anonymous letter in the mail.

Please find my grandfather's watch and give it to my son.

I have classes. I can't hop on a plane and fly to your house.

Please find my killer and bring him to justice.

Do you see me? I'm a twenty-one-year-old student. Not a cop.

Please tell my wife she's a no-good cheating whore, so I can rest in peace.

Wait. What? No. Hell, no. Now leave me *alone.*

My faith in humanity has been tested by the sheer number of the last kind. Ghosts trapped in this realm by bitterness and a need for revenge. I've taken to humming "Let It Go" as my answer, which works much better on modern ghosts.

Then there are the ghosts who treat necromancers like an Internet connection. They want us to pop off an e-mail. Or check the stock market. Hey, you there, necromancer, can you tell me how the Cubs are doing this season? Can you tell me how my favorite TV show ended? Simple requests, easily completed, but once you start doing them, you never stop, and pretty soon, you have a dozen ghosts wanting weekly coffee dates, during which they watch you creep on their family and friends' social media accounts.

Just say no. The mantra of necromancers everywhere.

So I say it to this guy. And I keep walking until he leaps into my path with "It's a matter of life and death."

"It usually is," I murmur . . . and walk through him.

He swings around to get in front of me again. "No, seriously. It's my little sister. She's—"

"No," a deep voice rumbles behind me.

I glance over to see a guy stalking our way. Now, I'll be blunt— if I didn't know Derek Souza, he'd send me scurrying away a whole lot faster than this ghost would. Six foot three. Built like a quarterback. With a scowl known to send small children running. Shaggy dark hair and a broad face, rough from old acne scars. Derek is . . . well, I think he's the hottest guy ever . . . which puts me in a fan group of one.

"Did she tell you to go away?" he says.

The ghost sputters.

"Yes," Derek says. "She did. Now go."

The ghost glances at me. "How can he see—?"

"I can't," Derek says. "Can't see you. Can't hear you. Doesn't mean I don't know exactly where you are and exactly what you're saying. Now piss off."

I lay my hand on Derek's arm. "I'm giving him two minutes."

Derek's jaw works, but he only eases back with a curt nod.

I turn to the ghost. "I mean that. Two minutes." I lift my watch and hit a timer. "Go."

"It's my sister. I . . . I died last night. Not really sure how." A strained chuckle. "Well, I may not know how—that part's a blank— but I do know why. I got mixed up in . . ." He swallows. "Can I have three minutes? Please?"

"Just talk."

He rocks back on his heels. "It's just me and my sister. Half sister. She's thirteen. Our mom died last year. I've been trying to take care of my sister—Gina—and I got mixed up in . . ."

He stuffs his hands into his pockets. "I agreed to move some product. Drugs. A onetime thing. A buddy convinced me it was easy money. As you can see"—he throws up his arms—"not so easy. I got the drugs, and then they disappeared. When I explained, the dealer threatened to go after my sister. I freaked out and . . . and that's the last thing I remember."

The ghost inhales deeply, those habits of life slow to fade.

"Now she's in danger. She was staying at a friend's house last night. I've been haunting the apartment, waiting for her. She came home at lunch and found two guys searching the place. So she ran. They went after her. I followed as long as I could. Then I lost her. Now she's out there, and they're hunting for her, thinking she knows where to find the drugs, and I can't even explain to her what's going on."

"You want me to tell the police?" I say. "Explain it to *them* so they can find her?"

"Normally, yes. Absolutely. But this dealer gets his drugs *from* a cop. Stolen from evidence."

"So you're asking me to . . ."

"Find Gina. Tell her what's happened. Help her. Please. And tell her I'm sorry. Tell her I'm so, so sorry."

>‍><‍<

Derek and I are in our apartment. I told him the ghost's story on the way up. As for the ghost himself—Justin—I told *him* I'd think about it and took down the information he provided, in case we followed up. I'm afraid that was an excuse, empty words blurted to let me flee like a coward so I didn't have to tell him no.

Now I'm curled up on the sofa with Derek, my back against him, his arms around me. We aren't talking. We haven't talked since I finished the story. I'm holding back the plaintive cry of "We have to do *something*," and he's holding back the ugly truth of "There's nothing we can do."

No, there's nothing we *should* do. That's the problem. If we couldn't honestly do anything, we'd just feel bad. *Refusing* to do anything is so much worse.

Finally, he says, "I'll let Sean know. His people can look for her."

Sean Nast is the guy who took us in, who built an entire wilderness community for the Edison Group subjects, where we could grow up in safety. He's also the one who sends our "parole officers" to check in on us. As the co-CEO of a supernatural Cabal, he has entire security departments at his disposal. He can—and will—send investigators to find this girl.

But when? How long will it take to reorganize missions and dispatch help? Too long for a thirteen-year-old girl with a murderous drug dealer on her tail.

"We can't get involved," Derek says. "This is a dealer. A guy who obviously has no problem killing anyone who gets in his way. We'll tell Maya and Daniel about it."

I don't answer. He doesn't expect me to. While our friends would happily fly from Vancouver to help, we can't dump this on them.

"We'll . . . figure out something," Derek says.

I nod and push to my feet. "I'll start the spaghetti."

He nudges me back down. "I've got it. You write down what Justin told you. Get all the details out while you remember them."

I kiss his cheek. "Thank you."

He hugs me, murmurs again that we'll figure something out, and then pads off to the kitchen to start dinner.

>—><—<

Between readings that evening, I look up Justin's story. That's the first basic step, and there's a good chance it'll be the last. He wouldn't be the first secret supernatural—living or dead—to try luring us into trouble with a sob story. That's what I'm hoping for here. That I'll find no evidence to corroborate his claims and we can leave it at that.

I find the story right away. The body of a young man discovered in the ravines this morning, dead of a gunshot wound. Lacking ID, the police are circulating a sketch and description. It's Justin. While the police aren't speculating on the manner of his death, someone in the comments points out that the spot where he was found is known for drug activity. Also, in Toronto, gun-related death usually means organized crime of some variety.

So Justin's story checks out. I tell Derek. He grunts and keeps working, soldering circuits for a project. That doesn't mean we've dropped it—just that we're letting it slide for now. Taking time to think this through and make our decision in the morning.

><<

Derek and I have been together since I was fifteen. Thus followed years of impatiently waiting for the day when we could start sleeping together. I don't mean sex. Even in a community as small as ours, it was easy enough to find private time. What we longed for was the actual "sleeping together." Not needing to part at the end of the evening. Going to bed together and waking up together and truly feeling like a couple who planned to *be* together for the rest of their lives.

For us, it's more than simple nighttime companionship. It's about feeling safe and knowing the other is safe. We sleep curled up and entwined, his arms around me, my head against his chest. This means that if one of us slips from bed, the other almost certainly notices. So that night, when his warmth and his heartbeat disappear, I wake to hear the soft swish of him pulling on his jeans.

"Going for a run?" I ask.

The sound stops, and I crack open one eye to see him poised in a sliver of moonlight, his chest bare, jeans half on.

Derek's "runs" aren't jogs through the streets of Toronto. We have a car, which spends most of its life in a very expensive parking garage, the advantage of having a rich father who tries to cushion my life with stacks of cash. That car usually comes out only when Derek and I go to the ravines—or outside the city—for his runs. If I'm swamped with work, he'll insist on going alone. I'm not currently swamped with work.

Still, he could say yes. When *he's* swamped with work, he sometimes needs the stress release of a run, and he wouldn't wake me at two a.m. to accompany him. It'd be such an easy lie to tell. Yet once we start lying to each other—even for the best reasons— we erode the thing we treasure above all else. Trust.

We have a small circle of people in our lives that we trust, but none so implicitly as each other. In this life, we need that. The one person who would never betray us, never hurt us, never lie to us.

"I'm restless," he says. "Not sleeping. No reason you shouldn't."

I lift onto my elbow. "So you're going for a walk?"

"Yeah."

"Over to Justin's apartment to see whether you can pick up his sister's trail?"

When he's quiet, I sit up. "Answer carefully, Derek. Because if you say you just need air, and then I find out you ended up three miles away at their apartment, I'll sleep on the sofa for a month."

One brow rises. "Shouldn't I be the one sleeping on the sofa?"

"You'll feel worse if I do."

A low rumble of a laugh. "True." He sits on the edge of the bed and tucks back a lock of my hair. "I wasn't planning to follow her trail, necessarily. To do that, I'd need her scent. I was going to see whether Justin was right about the key being in the garden."

"And if it was?"

"I'd go in and find a scent source."

"Then come straight home without trying to find her trail? Leave that until tomorrow because it's so much easier sniffing city sidewalks in broad daylight?"

He sighs and leans against the headboard. "Yeah, I guess I'd have checked it out. I just wasn't thinking that far ahead."

"You always think that far ahead, Derek. You just weren't committing to trying to find her. Baby steps. With any luck, there'd be no key, so we could stop there. Or you wouldn't be able to find a good source of her scent in the apartment, so we could stop there. Or the trail would be cold, so we could stop there." I shift up beside him. "Not that you'd actually be happy if we had an excuse to stop. The excuse is telling yourself you were looking for an excuse."

He sighs again, deeper. "We don't need this shit."

"We don't."

"It doesn't involve us."

"It doesn't."

"We could get hurt."

When I don't answer that, he manages a still deeper sigh, one that shudders through him. "Fine. Yes. I wasn't thinking that I could get hurt. I was thinking *you* could. I was leaving you behind, which is stupid. I should have backup. Second pair of eyes and all that. And if I *had* managed to sneak out, you'd have been very cross with me."

I sputter a laugh. "Which is *terrible*."

"It is." He glances over. "I'd rather you fought, like Maya. Lose your temper. Yell at me. Maybe throw a few things. Kick my ass. Your 'very cross' is so much worse. Almost as bad as 'quietly disappointed.'"

I hug him. "Well, you got away with 'mildly exasperated' this time. Now let's go see if we can find a scent source. We'll be fine. Remember, the couple that breaks and enters together goes to prison together."

He shakes his head and pushes out of bed, and we get ready to go.

>―<

The key is where Justin said to expect it. He and his sister live in an old house that's been converted to apartments, and they keep a key under a garden rock. From there, it's just a matter of climbing rickety external stairs and opening the apartment. Inside we find a photograph with a woman—their mother, I presume—looping her arms around a teenage Justin and a preteen girl who must be Gina.

I'm stepping outside when Derek yanks me back and shoulders past me without a word. At one time, I'd have grumbled at him wanting to take the lead, put himself between me and the oh-so-dangerous world. That's changed—for both of us. If he pulled me back, it's because he saw something.

He stands on the tiny stoop and scans the narrow laneway below the stairs.

"Is there another exit?" he asks, his voice a low rumble.

"A window. I could take that."

I don't suggest he go out the window—he wouldn't fit. He pauses, weighing the safety of sending me another way against the danger of me going it alone.

"Do you see something?" I whisper.

"Heard. Footsteps."

His gaze sweeps back and forth like a searchlight. The lane is dark and silent. Or it is to me. His night vision and werewolf hearing mean he's rightly the person who should step out first.

"You think someone's staking out the apartment," I whisper.

"They killed the guy who lived here. After he ripped them off.

Now they're after his sister. Who also lives here." His voice drops to an almost inaudible mutter. "Why didn't I expect this? Fucking stupid."

"We both didn't expect it, because dealing with drug dealers isn't really our thing."

Another muttered profanity. Then, "I'm going down. As soon as I give the all clear, follow. Or if you hear a fight, get over to that coffee shop on the corner. I'll meet you inside."

I want to argue, but he's right. Before he can leave, I catch his sleeve.

"These aren't supernaturals," I say. "They may have guns."

"Yeah, I know. Be careful."

He slips down the rickety steps, somehow managing not to creak a single one, despite his size. I withdraw into the shadows of the doorway.

Below, the lane remains silent and still. Derek pauses and sniffs the air. A sharp shake of his head has me stifling a laugh. Sniffing an alleyway on a warm night is never the best idea.

He rubs his nose and then inhales again. His head swivels, as if he's caught a sound. It's coming from farther down the laneway. He takes one step in that direction. Then he pauses and peers toward the street. A car passes. That must be all that caught his attention, though, because after it's gone, he's making his way down the lane.

I lose sight of him three steps into the darkness, and my pulse quickens. I resist the urge to try getting a better look, and I strain to listen instead. This is one thing that living with a werewolf has taught me—use all your senses. Hearing works here, especially when I close my eyes and focus.

I don't hear Derek's footsteps. That's normal. If I were a werewolf, I might pick up the faint scuff of his shoes, but to a human, he moves silently. Right now, silence in general is good. It means he hasn't found anything. Then comes a cry of surprise, too high-pitched to be Derek. The smack of fist hitting flesh. The thud of a body slamming into a wall. Grunts and groans, none of them my boyfriend's, but that doesn't keep me from bouncing on my toes, wanting to clamber down those stairs and see what's happening.

I know what's happening. I can tell by the sounds. Derek got the jump on whoever was watching the apartment. Time for me to run. Get to that coffee shop.

That's the plan. And the plan, frankly, sucks. It's the antithesis of what I imagined in those movies I'd write someday, where the girl never needed to run while her boyfriend fought the bad guys. But this is the story I'm stuck with. He's the genetically modified super-soldier, and I'm the girl who can talk to ghosts. One of these things is always better in a fight. The other can fight, but having her there worries and distracts him. That stings, and it will never stop stinging, but the best way to keep him safe is to do as he said—use this diversion to get to safety.

I scamper down the stairs as quietly as possible, which isn't quietly at all. Derek hears me. I can tell when words punctuate the sounds of fighting. "Why were you following me?" "What do you want?" Meaningless dialogue as he makes sure they don't hear me.

I creep toward the end of the lane. Duck around the corner, onto the street and—

Hands grab me. I yelp, but one of those hands slaps over my mouth, and before I can even process what's happening, I'm propelled into a shadow-shrouded doorway and shoved up against the wall. A guy's face lowers to mine. Pale skin glows from the depths of a hoodie, and that's all I see. No gun, though. Not in his hands, at least.

"Where's the girl?" a man's voice says.

"G-girl?"

"What did you want in that apartment?"

"N-nothing," I say, faking my stammer. "M-my b-boyfriend said a f-friend of his—"

The guy gasps, head jerking up. I slam him backward, and he stumbles, hand clapping to his stomach, where blood oozes through his fingers.

"You—you—"

As I brandish the switchblade, my attention stays on his hands, watching to see if he'll go for a gun while I back out of the doorway onto the sidewalk. A passing car doesn't even slow.

The guy advances on me, one hand pressed to his wound, the other jabbing at me. "You think you can get away with that?"

"Kinda, yeah. The real question is whether you're going to get away with *that*." I nod at his injury. "Or do you want more?"

It's pure bravado. Laughable even, and his face twists. Then he freezes. Blinks. Backs away, hands rising before he wheels and tears off down the street.

"You're right behind me, aren't you?" I say.

"Yeah."

I turn to see Derek. He's in half shadow, a massive dark hulk with blood dripping from a cut lip. It's his hand that sent the guy running, though. It's misshapen, the nails thickened to claws. A localized partial Change makes a very nice weapon, but—when dealing with humans—it's even better as a pure "What the hell?" scare tactic, especially paired with the blood dripping from his mouth.

"Is the other guy gone?" I say, nodding to the alley.

"Both of them, yeah."

I arch my brows.

"Seems I interrupted a drug deal," he says.

"Ah. Well, maybe you scared them straight."

A rumbling chuckle. "Doubt it." He shakes his head. "First I didn't think to see if anyone was watching the apartment. Then I missed the *actual* guy who was. I'm screwing up all over the place, and we've barely started."

"*We're* screwing up. If they were Cabal half demons sent to kidnap us, we'd be fine. This is not our wheelhouse." I glance back toward the apartment. "I'll understand if you want to quit. You're already injured."

"Just a bloody lip. If you're okay to keep going . . ."

"I am. We just really need to make sure we aren't being followed, or instead of rescuing this girl, we'll lead the bad guys right to her."

"Agreed."

➤➤◄

There seemed to only be the one guy watching the apartment, and we follow his trail a half block where it disappears at the curb, as if he called a friend or a cab. If he's smart, the hospital will be his next stop. We don't see anyone else around, but we keep our eyes out as we backtrack to the apartment and start following Gina's trail. Well, Derek follows it. He hasn't shifted. Whatever the hour, a two-hundred-pound black wolf in downtown Toronto is kinda noticeable.

Wolf form *would* be easier—Derek could just walk with his nose down. Being in human form requires stopping for a sniff check at every corner and backtracking when he loses the trail, woven through a hundred others.

Justin warned us that Gina had no place to go. She had no idea where her father was. More distant relatives were indeed distant, living in the prairies and long out of contact. There'd been a teacher she'd been close to, but she'd retired last year. Their social worker was new, and Gina didn't feel comfortable with her yet. While she had plenty of friends, she wouldn't bring trouble to their doorsteps.

Her trail confirms the sad truth of her situation. After she fled the apartment, she'd moved from public space to public space. A coffee shop. A library. Another coffee shop. Eaton Centre mall. Derek loses her outside the last. Too many scents and too many entrances.

We're standing on a street corner, waiting for the light to change—despite the complete lack of cars—when Derek's head jerks up. After making sure there's no one around, he drops to one knee and sniffs near the sidewalk.

I'm about to ask whether he smells something when a movement catches my attention. Someone's crossing the road a half block down. Just as I lay my fingers on Derek's shoulder, the woman moves under a streetlamp, and I see her A-line polka-dot dress. A car turns the corner and heads straight for her, and she only glances at it. The car whooshes past, close enough to ruffle her skirt, which stays perfectly flat.

The ghost crosses to our side and strolls our way. I press the amulet under my T-shirt. A family heirloom, it douses the glow that marks me as someone who can hear the dead. For an ordinary necromancer, it would cover that light entirely. For me, it just turns my neon pulsing *Necromancer Here!* sign into a gentle glow. If ghosts do see it, experienced ones presume I'm a very weak and untrained necromancer, lacking the power to help them.

"Gina came this way," Derek says as he rises.

"Oh? Great. All right, then. Can you tell which way she went? I know it's hard to determine scent direction."

His brows rise only for a split second before he recognizes my blather as cover.

Why hello, ghost lady who is walking straight toward me. I'm afraid I don't see you there. I'm just so busy talking to my boyfriend. Deep in very important conversation.

It isn't necessary. The ghost doesn't seem to see me. She just strolls along, humming under her breath, ignoring the humans at the streetlight.

"The girl by the city hall skating rink," she says as she passes.

I blink as she keeps going. "Wh-what?"

She stops and looks over her shoulder. "You are looking for a girl, yes? That's what I thought I heard when your boyfriend was sniffing around earlier. Werewolf, I presume?"

"Uh, yes . . ."

She smiles, lipstick glowing a cartoon red under the streetlight. "Haven't seen one of those in ages. As for the girl . . . Thirteen, maybe fourteen? Running from someone?"

"Not us."

She gives a tinkling laugh. "Ah, sugar, I had no doubt of that. Neither of you strikes me as the sort who goes around frightening children." She glances at Derek. "Not on purpose, anyway. Go help the girl. Poor thing's putting on a brave face, but she's scared out of her wits. This town ain't too bad, but no place is good for a girl like that on her own."

"Thank you." I pause. "If there's anything I can do—"

Her tinkling laugh cuts me short. "Not looking for quid pro quo, sugar. Just a fellow traveler in the night. You take care of yourself now."

With that, she's gone, sauntering along the dark street.

I tell Derek what she said.

"Seem legit?" he says.

"Yes, but after earlier, we can't take chances."

"Let's go check it out, then. Carefully."

>—<—<

It isn't a trap. There's a girl huddled behind the giant *TORONTO* sign in Nathan Phillips Square, and she's the one from that photograph in Justin and Gina's apartment. She has her back against the sign, arms wrapped around her knees, backpack at her side. As we watch, a passing homeless man spots her and gives her wide berth. A woman pushing a cart walks over and exchanges a few words before moving on.

"She was telling Gina where she can find a shelter for teens," Derek says.

"Not exactly well hidden, is she? No wonder that ghost noticed her."

"You think that's suspicious?"

I shake my head. "I think she's even worse at this sort of thing than we are. She's tired and scared, and at least here, if someone does grab her, she might be able to scream and bring help."

Tucked behind that sign next to the out-of-season skating rink, she's on the doorstep of city hall, in the heart of downtown. Did she really pick the spot because it was safe? Or because she's hoping someone will notice her, someone who can do more than direct her to the nearest teen shelter?

At least this makes our job easy. Not like we need to worry about her bolting. Well, not unless . . .

I glance at Derek.

"I'm staying here," he says. "I've got your back, but yeah, I'm not exactly the friendly face she needs right now."

I put my arms around his neck and rise up to kiss him. A quick squeeze, and then I'm off. I get halfway there before Gina sees me coming. She doesn't tense. Doesn't grab her backpack. Just watches me approach.

"Gina?" I say.

That has her stiffening. I put out my palms and stay back. She gives me a once-over and relaxes. I might not have Derek's brute strength, but there's power in being able to lower people's defenses, too.

"Don't go back to your apartment," I say. "There's a guy watching it."

"I know." Not defensive. Not sarcastic. Flat, emotionless, empty. Defeated.

"Do you know what happened to your brother?" I ask.

Every muscle tenses, and grief flashes before she ducks her face, letting her light brown hair curtain it from view.

"I saw the news," she says. "After . . . after I realized Justin hadn't come home, I knew—Fuck!"

The word takes me by surprise as she slams her fist into the ground.

"He was stupid," she says. "Always so fucking stupid. And see, Justin, now that you're gone there's no one to tell me I shouldn't swear, is there?"

Tears well up as she continues. "You and your stupid, stupid schemes. We didn't need the money. We never needed it, but you had to have it. Dad sent enough. Then you lost your job and suddenly you're being stupid, doing stupid things and treating *me* like the stupid one, too dumb to figure it out."

She swipes at her face. Then she looks up at me. "It's true, isn't it? What was in the news. That was him."

I crouch to her level, staying an arm's length away. "It is. I'm sorry."

The tears burst through then, streaming down her face as she begins to sob.

>≻≺<

We have a problem. Well, the first problem is what to do with Gina while we sort this out, but we can handle that. The bigger issue is that Justin lied. No one stole the drugs. He double-crossed the dealer.

According to Gina, everything had been fine while Justin worked in a sandwich shop. When the shop closed down, Justin said they'd be okay until he found a new job. Her dad sent them money every month, and it was enough to live on. Then Justin started sneaking around, making furtive calls, buying a second phone. She followed him and heard that he owed money to a guy, which he promised to repay soon. He had a plan. That plan, apparently, was double-crossing a drug dealer.

Gina had been following him when he took possession of the drugs. Then she watched where he hid them—inside the still-shuttered sandwich shop. That night, he told her to stay at a friend's place. Yesterday, she went home at lunch to find two guys searching their apartment. She'd fled and realized that whatever Justin was up to, it'd gone wrong. That was when she went to a library and found the story about the unidentified body.

So Justin hid the drugs and then told the dealer they'd been stolen, and the guy threatened his sister . . . and then shot him? Wouldn't they try to get his sister then, use her as leverage?

They're following Gina because they think she has the drugs. What's the chance that Justin's partner in crime is his thirteen-year-old sister? No. There's a reason they think Gina knows more, and I hate it. For Gina's sake, I really hate it.

><×<

We've put Gina up in a hotel. That seems oddly impersonal. She's thirteen—shouldn't we take her back to our place? No. One, Justin knows where we live, and I don't trust him. Two, while Derek would never complain, I know he's uncomfortable with strangers in his "den." I can easily afford to check into an upscale hotel, and that seems the safest place for Gina while we resolve this.

Then we need to confront Justin.

"Justin!" I call, as Derek and I stand in the courtyard behind our apartment. "Time for another chat."

The ghost doesn't show up right away. Usually, I have a spirit guide to help me with this sort of thing. Liz was another subject in our experiment, one who didn't survive. Right now, she's out of contact, enjoying her afterlife. Wonderful for her . . . lousy timing for us.

Justin must be within shouting distance, though. A few minutes later, he comes running into the courtyard.

"Did you find her?" he says. "Please say yes. I've been checking out her friends' homes and her favorite spots all night."

"Why are they after Gina?" I say.

He blinks. "Because they think she has the drugs."

"Which you hid."

"What? No. Someone stole them. I put them—"

"—in the sandwich shop where you used to work."

He pauses.

"They're still there," I say. "We just checked."

That's a lie—we may have made mistakes tonight, but we aren't stupid enough to risk being found near a drug stash.

Justin swallows. "I . . ."

"You thought you could double-cross a dealer. He figured it out, probably because you aren't the first idiot to try it. They threatened your sister, and when you didn't tell them where the drugs were, they shot you." I continue. "So why go after Gina?"

"Like I said, they must think she knows where—"

"Bullshit. You're not bringing your kid sister in on a plot like this. You aren't even going to admit you *have* a little sister. You told them she took the drugs. That's why they're after her. They think she has the stash."

"No. I wouldn't—I'd never—This was *for* my sister. So we could keep the apartment until I got a new job."

"Why is she with you?" I ask. "Why are you her guardian?"

His eyes bug. "She's my sister."

"It's the money, isn't it? The money her dad sends."

He stares at me. Then very slowly, he sighs and drops his head to his hands. After a moment, he raises it.

"There is no money," he says, quietly. "After Mom died, I got in touch with Gina's dad, hoping he might help out. He told me to fuck off. Said Gina probably wasn't his anyway, and . . . And he said a lot more. Nothing I was ever going to tell Gina."

"So you lied."

He nods. "I made up a story about why he couldn't come and said he was sending money. My job at the sandwich shop was part time, minimum wage, but a few of us had a little side hustle selling weed. When the shop closed, I lost both jobs. I got in debt just paying rent on the apartment. The guy who supplied the weed gave me this job and told me to pretend I got mugged and someone stole the stuff. Then he'd buy it at half price. He said because I was a first-timer, they'd buy my story."

"They didn't, and you blamed Gina."

His mouth opens. Then his face falls, gaze dropping. "Yes," he says with a shudder. "I panicked. I said I had a little sister. I didn't actually say she stole it. I said maybe she found it and hid it to teach me a lesson. I said I'd fix things—I'd confront her and get it back. The guy said he could do that himself, and I realized what he meant and started to say I lied—that I had the dope—but it was too late."

I say nothing.

He continues. "I panicked. That's no excuse, but it's all I have. It was the first thing I thought of. I'd tell them that, now that I think about it, maybe no one stole it and my sister hid it. Then I'd give them back their stuff and it'd be fine."

He meets my gaze. "Help me fix this. Please. I don't care if she knows what I did and hates me for it. Just help me fix it."

>—><—<

It's not yet dawn, and we're outside the sandwich shop where Justin stashed the drugs. Following his instructions, we've contacted the dealer to let him know where to find his product. The most complicated part of this operation so far? Finding a pay phone to make that call. But it's done, and now we're safely in a coffee shop watching the building.

We want to be sure the guy gets his product, but I don't know how much good that will do. It's a drug dealer—it isn't like we can produce video evidence of him retrieving his goods, demand he leave Gina alone, and expect him to follow through on the deal. We can only trust that once he has his stuff, he'll have no reason to bother her. We also contacted Sean to help navigate her through the system and get help.

As for Gina herself, she isn't sleeping. Can't say I blame her. She's been texting for updates. I told her what we're doing, and she's been silent ever since. I could hope that means she's gone to sleep, but I think she's just waiting for my next message—the one to say it's done.

Justin has been accessing the shop through the delivery door, which he still had a key for. We can see that from our spot, along with the front door. When someone finally shows up, it's the guy I stabbed last night. He's with a bigger guy, who stands watch. The wounded one doesn't bother with the delivery door. He jimmies the front one and slips inside.

"Please find the stuff," I whisper, as I clutch my now-cold hot chocolate. "Please find it."

"He will," Derek says.

Sure enough, the door reopens and the guy walks out with a duffel bag.

"Okay," I say. "We'll let him get out of sight and then—"

A police car appears from nowhere, sirens flicking to life. The two guys turn to run, but two foot officers are already closing in from both sides. The bigger guy reaches under his jacket. He doesn't get a chance to pull out a gun. The officers are on him, their own weapons drawn.

That's when I see Gina. She's standing on the corner, arms crossed as she watches the arrest.

I'm on my feet and flying out the door before Derek can stop me. He catches up, and we continue down the road. Gina doesn't see us coming. She only sees the police cuffing the guys. When we draw close, I slow, in case she bolts, but she only turns to us and grins.

"You called them?" I say.

She nods. "They shot my brother. I'm not letting them get away with that."

No wonder she'd been so keen to know what we were doing. I'd considered doing this myself, but we'd decided our primary concern had to be Gina, and if the guys escaped the police, she'd be in even more danger.

As she watches the arrest, she glows with triumph. The moment they're gone, though, she sags.

"It doesn't help, does it?" she says. "Doesn't bring him back."

"No, but it's still a good thing, making them pay."

She shrugs. "I guess so. I just wish . . . I wish I knew why he'd done it. Why the money was so important." Her voice drops. "More important than me."

I lay my hand on her arm. "I think there's someone you need to talk to about that."

>-><-<

We return to the courtyard where I first met Justin. While Derek keeps Gina occupied, I summon Justin and tell him what I'm about to do, make sure he's okay with that. He is.

I explain to Gina that I'm a psychic, in contact with her brother. She's far less shocked than one might expect. There's an accepted place in the human world for people who can speak to ghosts—far more than those who can turn into wolves—and I never risk much by admitting what I can do.

I have Justin prove it's him—Gina asking a question only he can answer. She didn't want to bother with that, but it'll be important later, when the adrenaline rush of tonight passes and she questions what happened.

Once we've established he's really there, I act as interpreter while Derek leaves the courtyard, giving them as much privacy as we can manage.

Justin admits the truth about Gina's father, and the truth about what he did—panicking and blaming her for the drugs, thinking the lie would give him a chance to fix it.

They say everything they need to say. The love and the anger and the grief and the forgiveness. They spend one last hour together, and then Gina sets him free, tells him she'll be fine and he needs to go someplace better, trusts he *will* go someplace better, that he deserves it. He does, and he will. I'm certain of that.

>✕<

That evening we're back in our apartment, right where we were when this started, on the couch with me curled up on Derek's lap, both of us sitting in silent contemplation. Gina is safely with one of Sean's people, who'll keep her safe while they figure out the next steps to her new life.

"You made the right call listening to this ghost," Derek says. "He's found peace, and his sister is safe, thanks to you."

"Thanks to *us*," I say. "Thank you for helping."

He snorts. "Like I'd just let you do it on your own. I want to help, too, Chloe. You know that. Sure, part of me would rather we holed up in a den I can protect. But that's not how you're wired."

"It's not how you're wired, either."

He lifts one shoulder in a shrug. "Maybe. All I do know is that it's been killing you to watch Maya and Daniel help others while we bury ourselves in our studies and pretend we don't have time for anything else. If they have time, we do, too. School comes first, but that doesn't mean we can't lend a hand now and then to someone who needs it as badly as we once did. Would that make you feel better?"

I nod. "It would."

He reaches for his phone. "Then let's see what Maya has for us."

I lean over to kiss him. Then we make the call.

TRAIN TO LAST HOPE

by Annie Bellet

A faint breeze rustled the curtains on the windows and brought the sound of the morning train into my kitchen. The air had held anticipation of summer storms all week, like a child holding her breath on a dare and then forgetting why, sending my weather-sense onto its last nerve. Baking in the sticky, expectant heat was faint help but it was something to do. I set the pan of blondies to cool as the horn pealed, almost drowning out the creak of my porch steps. The knock came in the stillness after. I took my time going to the door. When you're a witch living at the final stop before the world of the living crashes into the underworld, unexpected company is rarely a vacuum salesman or someone dropping in for coffee and gossip.

The visitor tipped the brim of her hat back as I stood a frozen breath away behind the screen door.

"Hello, Cassidy. You going to invite me in?" she asked, her voice as smooth and low as I remembered.

I shook my head and found my voice. "Even here we know better than to let Death into our homes." I couldn't find a smile in me to soften the words.

The train sounded again, stopping us both from talking for a long moment as we stared at each other. Stared into our pasts, I imagined. Raina was just as tall and lean as ever, but the sword was new to me. When she'd come back a decade before and told me what she'd done, what she'd given up, she'd still had warmth to her. Now she was just hard, her dove-grey eyes changed to an icy inhuman blue that sparked with inner fire. Her glorious hair was hidden beneath the brim of a stained and worn Stetson. Through the dusty screen I couldn't see her freckles, the constellations on her smooth, light brown skin. It didn't matter. If I closed my eyes I could still trace them all by heart.

I had a moment to wonder if she saw me the same. There was more grey in my black braids, more me on my hips and thighs in general I supposed. And still the space between us where everything had gone wrong, daughter-shaped and eternally aching.

"I found her trail," Raina said as the train faded into the distance. "I found it."

Her trail, but not Mairi, not our daughter. I knew that from the tightness of Raina's jaw, and from the raw certainty that hadn't left me since that dream, that final cold dawn when I'd known with every ounce of motherhood and magic in me that my baby was gone from the living. Ten years ago, but staring into Raina's expectant, even hopeful face, it was like it was ten minutes. Raina had never believed the worst. She'd never stopped searching.

"We can't do this again," I said, unable to meet her gaze. I remembered watching the hope die in her pale eyes once before. I wasn't sure the parts of me left would survive a second time.

"What if you're wrong, Cass?" Raina said.

I clenched my fists and turned away. It wasn't that I had given up, something she never understood. It was that I knew. I *knew*.

"Wait," she said, the word a command. "Even if . . . even if you were right, some kind of answers are more than we've got."

I'd known we all handle grief in our own ways. At first we'd searched for Mairi together, until all sign of her turned dusty and blew away and the space between us that had opened when her letters stopped coming grew from our hearts to physical. After, well, I'd come here to Last Hope, to the edge of living, waiting for the train to bring our baby's soul to the next world. Morning and evening, for years I'd made my way to the platform to watch the ghosts of the newly dead shuffle past until my heart broke from waiting alone in silence and disappointment too many times.

I had known my wife would keep looking, but I'd thought that our endless argument of fault and recrimination wouldn't be the end of everything, that she'd eventually realize some things had no answers. I'd thought she'd come back to me when she had accepted things how they were, and not how she wished they'd be.

But Raina . . . she'd kept going, straight to where the living should not go. She'd made a deal with Death and taken on the mantle of a Reaper, destined to hunt the earth retrieving wayward souls and escaped demons. Mairi's name wasn't on the scrolls, her soul unrecorded. So Raina searched, convinced our baby lived. Leaving me alone to bake away my grief and go on living. Go on waiting for all the empty parts of myself to scab over in time.

She stood on my porch, this woman I'd loved like my own heartbeat, two feet, a screen door, and ten years of pain between us, and repeated the words that would always break my heart even as I turned back to face her.

"I need you, Cassidy," she said softly. "There's places I can't go, people don't like to talk to me so much. Help me find her. Please."

Distant thunder rolled, the storm's far-off power licking along my skin with teasing promise. Wind rushed through the dry branches and rattled the screen like old bones.

"Give me a few minutes," I said. "I'll put some things together."

"Pack light, we're going on horseback and it's far."

I almost asked how far, but realized it didn't matter. Raina had come back to me, and though I knew only grief lay down this hollow road, she was maybe a little right about one thing. This had to be finished, for both of us, one way or another.

I traded my skirt for jeans and my slippers for boots. A spare shirt and socks in my bag. Needle and thread, candles, salt, and a small box with shavings of oak, rowan, and ash followed. As a last-minute decision, I put the butterscotch blondies into a tin and packed that. I tied my braids up and put a kerchief over them. I checked the windows one last time and then I was out of delay.

"Almost thought you'd changed your mind," Raina said as she leaned against the porch railing.

I locked the door behind me. "Where are the horses?" The gravel driveway was empty. In the distance the shapes of the town buildings grew indistinct as the herald wind kicked up summer dust. I took a deep breath and could almost taste the petrichor, though no rain had yet fallen.

Raina whistled and a cold tide of power washed over me. My ears popped as the biggest horse I'd ever seen melted into existence from the shadows beneath the spreading oak shading my little house. Its coat was black as ink, its eyes burning red like live coals, and its hooves struck sparks from the gravel as the horse danced up to Raina. It yanked her hat off her head and for a moment my heart stopped as her hair, waves of glorious rich black and silver curls, tumbled free of its twist.

I had no right, but I was secretly, selfishly glad she hadn't cut it.

"What's his name?" I asked, making myself walk toward them.

"She, and she's got none," Raina said, pulling her hair back into a knot before she jammed her retrieved hat back over it.

"Every horse should have a name," I said, tentatively reaching a hand out to stroke the horse's cold velvet nose.

"She's a Nightmare," Raina muttered. I raised my eyebrows and she added, "Hat Destroyer has a ring to it, I suppose. Be careful of your braids, she eats those, too."

Power, cold and foreign to my own, played down my hand. Neither painful nor pleasant, but the mare snorted when I pulled my fingers away. I risked another gentle stroke.

"What's in this? Rocks?" Raina asked as she stuffed my bag into her own saddlebags.

"Butterscotch blondies," I said. "You wanted a hearth witch, you are getting a hearth witch," I added when she shook her head at me.

Raina leapt effortlessly into the saddle and then extended her hand.

She still hadn't told me where we were going, but I looked at her outstretched hand, the same hand that had rubbed my swollen feet when I was pregnant, that had lifted our daughter up whenever she fell, and had held me through all our darkest nights save the last. Her strong fingers that had intertwined with mine a thousand times, and I figured, what was one more. I crossed the distance between us and let her pull me up.

Raina warned me that "she goes fast, hang on," and that was all I got before the Nightmare took off at a smooth but terrifying gallop. My arms went around Raina's narrow waist before I could stop myself, but I let go and grabbed for loose ties on the saddle to steady myself before she could say a word. I kept my eyes fixed on her back after a stomach-dropping glance to the landscape rushing by in a blur.

We were going too quickly to talk; the wind created by our speed would have whipped the words away. I gritted my teeth in frustration but decided to focus on staying on the Nightmare and not losing my breakfast. The ride gave me far too much time to chew over the past as memories I'd thought well-buried churned to the surface.

Mairi had taken after me in her magic, her love of living creatures great and small, of gardening. Also in her eyes, the color if not the texture of her hair, and the shape of her nose. But in all else, height, loose curls, and bullheaded desire to get her own way, she'd taken after Raina.

Mairi had left home at seventeen. Raina had wanted to go after her, but I'd stopped her. Mairi was like one of Raina's mustangs; I worried that if we tried too hard to tie her down, we'd lose her worse. I thought we could let her run and feel out the world a little, that then she'd come home when the money ran out and she realized that being alone wasn't freedom.

The letters started coming a few months after she left and they had felt like vindication for me while soothing Raina's anger. Mairi had joined a traveling carnival, working with the horses and learning acrobatics. She wrote detailed and funny accounts of her new friends, of the carnival life, and always at the end expressed that she loved us both and was glad we hadn't done, in her words, anything too rash about her leaving.

The letters might have calmed Raina, but I could see now, with the gift of a decade of heartache and self-recrimination, that the rift between us had started when our daughter left. Tiny stress fractures in what we'd always thought was a solid foundation. Mairi was careful to never mention places or too many names; she used nicknames for everyone, even the horses. She wanted to assure us she was fine, but she was wary of us dragging her home.

For a solid year, the letters came every couple weeks, not quite clockwork but regular enough to look forward to. Then I had the dream, the nightmare that ended everything. I'd heard our baby screaming for us and felt when she stopped. I'd awoken screaming. Raina refused to believe it was more than a mother's anxious dreaming.

But there were no more letters. It had been a couple weeks since the last when I had the dream, and week after painful week scraped by, no letters. I knew in my heart that something terrible had happened. Three weeks after, Raina and I started the search. We had little to go on from Mairi's words; it was clear a week into our search that she'd changed more details than we knew.

Weeks of dead ends and false trails before my tired soul couldn't take it anymore. We fought about every small thing, round and round as we hashed out the *what-ifs* and *could-have-dones*. Until Raina left me, riding off without so much as a backward glance and I retreated to Last Hope, baking and waiting for the train that might bring my baby past me one last time.

Tears stung my eyes and I told myself it was from the wind. The urge to press my cheek against Raina's leather-clad back so straight and strong in front of me was nearly overwhelming. She'd come to me, finally, asked me to take this journey with her one last time, but I knew it wasn't more, that some canyons can't be bridged. So I sat straight, blinked away my tears, and hung on.

The day fled past us with the miles and the sun was kissing the tops of lodge pole pines when the Nightmare slowed to a walk. The landscape had changed from the open prairie and oak-dotted land around Last Hope to rocky and pine forested, mountains I didn't recognize rising from dusk-shadowed foothills. Train tracks stretched alongside the hard-packed road we ambled up and I smelled wood smoke.

"Just ahead." Raina spoke for the first time as I shifted my sore body behind her. "There's a little town, got a hotel. I have a receipt signed by Mairi from there. It was in some things sold at a flea market, tucked in a book of western flora and fauna."

Raina halted the Nightmare and slung her leg over the horse's neck, dropping to the ground before I could respond. She offered her hand but I ignored it and dismounted with all the grace of a sack of potatoes. Sore, bitter potatoes.

"That's all you got?" I said as I peeled my dignity and my ass up off the ground. "A receipt?"

"It's more than we ever had," she said, arms crossed. "But the man who runs the place won't talk to me. He just locked everything up when I tried to talk to him, and then threatened me with a gun."

"Maybe you should have tried not wearing the sword," I muttered. The long blade was sheathed in black tooled leather that echoed her vest, the cold-looking sapphire in the hilt glinting with inner fire.

Raina put a hand on the pommel. "I think you'll have an easier time, people always liked talking to you."

"And I won't make any wards flare up," I guessed. From Raina's tight smile, my guess was right. The hotel owner was smart enough to at least salt his thresholds, which though meant to ward against evil spirits and demons would still cause a problem for a Reaper. After all, they came from the same place as escaped demons.

"The carnival came through here," Raina said. "I'm sure of that much. Someone will know where it went after." She set out up the road, walking with a confidence that said I'd follow.

I wasn't about to be left alone here an unknown number of miles from home, so I supposed her confidence was justified. "You check the next town up the road?" I asked as I fell in beside her, taking two steps for every one of hers until she noticed and slowed down.

"The road branches, as do the tracks. I checked both ways a while but all I got was closed doors and nervous looks." Raina's tense shoulders belied the offhand tone in her voice. A small muscle ticked in her jaw, one of her frustration tells. When that muscle moved, a fight was coming sure as wind rising before a storm.

"Nice to be needed," I said under my breath. I understood why she'd tried without me but I couldn't fully quell the hurt in my heart as it hit home how much coming back to me had been a last resort.

"You think Mairi is dead. I don't." Raina stopped so abruptly I walked three steps past her as she said the words. "Talking to you about finding her was like begging a river to run uphill. So don't get your panties bunched because I didn't come to you sooner; you made it real clear this wasn't a journey you were taking to the end."

I forced my fists to unclench as I spun and stared up into her face. There were a hundred things I wanted to say, but I'd said all of them before a hundred times.

"I'm here, aren't I?" I said after a couple deep breaths. I knew Mairi was gone, but I was willing to be wrong. Even if hope was breaking me into smaller pieces. Even if ten years was an alarming amount of time to go without writing her mothers.

Raina stepped back like I'd hit her and finally nodded. "Come on, then."

The Nightmare didn't follow. I assumed she'd go back to wherever it was she lurked until Raina called her. We walked side by side into the town. It wasn't that different from Last Hope, little bigger maybe but hard to tell from how many places were up among the trees. Lights were flaring to life as the sun sank into a red haze and a few people gave us wide berth as they went about their evening business.

The hotel stood a few buildings down from the train station, a big clean white sign with green lettering proclaiming what it was. The paint was scuffed but the steps didn't creak as I walked up them, leaving Raina behind me at the walkway. She handed me the carefully folded receipt: the linen paper scrap gone soft with age but the ink still visible. I didn't look too hard at it, not trusting Mairi's distinct swirling signature not to break my heart anew.

A bell dinged as I pushed through the door into a warm, somewhat shabby interior that smelled of tobacco smoke and faintly lemon-scented floor soap.

"Can I help you?" The man behind the long counter that appeared to double as a bar looked up as I walked in. He had a three-piece suit whose condition matched the hotel, wide brown eyes deep set into his pleasant face, and a nervously groomed mustache.

"I'm hoping so," I said, putting on my best Sunday potluck smile. "I'm looking for information on a traveling show that came through here, maybe nine, ten years ago?" I laid the receipt on the counter and smoothed it out. "Young woman with them, would have been working with the horses most likely. Probably looked like a taller, younger me, same coloring, but long hair and more big curls than mine. My daughter," I added as the man squinted at the receipt.

He rubbed his hand absently over his heart and shook his head, his eyes coming up to study my face. "Can't say I remember."

I wondered if he wanted a bribe but his expression had flat dismissiveness in it, not avarice. "This is from your hotel," I said, not making it a question. The name matched, the little drawn logo, all of it. The place had been fancier a decade ago, I imagined, glancing around at the polished wood and brass, the curtains clean but worn thin, the carpets likewise.

"Lot of people come through here, ma'am. I only remember the ones that make trouble or that come back. Guess your daughter wasn't either of those." His smile was bland as he studied the receipt again. "There was a carnival that came through I don't know, maybe a decade gone. They used our stables and the yard out back for a night, but they didn't stay. Can't say where they went, they just paid for feed and space for the night. Here, it's rubbed off mostly but you can see the line there."

The line was in a crease and whatever had been written was long gone beyond a few traces of ink. I didn't know if I believed him but I couldn't think why he'd lie to me. "Anyone else around during that time that might know where they went?" I asked.

He was about to answer when he looked past me and through the windows. The blood drained from his face, turning his light brown skin greyish, and he started reaching under the bar. Turning, I saw that Raina was wandering along the big porch, a shadow with blue coals for eyes and armed with a sword.

"She's not here to hurt anyone," I said without thinking as the hotelier pulled a sawed-off from beneath the bar.

"You with her?" He pointed the sawed-off at me but his finger wasn't on the trigger.

"She's also the girl's mother," I said, keeping my voice low and soft. "We're just trying to find our daughter."

"She's a Reaper. Came through here last week rattling the windows and yelling at folk. We're God-fearing people here, ma'am, we bury our dead proper and take no recourse from demons. We have no need for a Reaper here."

Oh, Raina. I sighed and took a slow step back from the counter, folding the receipt before sliding it into my pocket. "We're going, you can put away that gun. You'll want to see a doctor about your heart," I said.

"It's just indigestion," the man said, setting the gun on the bar. He kept his hand on it as though to reassure himself.

His aura and the way he'd been moving said otherwise, but I let it go. People didn't want us here, and I wasn't about to start revealing I was a witch to add any fuel to their suspicions.

I walked out onto the porch, keeping half an eye on the proprietor until the door was firmly closed behind me. Raina joined me.

"He doesn't know anything," I said, "though you walking around like that sure didn't loosen his tongue."

"She was here," Raina said.

"It's been ten years. The carnival only used his yard and bought some fodder for the animals. He doesn't remember Mairi and he doesn't know where they went."

"I knew her," said a soft, high voice. A girl with golden brown skin and wide-set brown eyes in a blue gingham dress who couldn't have been more than seventeen or eighteen came around the side of the hotel but stopped short of where she'd be seen from the windows. "Meet me on the other side of the station." She didn't wait for an answer before disappearing around the side again.

Raina gave me an "I told you so" look but mercifully held her tongue as we made our way to the train station and waited on the far side.

The girl showed up a few minutes later. She looked at Raina with curious, fearful eyes and stepped nearer to me.

"I'm Blythe," she said. "That's my daddy's hotel. I heard you asking about the girl with the horses, the carnival? You look like her. I mean, she wasn't fat or short but, oh, sorry. Mama says I can talk the ear off an earthworm." She flushed and ducked her head, her black rag-curls bouncing. "You a witch, too?"

My tired head hurt trying to follow the flood of words, and I nodded without thinking. "We just want to find Mairi," I said. "You remember her?" The girl couldn't have been more than eight back when the carnival came through.

"She was really nice. Said her name was May. She fixed my doll, wrapped this special string around her and said some magic words and it was like Ben had never broken her leg right off at all."

"Blythe," Raina said, pulling the girl's attention to her. "Where did May go? Do you know?"

"They went to White Water." She pointed down the tracks. "Follow the road and stay left, you'll see it in a couple days. It's not much now, just the train station and a few folk who stayed after the mines emptied. But May's friend Alice had a sweetheart there and she married him and they live in a big house. She'd know where May went after the mountain slid down."

"The mountain slid down?" I asked, dread pitching a tent in the empty pit of my belly.

"The old mine blew—well, part of it. Right when the carnival was there. Half the mountain came down. Missed the town, though. I remember we felt the shaking even from here. Nobody died," she assured me with a crooked-toothed smile.

"How do we find Alice's house?" I looked at Raina, but her face was a mask in the gloom, the flames of her eyes unreadable.

"Go into town and follow the small road until you see the creek. After that you'll see the flowers. You really can't miss it. Next year I'll be eighteen and then I can visit Alice. Mama thinks she's a witch 'cause of those flowers."

"Is she?" Raina said, amusement lacing her tone.

Blythe shrugged. "I don't know. Maybe that's why she and May were best friends."

We thanked the girl and started walking down the road without a word between us. The sun was gone, only a bloody smear of light remained to silhouette the trees.

"Once we're clear of town, we'll ride. Nightmare can do two days in a couple hours."

"We can't show up at night like this," I said, rubbing my arms for warmth. The heat of Last Hope was far behind me; the summer nights in this place were cooler with a promise of actual cold riding the light breeze.

"Let's go up the road a bit and camp till daylight," Raina said. I was surprised she didn't argue.

My ears popped again as the Nightmare emerged from the deepening gloom. I wasn't sure what supplies Raina had, or if Reapers even ate food anymore. Her lean, hard build told me nobody had been feeding her proper if she did.

Turned out Raina had a whole camp in those saddlebags. She pulled a bedroll from them, then a tin pot and cup, two cans of beans, and a hunk of smoked pork wrapped in waxed paper. She handed me my small pack and I fished out the blondies, nibbling one as I stood back and let her set up camp with the efficiency of a soldier. I lit the fire with a command after she made a pile of shavings for me, glad I could do one small thing.

"I have flint," she said, a hint of a smile playing at her lips.

"It's the most practical magic I know," I said with a shrug. For a while as we got comfortable around our small fire and filled our hungry bellies, things were almost amicable. I stopped short of saying I missed this, because it was a tiny step from that to saying I missed her, and that was a scab I was unwilling to pick. Even if it was already oozing just from having her solid and real beside me.

"I didn't ride far enough the last time," Raina said as she watched me set the wards.

"We'll find this Alice, tomorrow," I said as I finished walking the perimeter of our camp, my saltbox in hand. There was nothing out here but trees and small critters that I could sense, but a ward never went amiss. I looked at the pallet of blankets and thick felted pad she'd laid out.

"We can share, or I'll keep watch a while. I don't require much sleep."

That might have been a Reaper thing, but Raina had never slept well either. I couldn't count the nights I'd awoken with her pressed against my back, holding me in the dark of night, not sleeping, just watching the patterns on the wall turn from black to grey to blue. Sometimes we'd made love, her hands wandering my body until I was ready for her to press inside, but usually I'd pretend I was still sleeping, letting her hold me as she kept an eye on the dark hours.

"Sharing is fine," I lied. I was a grown-up, I could sleep next to someone and let the past be the past.

The fire banked, she lay down beside me, staying outside the wool blanket though I lifted a corner in offer. I closed my eyes and closed my heart, curling on my side away from her, trying to wish the night to pass.

"You ready to admit you might be wrong?"

"We doing this again?" I rolled onto my back and stared up at the shadow of her face as she leaned over me, her eyes like tiny blue stars. "Let it go. I'm here, I'll see it through with you, but hearts can't survive in pieces. I know what I know and I'm sorry I don't know how to show you." I wasn't sorry. I worried the pain of knowing the truth would kill all remaining light inside her.

"You should've let me go after her. Hell, before all that you should've told her the truth about her asshole fiancé."

The trouble with our daughter had started before she ran off, when she was fifteen and fell in love with a man ten years her senior. When we'd confronted him and told him he had to wait to marry our daughter, he'd asked for gold if we wanted him gone. I'd never let Raina tell Mairi the truth, preferring her angry at us for running him off than to let her live with a broken heart knowing her first lover played her false.

I closed my eyes as my nails bit into my palms. "She wasn't a doll we could keep on a shelf. We did what we could to protect her once and she hated us for it. If we'd gone after her, we would have lost her forever."

"If you are right," Raina said, the words hard and cold in the dark beyond my eyelids, "we lost anyway."

I said nothing because there was nothing left in me to say it.

We rode through the damp mist the next morning at blinding speed, only dismounting when we got to a sign telling us White Water was ahead. That final mile was walked in tense silence as well, neither of us feeling like fighting when a real answer might be over the next hill.

Blythe hadn't led us wrong; Alice's house was a pretty log cabin set among an explosion of blooms, many I recognized. A sweet hint of magic rode the air, so faint I nearly missed it and might have if it hadn't been so familiar to me.

"Mairi," I whispered, feeling the dance of her power on my skin. She'd used a lot of magic here, had a hand in this bounty. I practically ran down the path, Raina jogging behind me.

For a moment I believed in miracles; in that space between when I knocked at the door and it opened, I allowed myself to breathe in the scents of magic and life and to hope I was as wrong as I'd ever been.

Then the door opened and the woman who stood there had pale skin instead of brown, gold hair straight as straw instead of curls, and blue eyes instead of hazel. There had been no Alice in Mairi's letters, but she'd often mentioned a woman a few years older than she was, calling her "Goldie."

"Alice?" I asked.

"You're Cassidy," she said, wonder in her voice. "And Raina?" She looked behind me and her smile wavered. "You'd both best come in."

We sat at her kitchen table as she bustled around offering us coffee until finally she settled. "You're wondering about May? She spoke of you often and it's easy to see the resemblance, that's how I knew."

"Your garden?" I said, not sure where to start. "Mairi, that's May's full name, she planted it?"

"She helped me with the seeds, did her witch thing, well, you know," Alice said with a laugh. Then her face fell. "Did May send you here? Is she all right?" She looked between us, her eyes not quite meeting Raina's.

"We haven't heard from her in over ten years," I said softly.

"She was coming home?" Raina folded her hands on the table.

"Oh." Alice's face fell and she took a deep breath. "She said she might. But then things went bad here and I figured she'd gotten on the train like she talked about. Lot of us did, after the carnival burned."

I held up a hand to stop Raina from speaking. "Maybe you'd better tell us the whole story, Alice."

She did, at first in halting, scattered sentences as though she wasn't sure where to begin. She'd fallen in love with a man and planned to stay here in White Water since he worked on the trains all over but had family and land here. Her husband and her two kids were with their grandparents down the mountain a ways going fishing this week, which was why she was there alone.

She'd been an acrobat, dancing with the horses same as Mairi. Our daughter wasn't happy with the carnival since the owner's brother, Paulie, had arrived to help run it, but Alice wasn't sure why Mairi hated the man. She speculated that he'd been making passes at our daughter but said that May wasn't one to complain.

The trouble in White Water came when the main carnival tent caught fire, stalling them from moving on, though nobody was hurt. Then dynamite had been found on the tracks by the train bridge that crossed the Grand White River gorge.

"That was the last time I saw May," Alice said. "That night. She said something about the train schedules, seemed real upset. I asked my husband later, he said that the payroll was due to come through early the next morning. There were a lot more people around back then, though the town was already draining on account of the mine being low."

"Someone was planning to blow the tracks and rob the train?" Raina asked. She drummed her long fingers on the table and I reached out without thinking and stilled them with my own. I knew she wanted answers about Mairi, but people had to tell their story at their own pace.

"I think May knew about it," Alice said. "She was acting weird that day and then she said she had something to do. After that I guess somebody left a note for the train marshal to check the tracks and that's when they found it."

"The marshal listened?" Raina raised her eyebrows.

"The note was wrapped round a stick of dynamite, so yeah, he listened. My husband, he was just an apprentice then, he saw it. Said the handwriting was real loopy, like a fancy woman might write."

My heart began to dance inside my rib cage as a lump blocked my throat.

"That's why you think it was Mairi." Raina said what I couldn't find the voice to.

"She went up the mountain and later that night the mountain came down. A section of the old mine collapsed, everyone said it was probably an accident, but the timing wasn't too accidental. They dug for days but found no bodies. There's an old lodge up there and the rock slide missed it by inches. Paulie bought it, still runs the place as a gambling hall." Alice made a face. "He's not likely to give you answers. Maybe you're scary enough to make him." She said that last to Raina.

"I'll go and ask him," Raina said, baring her teeth in a grim smile.

"The flowers keep blooming," Alice said, her blue eyes fixing on my face. "Even in winter, right through the snow. That's why I'd hoped that . . . that May was all right. But she isn't, is she? Not if you're here."

I didn't know what the flowers meant. We witches can learn the words and focus our will and pull the life force from inside ourselves, use the right materials to try to invoke the power we want to exert on the world, but sometimes the magic doesn't work and sometimes it works in ways we'd never expect. Being a witch was more art than science. All I knew was that Mairi had left a piece of herself here, high in the mountains, in a garden overflowing with color and joy.

"I think I'd best go talk to Paulie," Raina said, standing up.

"Follow the trail after the station, you'll see the sign with the dice on it. I don't know what he'll have to say, though. Not much good goes up or comes down that mountain."

"I'll fit right in, then," Raina murmured.

I followed her out of the house, waiting until we were alone outside before I said, "You didn't say *we*."

"That's cause you're not going with me."

"Hell I'm not," I said, hands on hips. "You said we're seeing this through."

"Something bad is here, Cass," Raina said. "I smell the rot in the breeze. I don't know what I'll find up the mountain, but trouble is *my* job."

So she'd used me to talk to people and now she was done, back on her crusade, leaving me to wait. I took a deep breath of the flower and magic around me, pulling its warmth into my chilled bones.

Raina dropped my bag at my feet and leapt up onto the Nightmare's back, taking my silence for agreement. I could no more have stopped her riding away than I could hold the wind in my hands.

But I was done staying behind. I picked up my bag and started walking.

"Cassidy." Alice's voice stopped me as I reached the edge of the garden. "May saved a lot of people, you know. She probably saved my husband's life. He would've been on that train. If it had gone down into the gorge, I don't know how many would have died. Maybe all of them. I didn't know if I should say anything since I didn't want you going up there, but if you're going to go anyway, well, Paulie and some of the muscle he always hung around with went up the mountain that night. He didn't help with the search either, even though he was already at the old lodge."

I turned to Alice but couldn't manage a smile. "Thank you," I said. "I think this garden blooms because she loved you and love doesn't end, even when we're gone." I held out my hand and Alice put her palm in mine, her eyes bright as the summer sky with unshed tears.

"Be careful," she said.

I let her go and turned to face the mountain.

Raina would get there ahead of me, but it didn't matter. I was here, and I was going to see this through for the sake of my stubborn, beautiful wife and my stubborn, beautiful daughter. I was done waiting.

There was no sign of the Nightmare outside the lodge as I stepped out of the towering pines into a huge clearing. The signs of the rock fall were still evident in the large boulders and swath of treeless land cutting like a gash down the mountain. The lodge itself was a two-story log and stone building that had seen better days. Three horses were tied, untacked, to posts outside, their tails flicking lazily in the morning sun.

The silence warned me back, something unnaturally still and empty even though three live animals stood waiting patiently where they'd been tied. Not so much as a stick cracked to warn me as cold metal pressed to my neck even as I hesitated.

"How about you come inside, lady," a low male voice said. "Drop the bag."

I didn't need magic to know that was a pistol at my neck. A number of small tricks I could try to get him away from me flashed through my mind, but I didn't know if his finger was on the trigger or what startling him might accomplish, so I set the bag down, trying to bend away from the gun as I gathered power inside me.

The butt of the pistol came down on the back of my head and then the only thing going through my mind was nauseating pain and dancing red spots. He hit me again and I slumped, not quite unconscious but all the strength sapped from my limbs. I tried to struggle as he lifted me and half dragged me across the clearing, but a second, bigger man came out and grabbed my legs. Something wet trickled down my neck and I was sure it wasn't sweat.

The main room of the lodge had a bunch of tables pulled to the sides with benches stacked on each other. The men dumped me in the middle of the room like a sack of grain and I struggled to my knees, tentatively feeling the back of my head between my braids. My hand came away bloody.

"Hello, little witch." A man approached me, his posture and the way the four others followed him with their eyes telling me he was likely the boss. *Paulie.* I could see why our daughter hadn't liked him. His face was narrow and mean with a pinched look that came from temperament and not breeding; his pale eyes were bloodshot and held no warmth. It was the hunger on his face that scared me the most, that and the spiky red aura around him that was like nothing I'd ever encountered before.

"You're Paulie," I said, the room swimming in and out of focus. I tried to stand but slipped down again.

"You look like her a bit, mother maybe? Your little bitch ruined my life. But I guess you are here to make it all better." He chuckled and bent over me, gripping my chin so tight I felt my teeth shift.

"What did you do to my daughter?" I spit out, trying in vain to dislodge him.

I was too disoriented for magic, nothing but my own blood on my hands making them slippery as I clawed at his arm. Where in the cold hells was Raina? She should have beat me here. Rot filled my nostrils and heat traveled down my arms as Paulie's aura turned to crackling rusty lightning.

"How about I show you?" His eyes bored into mine and a headache that had nothing to do with the blows I'd taken exploded between my ears.

The room swam and re-formed. The tables were gone, the walls bare of hangings and mirrors, the floor dirty with a layer of grime saying the empty place hadn't been well-trafficked in years.

Mairi stood right in front of me with a revolver in her hand, so real I could almost touch her, but when I tried my arms ghosted straight through. I heard Paulie laugh but it was a younger, less worn down and sallow version of himself who confronted my daughter, standing where I had been standing.

"They know, Paulie," Mairi said. Her face was bruised, her lip swollen and bloodied, but her eyes were clear and focused. "You're done. There'll be no robbing that train, and there will be no leaving here, not for you."

"You ain't strong enough to hold me, baby witch. You should have minded your own business."

"I know what you are, demon," Mairi said, her words striking me to my soul where I hovered inside a memory not my own.

He moved so quickly it was a blur but she evaded him, flipping to the side, her head cocked as though she was waiting on something. A distant rumble filled the air, like thunder from a storm not yet arrived.

"With blood I bind you," Mairi said, spitting her own blood at the demon.

He howled and came at her again, managing to knock the revolver from her hands as two other men closed in behind.

"With wind I bind you," my daughter gasped as she forced the air from her lungs in a gust aided by her magic.

"Hold her down," Paulie yelled in the memory as the men dragged my baby to the floor. The rumbling grew louder and with it the sound of kindling splitting and snapping. Trees caught in the rock slide, I realized.

Over this din, Mairi yelled the final words of the spell. "With earth and fire I bind you, demon." Her blood, the power of the explosion she must have set before confronting him, it was enough. I felt what Paulie had felt those ten long years before as the spell found its target and iron bands of power locked around the demon, binding it to this place.

Only a Reaper could kill a demon and send it back to the underworld, but our daughter had found the next best way, trapping the demon in a body that would age and rot until Death could reclaim it.

Paulie's memories skipped around as the demon exited my brain and I used that moment to grab hold to what I could, searching for Mairi in them, taking more than the demon wanted me to see. I saw her fate, what he'd done to her after the roar and tumble of earth and stone stopped. I saw too, just before he shoved me backward and his hand descended to strike my face, what he intended. He was going to try to take my body and walk free of Mairi's spell with my witch powers.

"You're going to fail," I said to his gloating face. I spit blood at him, trying to summon enough sense and power to do anything. I had no salt nor my sacred wood and I'd never been as easy with magic without proper ritual as Mairi had, but I could always start a fire.

I spit again, using my rage and pain to fuel the flames of magic. My blood hissed like sparks from a campfire on wet wood as the droplets spattered the demon. Smoke trailed from his shirt. Orange flames flickered to life, then caught.

"Put it out," the demon hissed as flames I'd conjured licked at his shirt. They leapt from him to the man next to him as my will directed. I struggled to my feet, knowing the magic wouldn't last long.

This time when the man behind me tried to hit me with the butt of his gun, I was ready. Twisting, I slapped the gun to the side and launched myself into him. I got my hand around the revolver as we wrestled with the gun between us. He kicked my leg and I nearly let go, the barrel swinging back. Pointing straight at my chest.

Then the doors exploded inward and Death came to save me.

Raina flowed into the room like a river of steel and vengeance, her long body and sparking cold eyes an extension of the glowing blue blade in her hands. She cut through the two men in front of her without stopping before they even had a chance to reach for guns. Distracted by the arrival of his doom, the man I was struggling with let go of the revolver and I fell backward.

"No you don't," I said, pointing it at him as he tried to run. I recognized this man's face from Paulie's memories. He'd been there, he'd been one of the ones who dragged my daughter away.

Crackling lightning bringing a smell of ozone and rot flashed through the room and I ducked, clutching the gun. Icy flames met the hellfire, bursting in blue arcs from Raina's sword as she clashed with the demon. They fought to a standstill, power against power, the demon moving too swiftly even for Raina's deadly dancing blade. Desperate, I fired a shot that went far wide of either, but Paulie's rage-filled face turned toward me for a moment at the burst of noise.

I raised the gun again, the metal heavy in my hand. The demon's eyes flared with dull fire and I saw my end kindled in them.

Raina's blade flashed, separating the demon from his head. For a moment, his body seemed to hover as his head collapsed in a smoking ruin. Then the rot and fiery red aura fled the room in a burst of cold that froze my breath into pale mist. Paulie's body slumped with a thud, and left only silence in its wake.

I pointed the gun back at the cowering man, but my bloody finger slipped off the trigger as I stared into his fear-panicked eyes.

"Cass, give me the gun." Raina's gentle voice penetrated the haze of my mind. She pried the pistol from my ice-cold fingers.

"I saw her," I said. "I know what they did to Mairi. I know where she is. He was part of it. He hurt our baby."

"You're no killer," Raina said. She squeezed the trigger, the shot intensifying my already aching head as it cracked the heavy silence, leaving worse in its wake. The man's body slumped to the floor.

"Help me up," I whispered, not trusting my voice or my balance.

"I was waiting for nightfall to confront the demon," Raina said. "Cassidy, when I realized, God I thought I was going to lose you forever." She looked like she wanted to say more, but I clung to her arm and started pulling her toward the door.

"Let's go get our baby."

We found her up the mountain, Raina prying the boards off the old mine shaft I'd directed us to. They'd dragged Mairi here and chained her inside, then boarded it up and walked away.

Sunlight cast long beams into the small space, shining like a spotlight onto the grey-white bones jumbled at the base of a tarred and scarred length of wood. Her wrists were still in the manacles, the rusted metal holding them upright in a cruel parody of life, the bones of her hands laid as they would have been against the stone in supplication.

Mairi had died alone in the dark, struggling against the iron binding her, injured and drained of magic, slowly losing the battle with hunger and thirst and finally life. Locked in here, abandoned, her bones unmourned, her soul tied down by her tragic end.

Seemed that although she'd given up some of her humanity, Raina could still weep. We worked in silence, tears running down our cheeks, as we gathered our daughter's bones into my bag, making sure to not miss a single one. Then we rode down the mountain, back to Alice's garden, where she met us with concerned words and a flurry of help.

We buried Mairi there beneath the flowers her love and magic had seeded. As the earth was tamped down over her body, light that had nothing to do with the afternoon sun glimmered and formed a vague shape that became more and more solid as I clung to Raina's arm, my tears flowing anew.

Mairi held out her hands to us with a smile on her face. Her ghostly lips formed words that I'd longed to hear and though no sound issued, I read them with my heart.

"I love you, too, baby," I said, stepping toward her. Her hands were warm mist, light glittering on my skin.

"Mama's going to take you home," Raina said.

My ears popped and Alice gave a little shriek of surprise as the Nightmare stepped up beside Raina.

"Don't worry about me," I said when Raina's gaze met mine. "Bring our baby to rest. I'll catch the train."

Raina sprang into the saddle and Mairi's ghostly form leapt just as gracefully up behind her, glittering arms wrapping around Raina's waist, mother and daughter long and lean and beautiful riding together one last time. Alice and I stood in the sunlit flowers long after the Nightmare and her riders had faded into the trees.

A week after I'd made my way home, I heard the creak of my porch steps. This time my heart wasn't hollow and I went to the door, tossing the screen wide. Raina sat like a long shadow on my porch swing with her hat tipped down low over her cold fire eyes. Her sheathed sword leaned against the porch rail.

"I made cobbler," I said, leaning against the open door. "If you want to come in."

Raina unfolded from the swing and then cocked her head as though listening. My heart was pounding in my ears so loud that at first I didn't hear it.

"Train's coming," she said.

"Train's always coming. There'll be another." I held the door open and backed up over the threshold.

"You sure?" Raina said, and I knew though she was eyeing the physical distance between us, it was a different kind of space she was minding crossing.

"Come on in," I said.

Raina dropped her hat onto the swing and shook down her hair, inky waves falling in shining curls that glinted ebony and silver in the sunlight. Then she stepped across the threshold and into my arms.

FIRE HAZARD

by Kevin Hearne

The most important question in this life, I've heard it said, is whether you have the sausage to achieve your goals. Sausage being a metaphor for courage, in this case, instead of the many other things it could be, including actual sausage.

Okay, okay: I've never heard that said. I'm the one who said it—or at least thought it, because I can't vocalize like humans do. Irish wolfhounds are okay at barking and howling, but speaking English, not so much. Druids can hear my thoughts, though, and my personal Druid agrees with me that sausage can be a metaphor, thereby making it the finest of all foods.

I'm equating sausage to courage because Atticus told me to think about the nature of courage, and I realized it was so much easier if I just thought about sausage instead. This is working out great and I can understand why humans like metaphors so much. I think about courage as sausage pretty much all the time, so I expect to be recognized as an expert on courage any minute now.

Apparently I'm going to need some courage because we're going to Australia and it's on fire. Really on fire, Atticus said, not metaphorically.

<Why?> I asked him through our mental link.

"Why? Because there's a terrible drought. There are lots of fires and not enough firemen to put them out, so they need some rain to help them extinguish the flames. But the drought means there won't be rain for weeks, or even months, and in the meantime all this habitat is being lost for Australia's creatures."

<No, I mean, why are we going if it's really on fire?>

"Because we're in a position to help, so we should."

<We are not positioned in Australia.>

"We technically are. We're in Tasmania and it's considered part of Australia, even though it's an island off the coast. We can get to the main continent without too much trouble."

I knew that Atticus was leaving something out. <Hold on. *Without too much trouble* means there's going to be at least *some* trouble. What kind of trouble is it to get there?>

<I don't want any trouble!> Starbuck said, sneezing at the end of his sentence. He's my snorty Boston terrier buddy and he shares the mental link with Atticus too.

"We're going to take a ferry and cross the ocean from Devonport to Melbourne. It's nine and a half hours, and they will put you two in kennels for the journey. You can just sleep through the night."

<So it's just one night?> I had to ask for clarification on that because I'm not very good with time, except for two bedrock principles:

- It keeps passing, and
- There is no time like the present for a little something to eat.

Hours and months and seconds and weeks and minutes, however, tend to confuse me.

"Just one night," Atticus assured me.

<Are the kennels big enough for me?> I'm a pretty big dog—pretty much the biggest—and have discovered through experience that most places haven't planned for me to be there.

"Yes, they'll be fine."

Of course there was more trouble than that, though Atticus insisted it was all not too much. There were farewells to deliver to Inspector Rose Badgely in Launceston, who liked us a whole lot and made very high-pitched sounds for a human whenever she snuggled with us. She liked Atticus too, and he liked her back, but she made different sounds with him.

Starbuck and I overheard him explaining to her that he felt he had to go volunteer, and it was a tricky business because he couldn't reveal that he was a Druid and bound to the earth, and he truly needed to help the elementals when they said they needed it. We'd been in Tasmania to prevent the Tasmanian devils from going extinct because of a contagious face cancer, for example, and while Rose knew about that, she didn't know Atticus was actually curing them and helping them develop a resistance to it. She thought he was just counting the population, identifying diseased dens, stuff like that. Fighting wildfires was a completely different sort of thing. To Rose, it must have sounded like he was looking for an excuse to leave. She said these weren't as bad as the fires of the Black Summer of 2020, whatever that was, and Australia always burned in the summer.

"I'll be back when the rains come," Atticus said.

"What are you gonna do, exactly?" she asked, her Australian accent tight with tension. "You're not gonna be on the front lines, are you?"

"No, no. I can hardly use a shovel well with only one arm. But I can provide support in other ways."

Atticus was doing pretty well with his disability since losing his right arm. He focused on what he could do instead of what he couldn't, and he did quite a lot. We couldn't move around the world quickly anymore, and he couldn't shape-shift into animal forms like he used to, but he still had all his other powers and—most importantly—access to meats.

"So you'll still have work to do here afterward?" Rose asked.

"Yes. There's always something to be done. I may have to travel to mainland Australia from time to time for emergencies like this, but other members of my organization can handle problems in the rest of the world. My plan is to stay in Tasmania as long as the Australian government lets me. Part of that means periodically leaving the country for a while and then returning, until I can get a work visa that lets me stay longer."

His organization was a nonprofit nature charity he made up so that he and the other Druids would have an excuse to show up wherever disasters were happening.

Rose seemed reassured by that, but her eyes slid over to me and Starbuck.

"You're taking the dogs with you?"

"Yep. They go where I go."

<Yes food!> Starbuck said. He had difficulty separating the two words since he always approved of food.

"Can they go outside for a bit, if this is the last time I'm going to see you for a while?"

<Come on, Starbuck,> I said. <That's our cue to leave. They need to perform human mating rituals.>

Gods below, Oberon, Atticus said via our link, *I really wish you wouldn't call it that.*

<Sorry, Starbuck. I meant to say he needs to do sex to Rose.>

That's worse.

<You want me to use euphoniums?>

You mean euphemisms? No, I don't.

<I think I know some, though. One of them is "knocking poots." He's going to knock poots with Rose.>

<Yes food!> Starbuck said.

The phrase is "knocking boots," Oberon, and please, just . . . don't mention it.

I left him alone after that because I'd managed to embarrass him sufficiently. Rose drove us to the ferry the next day in Devonport, and we endured the kennels in the belly of the ship like very good boys by sleeping through most of the ride over, and spending the rest of the time discussing what kind of food we'd get as a reward for being so good. Starbuck was convinced we'd get steak, but I didn't think so. We were going to arrive in the morning and humans didn't eat steak for breakfast as often as they should. They preferred sausage, and that was just fine by me.

We didn't get anything super special, though; Atticus hired a car once we deboated (is that a word? I know you can deplane but can you deboat or dejetski or demotorcycle?) and he had the driver take us to a drive-thru to get sausage breakfast sandwiches.

After that he had the driver stop in a forested mountainous patch of country called the Dandenong Ranges. It smelled like flowers and butterfly dust and wombats underneath all the smoke. We could smell the fires even though they were miles away. Atticus stepped out on the side of the road and we got out with him.

<Is this a potty break?> I asked him, even though Starbuck was already turning it into one by lifting his leg on a nearby tree.

Yes, but also a chance for me to talk to the elemental and figure out where exactly we're going. Give me a few minutes of quiet, and stay close, please.

He stood still and faced the forest, his sandals kicked off and his bare feet planted on the earth. He shoved his hand into his pocket and remained still, closing his eyes as he established communication with the elemental. The driver was looking at him with a worried expression, perhaps wondering what kind of client he had picked up, but after a few seconds of staring he shrugged and got out his phone, probably concluding that Atticus was paying for the time so he could stand around doing nothing if he wanted.

But Atticus was bound to the earth, the tattoos on his right heel allowing him to speak directly to the local manifestation of Gaia, so he wasn't doing nothing. He could get a bit lost in that communication sometimes, though. That was why I always made sure to stand guard when he did that so nothing could sneak up on him. He said I didn't need to worry, no animals would ever try to hurt him, but I wasn't worried about animals. I was worried about other humans, which is what everyone should be worried about.

When Atticus moved again—it was only like fifteen years or five weeks or something—his face was tight with stress and stuff. I don't always get human emotions perfectly right from just looking at their faces, but I knew he wasn't happy.

"Let's go, pups," he said, even though we weren't pups. We piled back into the van and Atticus gave the driver better directions. We were going to someplace called Kanangra Walls in New South Wales, whatever that was. Once we were moving again he leaned back and spoke to us in our minds.

We have a bit of a journey ahead of us. Eight hours or so. Would you like to hear a scary story?

<Yes food!> Starbuck shouted, his mouth opening and his tongue lolling out in a smile. He loved stories.

<You bet!> I said.

The story was about snakes, and we loved it when he told us snake stories, because you got to eat the scary poison bad guys at the end and it was a delicious victory that tasted like chicken. Plus the heroine of this particular snake story was a fluffy entrepreneurial poodle named Gwyneth, who had made her fortune by hiring some humans to manufacture candles featuring the scent of her own ass.

<Wow, you mean you could just light a candle and sniff her ass in the comfort of your own home? You wouldn't have to meet her at the dog park?>

That's right.

<An ass candle! Holy shrieking cats, that's genius! Why didn't I ever think of that?>

Well, you're not Gwyneth.

<Can we get one?>

They're all sold out, unfortunately.

Starbuck and I whimpered softly at this disappointment, but we thrilled at the adventures of Gwyneth the snake slayer and admired her courage. Atticus reminded us we'd need to be every bit as courageous as Gwyneth when we got to where the fire was.

We could tell we were getting closer because the smell of smoke got worse as we went, penetrating the vehicle. I couldn't tell how long the ride was, unfortunately, but it seemed like a good while, and we stopped again in a town called Albury to grab some food and stretch our legs. Atticus also visited a hardware store and returned quickly with a hatchet. The driver looked at him a bit more suspiciously after that, and I wondered what was up too.

<What's that for?> I asked him.

It's for unnatural causes, he replied, but I think he realized that didn't answer my question very well, and he explained. *Most of the fires raging across the country right now are naturally occurring. That is to say, they got started as a lightning strike or something like that, even if the conditions that make them burn so long are a result of human action. The problem is that all these fires may have attracted some other beings that like to watch things burn, and if so, they're making an already terrible situation just a little bit worse. That's what the elemental is worried about.*

<The fires *may* have attracted other beings? The elemental isn't sure?>

The elemental is weak and suffering tremendously right now. A couple of years ago they had unprecedented fires during what they now call the Black Summer. The damage done was incredible; billions of plants and animals died, and their collective lives were giving the elemental life. And now it's happening again.

<Billions are more than hundreds, right?>

Right, sorry, I forgot your difficulty with numbers. Let's just say the elemental is very sick, and because of the sickness they're not sure whether something is encouraging the fires or not. There could be a legitimate otherworldly threat ahead. Or it could be the equivalent of delirium, a fever dream, something the elemental imagined. They're just not sure. Our job is to make sure.

<Okay. Whatever you need us to do, we'll help. Right, Starbuck?>

<Yes food! Help animals!>

After another long drive, during which Atticus told us some more stories about a band of noble dog rangers battling an evil council of squirrel wizards, he asked the driver if we were outside Kanangra-Boyd National Park and we weren't quite there. They talked back and forth a lot about some specific spot Atticus was looking for, a landmark of some kind, and eventually he thought he saw it and pointed into the haze.

"There. Drop us off there, please." He indicated a huge mountain ash tree with a boulder in front of it. I thought either or both would be pretty good places to pee.

The driver looked worried. "You sure?"

"Absolutely."

"It's nasty here, man. Not safe."

I agreed. The smoke was really bad and kind of burning my nose from the inside, even though we were still in the van.

"I'll be fine, thanks."

"You need a tank of oxygen, mate, seriously. We're too close to the fire. I don't feel comfortable leaving you here."

"I have an oxygen mask for both myself and the dogs cached behind that boulder," Atticus lied. I knew he was lying because who buries oxygen masks in Australia just in case? Well—hold on. I bury bones sometimes just in case. But that's because they're delicious, and as far as I knew, oxygen masks weren't. Still, Atticus has done weirder stuff.

"Oxygen masks for the dogs?"

"Modern times, man. We have all the things for pets we could ever need."

"Whatever, mate." He pressed his thumb on his phone and then held it up to Atticus. "Do me a solid and put it on record that you want me to leave you here and not hold me responsible for whatever fiery death awaits you."

Atticus basically promised not to blame the guy for anything that happened to us and we got out. The smoke made me and Starbuck hack, and Atticus suggested we hold our breath for a bit. Once the guy drove away, Atticus started speaking in Old Irish and doing his binding thing. He can bind most anything to anything else, really, as long as it doesn't have a large iron content, and in this case he bound the smoke and ash particles in the air to stay out of our noses. He created a little bubble of clean air around us, and our eyes stopped stinging once it retreated and we could see clearly.

<Gah. That's better. Thanks, Atticus.>

<Good human!> Starbuck added.

"We need to wait here for a while," he replied, "because we're meeting someone. But I'll keep making sure the smoke doesn't bother us."

<Okay,> I said. <Is this the Wall place you mentioned earlier? Because I don't see a wall.>

"No, it's going to be a bit of a hike to get there. We'll move as quickly as we can and hopefully get there before sundown."

I was just about to ask who we were waiting for when he showed up. He startled me and Starbuck by shifting planes from Tír na nÓg, causing us to flinch and yip in surprise. I recognized him by scent as much as by sight: Coriander, Herald Extraordinary of the Fae Court, smelled like a light puff of lime and cilantro that always reminded me of street tacos. Atticus told me that humans considered him to be a very pretty man, sort of like Legolas in the Lord of the Rings movies, his flawless features always ready for a high-definition close-up.

"Greetings, Siodhachan," he said, addressing Atticus by his original Irish name. He held up a bottle of ink and a fine-tipped paintbrush one might use for detail work on a canvas. "I've brought the requested materials."

"Excellent," Atticus said, and laid his hatchet down on the boulder. "Apply it to that blade, if you please."

<Man smells good,> Starbuck observed. <Does he have food?>

<Unfortunately, no,> I said. <That's a bottle of ink in his hand.>

<Unfair! Is he a super bad cat person?> he wondered. My Bos-

ton buddy tended to be suspicious of people who did not have any food for him and assumed that they must be allied with cats.

<I don't think so. He doesn't seem like the type of person who thinks about dogs or cats at all. Not bad, but not good either, as far as we're concerned.>

Coriander stepped forward but really floated since his feet didn't quite touch the ground. He unstoppered the ink bottle and dipped the brush in there. I snuck forward to see what he was doing. He drew some squiggly knots on the blade of the hatchet and Atticus asked him about it.

"So this sigil that you're applying here—how do I activate it?"

"It activates on contact with any denizen of hell," the faery replied.

"There are no words required to initiate the unbinding?"

"None. Merely embed the blade in the flesh of your target."

"Right."

<What are you talking about, Atticus?>

Coriander has drawn a Sigil of Cold Fire on my hatchet blade to unbind any demons we might run across.

<Cold Fire? Isn't that a thing you can do yourself? That one lady with the red hair gave you the power once, right?>

Brighid, yes. She granted me that power. But when I use it, the unbinding weakens me to the point that I can hardly move. That's suboptimal in the middle of a fire. This sigil will do the job for me.

<Sigils are just painted swirlies?>

They are magical bindings made with potent inks, but they are also painted swirlies. We're going to paint some on you. Or your collar, anyway.

<We are?>

Well, Coriander is going to do it.

The faery discarded his brush—it was just wood and horsehair—and put the stoppered bottle of ink in a pocket. He removed a different one and produced another brush and came over to me.

"Hello, Oberon. Please remain very still while I apply a Ward Against Fire to your collar."

<Okay,> I said, though I don't think he heard me. Atticus told him I understood, though.

"That cold iron talisman you have dangling from your collar will protect you against hellfire," Coriander explained as he worked, "because that has a magical origin. But this is regular old fire you're walking into, so we need a bit of magic to protect you against that."

I didn't feel any different when he had finished, but Atticus said I wouldn't. *I think you'll appreciate not getting burned, though,* he told me. Coriander repeated the process for Starbuck and I was proud of him for remaining still the whole time and not sneezing. That's really hard for him to do.

Coriander and Atticus bowed to each other afterward and the faery wished us well before shifting away to Tír na nÓg.

<Hey, Atticus, why doesn't he just do this thing we're going to do, if he has all the potent inks and sigils and things?>

"The Fae are supposed to limit their presence on the earth, and directly engaging beings from other planes would violate some treaties and maybe even start an interplanar war. If there is anything ahead of us to be banished from the earth, it's my responsibility."

<Because you're a Druid and bound to the earth?>

"That's right. Let's go. Stay close to me and I'll keep the air bubble moving with us."

We jogged for about six thousand feet or six hundred fathoms or furlongs or whatever, yeah, I'm not good with distances either.

But we saw a whole lot of animals running away from what we were running toward, and one wallaby clearly thought we were just uninformed and tried to warn us with some strangled sounds that there was a fire up ahead. We kept going.

I have to admit that I had an idea of what a forest fire might be like, but the real thing is so much more powerful than the two words imply. It's a forest—all its life and energy—violently transforming itself to heat and light and poisonous fumes. And up close, it's terrifying.

When I saw the wall of flames silhouetting the eucalyptus trees like blackened matchsticks and felt the heat on my nose and fur, threatening to singe both, I realized that there is quite a lot of difference between sausage and courage. They are, in fact, not the same thing at all, and metaphors can only take you for a short walk on a tight leash. Wait. Is that a metaphor too? Whatever. I didn't want to walk into that fire, even if Atticus somehow made a path through it and kept a bubble of air around us and I was supposedly protected by magic swirlies and a cold iron talisman. All my instincts screamed at me to turn around and run away, like all the wallabies and wombats and koalas were doing.

<No squirrel!> Starbuck said, summing up his feelings about going forward. Just as he had trouble separating the affirmative from food, he had difficulty separating the negative from squirrels.

<Any chance that the thing you're after will come out of there so we don't have to go in?> I asked.

"Unfortunately not. We have to go in. Or at least I do. Would you rather wait here?"

<Yeah, I would. But I'm not going to. I go where you go,> I told him. And apart from that, if there was something behind all this destruction, ruining the homes and lives of so many creatures, it needed to get got.

<Me too. Go with friends!> Starbuck said.

"Okay. I'm going to have the earth smother a path through the fire for us and we're going to run through, single file. Once we get through this first leading edge, we should reach a burned-out area where it won't be so hot."

<You're sure there's something to find in there?>

"Pretty sure."

<I wish we had one of Gwyneth's ass candles right now. It would make me feel better about all these open flames.>

There was nothing else we could say. Mostly because Atticus didn't give us a chance. He bound the earth to rise up and smother a strip of land ahead of us, effectively churning it so that what was underground was now on top and all the burning leaves and things were buried. It was kind of a biblical event, if I were the sort of hound or human who read the Bible—and I wasn't—but I knew it wasn't the sort of thing you talked over. The flames still rose in a wall on either side of that narrow strip, though.

Atticus took off, hatchet swinging in his left arm, and hollered at us to stay on his heels. We trotted easily behind, ears back, sphincters puckered. Great green gobs of catsick, the heat was terrible! It dried out my nose and eyes, and my skin felt like it was going to ignite. I didn't think I would ever stop panting once I started.

<Hard! To breathe!> Starbuck said, and I worried about him. Bostons don't do well in the heat. Their smashed faces don't allow them to cool off very well.

But the intensity lasted only a short while, I think, because we got through the wall, and the firescape changed to isolated trees still burning while the ground cover was all turned to char and ash, and then past that it was a blackened, smoking wasteland where it still felt hot but was cool by comparison to the inferno. Atticus paused there to check on us.

"My goodness. Your fur is smoking a bit."

<Very hot! No squirrel!> Starbuck said.

<You're smoking a bit too,> I told him, but left out the part that his eyebrows were pretty much gone and some of his hair and goatee had curled up and crisped.

"Let's do something about that."

He did more of his Druidry, moving the earth again in front of us, but differently this time. A circular sinkhole formed and deepened and I realized he was drilling down to reach the water table. Once he hit it, he pulled some out to rain down on us, and it was marvelously cold. My nose was wet again, and I felt like I could breathe once more.

<Good human!> Starbuck said. He was still panting but didn't look as distressed. <Much better!>

"Okay, we're looking for anything moving, basically," Atticus said. "Because nothing should be alive here unless it's up to no good."

<Well, we're up to some good, aren't we?>

"I hope so."

<Did the elemental tell you where to look?>

"Somewhere in this area; it's been some time since it felt a hint of what might be hellish." He gave us one more splash of water and petted us a bit and then stood up, surveying the ruin. We weren't inside a perfect circle or anything; the shape of the fire was a splattery business many acres or meters or whatever long.

Atticus pointed to the west, where we could dimly see flickers of flame beneath billowing clouds of black smoke. "We are basically on top of Kanangra Walls here, but in that direction they fall off into a gorge. If I were going to be busy doing evil, I'd want a view of the destruction. So let's head that way. Tell me if you see or hear anything."

We trotted to the west across a blasted landscape, stumps and twigs looking like scorched French fries. That made me think how nice a basket of poutine would go down right then, but I doubted I'd be getting any of that here.

Atticus saw it first and told us to hold up. He squatted down next to us and pointed with his hatchet, whispering. "See that moving through the trees?"

We all went still and watched. Something was there, but it wasn't any animal or human I've ever seen before.

<It's like . . . an avocado wearing a plague mask walking around on blackened chicken legs?>

<Yes chicken!>

Okay, good, I'm not imagining it, Atticus said in our minds. *Let's move closer, but slowly and quietly. No barking or growling. I think it's holding something.*

Atticus stayed low and we crept along next to him, keeping our eyes on the target. The intervening trees kept me from seeing what it held in its hand—I couldn't even see arms, most of the time. But then it moved slightly and I finally caught a glimpse. Its arms were as thin and sticklike as the legs, but the hands held a squishy accordion thing.

<I think I see it. But I forget what that thing is called. Blacksmiths use them to make their fires hotter. I think it blows air?>

It's called a bellows. That's exactly what it is. I think I know who that is, and he's definitely trying to make the fires worse.

<Who is it?>

If I'm not mistaken, that is Xaphan, a fallen angel who is supposed to be fanning the furnaces of hell.

<An angel? I thought they were supposed to be pretty.>

The ones who fell mostly lost their beauty during the fall. Lucifer was an exception.

<Stinky bad angel,> Starbuck observed. He'd noticed, like I had, the smell of sulfur that accompanied most anything that came from hell. They should definitely not be allowed to have any artisanally crafted ass candles made of their scent.

<Why is he here, Atticus?> I asked.

I don't know. Maybe the new furnaces of hell are just . . . Australia in the summertime. This Blue Mountains region was already hit hard in the Black Summer of 2020 and maybe he's come to finish the job.

<The Blue Mountains? Isn't that where the special koalas live?>

What do you mean?

<I mean the only ones without chlamydia.>

Oh, yes, I think that's right. How'd you hear about that?

<You always turn on the nature channels for us when you and Rose are busy.>

Right, right. Okay. I'm going straight at him because he has to go. Circle around to his flank but do not engage unless I'm in trouble.

<Please don't get in trouble.>

<No squirrel trouble!> Starbuck added.

Atticus set off in a sort of duck walk, trying to stay low and unobserved to surprise Xanax or Xaphod or whatever, I'd already forgotten his name. I nipped at Starbuck to get his attention and the two of us took a course headed to the right, which would eventually intersect the fallen angel's path if he kept going. Atticus would engage him before that, though, and once he faced Atticus, we'd be coming at him on his left side. That was usually what you wanted if you were tracking humans, since most of them were right-handed, but I didn't know if that was true for angels. Were they all ambidextrous?

I didn't need to wait for a signal because there wouldn't be one. When Atticus decided a thing had to be done, he did it. And he wouldn't try to engage the fallen angel in negotiations to leave peacefully, because that would never happen, and he wouldn't seek a fair fight either, because there was no honor to be had here. There was only a forest to save, and all the creatures who lived in it.

The best possible outcome would be that Xaphoo never saw Atticus coming and he'd just get an axe in the back and that would be it.

The best possible outcome never happens, though.

The fallen angel heard Atticus coming—or maybe smelled him, because what I thought was a plague mask beak from a distance was actually a super long nose—and whipped around to face him. Atticus rose and charged at that point, the element of surprise lost. But he was too far away. The beanpole arms hefted the bellows and pointed it at Atticus and squeezed the handles together. I immediately sped up to a sprint because that looked like trouble if anything did.

A powerful stream of air shot out of the bellows and ignited like a flamethrower and the evil thing laughed as Atticus was blown backward off his feet in a gust of fiery wind. He lost his grip on his hatchet and that was most definitely trouble.

Atticus didn't make any sound, but he was rolling to extinguish the flames. I hoped his wards and cold iron aura were working properly. Xaphudge laughed, a screechy cackle, and pried apart the handles of the bellows for another go. He never saw me coming until I was a blur of motion in his peripheral vision. He made a startled noise and started to turn my way as I was in midair. It was enough to make me miss him, but I tore the bellows right out of his grasp and ran with it grasped in my jaws. His cry of outrage was epic and he gave chase, so he missed a couple of things: one was Atticus getting to his feet, his clothes all crispy and his hair smoldering but otherwise okay, extending a hand toward the fallen angel and saying something in Old Irish, and the other was Starbuck coming up behind him to nip at his chicken legs.

They weren't really chicken legs—he had feet instead of talons, it's just that they were super skinny and appeared to have no muscles. Starbuck's efforts were enough to trip him up and he executed a graceless face-plant accompanied by a roar. He really did look like a large avocado that way and I dreamt for a fleeting moment of smashing him to guacamole.

I paused to look back and saw that not only had the fallen angel fallen, but Atticus had too. He'd just been standing a few seconds ago, so I didn't understand what had happened. Xantac rose and whirled around, locating me and then Starbuck, who was barking at him not far away and calling him a terrible cat person. His scarecrow arms rose and hellfire gushed out from them, one stream for Starbuck and one for me.

There was no avoiding it.

The sulfurous heat blasted over me and I squeezed my eyes shut and hoped it wasn't my time to die.

<Thanks for all the poodles,> I said to Atticus, because if this was the end, I wanted to be grateful for the good times and not say something obvious like <Ow! It's hot!>

I did let loose with a yipe, because it hurt more than anything ever had, and Starbuck did the same, but after a second of intense heat, most of it was gone. That cold iron talisman I wore on my collar had warded off the hellfire, leaving me and Starbuck very toasty and with lots of singed fur, but otherwise unharmed.

The fallen angel couldn't believe it. His jaw dropped open, some pink and off-white bits in there like jagged landscaping rocks, and he looked at both of us to make sure we were still alive, and then he looked down at his hands, wondering how they could have misfired so badly. He snarled and clenched his fists as he looked up at me, clearly deciding he should just try again. He said something in a language I didn't recognize—maybe the fell speech of Mordor or something, because it sure wasn't French—and then his eyes popped open in surprise and he belched. And shortly thereafter, he screamed, as much in surprise as in pain, as his avocado body began to bubble and hiss, and I understood what was happening: he was being consumed from the inside by Cold Fire. Atticus had gotten him after all, and that was what he'd done before he collapsed. Something about that particular unbinding drained my Druid like nothing else.

Fissures appeared in the fallen angel's body and yellow goo squirted out from them, which caused Starbuck to leap backward in alarm. Xaphig pretty much exploded after that, quickly turning into molten yuck that cooked down into greasy slag.

Starbuck? Oberon? Are you two okay? Atticus asked in our minds.

<Yes food!> Starbuck said, then added, <Stinky bad cat person went boom.>

<I'm okay, Atticus,> I replied, trotting over to him. He was lying spread-eagled on his back. <What about you?>

I'm wiped out. The hatchet wasn't much use after all, and I had to use my own strength to cast Cold Fire.

<What does that mean, then? Can you move?>

Not much. My muscles don't want to work at the moment, but I'll recover eventually.

<Remind me how long eventually is?>

It could be a good while. Overnight, probably.

<Overnight here? In the middle of a forest fire?> The sun had pretty much set and there was some farewell light in the sky, the kind that allowed you time to reflect and judge the kind of day

you'd had before darkness fell. We wouldn't get full dark, of course, because of the fire expanding all around us. Our little pockets of air were still okay, but it remained hot and uncomfortable.

I agree that it's not ideal.

<I'll say! You don't even have dinner on you!>

<Emergency!> Starbuck hopped around. <Emergency! Call for food! Human must use smart phone! Delivery now. One greasy bag of hamburgers please. Extra grease, yes food!>

We had to explain that no deliveries of any kind could be made to where we were, and Starbuck shivered as he realized what that meant. <Does that mean dinner won't happen? Is this the end of all good things?>

Dinner can still happen. It just can't happen here. You have to get me to where the food is. Through the fire, in other words.

<No squirrel!>

<How can we do that, Atticus?>

I'm going to bind together some torched wood to make a rough sled—a travois, really—and you're going to pull me out. It's going to be a lot of work for a long time, but I'll try to give you energy.

<Can't you give yourself some energy to get up and walk?>

Some. But this fatigue isn't something I can recover from quickly. This is why I would have preferred to use the hatchet with the sigil. Speaking of which, I need you to find that and bring it with you. The bellows too. Can't leave those here.

I knew where the bellows was and Starbuck found the hatchet after a bit of a search. Atticus used his Druidry to move some charred wood around and bind it together into a travois, which looked like a sort of torched trellis when he was finished. That took a while, and then we had to help him roll on top of it, pulling on the shreds of his clothes. That was how weak he was.

It was designed with a couple of branch leads and then a short branch connecting them that I'd have to take into my mouth, which would allow me to pull him behind like I was a horse. As a test, I dragged him a little way to the sinkhole he'd made earlier. He pulled up more water and got us all good and soaked, and then he had Starbuck crawl under his shirt so he'd have a wet layer of cloth around him as we entered the fire.

That was the part I didn't want to think about. When I came through it the first time, I was following Atticus. And when the fallen angel zapped me, I didn't have a chance to think about it. But now I had to enter the fire on purpose by myself, and I wouldn't be able to run at full speed.

There was a yippy Chihuahua voice in my head that said, *Don't do it, just go hungry for a night and maybe skip breakfast too and wait until Atticus can move on his own.* But what kind of wolfhound would I be if I listened to my inner Chihuahua?

The voice got pretty loud as I got nearer the fire, though. It burned with the rage of five grizzly bears on energy drinks fighting to drink the last one of a six-pack. I was thinking that maybe this one time, the Chihuahua was wise.

But then Atticus said, *I don't think I told either of you how awesome you were back there. You saved my life and ran through fire for me, and now you're going to do it again. You helped me protect the earth. There simply aren't any better dogs than you. You're the best.*

Well, I couldn't listen to the Chihuahua after that, because I was the best dog.

But fire wasn't a Scooby-Doo villain that you cease to fear once you pull the mask off. It's an elemental force against which my only chance of survival was to avoid it. No matter how much I told myself that I was the best hound, my instincts insisted that I run the other way.

I found the path through the fire that Atticus had made before and slowed, because I couldn't see the end. Smoke and distance made the flames seem to close up in an impenetrable wall.

<Atticus? Are you sure that path is still clear?>

It should be. Hold on. I dropped the lead out of my mouth and turned to see what he was doing. He twitched his foot onto the ground so he could check things out with the elemental.

It's clear, he confirmed. *Even if it doesn't look like it. Just take us through as fast as you can.*

That was when I learned the true difference between courage and sausage. A big plate of sausage might fill my belly, but it wouldn't help me take a single step toward that fire. I needed courage first, and then, if it served me well, I might get served some sausage on the other side.

I picked up the lead in my jaws again and flattened my ears against my head.

<Hold on,> I said. <Here we go.>

My first two steps were small things, not very courageous at all. But I realized that if I took small steps we'd all die from the heat and lack of oxygen if not the actual flames. The best hope we had was for me to use the full stride of an Irish wolfhound.

I leapt forward, startling both Atticus and Starbuck at the sudden lurch, but toppling neither. I pulled as hard as I could, fully aware that the weight was slowing me down, but still going at the top speed I could manage, right toward the most frightening thing I could think of besides a world ruled by squirrels.

I tried to think about things that made me happy, like belly rubs and poodles and gravy and every single time Atticus told me how good I was. I've had a very long life thanks to him, and a super delicious one, but I supposed all good things must be paid for somehow. The bill for our blessings always comes due in some fashion, and there's no way to avoid it.

The fire did its best to burn everything away as I plunged into it, flames rising well above my head on either side. My memories, my fine gray coat, the best human ever, my snorty Boston buddy, and my courage: it wanted everything to become ashes.

The ground scorched the pads of my paws and I could hardly breathe, the flames sucking up all the air, but there was nothing to do but churn forward.

Courage, I realized, only revs your engine at the starting line. It doesn't keep you going for the long haul. What keeps you going is something else: stubbornness, perhaps, or fear of what would happen if you stopped. In my case it was probably a whole lot of both. Once into the suffocating heat of the inferno, the only answer to any of my thoughts—like *it's too hot, I can't breathe*, or *I'm so tired*—was to keep going until I got through it.

It spurred me everywhere, not just on my flanks.

It toasted me from nose to tail.

It threatened to kill me. And Starbuck, despite being soaked and protected by Atticus, had trouble breathing, and let me know. <Very hot! No air!> he cried.

I needed air too. And if I gave up it wouldn't just be me who burned away—my best friends in the whole world would die as well.

The path kept going and going the way pain keeps going, hot and orange and urgent, until it suddenly stopped. And when it did, the relief was so acute I almost wondered why I ever felt distress, like the pain was a hallucination or something.

When we got past the leading edge of the fire, Atticus told me to stop and he did his water trick again to cool us all down.

Thank you, Oberon. You saved us all, he said, even though he had saved me from death too many times to count.

<Yes food thank you!> Starbuck said.

Then Atticus declared we could move at a slower pace to get to a ghost town called Yerranderie many miles away, where there was shelter, at least, if little else. It was deep night or early morning when we got there, and we crashed underneath an old tree until dawn, when Atticus could struggle to his feet and call for help to other humans who might have food or water but mostly food.

There were only a few buildings around, but an oldish woman eventually appeared and asked what in God's name had happened.

"Fire," Atticus said, though he didn't say it in God's name, and that was enough. Nobody was unaware of the fire. She invited us back to her place, where she gave me and Starbuck sausage and gave Atticus this stuff called Vegemite. Sausage is vastly superior to Vegemite, in my opinion, so I felt a bit sorry for Atticus, but he didn't appear unhappy.

He spoke with the lady for a long time while I lounged outside with Starbuck.

<You were a very strong hound. Super brave. Thank you for saving us,> Starbuck said. His tongue licked out and lapped once against my snout. Then he turned and curled up next to me, sorting himself along my side between my front leg and my back leg.

<You are welcome,> I said. <You will meet many dogs who say meat is why we live. But I don't think that's true. Friends are why we live.>

<You are right. Other dogs are wrong,> Starbuck said, and he sighed once before settling into a comforting series of snores.

I laid my head down between my front paws for a nap, knowing that Atticus would wake us when he wanted to leave. As I drifted off, I thought: I have courage and sausage and friends. If I ever get an ass candle, I will have it all.

GRAVE GAMBLES

by R.R. Virdi

There are a lot of garbage ways to wake up in someone else's dead body, but a full dumpster is at the top of the list. Especially if you're buried halfway down. If luck existed, it came in the form of every bit of refuse being neatly packed away in bags. Small blessings. I didn't need filth soaking me. The dumpster smelled like it'd housed a dead body for days, though, that could have just been me.

I wriggled around the bags, pulling them with care to not rip any. My effort paid off in gently padding more of the garbage below and bringing me closer to the lid. Among all the ways I've woken up in a victim's body, this had to be the easiest. Most involved escaping whatever horrible situation the stiff had been left in. The only saving grace to that was that every body I ended up inhabiting was restored to its healthy living condition prior to the murder. Which didn't do much for me since I still had to track the killer down and bring them to justice.

And in my cases, the murderers are always monsters. I don't do normal.

A quick kick lifted the plastic roofing by an inch before it fell, letting me know it wasn't bolted shut.

I placed both hands against the lid and pushed. Something *clanged* hard against both sides of the dumpster like it had been struck by a pair of metal rods. The bin shook once before moving in a steady motion. My eyes widened as I realized what had happened. I smacked the lid open, whipping my head around as I tried to situate myself.

"Well, shit." I hate being right.

A garbage truck had clamped onto the dumpster, lifting it two-thirds of the way to the top. The angle of the bin reached the point where bags pressed against me, threatening to tumble past into the truck's bed.

I scrambled forward and let momentum do its thing. My fingers fought for purchase as I tipped out from the dumpster. The inner lining, a bit slick, kept me from getting a decent hold. I slipped down, thumping the lid as I twisted to avoid tumbling into the sea of trash below.

Panicked decisions don't always pan out. I managed to divert my fall toward the outermost edge of the truck's bed frame instead. Metal met the side of my jaw and cheek like a sledgehammer. Bands of white and red streaked my vision as I pancaked onto the hard asphalt.

The landing didn't help my head as I tried to shake myself clear. Salt and copper filled the inside of my mouth. I spat and saw flecks of carmine tinge my spittle as it pooled with what water had beaded along the road. That, coupled with the humidity in the alley, let me know it had rained not too long ago.

The truck groaned as it finished emptying the dumpster.

"Damn, man! Are you all right?" Footsteps sounded behind me.

I got to my feet and turned to regard the source of the voice.

The guy couldn't have been out of his early twenties; he was Latin American and well-bronzed, likely from his job. He had a solid build, filling out most of the canvas uniform you see worn by sanitation workers. A good sign the man made time to hit the gym after a day of work. His hair was shaved close to his scalp and he showed a few days' worth of dark stubble over his face. A name tag was stitched onto his outfit just over his left breast, reading *Jake*. His eyes were the color of dark bourbon and held a clear note of concern for my well-being.

"Yeah." I shook my head, running the back of a hand across my mouth to wipe away some of the blood and drool. "Rough night . . . rougher morning."

Jake looked me over again. "Looks like. You sure you don't need anything, man?"

I thought about it. I didn't have my bearings yet, making my job harder than necessary. "There a church nearby?"

Jake glanced over his shoulder to the dumpster, then gave me another look-over, pursing his lips. "Yeah, I guess you could use one, huh?"

Ouch.

I cleared my throat and arched a brow—waiting.

Clarity returned to him a second later. "Right, there's one a bunch of blocks down from here." He gestured in the direction for me to head. "Just stay on the outside sidewalk of the strip mall and you'll hit it if you keep walking for a bit. See it all the time on our route." His eyes widened. "I gotta get back to that." He thrust his chin up in a curt nod and clambered back up to his spot on the garbage truck.

I put two fingers to my forehead, tipping them in a salute as I made my way out of the alley.

Jake's instructions would be simple enough to follow. I made my way onto the corner of a sidewalk in the small mall, looking over my surroundings to situate myself. As I did, I caught sight of a pair of rainbows arcing from the roof of one of the buildings to about a block or two away.

The strip looked to be the usual fare for local businesses: a barber, a nail salon, a doughnut shop, and the closest building to me being a veterinarian's office. I made my way toward it, hoping to bum their bathroom to clean up.

The windows were tinted a dull black that kept me from catching sight of my reflection, meaning no luck on figuring out anything about my new body. I placed a hand against the glass, trying to peer into the place, but couldn't make out a single thing. A tug on the door elicited a low rattle as it jerked, refusing to open. A piece of paper sat taped to a boarded-over pane on the other side of the door. It featured an image of a young boy. The kid was seven years old. Dark haired and dark featured with bright eyes. Andy, and he'd been missing for a few days now. Another sign next to it told me the building had been shut down for a month.

I sighed, resuming my walk. I'd have to try my luck somewhere else. The quicker I could get any bit of info on whose meat-suit I wore, the faster I'd get to the bottom of what monster had killed him and hit my next case.

A lance of pain shot through my temple like someone had spiked me with an ice pick. My vision cut again and a percussive beat went off that silenced me to anything other than drumming agony. I placed a hand against the masonry for balance as my legs threatened to give out.

Images flooded my mind. I sat at a round wooden table, its stain washed and worn down to reveal pale streaks. It could comfortably host three people around it at most. Someone sat opposite me, but the edges of my vision blurred, obscuring them in a haziness. Pressure built in my right leg just above the knee as my fingers dug into the meat there, squeezing harder than necessary. My other hand rested inches from the side of my head and trembled. A weight filled it and I couldn't peg what it could be from.

The world rocked and blackness followed.

I blinked clear of the dream, smacking the heel of a palm against my skull to reorient myself. A courtesy of the few gifts I've got on account of being a body-hopping soul. I end up collecting the memories and skills belonging to the bodies I bounce through. The problem comes when those memories flood you without control and vivid realism. They were some of the only clues I ever had, though.

I found my balance and staggered forward toward the doughnut shop, figuring I could grab enough of a quick meal to bounce back from the trying memory and give myself a proper look-over. I pushed the door open and went inside.

The counter and display took up most of the space, running from one wall of the shop to eight feet short of the other side. All manner of delectable doughiness caught my eye, promising me the perfect sugar bomb to keep me going. My stomach tightened in anticipation. I placed a hand over it and strolled over to the glass housing, taking a better look at the shop's offerings. I spotted a row of cake doughnuts drizzled in white frosting with countless sprinkles on top.

"Want me to grab you one?"

I looked up to see who'd spoken.

The young man couldn't have been out of high school. He had dark skin and short-cropped hair. Past that, you'd be hard-pressed to pick him out of a crowd of teens at the mall. He wore a collared shirt the color of the frosting with blue pinstripes running down it.

His question drove me to consider something I hadn't earlier. I gave myself a quick pat-down, hoping my new body had been disposed of with a wallet. Something pressed against one of my hands as I slid it along a pocket on my hip. I plunged my fingers in, fishing out a few crumpled bills, a single quarter, and a lone key that had been oddly filed down in places along the teeth.

It had been too much to hope for the wallet. Most monsters don't leave anything behind on a victim that could be used to identify them later.

I looked back to the doughnuts. White frosting with sprinkles. No self-respecting paranormal investigator would choose those. I glanced back to the kid and held up a pair of fingers. "I'll take two."

He nodded and plucked up the treats with a pair of tongs, slipping the desserts into a paper bag. "Coffee, something else to drink?"

I eyed the cash in hand. Three bucks and twenty-five cents. "What'll this get me?" I waved the money, giving the kid a second to tally it up.

"Small dark roast or decaf."

I nodded as I made my way down to the register, plopping the cash down on the counter sans the quarter. That ended back up in my pocket.

Maybe it was a little superstitious, but a lone coin's a lucky thing to some. And in my business, a little luck can go a long way. Especially when dealing with the supernatural.

"Holy shit, I won!" A man leaped to his feet, clutching a sliver of paper between his fingers.

The employee sighed from behind the counter. "That's like the twentieth one."

I eyed him, asking a question in silence with my look.

"People have been winning big cash from scratchers all week

in the mall. I don't get it, man. My luck's not that great." The kid scooped up my cash, running the total and passing me my change.

I waved him off. "Keep it." *I won't be around long enough for it to do any good anyhow.*

He shrugged and passed me the bag with my doughnuts, leaving my coffee for me to pick up.

I spotted the bathroom and headed toward it, bumping the door open with my hip. The sink had a wooden board running over it where a mini soap dispenser rested. There was enough room for me to place my drink and food down while I washed my hands.

The mirror above the sink sat at an angle, its metal frame crooked. But it gave me what I needed. A chance to make out my newly borrowed body and identify the victim.

The face staring back at me looked to be in its early forties. I had a decent tan and wrinkles around the dark brown eyes that could have come from lots of time in the sun as well as age. A few rogue bands of gray streaked my finger-length dark hair. More salt than pepper made up the stubble lining my new face's solid jawline.

There were no visible signs of what could have killed me. Both the blessing and the curse of my situation. Any body I inhabited was restored to its state prior to death by a higher power, and I healed a good bit faster than the average vanilla mortal. It wasn't comic book crazy, but if something didn't kill me outright, there was a good chance I'd bounce back to one hundred percent given enough time.

I took in my clothing next. The kind of dark blue overalls that could be found on mechanics and other industrial laborers. A white oval had been stitched just above the left breast pocket and a name had been embroidered into it in red thread: *Curt.*

At least now I had the start of his identity and maybe a guess at what kind of work Curt might have been in. None of which got me any closer to what sort of monster killed him and, more importantly, why?

I finished my business and grabbed up my food, leaving the shop and hitting the streets in the direction of the church. A few minutes passed before the inevitable hunger pangs of taking on a new body hit me. It's a coin toss between what growled louder, me or my stomach.

I plunged a hand into the paper bag, snatching a doughnut and scarfing it down. The frosting had caked up in a few places, and some of the sprinkles had softened like they'd been out for a while, but it was the best damned thing in the world to me. The coffee hadn't cooled quite enough for me to take a sip without burning myself. I chanced it anyhow, giving the lip of the cup a quick blow before tipping it back. The brew tasted smoother than I would have guessed for strip mall coffee, not carrying much of a bitter bite.

The rest of the walk went by in a blissful blur as I reached the church just as Jake had described. The place looked like what anyone would expect of a church just outside a strip mall. It could have been a small barn at one point that had been converted and fixed with a steeple at the front. The whole of the building was painted a shade of white found on classic picket fences. An unassuming place not worth remembering.

I leaned against one of the brown double doors and pushed my way in to find the building unoccupied. Not a surprise. Every time I entered a church on a case, it'd be remarkably empty save for one person.

I let the door shut behind me as I made my way over the burgundy carpet and by the old worn pews. The inside had been painted a softer, muted white than the outside. "Hello?"

"Vincent."

I jumped a foot away from the source of the voice and almost dropped my coffee. "Christ, don't do that!"

The man who'd spoken had the sort of looks where you weren't sure if he was prettily handsome, or handsomely pretty. Fair-skinned, lean build, and tousled golden locks that fell to his chin and framed his face well. His eyes were a deep and cold blue like the waters just below the surface of a frozen lake. He wore a pair of black glasses that only added to the nerd chic look all made worse by the khakis and pale blue dress shirt he'd tucked into his pants.

His lips pulled into a thin frown as he looked me over. "Please don't say that name in vain here, Vincent."

I grimaced when he said my name. Not the one of the man whose body I was occupying, but the only name I'd had to cling to when I started this gig. The name I'd given myself, Vincent Graves. Doing this job, my soul bouncing from body to body, all came with a cost. I'd accrued so many borrowed memories and skills from the people I'd been in that I'd lost track of my original ones, including my name.

I'd once asked the blondie in front of me for his own. He thought it funny to take a look around the church we'd been in then and name himself that.

"I'll stop that when you stop the Batman act, Church." I arched a brow and shrugged. "So, where am I this time?"

He waved a dismissive hand. "A small town outside of the counties that make up what's known as Northern Virginia. Somewhere you won't likely be back again any time soon." Church held out a hand expectantly.

I sighed. It was as good as I was going to get on info. He wasn't a chatty guy.

"I'm chatty enough when I need to be."

I squinted. He also had the unnerving habit of being able to guess my thoughts.

He smiled, saying nothing. The look could have easily been the sort of smug satisfaction that'd get a guy punched in the nose.

I set the drink and paper bag down, rolling up the sleeve of my left arm as I presented it to him. "Don't suppose you'll be nicer with the timeline this time around?" I flashed him a lopsided grin. "I brought you coffee and a doughnut."

He rolled his eyes as he clamped onto my forearm with both hands. "Coffee you've already sipped and a doughnut you bought for yourself? Besides, I'm trying to watch my figure and sugar is bad for you."

I opened my mouth to say something brilliantly witty when searing pain engulfed my arm. It felt like the tissue had been pressed to a hot grill and held there for a handful of seconds. When I pulled away from his grip, a big black number 1 sat emblazoned into the center of my forearm. The surrounding area had turned a bright red and still burned.

One hour. That was how long I had to solve the case of what monster killed Curt and how long my soul could occupy his body. If I failed, justice wouldn't be done for Curt and a monster would still be roaming the world. I'd be shuffled along to the next body and case having to live with that. And there was always the chance the freak behind this got the upper hand and killed me.

At the end of the day, I can die just like anyone else.

I shook my head clear of that thought and eyed Church. "What gives with the short deadline?"

His face remained perfectly impassive, but a light filled his eyes like he was refraining from smiling. "You won't need it."

I raised a brow higher than earlier. "Why's that?"

"Because I'm going to give you what you need. Your name is

Curtis Brown. You're a local HVAC technician, former locksmith, who also volunteers as a handyman for the daycare center across the street, all out of the goodness of his heart. That's where you should start, and maybe consider looking into the children's playground at the back."

I blinked. Church didn't have a habit of being overly forthcoming with info on my cases. Now he'd practically handed me what I needed. "What gives?"

"Children." His eyes hardened and, for a second, I could have sworn the light behind them brightened a bit. Storm clouds brewed behind that stare.

I had to look away as I took in what he'd said.

Kids. Both he and I had a particular hard rule about that.

Never mess with children, whether you're a monster or human. You don't do that around either of us.

I clenched a fist. "Fair enough." I looked back to where he'd been standing to find nothing.

Silence. You'd have never known anyone else had been there with me.

I exhaled, reaching for the bag with the doughnut. "That shit gets really tiring, you know?" I paused when I glanced at where I'd set the drink down. It had vanished as cleanly as Church, but the bag remained. "Really, my coffee?" I grumbled, going through countless iterations of what kind of ass Church was as I snatched up my doughnut and headed out of the building.

>—><—<

The place across the street had been painted a shade of taupe that made me fight down a yawn just looking at it. Bright rainbow lettering over the front listed the phone number and the words *Daycare Center*.

I made my way to the front door and pulled on one of the handles. It budged a micro-fraction, clicking in resistance as it refused to open. I squinted at the door, then noticed a buzzer to one side. It chimed before I could jab it with a thumb and I gave the door another pull. It opened and I slipped inside.

The room was more along what I expected out of a kids' center. Plush carpet, the kind that wouldn't be too bad to fall on but would still give you a decent rug burn if you weren't careful. A few building blocks littered a corner to my right. The desk ahead had been peppered in loose sheets of paper filled with crayon scribbles. A young woman sat behind it who looked like she belonged in college.

She wore a pale blue blouse and had her brown hair pulled into a neat and tight bun. Her mouth pulled into a tired smile when she saw me. "Hi, Curt."

I inclined my head, figuring it best not to speak since I couldn't recall her name through the muddle of Curtis's memories.

"You look rough. Bad night?"

"Trashy one, same with the morning, I guess." I mirrored her strained smile as I tried to navigate the conversation to what I needed. "Anything unusual up? Something need fixing?" It made sense to lump in asking for gossip along with a bit of work questions. I moved closer to her, reaching the edge of the desk and propping my elbows onto it.

She gave me a thin frown and the expression brought out creases in her forehead she was too young to have. "Some of the kids are still missing. A few of the parents told us the police haven't turned up anything yet. I've been trying not to think about it too hard." Her voice had cracked near the end.

"I'm sure they'll turn up something." *Or I will, at least.* I raised the little paper bag, giving it a shake. "Doughnut?" I hoped the offer would cheer her up even a small bit.

"Oh, God. I can't—shouldn't. I've been bingeing pizza and beer the last few nights while cramming for midterms." She shook my offer off.

I drummed a finger against the desk as I looked to the far end of the room, trying to peer through the windows and into the playground outside. "Mind if I go out back and check on the equipment? I want to see if anything's at risk of falling apart. Don't want a kid to get hurt."

She gave me a tense nod.

I moved by her, heading toward the back.

"Curt, wait. You left your keys here two days ago."

I turned, processing what she'd said. So he'd been missing for a pair of days, and in that time, he'd wound up dead. He couldn't have gone that far from here to manage that. Meaning the monster had to be close. I flashed her a more sincere smile than before and held out my hands as she stood up, leaning over the desk to plop them into my hands. "Thanks." I tilted my head, pretending to stifle a yawn as I managed to catch sight of her name tag. "Jeanine. I don't know how I lost them, guess I've been unlucky of late."

Jeanine blew out a breath as she sank back into her chair. "Yeah, well, people's luck's been weird the last week, right?" She'd spoken as if I was supposed to be in on the context.

I arched a brow and waited.

She watched my passive expression and then blinked, mouthing for a moment without words. "Come on, like Tyler's parents? One moment they're the perfect couple, then the next"—she clapped her hands—"divorced. She wins the Powerball. He's lost everything on the stock market? My car broke down yesterday and I was freaking out how I'd get here. My mom offered me a ride and turns out she'd been sitting on a huge birthday check from my grams. You hear about how many people have been winning scratchers over in the strip?" Jeanine hooked a thumb in the direction I'd come from earlier.

I grunted, not bothering to draw out the conversation any more than needed and headed toward the back door.

The playground lived up to what you'd want for your kids. A wide patch filled with wood chips and some swing sets. A solid plastic slide to zip down. Monkey bars and rungs to clamber over the way only little children could. A few rocking horses sitting on heavy-duty coiled springs. Hoops set low enough for kids to have a hope to make them. A mini blacktop area off to one side that had clearly been built for the children to have somewhere to spill paint and scribble chalk over.

A band of tykes was being led along in a line, clapping their hands, by a woman who I pegged to be somewhere between her late thirties and early forties. She had the skin and dark features that could have marked her ancestry as coming from somewhere in Southeast Asia. Her dark hair had been braided into a neat and out-of-the-way tail that hung past her shoulders. She was dressed comfortably in a pair of slacks, loose-fitting shirt, and well-worn sneakers.

Her eyes widened when she saw me.

Bingo. When someone reacts like that to a body I'm borrowing, there's usually a good reason why. And I decided to go find out what that was.

A boy, likely no older than six, tugged on the woman's pants just below the waistline. I drew closer as the lady bent to listen to him.

"Miss Chaudhry, can we take the ball and play?" The kid gestured to another child behind him who held a purple rubber ball.

It was the kind of thing that would have packed a wallop whether kicked or thrown. "And do you know when Andy will be back?"

She frowned before putting on a forced smile. Miss Chaudhry ushered the kid forward, saying something I couldn't catch but had to take as an affirmative. The boy burst with delight and ran off shrieking with the enthusiasm only someone his age could muster. The rest of the kids broke out of the line and followed behind.

"Miss Chaudhry." I inclined my head before turning to watch the kids punting the ball back and forth.

"Curtis . . ." The pause lingered for a bit longer than I would have expected. That told me something.

I let the silence drag out until it weighed on the pair of us. "You looked surprised to see me."

She gave me a thin, strained smile. "I am."

"Didn't expect to see me, then." It wasn't a question. I watched her, waiting to see her reaction.

Miss Chaudhry sniffed. "No. And since none of the missing children have returned, I don't know how you could have either?"

I blinked. That meant she knew Curtis had gone looking for them, which meant she had an idea of what was going on. And that was a damn sight more than me. I matched her thin smile from moments ago. "I'll show you mine if you show me yours."

She gave me a level look. "You're not Curtis, are you?" It came off more as an accusation than a question.

I matched her stare. "You ever hear of the name Vincent Graves?"

Her body stiffened like an icy rod had gone through her spine. She licked her lips before speaking. "Some of us have . . . the supernatural, I mean. The spirit, bouncing around solving murders, killing some of us."

Some of us. Meaning she was walking on the monster side of things. Question was, what was she?

Sometimes the best thing you can do is just ask. So I did.

"And I'm here to put another monster down. Which brings me to this: are you the one I'm looking for? If you're not, then you might want to tell me what you are and why I shouldn't find a way to gank you."

She didn't miss a beat. "Yaksha." Miss Chaudhry waved a hand to the widespread thicket of trees at the edge of the park. "I preside over this small bit of nature. I'm the local luck spirit, *trying* to do what I can to look after the little ones." She gave the kids playing ball an affectionate look.

I hadn't expected that. Yaksha were nature spirits that could manipulate luck on a small scale, granting it or taking it away. They weren't known for being malicious unless provoked. But minor spirits across many religions were usually tied to some small chunk of land they couldn't leave without giving up serious bits of their power, meaning she couldn't interfere or help. Some lore argued that yaksha had a soft spot for kids.

And nothing's got more luck than a child's luck. They're innocent, pure, and damn near magical as anything can get. Which meant . . .

"I'm going to ask you something, and I'd like you to answer honestly." I didn't give her a moment to consider anything else. "Do you know what is taking the children? And is it after their luck?" I thought back to the odd happenings in the town concerning twists of fortune. There wouldn't be any more obvious reason to go after the kids, and sometimes the supernatural are just that damn simple.

She bowed her head in a silent yes.

"What is it? Where is it?" I may have taken an unnecessary

step toward her and lowered my voice to a growl. It wasn't intentional, but when kids are involved, I see red easier.

Miss Chaudhry pointed at an angle to the sky.

I followed the gesture to a pair of rainbows arcing from the parking lot of the daycare center back toward the strip mall. "Oh, you've got to be fucking kidding me."

>—•—<

Leprechauns. Freaking leprechauns.

Lots of their lore got twisted over the ages—perverted, but some bits were true. The meddlesome monsters were definitely lucky, and they could play with luck too, for good or bad. But it came with a cost.

Fortune always does. Never forget that.

I'd seen people try to twist luck to their ways before and it never went well for the people who'd made the deals.

I grumbled under my breath as I moved toward the strip mall, bothering to take a peek at my forearm.

It hadn't changed—one hour left, but just how much of that hour remained? My tattoo didn't take minutes into account.

That galvanized me into doubling my pace until I fell into something just short of a run. My gaze kept flicking to the sky, tracking the double rainbow in hopes of pinpointing exactly where it ended.

I made my way onto the asphalt of the strip mall and caught sight of what I believed to be the end of the twin beams. The location brought me to a stop.

The clinic I'd first tried to catch a glimpse of myself at. A familiar piece of paper stared back at me. The one with a young boy's face on it—Andy's face.

My fingers tightened against the mouth of the paper bag holding my last doughnut and I resolved to treat myself to it after kicking Lucky's ass.

I rushed over to the door to the vet, giving it a forceful tug. It didn't budge. A quick look around the strip revealed two people leaving the doughnut shop. Smashing my way through the window wasn't an option. The noise would draw more attention than I could afford and—

My vision tilted before images flooded me. Curtis's hands slipped an odd key into the deadbolt of the door before me, giving the tool a jiggle before smacking it hard. Clarity returned seconds later along with a migraine like someone had taken a bat to my temple.

I recognized the key from my vision and sent a hand fumbling through my pocket. My fingers slipped over the piece of metal and I plucked it free, turning it over in my grip. It took me another second to realize what I really had in my hand. A bump key.

They were tools fashioned by criminals more than anyone else to help circumvent a lock. Genuine locksmiths didn't have much use for one outside the novelty . . . and that they could work in select situations.

The principle is simple. They're filed down just enough to slip into any lock. You put them in, apply pressure, give them a good bump, and the impact jars the pins of a lock into place for a fraction of second. You can usually get through a single lock that way.

And then it clicked. Curtis had used his background to fashion this to get through the door before me.

I slipped the key in just short of all the way, then pulled off a shoe, applying pressure to the broad face of the key with a thumb so it would try to turn the lock. A smack from the heel of my shoe slammed the key in. *Click.* I tugged the door open, slipping inside without bothering to put my shoe back on immediately.

It took me longer than I would have liked to adjust to the darkness of the boarded-up interior. I moved past the small reception area, heading toward the back. That was when I heard it.

Sniffling. A few moans. The kind that could only come from one source. Little kids. You know the sound if you've ever heard it before.

I gritted my teeth, opening the first door on my right.

A child who couldn't have been more than eight lay strapped to a bed. He'd been blindfolded.

Crimson streaked my vision and I rushed to help him.

Well, I tried.

Something barreled into my midsection, slamming me into the door hard enough to threaten tearing it from its hinges. The paper bag slipped from my grip. Instinct drove me to twist and drive an elbow down into the back of my attacker.

The blow connected, forcing him to his knees, but I must have had a moment of bad luck as the inside of my joint struck a bony bit of his spine. My arm went numb, tingling in odd places. I'd struck my funny bone in the attack.

My assailant used the pause to right himself, swinging a fist toward my ribs.

I pivoted and stepped to the side, hoping he'd slam his hand into the unforgiving metal door. I didn't pay enough attention to my surroundings, though. My haste led me to shove a foot against the protruding doorstop and I tumbled to the ground in another bit of misfortune.

A laugh sounded from above me.

I rolled over to take stock of my attacker.

He stood at five-six. Dark hair and eyes, blotchy pale skin. He had a lean body carved from gnarled wood. I could tell he knew how to scrap even if he didn't have much muscle. He wore a gray tank top and a pair of jeans that only stayed on because of the belt. His nose had the sort of crookedness to it that came from being repeatedly broken and never once set right.

I slowly got to my feet as he watched me. "I'm guessing you're Lucky, huh?"

He gave me a toothy smile. "Bad stereotype. And I thought you died the first time you tried this."

Which answered my question.

"Round two will go differently." I flashed him a wolfish grin.

He tilted his head to one side. "That so?"

"Yeah. Ever hear of Vincent Graves?"

His eyes widened and he screamed, bull-rushing me.

Guess he has.

He collided with my torso, trying to take me down.

I'd braced a heel against the wall behind me, using it to keep my balance. When his attempt failed, I capitalized on his lack of momentum and drove a knee into his sternum. The strike landed home but a dull ache manifested in the muscle around the joint. I winced. "What gives?"

Lucky pulled away from me, grimacing as he massaged his chest. "Haven't figured it out yet?"

Son of a bitch.

"You're manipulating chance, any bad thing that can happen in this fight is happening." I glared at him.

He waggled a hand. "It's more likely to happen." His smile from earlier came back, widening.

I ran a tongue over my teeth. "If that's the case, there's got to be a limit. No monster's perfect, and there's only so long you can keep that up."

His smile faltered, just for a moment, but enough for me to know I'd been right.

"So, how long do we do this dance before your luck turns

sour?" I recalled a bit of lore I'd once read concerning leprechauns. The more they manipulated luck, the higher the chance they also had of incurring bad luck to the degree they'd altered. It was a karmic clapback of exponential proportions.

"That's the thing about luck, spirit, you never know when it will turn. It could go poorly for you before you ever manage to turn it on me. It did for the last guy." He winked.

"That's why you're feeding off kids? Trying to stockpile fortune for a rainy day?"

"Something like that. It's not all bad. I've been throwing random bones here and there to the locals." Lucky rolled his shoulders once.

"Yeah, I bet. So how about we settle this?"

"Thought you'd never ask. Follow me." He stepped backward out of the room, turning to move down the hall.

I hadn't expected that.

I picked up my fallen bag and followed him to a back room.

The room at the back had been cleared away but for a table . . . and cages. Three guesses what was inside them. More kids.

And I recognized one of them. The boy and I locked stares and he was a kid of dark hair and eyes—six years old at first guess. Andy. He gave me a look of silent plea. Wanting help. Wanting rescue.

My fingers dug into my palms.

I counted at least six more kids and it took everything I had not to throttle the monster on the spot. He probably would have expected it and turned it on me somehow.

"Sit." Lucky motioned to a round table with two seats opposite each other.

"We going to talk this out like rational folk?" I pulled out a chair and sat.

His mouth pulled to one corner. "Something like that." He went to a small shelf that came up to his waist, pulling a revolver from the top of it.

My eyes went owlishly large. "Oh you dirty, cheating son of a—"

He raised a hand to stop me before smacking the gun down in the center of the table.

I paused. Then it registered. "This is how you dealt with Curtis." The first vision I had of how he'd died, a game of Russian roulette. "Fitting, I guess. Gets your rocks off, playing with luck and danger." Another realization hit me.

He opened his mouth to speak, but I cut him off.

"You're right. I don't know if I can beat you in a straight-up fight, especially when you can twist luck. But if you want to do it this way, you'll have to swear on your power you won't manipulate here. Besides, if you do, never know when it can go all wrong, huh?"

Lucky frowned, glancing down at the gun, then back at me.

"What's the matter? Not feeling as lucky as you claim to be?" I glanced at the kids in cages, clenching my jaw hard enough to make my gums ache. "I've gotten this far without a whit of luck, so maybe yours isn't all that it's cracked up to be if you need it? Can't play fair? Or maybe the only way you have any luck to throw about is when you steal it from some kid? Doesn't say much for you, does—"

One of his fists slammed into the table. "Enough. Fine, you want to die that badly? We'll play it that way. I swear on my power that I won't use an ounce of my luck till this is over and one of us is dead." He narrowed his eyes in a look that made it clear he believed I'd be the one to bite it.

Say what you will about the paranormal, but they've got just as much hubris as any mortal. Sometimes more. And if you can ding that, go for it. There's a reason it's a sin and a downfall of many. And I meant for it to be his.

By swearing on his power, he'd ensured he had no choice but to play fair. Violating that oath would cause a nasty magical or psychic backlash that could rob him of his powers, hurt him, or even turn them against him. It wasn't much, but I'd leveled the playing field.

Now all I had to do was win.

In a game totally down to luck.

He raised the revolver, thumbing the cylinder open to show a single round inside. Lucky snapped it shut, slammed it back to the table, and spun it.

It rotated till its point faced me. *Of course I'm first. Lucky me.*

The leprechaun grinned, a maniacal light in his eyes.

I inhaled, raised the gun, and pulled.

Click.

Phew. I breathed out and put the gun back down, giving it a shove to send it spinning.

Lucky's turn. He raised it to his head without hesitation, grinning, and then pulled the trigger.

Click. Nothing.

Of course it wouldn't be that easy.

He spun the gun.

My turn. I brought it to my head, casting a sideways glance at my tattoo. Still said an hour, but how much of that had slipped away? Was I gambling away time? Did I have a chance to turn this around in a fight?

"Stop stalling and pull."

I did.

Click. I slammed the gun back down and stared. "Your turn, Lucky."

He bristled in his seat. Guess he didn't have as much faith in his luck as he'd thought. He didn't grab the gun, choosing to lean forward instead. "You can't win."

"Maybe. Won't know till you pull. Go." I held my stare.

He leaned back, giving me a nonchalant shrug that carried a hint of stiffness in it. "I've done this before."

Poker face, huh? Two can play that game. "You have. But not against me. Pull."

He grabbed the gun and aimed at me.

. . . oops? I should have seen that one coming.

"What are you doing?" I placed a hand under the edge of the table, hoping I could flip it over in time in case things went from bad to worse.

"Thinking that maybe I could save some time and end this now." He steadied the gun.

Guess my poker face needed work. "Save face, you mean. Your luck must not be as hot as you thought, huh?"

Lucky narrowed his eyes and the gun shook. "What did you say?"

I smiled, but beads of sweat built on the back of my neck. Hubris had gotten me into this, maybe a touch of my own, but maybe it'd get me out, with a little luck.

An idea struck me.

"I think you're scared and can't live up to what you said earlier. What if I raise the ante?" I didn't give him a chance to reconsider as I fished a coin out of my pocket, rolling it between the first two fingers on my right hand. "I toss this coin, you call it, we finish the game. You call it right, you get my soul."

Silence.

And I knew I had him.

There are few things more magical in this world than someone's soul. It's damn near a nuclear reactor of magical potential. For a creature wanting power—luck, he could do worse than my soul.

Hunger flooded his eyes and the gun shook more. He licked his lips once and put the gun down, not relinquishing his grip on it.

I raised the baggie in my other hand, giving it a shake.

"What's that?"

"Just sweetening the pot." I pulled the doughnut out, setting it down on the bag as I pushed it to the center of the table. "My soul and a doughnut . . . with sprinkles, so long as you're around to collect. Think you're lucky enough for that wager?"

Lucky's lips pressed tight like he was fighting a smile. "Fine by me. Toss."

I did and hoped I was right about how this would go down. A look at the kids told me I didn't have much choice now that it'd come to this.

I had a job to save them. I wasn't a hero; that was what Curtis was. He had zero clue about this world and still stepped into it to help these children. But sometimes the heroes are dead and we have to fill in. It's not something you're born to. You just lace up the boots and walk in 'em when the moment calls for it.

I tossed the coin. "Call it and pull!"

He raised the gun to his head, grinning wide enough to make a shark jealous. "Heads."

The coin landed heads.

Lucky's smile grew further. "Guess I still had enough luck to sway that, huh?"

Yeah, and I was betting you would.

He pulled the trigger, eyes widening just as he caught on to what I'd done.

And bad luck came to collect.

Bang. Red ichor and gore spurted from the side of Lucky's head before he thumped against the table.

He shouldn't have used his luck to alter the toss, but he'd gotten greedy. Lucky had made a pact, swearing off from using his powers, and the second he did, his luck turned on him—badly.

He might have won my soul, but he wouldn't be around to collect.

I gave one look to the kids in cages. The risk had been worth it.

The frosting of the doughnut stole my attention and I snaked it up, glancing at Lucky as I bit into the dessert. "You know"—I took a moment to chew and swallow—"these things can kill ya." It tasted just as good as the first one had.

>>‹‹

I set about freeing the kids, starting with Andy.

His eyes were red and a hint of moisture welled along his lids. "Am I going to be okay?"

I held him tight for a long moment. "Yeah, kid. You're going to be fine. You're going home."

A quick search of the place revealed an old office phone still connected. A simple 911 call did the rest. I wouldn't stick around for the authorities to show up, knowing they'd get the kids taken care of.

Sometimes the usual heroes aren't around to save the day. You've got to hope someone else comes along, and if they don't, you've got to hope you can do it. And in my experience, hope works, and we can all be the heroes someone else needs.

I headed back to the church to wrap up my case.

SILVERSPELL

by Chloe Neill

1

We'd made mistakes. And we were paying for them.

Shards of pink cardboard were spread before us. Only hours ago, they had been a glossy box holding a dozen donuts shipped from Lulu's parents in Portland to our loft in Chicago. Now they were compost.

Beside me, Lulu sighed, hands on her petite hips. She had pale skin and a dark slice of hair down to her chin, some of it now falling across eyes I knew were as furious as mine. She was a sorceress who didn't practice; I was the vampire she allowed to share her home.

"This is your fault," she said.

"You can't blame me every time she has a tantrum."

The aforementioned "she" was Eleanor of Aquitaine, the sleek black cat who ruled this particular roost. Eleanor of Aquitaine had no fear. But she had a canny sense of entitlement and punishment for presumed wrongs.

"This isn't a tantrum," Lulu said, and picked through the cardboard, looking for remnants. "It's a shot across the bow. There was one glazed left, and I'd been saving it."

I narrowed my gaze at the cat. She sat in her usual spot—atop the window radiator—tail swishing as she watched us, boredom in her green eyes.

"Have a banana?"

Lulu looked at me, gaze dry as old toast. "Seriously?"

"Until she adopts a new personality, that is my only suggestion."

My screen buzzed. I pulled it out, and found a message from Roger Yuen, the city's supernatural Ombudsman.

SUP DEATH IN SOUTH LAWNDALE, the message read, and gave an address on the south side. SHIFTER, he added. CA PACK.

I was Elisa Sullivan, daughter of two of Chicago's most prominent vampires, born because magic and fate twisted together. Me and my partner, Theo Martin, were associate Ombuds, liaisons between humans and sups: problem solvers, mediators, and occasionally investigators.

CA was an abbreviation for Consolidated Atlantic, the shapeshifter Pack that controlled the Eastern Seaboard. And that explained why Roger had tagged me, even though I was off tonight. Chicago was the territory of the North American Central Pack, led by Apex shifter Gabriel Keene. And Connor Keene, Gabriel's son and the heir apparent to the North American Central Pack of shapeshifters, was my boyfriend.

If Roger's information was correct, the shifter wasn't one of Gabriel's wolves, but the death of a stranger in NAC territory almost certainly carried its own complications.

ACKNOWLEDGED, I messaged back, knowing he'd given me the

information to prepare me for what I'd see—to assure me that it wasn't a shifter I knew. I was doubly glad of it when he sent the image: a wolf lying inside a pale white circle drawn on the street, its gold-tipped beige fur stained with blood.

I blinked, looked closer, and sent another message. IS THAT A SALT CIRCLE?

LIMITED INFO, Roger responded. YOU AND THEO TELL ME.

That was fair, I thought, and put my screen away.

"What is it?" Lulu asked.

"A shifter is dead," I said. "And it looks like magic was involved."

Lulu's eyes went flat. She refused to use her own magic, despite her parents being two of the most powerful sorcerers in the country. Her mother had overcome an addiction to black magic, but not before wreaking havoc on Chicago. My mother, Sentinel of Chicago's Cadogan House of vampires, had had to deal with it. As a result, Lulu tried to avoid supernatural drama.

"Why magic?"

"Salt circle."

"Ah." She nodded and began to pick up the pieces of cardboard. "You should talk to Petra."

"I will," I said. Petra was also an associate Ombud, insatiably curious about all things supernatural, and an aeromancer in her own right.

"I'll let you know if I'm going to be late," I told Lulu. "Or not at all."

"If you're talking about sex, I don't need the details." She paused. "Unless they're exceptionally good ones."

"They usually are," I said with a smile.

➤✕◄

I grabbed my jacket and scabbarded katana, pulled my wavy blond hair into a knot, and called an Auto. I messaged Petra about the salt circle while the driverless vehicle transported me south through Chicago.

When it pulled to my stop, I climbed out and belted on my sword.

The street was silent here, sandwiched on one side by an empty lot and on the other by a park that needed serious rehab. There was a chill in the air, a harbinger of autumn. Death didn't care about seasons; it took its fill throughout the year.

Magic peppered the air, either from the spell that had been worked here, or the spill of shifter blood, which carried its own unique power. And beneath both, something darker. Something oilier, that left a stain on the air.

This was dark magic—dangerous, painful, risky; magic that tipped the balance of the world.

As if in answer, thunder rumbled from sickly green clouds, spinning overhead. "Not at all ominous," I muttered, and flipped the thumb guard on my katana, just in case.

The salt circle was twenty feet away, the wolf lying still in its center. I crouched outside it, careful not to disturb the scene.

There was a gap in the circle near the wolf's head, a spot where the salt had been smeared, the circle broken. As I understood it, breaking a circle had a magical effect—either to end the spell or to release whatever creature or power had been bound inside it. So was this accidental or intentional?

The cause of death seemed obvious—the dagger still protruding from its belly. I couldn't see the blade, but the handle was ornately carved wood with a glinting silver guard. Shifters in wolf form were larger than the natural variety. This one seemed pitifully small: as if death hadn't just been an insult but a reduction.

"Lis."

I stood, looked back, and found the prince emerging through darkness.

Connor strode toward me, blue eyes gleaming. His hair was dark and permanently tousled, his skin sun-kissed, his generous mouth worthy of an ancient god. He wore an NAC Pack T-shirt and jeans over boots.

I enjoyed watching him move, powerful and confident, and felt my blood begin to race. He put a hand on my arm, the touch warm and soothing, then pressed a kiss to my forehead. He gave ferocity to the world; the tenderness was just for me.

"Hey," he said.

"Hey. I'm sorry for this." I glanced back at the wolf.

"So am I. Didn't know him, but I'm sorry just the same." His eyes went dark. "No one, shifter or otherwise, should die alone in the street."

"Not entirely alone," I said, gesturing to the circle. "Someone was here, and we'll find out who that was. What was his name?"

"Bryce. Jason Maguire sent a picture."

Maguire was the Apex of the Consolidated Atlantic Pack. Connor pulled out his screen and showed me a photograph of a smiling young man with pale skin, blond hair, and green eyes.

"So young," I said. "What's a CA shifter doing in Chicago?"

"Visiting friends," Connor answered while putting the screen away. "He was at The Raucous Wolf, a bar near McKinley Park. He went outside to chat up a woman. His compatriots didn't hear from him for a couple of hours, thought he'd gone home with the girl. Someone sent them a picture of that," he added, casting his gaze back to the wolf.

"The killer?" I asked, my pity a tightness in my throat but little comfort to Connor or Bryce now. "Why draw attention to what you've done? Was this for revenge?" I wasn't asking him, but talking through the issues aloud.

"I don't know." Connor's voice was quiet. "I'm told he was well-liked, had no obvious enemies. Easy to get along with. Do you know anything about the magic?"

"Only that this looks and feels like dark magic," I said quietly, and he nodded.

"Death, blood, power," he confirmed. "And it's strong. Reminds me of the time a sorcerer in Memphis tried to open a gate to hell."

"Because the blues and barbecue weren't enough entertainment?"

"It takes all kinds," he said philosophically. "And it felt a lot like this."

He walked toward the wolf and stared down, hands on his hips and a furrow in his brow. "The dagger is silver. I can feel the interruption in the magic. As if splitting him open wasn't enough, the silver could work its punishment too." His words were hard and angry.

Saying *I'm sorry* again seemed inefficient. I brushed my fingers against his, our touchstone. He met my gaze, nodded once. Acknowledgment. Confirmation.

"You sense anything else?" I asked. "Any indication someone was here?"

"Not at the moment." A corner of his mouth lifted. "But I'll tell you if I do."

I nodded, crouched to take photographs of the circle, the smear of salt, the wolf, and sent them to Petra. And saw something stuck in the blood beneath its fur. Before I could reach out, the sound of a vehicle rumbled through the night.

I rose as a CPD cruiser rolled up and parked diagonally in the street.

"Your cavalry," Connor said.

"They'll work for Bryce," I reminded him.

Theo emerged from the passenger side in his typical uniform, jeans and a button-down shirt, this one in checks of white and periwinkle. His skin was dark brown, his hair black and twisted into small, short whorls. Grimness narrowed his brown eyes.

A woman emerged from the driver's side. She was Detective Gwen Robinson, the CPD's supernatural expert. She strode forward, her dark brown skin glowing against a trim suit in dark navy. Her dark hair was loose today in soft waves that framed her face. And although her wide brown eyes were cop-blank beneath angular brows, there was sadness there.

"Our condolences," Gwen said when they reached us.

"Thank you," Connor said. "He's from the Consolidated Atlantic." He gestured toward the vehicle. "No cruisers? No lights?"

"Our bosses thought it best to keep it quiet, given the magic," Gwen said. "What do you know?"

Connor told her what he'd learned as she moved around the circle, occasionally crouching, and taking her own photographs.

"And I think I see something," I said, and crouched beside her, pointed to the white fragment beneath him. "Do you have an evidence bag or . . . ?"

"Right here," Theo said, as he set a kit on the ground, opened it, and pulled out gloves and a bag, which he offered to Gwen.

"You're a very handy assistant," Gwen said, without looking back.

Theo snorted. "Ombuds are not assistants. We're liaisons. I'm liaising."

Rolling her eyes, Gwen pulled on the gloves, then carefully extracted a piece of paper from beneath the wolf with a pair of tweezers. She slipped it into the evidence bag and held it up to the light. It was white, about five inches high, cut roughly into the shape of a wolf.

Gwen swore.

"What is that?" Theo asked. "A paper doll?"

"Possibly a kind of effigy," Gwen said, rising again. "The second one we've found. A human was killed two nights ago. Stabbed by a dagger, a human-shaped effigy beneath him."

Theo put his hands on his hips, looked at me. "We didn't hear about this."

"No," I said. "We didn't. Was there a salt circle in that one?"

"No," Gwen said. "Which is why it wasn't flagged as supernaturally involved."

Connor frowned. "It rained two nights ago."

"So it did," Gwen said. "Washing away whatever evidence might have remained. So these crimes might be connected, by perpetrator or magic or both."

"Dark magic," I said, and they all looked at me with grim acceptance, and concern for whatever the consequences might be.

The silver ring of a bell echoed through the street, and we all glanced at each other.

"Did we all hear that?" I asked.

"We heard it," Connor said, gaze narrowing on the shadowed trees in the park on the other side of the street. "It wasn't magic. Maybe part of the ceremony. Maybe intended to scare us away."

"Very high creep factor," Gwen said.

"So what's going on here?" Theo asked. "Some kind of sacrifice?"

"You kill someone in a salt circle with a silver dagger, it definitely seems ceremonial."

"And what's next? Vampire? Fairy? River nymph?" I looked at Theo. "We need to warn the Houses. Just in case." My father was Master of Cadogan House, one of Chicago's four vampire Houses. The man who'd stood as my uncle for most of my life was Master of another. I didn't want to find any of them—or any of their people—like this.

He nodded. "Roger will get the word out."

Gwen removed the gloves, pulled out her screen, did some swiping. "I'm going to call the forensics team, have them pull the dagger and get samples of everything else for the lab." She looked around. "There's a reason this was done here. No security or traffic cameras. Very few people."

When she was done, she looked at Connor. "Legally, the Pack has no authority to participate in an investigation. But," she added, holding up a hand when I opened my mouth to argue, "I'm also aware how valuable your contributions have been to the Ombuds and the CPD. So I'm willing to give you some latitude, as long as you don't impede our investigation. Or break any laws."

"I'm here to help the Pack, not impede the CPD or the Ombuds," Connor said. "Obfuscating the truth isn't going to help us find justice for Bryce." He glanced at me. "And I have every reason to help."

Gwen nodded. "That's good enough for me. And if you cause trouble, I'll sic the Ombuds on you."

Connor's smile was sly. "That's no punishment, Detective."

"Returning to business," I said, before a flush could heat my cheeks, "we should check out the bar where he was last seen."

"Why don't you take him?" Theo asked, nodding toward Connor. "He might get more out of shifters, and I want to hit the magic angle with Petra."

Connor nodded. "Fine by me."

"Then we'll let both of you know if we find anything," I said.

Gwen nodded. "I know you will. Probably right after you feed your coffee addiction."

I shifted my gaze to Theo. "Narc."

His grin was wide, smooth. "Are you going to get coffee right now?"

Only if the universe was just.

2

The universe was just.

We found a drive-through Joe's—my favorite Chicagoland coffee hookup—not far from the scene. I got a coffee, Connor went for the water, and we split a blueberry scone.

"They're changing my opinion of scones," he said, licking blueberry juice from his thumb as he drove, that small act sending a bolt of desire through me. "I used to think of them as the biscuit's lesser British cousin."

"That's because you were born in Memphis. Southerners and biscuits have a very special relationship. These taste like butter and blueberries, which is a winning combination in any book."

Chicago being what it was, we parked on the street two blocks away and hiked back to the bar through darkness.

The Raucous Wolf was not what I'd expected. Most shifter establishments were heavy on the leather, cheap booze, and loud music, but very light on inhibitions. This was the bespoke, artisanal, shade-grown version. Gray wood floors and walls with metal panels and enormous letters from old shop signs. Tables were communal and the bar industrial, with a full array of expensive and small-batch whiskeys behind it.

"Huh," I said, looking around.

"We are a complex people. And occasionally we like good bourbon and truffle fries."

"I guess." I glanced at him. "Was I sheltered? Or is this another case of sups preferring that vampires not be in the know?" I'd only recently found out that the Taco Hole, a dive bar with mouth-searing tacos, served as a supernatural neutral ground.

"Both," Connor said, and smoothed a hand down my hair. "But I like you just the way you are. Or mostly."

"Careful, puppy," I said, and looked around at the patrons. "With whom should we speak?"

"Let's start there," he said, gesturing to a broad-shouldered woman standing behind the bar. She had suntanned skin and salt-and-pepper curls that just reached her shoulders. She wore a T-shirt with the bar's name and cleaned the counter with a rag.

"You know her?" I asked.

"Not yet."

We strode toward her, Connor in the lead, and I watched with amusement as virtually everyone in the room paused to get a look at him. They knew power when they saw it and didn't bother to hide their appreciation.

The bartender smiled broadly at Connor as we approached. Human, I thought, given the lack of apparent magic. But powerful magic could hide a lot of sins.

"Mr. Keene," she said, putting her hands on her hips. "I'm Lucy Dalton, and very pleased to see you in my place. What brings you here? Can I get you a drink? Or something to eat?"

"There was a shifter in the bar last night," he said, then showed her the photo. "Do you remember him?"

She frowned, nodded. "I do. He was cute." She filled a glass with ice. "Young enough to be my son," she added with a laugh. "But very cute."

She added water to the glass from a pump, then drank deeply. "I think he was here for about an hour? We were pretty slow, and he was with a boisterous group."

"Did he leave alone?" I asked, and for the first time, the woman seemed to actually notice I was there. And didn't seem to like it.

"How could I possibly know that?" Her tone had changed, become guarded. Which I dutifully ignored.

"Did you talk to him?"

"He didn't come up to the bar."

"That's not an answer," Connor said.

She looked at him, smiled thinly. "No, I didn't talk to him. I don't talk to every customer who crosses that doorway. What is this?"

Connor ignored the question. "Did anything unusual happen while he was in the bar?"

"No, why? Did he get arrested?"

"He's dead." Connor's voice was flat, and her eyes went flat. But he continued before she could respond. "Who served him?"

"We didn't do anything wrong here."

"I didn't state otherwise. Who served him?"

After a moment of frowning, she looked toward a waitress on the other side of the bar delivering drinks on a tray. The woman was leanly built with light brown skin and long, dark, curly hair. She wore shorts, tennis shoes, and the same bar T-shirt as Dalton.

"She did," Dalton said. "You're welcome to talk to her but try to keep it fast. We're short-staffed."

When a shifter tapped a glass on the other end of the bar, Dalton gave Connor a smile and left us for the customer.

"Hmm," I said, and Connor nodded.

For a moment we watched the waitress and waited until she headed back to a swinging door with a tray of empty glasses.

We reached her just before she disappeared into the back, and I realized the woman looked familiar. Very familiar.

"Ariel?" I asked.

Ariel Shaw was a necromancer, or the daughter of one, at any rate. I'd never seen her practice. But I could feel the magic, cold and heavy as a tomb, that surrounded her. Her mother, Annabelle, had helped my parents with issues now and again, and Ariel and Lulu had been friends as teenagers. I'd been a fan of rules and order growing up; Ariel hadn't, and had tried to steer Lulu down the same rebellious path. They'd eventually grown apart, which was fine by me.

Ariel looked at me, brow knit, when something flashed in her eyes. It was gone in an instant, but not before I registered concern.

"The prince and princess come to visit the commoners?" Her tone was derisive, as was the expression she donned. "Vampires slumming with shifters these days?"

"Since you're working in a shifter bar," Connor said easily, "you might want to lose the attitude."

"Working," she said, "and I need to get back to it."

"Tell us about this man," Connor said, and showed Bryce's photograph.

"He was a shitty tipper," she said, tone edged with irritation, but I saw that hitch in her eyes again.

"What else?" Connor asked, putting his screen away.

Ariel gave a haggard sigh and rebalanced her tray. As she moved, I caught the edge of a black tattoo on her arm—a thin line with short hash marks, at the edge of her sleeve. When she saw the direction of my gaze, she shifted her body to block my view of it.

Totally not suspicious behavior.

"He was a customer," she finally answered. "I served him."

I bet that wasn't the entire story, so I took a chance. "And what happened when you went outside with him?"

She jerked, and the glasses rattled. "I don't know what you're talking about."

"You clearly do," Connor said. "Would you rather talk to us or the CPD?"

She met his gaze. "I'm not one of your subjects, and you don't own me, *prince*." There was teenage petulance in her tone.

"He's dead," Connor said. "He was killed with dark magic, or because of it. You have magic, witch. Did you kill him?"

"My coven is good. We don't practice dark magic." She started to move away again, but Connor took her arm, stared down at her with the threat in his eyes plain and clear.

Before he could speak, my screen buzzed. I found a message from Theo—an address only a block away, and a message: THINK WE FOUND HIS CLOTHES.

I showed it to Connor, who nodded, then looked at Ariel again.

"A shifter is dead," he said, fingers still wrapped around her arm. "If you were involved in that, it won't matter that you're a witch, or if your mother was good, or if we were friends once upon a time. I'll find out. And you won't like how that conversation ends."

He lifted his hand, and she pushed through the door, where glass rattled again.

Connor took my hand, and we walked back through the bar together. This time, the gazes weren't just on the prince, but on both of us, and our linked hands.

>—<

We found Theo in McKinley Park proper. He stood beneath a tree, flashlight aimed on the ground—and a pile of clothes tossed there.

He nodded in greeting when we reached him. "You get coffee?"

"Not enough," I said.

Connor kneeled, looked over the pile of clothes. The shift between man and animal—whatever form that took—was magical and physiological; it didn't affect clothing. So a shifter either sacrificed their clothes, which would be shredded in the transition, or took them off before shifting and dressed again afterward.

"These are from Bryce," Connor confirmed. "They have the same scent as the wolf."

"Can you smell anyone else?" I asked. "Anything else?"

"No." He lifted his gaze to Theo. "How'd you find them?"

"Anonymous tip."

"Interesting."

"I thought so."

"You go through them?"

"Not yet," Theo said. He took a plastic bag and a set of gloves from his pocket, then pulled on the gloves. We moved aside while Theo crouched and searched the T-shirt, jeans, and boxers, looking for anything that might have been tucked inside.

"Gwen?" I asked.

"Working with the lab," Theo said, frowning as he inspected

the jeans' front pocket. He pulled out a rounded square of thick paper.

"Bar coaster," he said, flipping it over. "For The Raucous Wolf." He slipped it into the evidence bag and, when it was protected, offered it to me.

The bar's wolfish logo was, in a bit of gruesome irony, tucked inside a circle on the front. The reverse side advertised a beer company with a curvy pinup. But there was something else—what looked like a tiny bit of writing on the bottom corner. A phone number? I wondered.

"Flashlight," I said, and held out my hand, expecting one of them would fulfill the request. Connor got there first, putting a penlight into my hand. I flicked it on and shined it on the spot, illuminating a simple mark of lines and dashes inked so heavily into the coaster they'd left a groove in the paper: two lines crossing in the shape of an X, and a series of shorter marks that crossed them both or individually at intervals.

"It's a stave," I said.

"A what?" Theo asked, moving closer.

"A symbol that makes up a spell. Nordic in origin. I studied staves in college—supernatural sociology," I reminded him. "I don't know what this particular stave symbolizes, but each mark has meaning, and when you put them together, they have a magical effect. Combine that with a little blood, a little salt, and a little paper, and you've made magic." I looked up. "I think Ariel has one of these tattooed on her arm. I saw it when she moved her tray."

"Ariel?" Theo asked, and we told him what we'd found at the bar.

"The lines," Connor agreed with a nod. "I saw that, too."

"We need to talk to her again."

"We do," Theo agreed. "And good catch. Petra couldn't do much with the salt circle, it was too general. But added to this, we might have something." He pulled out his screen and sent her a message.

I rose at the scritch of shoes on pavement behind us. And along with it, the low buzz of magic.

I turned back. Connor positioned himself toward the sound, toward the threat. Theo slid the wrapped coaster into his back pocket and moved to put himself between the bundle of clothes and the interloper.

I knew the man who approached. Tall and lean, with blond hair, eyes the color of good bourbon, and a rather beautiful mouth. Not that I'd admit that to anyone in the present company.

Jonathan Black was part elf, evidenced by the delicately pointed tips of his ears. I wasn't certain about the rest of his genetic origins. He appeared human but exuded more magic than part elf would account for. And unlike the first time we'd met, tonight he'd made no effort to use his elf-born glamour to hide his magic. It all but swirled around him.

I'd met him outside the Ombuds' office one night and enlisted his help in dealing with the Assembly of American Masters, the ruling body of American vampires. He represented certain supernatural interests in Chicago but was cagey about who or what those interests were.

He looked at me, and while his smile was pleasant, it didn't reach his eyes. Grimness had taken firm root there. Quite a change from the last time we'd spoken, which had been before my promotion to a permanent position in the Ombuds' office. He'd been all charming smiles and flirty words then.

"Mr. Black," I said. "What brings you to McKinley Park in the middle of the night?"

Recognition sparked in Connor's eyes, and then his gaze shifted to take in the ears.

Jonathan didn't answer, he just slid his gaze over Connor, then to Theo. They all looked at each other in hard silence, as if each waiting for the other to blink.

Alphas, I thought with a sigh. "Connor Keene and Theo Martin," I said, making the introductions they'd apparently been too stubborn to make on their own. "This is Jonathan Black. Why are you here?" I asked again.

"My clients requested I come here and see what might be found."

Theo crossed his strong arms. "And what did you expect to find?"

"Not that my clients' instructions are any of your business," Jonathan said, "but I wasn't given specifics. I was only asked to take a look."

Silence fell as we waited for him to elaborate. When he didn't, I sent a little magical persuasion his way. Just a touch of vampire glamour to make the confession easier.

His expression didn't change. "I like you, Elisa, but glamour won't have me break my promises."

Beside me, Connor shifted. I wasn't sure if it was the magic or the *I like you* that had him moving closer.

"How about an arrest for obstruction of justice?" Theo asked mildly.

"For having clients?" Jonathan said, and lifted a shoulder carelessly. "I suppose you could try to make that stick." But his gaze darted around the park, searching. Seeking.

"Jonathan," I said firmly. "A shifter is dead. He wasn't the first and may not be the last. We need whatever information you've got."

That got his attention, as his gaze snapped to mine, eyes narrowing. "What do you mean he wasn't the first?"

"Information for information," I said. "Quid pro quo. Even if we can't take you in, withholding information will make you an enemy of the Pack. I'm betting your clients wouldn't like that at all."

He lifted his gaze to the dark sky, as if contemplating or irritated. Likely both. But when he sighed, I knew he'd relented.

"I have very little information," he said. "Only that they're aware magic was used—dark magic. They felt it along the lines."

"The ley lines?" I asked. The lines of magic and power ran beneath the world; Chicago was a crossing point for several, making it a city of power and consequence.

He nodded.

"Your clients are sorcerers?"

"I'm not obliged to provide that information, and won't. How many more are dead?"

"This is the second," Theo said. "The first was a human."

"A human," Black repeated, as he considered it. "That explains why they weren't aware of it."

"What's going on?" I asked. "Are people being killed to invoke some kind of magic? Are they sacrifices?"

"I don't know," he said, and looked earnest. But I already knew he could lie. "I've told you what I can," he said, and looked beyond Theo, finally saw the clothes on the ground. "And I'm guessing you aren't going to let me take that."

"We are not," Theo said pleasantly. "But you're welcome to report that to your clients. They know how to reach us."

><><

We tried a few more questions, but Jonathan provided nothing else. He left unsatisfied. He didn't say as much, but it was clear in the hard set of his shoulders.

"He's in a mood," I said, and felt Connor's gaze on me.

"What do you know about his moods?"

"Fair question, and very little. But he's been very collegial when we've talked." I glanced at Theo. "Same when he's come to the office?"

"Same," Theo added. "And always a smile for Petra."

"Unrepentant flirt," I agreed. "At least usually. So what's he gotten himself into?"

Theo's screen buzzed, giving us a respite from wrangling with that question. Given the possibility we weren't the only eyes on the park, we climbed into Theo's nearby vehicle when Petra offered an update.

I took the front, Connor the back. And by some technological miracle, Theo shifted Petra's image from his screen to the interior windshield, as if we were all squeezed into the car together.

"It's the Great and Powerful Oz," Theo said musically.

"I am the Great and Powerful Petra," she said, and snapped her fingers so a spark appeared. With tan skin and dark hair, currently in a bouncy tail, Petra could manifest lightning in her fingers. She usually wore gloves to avoid electrifying the unaware.

"You've found yourself a poppet," she said, tucking her long bangs behind her ear.

"A what?" Theo asked.

"A poppet, or little doll—in this case made of paper—for the spell. It's symbolic." Her image was replaced by the photo of the stave from the bar coaster. "And this beauty is an American stave." The image on the screen appeared with the previously black lines of the stave now shown in three different colors. "These parts of the symbol stand for auspicious, sacrifice, and calamity," she stated, pointing to each in turn.

We greeted that explanation with silence.

"Does that mean it's a good time to kill someone to avoid a catastrophe?" I asked. "Or a good time to kill someone to cause one?"

"It's dark magic," Petra said. "Blood magic, so I lean toward the latter."

"The stave doesn't tell us what the calamity is?" Theo asked.

"It does not. That's up to the words, the intentions of the witch, et cetera."

Behind us, Connor swore. "We need to find them and stop whatever this is."

"Or get them donuts and trophies if they're doing a public service," I said. "But there's really no way to tell."

"Not until we find them," Theo said, echoing Connor's words.

I glanced back at Connor and found his gaze on me, the same concern in his eyes. He reached out, brushed a lock of hair behind my ear.

"Oh my god, you guys are so adorable." Petra was back on the windshield, batting her eyelashes at us.

"Anything else?" Theo asked. "The magic's getting thick in here."

She snorted. "That's it for now. CPD's canvassing, but they haven't found any other evidence, any other witnesses. It's early yet."

It didn't feel early. Not with two people already gone and a storm literally gathering. And growing, I thought, glancing out the window at the sky. The ceiling of clouds seemed to be dropping, as if made heavier by magic. How long until we were all suffocated?

"We'll talk to Ariel again," Theo said, and turned on the vehicle.

But by the time we made it back to The Raucous Wolf, she was gone.

3

Her address was easy to find; one apartment in a fourplex not far from the bar. The yard and building were simple but tidy, the building dark but for her glowing window.

We moved inside, Theo in front, and climbed the stairs . . . and found her apartment door wide open. I flicked the thumb guard on my katana; Theo unholstered his weapon. Connor rolled his shoulders. His body was a weapon.

Theo put a finger to his lips, and he pushed open the door. We listened and heard nothing in the room in front of us. The soft sound of shuffling came from somewhere deeper inside the apartment.

Theo and Connor signaled each other and headed toward the noise. I moved through the front room, wondering about the girl who hadn't quite been my friend, and hadn't quite been my enemy. The building was old, the floors wood and doorways arched. The living room was dark and held mismatched furniture and a handful of plants. But there was nothing here that spoke of death or magic, no stain in the air. Just the ordinary home of an ordinary woman.

I felt a twinge of guilt that I'd somehow played some part in pushing her toward this, as if my excluding her as a kid had somehow turned her toward evildoing. But we'd only been kids, and her parents were kind and capable people. I don't know what I could have said or done to redirect her.

I told myself later that the twinge was the reason I hadn't sensed him coming for me.

A hand clamped on my mouth, his body at my back, his magic thickening the air. I couldn't see the man, but I could read the magic clear enough.

Jonathan Black had beaten us here.

I threw back an elbow. He dodged it, but his shift gave me room to scramble beneath his arm. I spun my katana and he kicked it away, then lunged toward me.

I pivoted and dodged, threw another elbow, connected with his torso. He swore, grabbed my arm, and twisted. The pain in my shoulder, only just healing from another fight, was red hot. I worked to push through it, tried to beckon the monster to join me, but she had no interest in the muddled magic Black was throwing off. So it would just be the two of us, at least until Connor and Theo heard the scuffle.

I wrenched my arm free, threw a jab, but he ducked, kicked, and managed a glancing blow off my hip. I sliced upward, smelled his blood—dense with magic—before I heard his groan of pain. He hit the ground, a foot-long laceration in the top of his thigh.

"On your knees," I demanded, chest heaving and shoulder singing, and pointed the sword at his heart.

Connor and Theo rushed into the room. "Lis?" Connor asked.

"I'm fine," I told him, but kept my gaze on Black. "We have a guest."

>—><—<

While Theo searched for bandages, Connor dragged Jonathan Black to a chair at a small dining table and pushed him down. Magic or not, Black made no effort to fight back.

He looked at me. "I'm sorry. I didn't know who you were."

A lie, but it hardly mattered now.

"Talk," Connor ordered, as Theo wrapped a kitchen towel around Black's thigh, used duct tape to adhere it.

"Fancy," I said, using another towel to wipe the blood from my sword.

"I'm looking for evidence," Jonathan said.

"For your 'clients,'" Theo said, using air quotes. "Unless Ariel's one of your clients, and we all know a waitress at a shifter bar isn't paying your fees, you have no cause to be in here."

"You don't have a warrant," Jonathan spat back.

"The door was open," Theo said helpfully. "We have a little thing called probable cause."

"Talk," I told him, "or we play with the katana again."

He cursed with impressive creativity. "The magic they're using is an ignition spell," he finally said. "It's intended to start an apocalypse."

We all stared at him.

"An apocalypse," I said. "Zombies, robots, locusts? War? Pestilence? What exactly are we talking about?"

"That depends on the caster," he said, which mirrored Petra's conclusion. "I don't know."

Connor's gaze was narrowed. "How do you know that's what it is?"

But I knew the answer before Jonathan had a chance to speak it, because I finally realized where I'd felt this kind of magic before: in my own house.

"You're a sorcerer," I said. No wonder he had so much magic and was so well-equipped at hiding it.

"Half," he said, and there was impatience in his tone. "Part elf, part sorcerer. Too much of both, and not enough of either."

"Why hide it?" Connor asked.

"I don't," Jonathan said, leveling his gaze at me. "But people see the ears, and they believe what they want."

Guilty as charged. "And why do your clients care about this apocalypse specifically?" I asked. "How are they—and you—involved?"

He looked at the ceiling, began to hum a tune as if bored by the entire proceedings.

"He got into the apartment," Theo said. "The door was open to us, but it wasn't busted, and the locks weren't scratched."

I looked back at the door, then Jonathan, and understood the point Theo was making. "Either the door was open when you got here, or you had a key." I saw the quick tightening around his eyes and understood. "Ariel gave you a key. You're together?"

"Were," Jonathan said. "Not anymore."

"You're lying," I told him. "You told me you'd just moved to Chicago."

"We were long-distance," he said. "We had friends in common, talked online. When I moved here, we started dating—actually dating. That lasted a couple of weeks, and then we broke up."

That was entirely plausible, and probably some of it was the truth. But not all of it. Maybe not even most of it.

"So you're pissed she broke it off," Theo said, crossing his arms. "And you're trying to get even?"

"No." His voice was hard now.

"Oh, we're listening," Theo said, "but nothing you've said makes any sense. If you broke up, how'd you find out about the magic?"

"My clients. I didn't know until one of them told me, asked me to investigate. And then I could feel it. Ariel's part of a coven," Jonathan explained. "There are five of them in the group, and I found out what she's trying to do. The leader of the coven said an apocalypse was coming, and they have to make sacrifices to stop it. That it's necessary to fight darkness with darkness. I'm trying to stop the spell."

"Why?" Connor asked.

"Because they're doing it wrong. Because the magic they're making won't stop an apocalypse; it will *start* the apocalypse. I told Ariel the truth. And now I think she's in danger because of it."

"She told you that?" I asked.

"She called me, for the first time in weeks. I didn't answer, but I found a message."

Something in his tone had goose bumps lifting on my skin. "What was it?" I asked, quietly.

"The sound of a bell."

The three of us looked at each other.

"You have to find her," Jonathan said. "And you have to stop them from completing this."

"Tell us where they are," I said, "and we'll be on our way to do just that."

This time, he met my gaze. "I don't know where they are."

I watched him for a moment. "That might be the first honest thing you've said since we came in here."

Magic pulsed, faded. Either he didn't think it worth the trouble to challenge my assessment of his character, or he didn't think the odds were in his favor.

"Look around," Theo said. "See if we can find something that tells us where they might have gone. Grimoire, notebook, another screen, a grocery list for bells and candles. Whatever."

Jonathan moved to rise, but Connor's hand on his shoulder kept him in place. "You stay. We look. And if you so much as consider standing up, Elisa will show you what else she can do with that sword."

>—<—<

He stayed and we looked, but found nothing in old journals, new notebooks, a beaten desk, or the junk drawer in the kitchen. I tossed through a stack of mail, checked pockets in a coat closet, and came up empty.

I cursed, looked back at Jonathan. He was still and silent but stared out the window beneath a furrowed brow.

"Where would the coven work?" I asked again.

"I don't know," he said again. "She mostly didn't talk about them. The rituals, she said, were for her, for them. Not for me."

Mostly truth, I gauged, and turned around. I ended up facing a chalkboard that hung between the coat closet and the front door. "Be kind!" was written in white script above a simple drawing of a daisy. And below, scrawled in handwriting so slanted and rushed it was nearly impossible to read, was a single word: ELEVATOR.

Memory hit me with the power of a punch.

Lulu, Connor, Ariel, me, probably sixteen or seventeen years old, in an abandoned grain elevator not far from McKinley Park. We'd thought ourselves urban explorers, had backpacks of water, granola bars, and flashlights. We'd climbed over the fence, then hurried to the tall concrete cylinders that once stored feed grain for waiting trucks. And we'd made our way into the main building—a long rectangle where metal chutes dropped from the tanks—and played a game of truth or dare.

"I dare you," Ariel had said, smiling at Connor. "To kiss me."

"That's not much of a dare," Connor had said, and he'd given her a chaste kiss on the cheek. It had been a tease, totally innocuous, and Very Connor.

But Ariel—whether driven by hormones or magic—had been embarrassed and furious that he hadn't kissed her properly. She'd ended up storming out with Lulu in tow behind her.

I'd found out later it had been her first kiss. And apparently not a very satisfying one.

"Connor," I said.

He came to me, put a hand at my back. "What is it?"

I pointed at the chalkboard, watched his gaze drop from flower to quote to the message scrawled below. And he blinked, frowned, blinked again, then looked at me.

"You think she left this for you? To tell us to go there?"

"I don't know. But this building doesn't have an elevator, she wrote it fast, and she had to know we'd come looking for her here." I looked back at the slanted letters. "It's a potent memory."

Connor went silent, considering. "It could be a trap."

"Or he's telling the partial truth," I said, dropping my voice, "and Ariel's in danger. Maybe she was trying to warn us off before, realized that wouldn't work."

"Because in the last ten years, she forgot how stubborn you were?"

I arched an eyebrow. "Do you have a better idea?"

"No," he said after a moment. "I keep half expecting a raven to come knocking at the window."

"Nevermore," Theo said behind us.

"We have to go," I said. "God knows I wasn't a fan of Ariel—and I'm still not a fan—but if the coven realizes she knows something, thinks she might try to stop them—"

"She may be next in the circle," Connor filled in.

That's exactly what I was afraid of.

>×<

We lost precious minutes waiting for the CPD and an ambulance to pick up Jonathan, more as we dodged through traffic. Theo had added a light to the vehicle, but that was hardly a deterrent to the Chicagoans still on the road despite the hour.

Clouds swirled like a typhoon overhead, and I wondered if

that was a gift of our magicking coven. With dawn looming and Ariel's life on the line, we needed to end this, and fast.

The grain elevator loomed over the south branch of the Chicago River like a six-pack of enormous concrete canisters. They were stained with time and graffiti but looked the same as they had nearly ten years ago.

There were no vehicles at the site, no obvious disturbance to the fence, no light that indicated anyone was here. But the magic was thick and felt oily on the skin.

"Are we thinking sharknado or hellmouth?" Theo asked contemplatively as he looked up at the sky.

"Hellmouth," Connor said with a grin. "I've always had a thing for Buffy."

"Hello?" I said, giving him a pinch on the arm. "It's exceedingly bad taste to mention your love of a slayer to the vampire you're currently dating."

"I love you more," he said with a wink.

"No pinching or winking on an op," Theo said, but he was smiling when he said it.

We snuck through a gap in the fence, crept toward the main building, and looked inside.

A spotlight illuminated something in the middle of the long corridor.

There, in the center of a glittering circle of salt, was Ariel.

4

I held my breath until I saw her chest rise and fall; unconscious but not dead. We still had time.

"Let's go," Connor whispered, and we moved forward across the stained concrete floor to the edge of the light.

A bell rang and I looked up to find a woman in black moving through the haze of magic.

"Son of a bitch," Connor murmured beside me.

It was Lucy Dalton, the bartender from The Raucous Wolf.

She ruthlessly pulled back her curls, slicked now into a tight bun, and wore a gown of black velvet that fell to her ankles. A silver cord made a belt, and on it hung a tinkling silver bell. Her arms were bare, the thin line of a stave tattoo stark against her skin.

Three more women, all in black gowns, stepped toward the light. They were different sizes, different skin tones, different hairstyles. But there was no mistaking the magic.

"Not what I thought I'd see when I climbed out of bed this morning," Theo murmured. "I am Theo Martin," he announced, the sound of his voice echoing through the chamber as he held up his badge. "And this is Elisa Sullivan. We're Ombuds, and we're ordering you to immediately cease and desist all magical activities. The Chicago Police Department is outside, and you are surrounded."

They weren't outside quite yet, but would be eventually. And hopefully soon enough.

The witches didn't move closer, but magic rose higher, the scent of sulfur staining the air and leaving bitterness on the tongue.

"Stop," Theo commanded. "We know you're trying to cause a disaster."

"We're trying to *prevent* a disaster. Darkness is coming." Dalton's gaze shifted smoothly to Connor's. "I'm sure you can feel it in the air, like a storm on the horizon. The pressure changes, and the storm breaks, and we will all be caught in its power. We will drown in its power."

"So you decided dark magic was the solution?" Connor asked. "Blood sacrifice?"

"The loss of a few is a small cost to bear."

I'd heard the AAM make that same argument, and I hadn't bought it then, either. "I bet the 'few' would disagree with you. And dark magic has consequences. You might actually be making the disaster worse."

Her smile was thin. "Unlike the Precursor, our understanding is strong."

Something went cold and sick in my belly. Did she mean Lulu's mother? The woman who'd become so addicted to dark magic she'd nearly destroyed Chicago in the process?

"I don't suppose *Expelliarmus* would work here?" Theo murmured.

"Wrong fairy tale," I said, and unsheathed my sword.

"We won't allow this to happen," Connor said. "You have to know that."

"You have no choice. You cannot stop this," she said, the magic growing thicker, as she pulled a gleaming dagger from her skirt and moved toward the circle. "If you attempt to do so, we all die. And that death will be ugly."

But if we let it proceed, she'd kill Ariel in front of us. Murder and apocalypse were both bad options, but I laid odds that the apocalypse wasn't going to happen today. "First problem first," I said, and darted toward the circle.

And without bothering to consider whether it was a good idea or not, I swiped a foot through the salt. As if freed by the magic, Ariel groaned.

Dalton screamed like a banshee, and magic blew through the

corridor like a hurricane, sending dust, salt, and shards of old glass flying.

I raised a hand to shield my face, used the other to point at the three young women who now looked utterly shocked to find themselves standing over Ariel's unconscious body—and facing down a sorceress with spells at her literal fingertips.

"Get the witches," I told them. "I'll take the boss." I smiled at Dalton and rolled my sword in my hand as she gathered up a swirling mass of green magic that resembled the clouds outside. She had been the source of the storm.

She tossed the first volley. Fortunately, katanas were fairly good weapons against fireballs. I raised my katana, used it to strike back. Magic bounced against the blade, spun off, and struck a metal support beam, which groaned in response, sending up a firework's worth of sparks.

I spun and swung the sword into a low arc, sending another shot high into the rafters. Bird's nests, and probably worse, snowed down around us. The concrete floor was dotted with kindling now, and it flared in the sparks that flew with each round of magic. Fires began to sprout in piles of detritus; it felt like we were fighting in hell itself.

Dalton's face was red with fury, her eyes like flame as she reloaded and fired again. These blasts were smaller, faster, and I swung the katana wildly to catch them. I needed to redirect them, giving Connor, Theo, and the other witches a chance to escape through the doors behind me.

I spun and felt the sear across my shoulder as magic grazed my arm. I looked down to see a bright red smear of blood through a rip in my T-shirt, the pain hotter than anything I'd felt before. I heard myself whimper but swallowed hard against a bolt of nausea, glad at least that she hadn't hit my shoulder.

Light blasted behind me and a growl rent the air.

Connor, I thought, my heart tripping in response as the great gray wolf barreled past me. He struck Dalton with enough force to send her flying back and into a pile of old lumber. Dalton screamed and tried to scramble away. He growled at her, lips curled back, human fury in his eyes.

She'd drawn my blood and would pay a price—this time, to him.

The sound of booted feet echoed through the room like an army on the move; its commander strode in front of them.

"We always arrive after the fun part," Gwen said, as a dozen officers in protective gear filled the space around us. "We are the Chicago Police Department, and you're all very under arrest."

>×<

It had started as a gentle coven, Ariel told us when we were outside. Four of them, led by Dalton, who worked minor earth and love magic to heal heart, water, and land. They all had specialties, and Ariel had learned to use her necromancy to comfort those left behind. Added to the waitressing, she made enough for her own car, apartment.

"But something scared her," Ariel said of Dalton. "She believed the end was coming, and we were the only ones who could stop it. We believed her. Maybe she added magic to it; I don't know. Stupid or not, we believed her. And we helped her."

"But you wanted out," I said, and Ariel lifted her gaze to me. "Jonathan Black got your message," I explained.

Her gaze darted away, full of emotions I couldn't read. "He has . . . power. Maybe more than he lets us see. Maybe less."

"And he is not well acquainted with the truth," I said.

"No, he isn't," she said. "He can be a real son of a bitch when he wants to be." Her smile fell away. "Anyway, Dalton told us about the poppets, the stave, the circle. Silverspell, she called it, because a silver dagger would be used each time to perform a small ritual."

She looked at me, and for the first time I could see her own magic in her eyes. "She said only a bit of blood would be needed. That it wasn't dark magic, because the blood wouldn't kindle the spell. It was just a gift to the earth. She performed the ceremony on the human without us. But she said the human wasn't enough, so we had to use a shifter the next time. We didn't know she planned to kill him. We didn't know she'd done it until he fell, and the dagger was—" She paused, looked away as if staring at the memory. "The dagger was in him."

Ariel breathed in, exhaled. "She said each death would help ward the city from whatever was coming. Would keep the destruction at bay. We told her she had to find another way, but she didn't believe us. So I sent Jonathan the message."

"The bell," I said. "And you put the coaster in Bryce's clothes, and left the message on the chalkboard for me."

She nodded.

"You did good, Ariel." I put an arm around her shoulder. "No one died tonight, and that's because of you."

"Tonight," she sobbed. "But I think she was right, and she was wrong, and I don't know what's coming next."

I held her until the tears were dry.

>—<

Theo gave us a lift back to Connor's vehicle, still parked at the bar. We said our goodbyes to Theo, watched him drive away.

And then Connor's hand was behind my head, the long line of his body pressing forward, and his mouth against mine. Taking and promising, comforting and seeking comfort. I sank into the kiss as he slid his fingers into my hair, felt love and desire and magic—vibrant and clean and full of life—rise between us.

After a moment he pulled back, leaned his forehead against mine. "I needed that."

I put a hand against his cheek; he turned to press his lips to my palm.

"We protect each other," I said, our mantra. "And we found the villain." I looked up at the sky, the green clouds all but gone, but the fear lingering. "We either saved the world, or we doomed it."

"Together," he said, his arms banding around me. "Whatever it is, we'll face it together."

TROLL LIFE

by Kerrie L. Hughes

"Mommy, it's an ogre!" a child said loudly.

"Alex, mind your manners," the woman beside him admonished gently.

Harzl barely glanced up at the human child as he restocked the vending machines on the platform of the Northwest Transfer Station. He knew what he looked like to the offspring of those who dwelled outside the Liminal Subway System. He was used to being gawked at, mistaken for an ogre, or worse, an orc. Never mind that ogres were never less than ten feet tall, and orcs were mythical cannibals.

On the other hand, he was five feet, eight inches tall and thick-limbed, with a shock of purple hair. His skin wavered somewhere between greenish gray and grayish purple, depending on his mood. Currently his mood was bothered, and his skin flushed a bit more purple.

The child ran over to Harzl. "Are you a troll?"

"Good guess, kid," Harzl replied as he guessed the child to be about seven and unafraid of asking questions. He surmised it would be best to give short answers and make no eye contact.

"Do you live here?" the child asked.

"I do not," he replied in a careful, even tone cultivated by a decade of customer service. Harzl didn't stop what he was doing; he had two boxes of snacks to restock and only fifteen minutes until the train arrived with the new station inspector. He wasn't supposed to know about the surprise inspection, but the trains were sentient and they liked Harzl, so they kept him updated on the gossip.

The Eastern Line train had told the Chicago Line, and the Chicago Line had relayed the information to the Northern Line, which had let him know ten minutes ago when it had dropped off its passengers. Harzl had gotten busy, stashing his mini-TV—which he wasn't supposed to have—sweeping the platform, and restocking the vending machines.

Normally, when humans or snobby wizards were on the platform, he would stay in the shadows of his service counter by the bulletin boards to avoid these annoying encounters. But he needed to make sure everything was perfect before the "surprise" inspection so he could have this temporary posting made permanent and be one step closer to becoming a station manager. Then he and his pet barghest, Snori, could move out of his cramped subway-level apartment and into a place that actually allowed a beast as large as him on the premises. Snori wasn't even the largest of his kind, he was no bigger than a St. Bernard, and didn't drool as much.

The vending machines wouldn't have been a big deal, but Harzl had a keen craving for chocolate, especially the Cheshire Chocolate Chews. He allowed himself one per day, but sometimes, when the stress of dealing with the public got to be too much, he had two or three, and then he owed money from his check to cover the difference. He'd been written up in the past for complaints about a lack of vending items in this section of the Liminal Subway, and the last inspector knew Harzl had a sweet tooth. He needed to make a good impression on the new one.

Snori, whom he also wasn't supposed to have at the station while on duty, loved the Carnivore Jerky Treats. It was hard bringing enough food down to keep his pup full and happy, harder still to afford the kind of food a beast like him deserved. Most barghests would hunt rats, rabbits, and the like, but Snori had already eaten all the vermin in the station.

Harzl hadn't planned on having a pet, but Snori had been left behind in a cage on one of the trains about six months ago. He'd been half the size he was now, with scratches and bites all over him. The poor thing was in sore need of a friend, so the trains had taken pity on him and brought the barghest to Harzl. A high honor considering the trains weren't just sentient, they were a sacred form of elemental shifter that his clans took care of in exchange for knowledge and cooperation.

"When does the Chicago Line come in?" the woman asked as she came up behind him.

Harzl finished the candy machine, locked it, and saw that the child was staring into the darkness of a seldom-used side tunnel where Snori was hiding. Kids always seemed to know where the dogs were.

The woman was young, with short, choppy dark hair, but she had the look of someone who might complain if he just told her to look at the posted schedule right next to the information desk.

"It should be about ten minutes, ma'am," he answered with a pleasant smile.

"And where are the bathrooms, please?"

Harzl pointed beyond the vending machines. "Over there, ma'am, right under the bathroom signs."

"Thank you. I wouldn't ask, but my glasses were broken yesterday. I can only see about five feet in front of me."

Harzl felt a tiny pang of guilt, and was glad he had been pleasant. "Sorry to hear that, ma'am, do you need me to walk you over? The platform is uneven in places."

"No, no, Alex will help me."

The little boy earnestly took the woman's hand, and Harzl noticed she had bruises on her neck. The child had a cut on his forehead peeking out from a bomber hat, the kind with ear flaps, but wasn't wearing a warm enough coat. Instead, he had on an oversized flannel shirt with a T-shirt underneath, and jeans with ripped knees. The thin woman wasn't any better dressed in a long skirt and a jean jacket. They didn't look related, but they were familiar.

Harzl inwardly cursed himself for not noticing earlier. They looked like a pair he'd gotten a notice about in the morning updates. Something about a missing child and his nanny.

With a whine, Snori crept out of the tunnel. He was dark gray with big green eyes and a crooked smile with one bottom fang that stuck out a bit. He was a well-muscled beast, but he was also a big baby and didn't like to be left alone, which was why Harzl brought him to work every day. If he left him at home, Snori just whined and scratched until the neighbors complained. And his neighbors were a witch on one side and a writer on the other—not people to disturb lightly.

"What's the matter, buddy?"

The barghest snuffed and huffed and shook his butt. He really did look like an oversized bulldog crossed with an undersized bear.

"I can't play right now, and you need to stay out of sight."

Snori whined even more at that.

"You have your blanket and teddy. Stay out of sight, Snori," Harzl said firmly.

The barghest whined a protest one last time, turned around, put his head down, and padded back to the tunnel.

The station was mostly safe, and looked like some of the older subway stations, with the smooth tile and clean architecture of the '50s. A large tunnel that could accommodate two trains going in opposite directions was off to the east side.

The old tunnel on the west side, where Snori was hiding in an unused alcove, was from the early 1900s. It was in use about a dozen times per month by the old trolleys that serviced some of the more rural stations. The trolleys were also sentient, but they were older and kept to themselves.

In between the tunnels, southward, was the service counter and bulletin boards. Northward was the vending machines and bathrooms. The two sides were divided by four long benches for waiting passengers. If someone missed a train they could catch the next one, but they couldn't stay the night. This station didn't have a night guard, and there were things deep in the tunnels that would kill a person if they weren't careful.

Harzl usually put the errant traveler on the last train before he closed up, and the train would take them to the nearest approved subway motel if they were humanoid, his apartment if they were a troll or aligned with the trolls. He didn't like it, but that was what was expected in his clan. Trolls helped trolls, and woe be the trollkin that was a poor guest or bad host.

Even though the city of Milwaukee above was busy, the station below was not. The schedule had a mere three stops per day per each of the four main trains, so Harzl saw less than fifty people on an average day. Many were regulars who commuted to work and back. A few were on vacation, or students. Occasionally you'd get the odd runaway or criminal either seeking or running away from crime.

Most people who rode the Liminal system knew the trains were sentient enough to communicate with the station managers, but they didn't seem to realize that the trains had a mind of their own. Only paranormal beings with proper authorization could use the subway stations, and even then they could only go as far as the trains allowed. The trains knew how far each person could go, and weren't shy about stopping someone trying to cross the dimensions into the outer protected realms. They didn't say much, they just dropped interlopers off at the major stations and informed the being on duty that the passenger was in violation.

All of the station managers were trolls, but the busiest stations were manned by witches and half humans who worked for the station manager. Harzl's oldest sister was in charge of the Denver station; his youngest brother was assistant to the one in Portland. His other two brothers were rangers that patrolled the rural stations on this side of the realms. It was their job to check in with the old trolleys, oversee repairs, and handle numerous problems that could come up when paranormal dimensional travel goes wonky.

His father, an elder of the Hellirverja clan, was a ranger on the other side of the realm and made sure no one crossed that was not allowed. His word was law, and he was disappointed that Harzl had yet to become a station manager or a ranger, and was considering calling him back home to work with him. Harzl didn't want to go back where he would be expected to get married, have children, and someday become an elder. He hadn't even gone home for the last few holidays. He just wanted to stay on this side, unburdened by family responsibility, watching television shows, eating junk food, and hanging out with his barghest.

Harzl took the refill box to his counter, put his mini-TV inside, and locked it in the cupboard. He hoped the inspector would just think it was extra vending products and make this a quick inspection. He was going to miss the next episode of *British Bakery* as it was.

Next, he took off his extra thick black hoodie and put on the itchy station master coat he was supposed to wear every day. It was the coat from the previous station master and too small across the shoulders, but he couldn't afford a new one and didn't like wearing it anyway. It was just too uncomfortable.

Then he went to the old fax machine and looked at the BOLO or "be on the lookout" list. Yes, there it was, a flyer of the pair, except she had long hair and the boy was more odd-looking without his hat. He had angles to his face that human children didn't normally have. He looked like . . . a gargoyle? As in, one of the lost clan gargoyles? Why would the flyer state they were human when they were not?

As Harzl stared at the flyer, the boy in question walked up to the counter without the young woman. Yes, he had a slight forehead ridge, his ears were a bit high, his cap covering most of the telltale signs. But the child had the pale skin of one of the French gargoyles, and his eyes were a startling blue from the side but looked normal straight on. The boy—if he was a boy, many gargoyles were sexless until puberty—was a child aligned with the trolls. Worse, he was probably being trafficked for the extra stone of his as-yet-undeveloped wings. They had magical properties prized by wizards who made dark artifacts. The oversized flannel was trying to cover that particular asset. Harzl folded the paper and stuck it in his back pocket.

"Nan . . . I mean, Mom fainted in the bathroom," the boy said with urgency.

"Arriving track one, Chicago Line," the Chicago train projected into Harzl's head. Which was his cue to announce it over the speakers and clear the tracks. "The station inspector is on board with three other beings; two are wizards, and the other a shifter. I don't like them. One has the odor of vampire."

Chicago Line, along with most of the other trains, despised vampires. They wouldn't say why, which was in keeping with the habits of the gossipy yet personally private trains.

The child ran to the bathroom as the sound of the approaching train filled the station. Could he hear the thoughts of the train? Trolls and gargoyles were of the same magick.

Snori peeked around the corner at Harzl from the other tunnel. This could cost him his job, but he had to do *something*. Harzl grabbed the "Bathroom Closed" sign from his counter and crossed to them while calling out, "Snori to me!"

Snori came running out with a grin. Harzl opened the women's room and saw the child over the woman. She was out on the ground. The child bent over her, trying to shake her awake.

"Kid, don't be scared. I'm Harzl Hellirverja, of the Cavern Clan. This is my . . . dog, Snori, he won't hurt you."

Snori stayed next to Harzl until the child looked reassured. Then he snuffled over and butted his head on the boy's leg. The kid tentatively petted Snori's head.

Harzl quickly walked to the woman and bent down. She was breathing, but pale and shivering. The bruise on her neck appeared to be more serious, like a vampire bite.

"Who's after you?" Harzl asked the boy as he took off his station master coat and placed it over the woman.

"Our master," he stated meekly, like one who was used to being meek. Then he straightened and said more defiantly, "We won't go back."

"What is the name of your master?"

"I won't say it, the spell might call him to us," the boy stated.

Harzl was proud of the child. Gargoyles had been enslaved for centuries. Most had gone into hiding until paranormal laws had been changed. It was now forbidden for one being to own another, but vampires and wizards were still under the impression they could do what they wanted to whomever they wanted.

"Can I know your names without harm?" Harzl asked in a fashion common among the Fae.

"You can call me Alex, she's Nancy."

Harzl was sure the names were fake, but it didn't matter. "Call me Harzl. Snori will watch over you until everyone is gone. I'm locking this door for your protection. I'm going to call for help. Stay quiet and keep her from panicking if she wakes up."

Harzl patted Snori on the head and walked out of the bathroom, locking the door from the outside with a master key and posting the closed sign on the door.

The Chicago Line train was parked and waiting for Harzl to give the "all clear" order. Three beings waited on the platform, and two of them, a man and a woman, looked his way. The man had the haughty look of a wizard. Overdressed, an imperious look on the face, eyes set in a manner that made regular beings feel like they were being judged. Rude.

The woman looked away. She was smaller, with curly brown hair, and wore a trench coat, dark pants, and loafers. It seemed she didn't want to be looked at directly. Probably the shifter. But what kind? Harzl guessed she was wolfen. They had to strip to shift, and often wore loose clothing.

The third person appeared to be the other wizard, a younger

one, but she didn't seem to be with the two. She was dressed in tight jeans and a puffy purple coat. She was using a glamour spell to hide who she really was; Harzl could tell by the slight blurring around her. Why? And where was the station inspector?

Harzl smiled his practiced smile and considered his next move. Pretend he was a passenger waiting for the next train, or reveal himself as the acting station manager? Which ploy would help him control the situation better?

"You there," called the male wizard, "have you seen the station manager?"

The younger female wizard was beginning to look behind the counter.

"He's fixing a pipe in the access tunnel, I'm the assistant. What can I help you with?"

Harzl noticed that the younger female wizard moved back from the counter and over to the bulletin board. She probably knew that trolls could see through glamour spells, but maybe not. She was acting suspiciously, and it was hard for him to track what all three were doing at the same time.

The male wizard crossed to him. The shifter stayed by the train with her back to him. Very close to the edge of the tunnel. She was looking out into the darkness.

"Have you seen these two runaways?" the man asked as he held out the flyer without introducing himself or asking Harzl his name. Very rude.

Harzl glanced at it and looked the wizard in the eyes. "No."

The wizard cocked his head for a split second. "Are you sure? You didn't even look at it."

"I saw that this morning when it was faxed to all the stations. If they came through, I would have seen them."

"Indeed. Well, there's a reward if they are found."

The flyer made no mention of a reward. Which meant the wizard thought Harzl was lying and would sell out for money. It also didn't say that the two were runaways. The wizard was lying about something.

"Try the Madison station," Harzl replied as he noticed the shifter was now on the other side of the train looking into the dark. She had to be wolfen to see well into the dimly lit tunnel without shifting.

"Why, have you heard something?" the wizard asked as he put the flyer into his outside coat pocket.

"Kids like Madison, most runaways from around here head there," Harzl replied as he went to his counter and reached for the phone he needed to call for an emergency team. Someone had cut the line, and cell phones didn't work in the Liminal. The glamoured wizard was clearly avoiding his dark stare now.

The man continued, "I see. Well these two aren't children and they aren't from 'around here.'" He was making fun of Harzl's vernacular. "In fact, I heard from the Chicago station manager that they had been seen on the train that arrived before ours did."

The female wizard glared at the male wizard, then stuck her tongue out at him. It was a strange gesture. She knew Harzl could see her, but the other two couldn't. She was communicating something to him. Was she here to help the two in the bathroom? Or did she know who the man was? And why would she damage the phone?

The man saw where Harzl was looking and turned to see what was happening behind him. The female wizard ignored him and pretended to read a bulletin.

The shifter was now by the vending machines. She was sniffing for the pair.

"If you need change I can provide it," Harzl offered.

She barely stopped what she was doing and glanced at the wizard, who gave her a slight nod. She went back to sniffing.

The female wizard walked between the man and Harzl, then stopped in front of the bathroom, blocking the shifter from her progress.

"I need to use the bathroom . . . please," she called out to Harzl.

Harzl took a few steps away from the man and toward the bathrooms. Was it his imagination, or did the female wizard resemble Nancy? "The women's room is closed. I can stand guard if you wish to use the men's room?"

There was a closet space in between the men's and women's rooms with a locked access door on each side. An accomplished wizard could unlock it with magick. If she was here to help, she could tend to Nancy, and if she wasn't, Snori would stop her.

"Is it gross in there?" she asked with feigned disgust.

"No more so than the women's room," Harzl replied with humor.

She laughed and went into the men's room.

The shifter was now over by the alcove where Snori hid when passengers came through. She looked back at him in surprise. No doubt recognizing the smell of a mutual predator.

"Can I help you with something, ma'am?"

The shifter narrowed her eyes.

"Pay no attention to Jana, she works for me," the man said.

"You said no names, Spencer," Jana snapped.

Jana clearly didn't like Spencer.

Harzl turned back toward the wizard to see that he had a wand out and pointed at him.

Stupidly rude.

"You don't know much about trolls, do you?" Harzl said.

The wizard responded with a knitted brow. The shifter laughed as she crossed behind Harzl and looked behind the counter. "Trolls are not affected by magick, Spencer, your wand is useless against him."

It was true. Trolls were immune to most forms of magick involving witches and wizards. They could only be compelled by certain kinds of shifter magick, and even then it was minimal. A being could use a human weapon, but guns did not fire in the Liminal; it was a permanent spell installed long ago. Someone could use a bladed weapon, but trolls had thick skin and were strong enough to beat down most attackers. Any kind of fight in the Liminal system wasn't smart, as the trains did not take kindly to violence.

Harzl crossed his muscled arms across his chest and stared hard at the wizard. "Why are you here?" he asked with a rumble in his voice.

The wizard looked momentarily embarrassed, then cleared his throat. "That pair are runaways who need to be returned to their parents. I've been asked to find and return them. Safely, of course."

"The flyer says the boy is a child and the female his nanny."

"It is . . . incorrect."

Harzl turned to the shifter named Jana as she stepped back from the counter and narrowed her eyes at the men's room. The scent trail probably told her that the girl with the glamour had cut the phone wire. Which was curious because a glamour spell had a scent a shifter could detect, and the young woman had been on the train with them.

"Why is he here? And why are *you*, a shifter, helping a wizard?"

"Say nothing, Jana," the wizard snapped. "I'll handle this."

The shifter glanced at Harzl as she walked back toward the train. "The two belong to a very powerful man who employs him. I'm here because I owe Spencer a favor . . . but I'm considering walking away."

The train door slid open as though offering her a way out. Jana stepped back in surprise, which was odd if she knew about trolls, but not trains.

Harzl realized the train should have already left the station and was waiting for him to give the "all clear" signal, but where was the inspector? Had he misheard the train?

Spencer crossed to Jana and put his hand on her arm. "You can't afford to walk away. Now please fetch those kids out of the bathroom where they are clearly hiding," he said in a surprisingly tender voice.

"No being owns another. Get on the train and leave," Harzl demanded.

"We can't," Jana said.

"The train will not leave unless I clear it to leave," Harzl stated.

"I will have you fired," the arrogant wizard stated.

"You can complain to my manager, *after* you leave."

"Oh, I will," the wizard said, and gave Jana a small push.

She locked eyes with Harzl, smiled slyly, and spoke a few words of Gothic as she began to take off her trench coat.

Her eyes were brown and gold, the pupils large, and they held his gaze as she disrobed. She was beautiful. What had she said? Something about enchantment? He should have paid more attention when his grand-auntie was teaching the old languages. Why couldn't he take his eyes off her? Why couldn't he move? Was she something more than wolfen?

Suddenly, she sprayed something into his face, and his eyes burned! Harzl pulled back, twisting away. He heard more words in Gothic, and his arms felt like lead. He fell to the ground and called out, "I unravel your wretched words!" It was a spell the witch next door had taught him. He didn't know if it would work.

A door slammed open. Snori barked and growled. A woman

screamed. The boy yelled and threatened. A thick white fog of something soothing formed around his head. His arms felt less heavy. He could hear a low hum of music. Something his grand-auntie used to sing. Was it Scottish? A woman's face formed in the cloud and reached a hand down to him, wiping his face. Was he dreaming?

Snori was giving someone a very hard time.

Harzl struggled up, his eyes mostly cleared; it had to have been bear spray. The mist was so thick he couldn't see more than two feet in front of him.

"Harzl? Should I go for help?" the train called into his head.

Alex screamed and cried.

"Stand by, Chicago Line!" Harzl roared his frustration and willed himself forward. He nearly tripped over the girl in the purple coat as she flew backward, out of the bathroom, as though she had been thrown.

The mist swirled around her on the ground; she was bleeding from the nose, but was alive.

"Snori!" Harzl called out.

The barghest responded with a mighty "Aroooo ro ro ro!" that shook the walls. The mist retreated, and Harzl advanced toward the bathroom.

The stupid wizard came out, wand drawn, the boy struggling as Spencer held him by the neck. Growling rose up from deeper within, Jana, and was met by Snori's deep warning. The shifter didn't know what she was getting into.

"Let us leave!" Spencer demanded.

"Let them go, and get on the train," Harzl responded, knowing the train would lock them inside.

Spencer aimed his wand at the boy's head. Harzl took two steps forward, pulled his arm back, and punched the wizard in the collarbone. The wizard screamed as he fell to the ground, releasing the boy and dropping his wand.

The wolfen charged out and leaped onto Harzl, knocking him backward, showing teeth and desperation. She launched off him and ran off.

Snori gave chase, nearly knocking Harzl the rest of the way to the ground. "Snori, stop!" he called out as the barghest chased the shifter into the tunnel that led north to Green Bay.

Snori didn't stop.

"Snori, come back!" he called out.

Alex was pulling at the girl in the purple coat on the ground. "Get up, Cortney, we have to go!"

The girl steadied herself and made eye contact with Spencer. They both scrambled to get the wizard's wand. She got it first and pointed it at the man. "You killed my sister, Spencer Beaumont."

"She committed suicide when she became a bloodbag," Spencer snapped back as he winced through the pain of his shattered collarbone.

Bloodbag was the derogatory word for anyone who allowed vampires to feed from them in exchange for money, protection, and prestige, or what the newer generation called the blood life.

Cortney aimed the wand at Spencer.

"Cortney, you know what will happen if you kill me. They'll hunt you down."

"What about Nancy? What justice does she get? Or do her precious vampires only care about what they want?"

Harzl didn't want to listen to this drama, and he didn't care why the wizards were working with vampires. He just wanted to fetch Snori before the barghest got hurt.

The mist re-formed and swirled around the three in front of him. "Calm yourselves," said a melodic female voice.

The wizards stopped what they were doing in shock. The mist flowed into the bathroom and Harzl followed. He cursed himself for not realizing that this was the inspector—and she was a banshee.

The banshee pulled together into its floating female form and reached down to Nancy. "She is alive, but fading; we need to get her to help, we cannot wait for it to arrive," she said in a lovely, haunting voice.

"I can get her on the train," Harzl said.

The banshee floated away from Nancy as Harzl bent down to scoop her up. She was as light as a wee child but did not smell of death yet, just vampires, blood, subway, and magick.

Cortney followed as Harzl placed her carefully on the longest seat in the back of the train. The banshee was now a fully formed being and sat beside Nancy. She was a mature, wispy woman with long white hair, very pale skin, and gray eyes. She wore a long dress of light gray under a matching uniform coat with an inspector patch and a name tag: *Gwyn Ivershae.*

"I am pleased to meet you, Madam Ivershae." Harzl greeted her in the manner of his clan, with a slight bow and his eyes on her eyes.

She returned the greeting. "I am pleased to meet you, Harzl Hellirverja."

The train door closed. Harzl, Cortney, and Gwyn turned to look as Spencer banged on it with his good hand. "Let me on, you stupid train!"

"He is very rude," the Chicago Line projected into Harzl's and Gwyn's heads.

"Very rude indeed," Gwyn agreed.

"I will hold him here until you send back help. I need to find the shifter and fetch back . . . that is . . . I need to get Sn—the child . . ." Harzl stammered. He'd nearly said Snori's name, and he wasn't sure if the inspector had seen him. For all she knew, two shifters had run down the tracks.

Gwyn held up her hand. "Do not worry, you have your obligations. I see one of them has just run away," she said, her gaze out the window.

Harzl looked out; the gargoyle boy was gone.

The wizard cursed, cradled his bad arm, and headed off toward the trolley tunnel.

Cortney started for the door behind Harzl. "We have to save him. The vampires will tear him apart for helping Nancy escape."

"Your sister needs a transfusion," Gwyn said. "I can do a magickal one on the way to the next station."

Cortney looked down at her sister, and then to Gwyn, and finally to Harzl. "Please save him. We owe him everything."

Harzl dipped his head. "Of course," he said, and left the train in pursuit. The sooner he saved the child, the sooner he could save Snori.

The wizard picked his wand up from the ground to see that it was broken in half. Harzl grabbed him by the good arm and pushed him into the men's room.

"Take your hands off me!" he protested as Harzl slammed the door shut and locked him inside. Then he went into the women's room and locked the closet on that side, effectively jailing the wizard until help arrived.

"Northern Line will be here in twenty minutes," the Chicago Line said as it slowly left the station.

"Great, that gives me fifty minutes to get the child, find my barghest, and disappear," Harzl said to himself. It had been a great job while it lasted, but he knew he would need to get both beings to the outer lands for safety. He didn't trust the paranormal or human governments to do the right thing.

Harzl grabbed three things from behind the counter: his hoodie, his knapsack, and a security flashlight. If there had been any of the chocolate left outside the vending machines he would have taken one for the road. He would miss this job.

The trolley tunnel was barely lit at the entrance, and would get darker as they went. The kid would be terrified somewhere between the end of the platform and the beginning of the older part. That was where a crossway turnaround would force him to make a choice: wander into the dark unknown, or come back.

Harzl heard crying from nearby; he shined his light along the ground but found nothing, then searched above. There he was, sitting on top of a brick ledge behind some of the power grid; it was a bad place to be.

"Alex, stay put. I'll come to you and help you down."

"No! I'm not going back!"

"Alex . . ."

"My name isn't Alex, it's Alazavier Marcelle duFrancdeparis, they just call me Alex because they don't want to learn my name. They don't want me to have a name."

"Hello, Alazavier Marcelle duFrancdeparis, I am Harzl Hellirverja of the Cavern Clan, and I will help you."

"You . . . said my name correctly?"

"Names are important."

"Do you know what I am?"

"I know you are a gargoyle, and from your name you are from the Paris clan."

"My mother was from the Paris clan. I am from nowhere."

"How old are you, Alazavier?"

"I'm seven in gargoyle years."

Harzl knew gargoyles counted time by the Gregorian calendar, but they didn't count the time they spent as stone. "What are you in human years?"

"As far as I know, thirteen. They keep me in stone as punishment. Now they want to sell me to that wizard's people so they can take my wings."

"Who claims to own you?"

"That vampire clan in Chicago, I can't say their name or they can track me."

Harzl knew who he was talking about, the Vertasoturi Clan. They claimed to be an example of modern vampire cooperation, but many of the paranormals knew it was just another trade-off. They had to join an unjust clan to escape violent human justice.

"Alazavier Marcelle duFrancdeparis, you are no longer a slave. The laws that allowed gargoyles to be enslaved were abolished before you were born. I am honor bound to take you to safety."

The kid looked hopeful. "How do I know you aren't lying?"

"I am a troll. I swear on my clan that I am telling you the truth."

It was a long few seconds of listening to beetles and rats crawling along the walls. Finally, the squeak of a bat seemed to prompt the kid. "Okay, I'm coming down."

"Careful, don't touch those cables," Harzl said as he reached up to catch him if he slipped.

Harzl waited until the kid brushed himself off. "Alazavier, before we leave, I need your help with something."

"What?"

"I need your help finding Snori. He went down the other tunnel chasing that shifter, and I have to rescue him and get him to safety too."

"What about the shifter? Will you kill her?"

"No, it is a part of the troll code. We do not kill unless we have to, and we only have to if it is to save ourselves or another being."

"What if they threaten someone? What if you know they will kill someone if you let them go?"

"That is a difficult choice, one that rarely comes up. It is a big thing to kill another being because you think they might do harm. Trolls believe we must persuade and protect without killing. Death should be a last resort."

"That's not what vampires think."

"I don't know much about them; perhaps you can tell me as we walk."

"I'd like that."

They didn't get ten feet down the tunnel before they heard Snori bellow, "Arooo ro ro!"

They both stopped and looked behind them.

"Did that come from behind us?" Alazavier asked.

Then Snori let out a high-pitched squeal: "Hiiiyipe!"

Harzl's heart felt like it leaped into his throat. "The tunnel intersects back that way; it's a dangerous section but shorter to the new tunnels."

"Then we have to go," the kid said, and led the way back to the intersection.

"Wait, I will take the lead; you watch my back and listen for anything that sounds suspicious," Harzl insisted.

"What would be a suspicious sound in here?"

Harzl wasn't sure he should list the many things that lived in subway tunnels, but decided to give the kid a chance. "Rats can grow large and a few hunt in packs; they make a scurry sound and smell like vermin."

"I'm used to that, mice crawl around in the basements of the Vertasoturi buildings. If you hold still long enough, you can kick them across the room."

The tunnel crossover was full of debris. Harzl could see that the old wooden rails had been stacked off to the left side in piles. He stopped and cast his light around. Water dripped from the ceiling ahead. Some of the ceiling tiles were in a suspiciously neat pile, as though someone was sorting them. The last time he'd been down here, they were scattered. And was that blood he smelled? It was hard to tell when both he and the kid had blood on their clothes.

"I wasn't torturing them; they would bite me when I slept," the kid said, possibly thinking Harzl was silent because he disapproved.

Harzl spoke quietly, "I was not judging you. I am suspicious of what's ahead. Stay close and be prepared for me to pick you up in case we—"

"There we go, and here you are, tarry not, you won't get far." A singsong voice with the inflection of a madman echoed down the tunnel. It seemed to come from farther ahead.

Something moved ahead, and then something else dragged.

Harzl crouched down and shut off the flashlight. Only the ambient light of the tunnel on the other side of the crossover helped them to see.

"What is happening?" Alazavier whispered. "Who's down there?"

"Tunnel ghoul," Harzl replied. "He is like a vampire, but not a vampire."

"What should we do?" the kid whispered.

"We wait."

Alazavier got closer to Harzl, and Harzl put his arm around him. "Courage."

"You cannot leave, you are now mine, be my lovely Valentine," the tunnel ghoul sang from farther ahead.

"Stop . . . please," said a very faint female voice.

It had to be the shifter. She sounded hurt. But where was Snori?

Harzl started to move ahead, but the kid held him back. "Shouldn't we go back?"

"No, he has someone, and Snori might be hurt. You can take the flashlight and go back."

"No, I won't leave you . . . alone," the kid said. Harzl was sure he was too afraid to go back by himself.

"You are brave, Alazavier. You helped your friends escape, and now you are helping me."

Harzl couldn't see the kid's face, but he was sure he would try to live up to the compliment. They both started creeping forward, the kid holding tightly onto the strap on Harzl's knapsack. It was tricky picking steps around the debris without the light. The kid stubbed his toe and almost cried out.

Harzl got an idea. He stopped and opened his knapsack, then took out his apartment keys and took off a small keychain light. "Here, take this, it doesn't give off much light, but you'll be able to see where you're stepping."

The kid took it and turned it on; it was an oval disc of neon green and the button had to be pressed constantly to work. "Thanks," he said as he shined it at the ground, making a one-foot circle of weak light.

They picked their way over the tiles and bricks until they came to the newer tunnel. Harzl held Alazavier back and handed him the flashlight. "This can be used like a bat; it has a flashing setting to alert incoming trains, but can be used to shine in the ghoul's eyes if he comes near you."

The kid took it silently and gave Harzl the smaller flashlight.

Harzl put it in his pocket and peeked around the corner to the north. Snori was lying on the tracks.

"I shall hang you with the twine, sweet and pretty, wolfen mine," the ghoul sang again.

It was coming from the crossover near where Snori lay. It sounded closer because that crossover used to be a turnaround when this was the end of the line. It formed a circle with an old office in the middle where winter supplies used to be kept.

"Alazavier, Snori is ahead, I don't know if . . . I don't know how he is. Take my knapsack. There is a water bottle and his favorite snack inside. I must go to the next crossover and see what can be done. You stay with Snori if he's alive and keep the Northern train from hitting him by flashing the light when you hear it coming. If I don't come back, or the ghoul comes for you, you run to the station and wait for the Northern Line, tell him what has happened."

The kid nodded and they moved out into the tunnel. The light was dim along the active tunnels, but it was better than the light in the crossover.

Harzl bent down and examined Snori. It looked as though the barghest was unconscious. His front leg was most likely broken. Snori moved a bit and sputtered out his soft snore. Harzl was never happier to hear his goofy buddy make his doggy sounds.

Alazavier shined the light on him and looked him over. "I think he's out cold; I'll try to wake him and get him out of here."

Harzl wasn't sure Snori could walk, but he didn't want to argue since he might not come back from facing the ghoul, and then the kid would have to leave Snori behind. He thought for a moment; he should just pick up Snori and take him back to the station himself, then come back for the shifter. It was stupid to go in without a plan and a weapon. He could try to at least get him off the tracks, back to the other tunnel.

"No . . . no . . . stop," he heard Jana say, and then start crying and choking as the ghoul chuckled.

"Try to get him to the tunnel," Harzl said to the kid as he leaped up onto the narrow platform and headed into the darker tunnel where the sound came from. He didn't know if ghouls were sexual, but he wasn't going to let the cursed thing kill her like this.

The platform was littered with bricks, and he picked one up. He knew from the Liminal wanted posters that the thing was the size of a thin human male and wore a tattered Victorian suit and top hat. He also knew it would bleed if you hit it. The Northern Line had said as much when it had thrown the ghoul against the wall after it had jumped on its back stairs and tried to attack passengers. They were still waiting for a ranger to come out and take care of the problem.

"I should have taken care of it myself," he grumbled as he found himself blocked by a stack of old vending machines.

He pulled the little flashlight out of his pocket and shined it down on the tracks before jumping. It was only a few feet down, but the debris made everything treacherous. He quickly headed to the old office.

A faint light gleamed inside, he didn't know from what. It was possible the ghoul was using an oil lamp or flashlight from the old supplies. The door had been torn off long ago and there was a large window on each side, but both were boarded up. He looked around for a weapon better than a brick.

Jana was whimpering; he couldn't be slow about this.

"Hey, asshole!" he yelled so the ghoul would stop whatever he was doing.

Everything was painfully quiet. The light inside went out.

"Whooo goes there?" the ghoul finally said.

"I am Harzl Hellirverja! Come out and play with someone who isn't hurt!"

"She's mine, fair and square, I won her from the bear!"

This was annoying, and the train would be here soon. Harzl couldn't speak with it until it slowed down. It wouldn't hear him over its own wheels. He needed to get Snori off the tracks.

He put his keychain on the platform and then set the brick on it so the light would stay on. Then he stepped back, moved to the other side of the door, and flattened himself down against the platform wall. "Come out and have a chance to run, or I'll come in there and beat you down!"

A train rumbled from far away.

Harzl saw the flashing light as the kid tried to stop the train. He hadn't been able to move Snori.

Jana howled like a wolfen.

Harzl stood up to charge.

The ghoul ran out and scrambled away from the light Harzl had planted, slamming into Harzl's chest. He heard something metal clatter to the ground. The ghoul tried to run, but Harzl grabbed it by the neck. It fought back, flailing its arms and legs against Harzl's stranglehold. The foul thing smelled terrible, like a pit of vermin. Harzl couldn't see him clearly but he didn't need to in order to break his neck, just like Snori did to the rats that infested the tunnels. He used both hands and twisted as the thing squealed as loudly as one hundred rats. The snap was not satisfying, but the cessation of its voice was.

A flashing light came running down the old tracks to Harzl as the train got closer.

"Harzl!" Alazavier called as the train surged by, air and light whooshing around him as he approached. The train hadn't stopped.

Harzl dropped the body of the ghoul to the ground and bellowed for the soul of his lost little buddy. "Snori!"

"Arooo ro ro" came back through the tunnel.

"I got Snori to wake up enough to get him to the other tunnel."

Harzl dropped to his knees and pulled Alazavier to him. "Thank you."

A whimper came from the office. The kid pointed the flashlight, and Harzl stood ready. Jana limped out in wolfen form.

"Stay back, I'll get her." Harzl went up the crumbling stairs and saw her fall to the ground; she shimmered and shifted back to human form.

He took off his extra heavy hoodie and wrapped her in it as he helped her to her feet. The hoodie was long on her, but he could see a deep gash in her left leg.

"Can you walk?"

"I think so," she said as she put weight on her leg and winced.

"What happened to you?" Alazavier asked.

She looked up, startled; she hadn't realized the gargoyle boy she was after was holding the light that illuminated her injury.

"That . . . thing, skewered me with a knife to . . . well, to trap me. It told me it was going to eat me. What was it?"

The kid answered before Harzl could, "A tunnel ghoul, it's like a vampire but not a vampire."

Harzl looked around his feet and located the bloody knife. It was short but sharp and had a handle carved into an intricate wolf. Jana stepped backward when he picked it up.

"Did you bring this with you? It has a wolf carved on the bone handle and the blade is silver." Silver would have kept her from shifting.

She didn't answer. It was clear she was more than wolfen. One of her parents, or grandparents, had to have been a witch. It would explain how she knew the old language and had been able to enchant him.

"I'll give this back to you once we get Snori to safety," Harzl said as he descended the stairs and then stopped to wait for her.

She tried not to wince as she came down the steps, holding on to the railing.

Alazavier stepped forward. "You take the flashlight, I'll help her. You'll need to carry Snori."

"A good plan," Harzl agreed with pride as he took the flashlight and put the knife in his knapsack side pouch.

"Why are you helping me?" Jana asked with suspicion.

Again Alazavier spoke before Harzl could answer. "Because it's the right thing to do."

He was a good kid. Harzl committed to getting him to his father for protection.

They made their way to the barghest, and Harzl bent down so he could hug his best friend. Snori held his injured leg close, but wiggled his butt and tail in excitement. He whined and yipped greetings while Harzl looked him over. "What happened to you, buddy?"

Jana supplied the answer from a safe distance; she was leaning on Alazavier's shoulder. "He chased me down the tracks and tried to corner me; we tussled and I unshifted. He didn't know what to do when I was naked. Then that ghoul attacked your . . . dog . . . with a shovel and I ran. I'm sorry."

"How do you carry that knife when you're, uh, naked?" Alazavier asked.

"An arm strap."

"How'd the ghoul get you if you ran?"

"He threw a brick at my head."

Harzl had had enough of the questioning. "Northern Line, can you hear me?"

"Yes, what do you need?" it projected into his head.

"Please come back through the tunnel slowly. Snori has a broken leg, another passenger has a deep wound, and I need to get them help."

"I will be there momentarily."

Snori growled.

"Don't move," came Spencer's arrogant voice from the darkness of the crossover tunnel. Then he emerged, a wand in his good hand, aimed at Snori.

Harzl stood up and stepped past Snori, blocking off the rude wizard's aim. "Your wand was broken, wizard."

"It's Nancy's wand. I assure you it will work as well for me as it did for her."

"That's not Nancy's or Cortney's wand," Alazavier stated.

Harzl could see on Spencer's face that the kid was right. "Did you use the duct tape from my counter?" he asked as he noted that the Northern Line train was edging toward them.

"Shut up, it worked well enough to muffle my footsteps, it will work well enough to blast your pet monster."

Harzl took a step forward; Spencer stepped back, tripping over his own feet and falling to the ground. He did his best not to cry out at the pain from his broken collarbone, but failed.

"Stop being a dick, Spencer, you've lost," Jana said. "The girls are gone and you can't take the boy. I won't let you."

"Damn it, Jana, you know what will happen if I go back. Those accursed vampires will kill me, and they won't be quick about it."

Jana hobbled over to him. "Look at me, Spencer."

"Oh god . . . what happened to you?"

"A tunnel ghoul got me and these two saved me. Spencer, we

have to walk away from this. Let me help you. We'll find another way to get you out of this mess." She put out her hand.

Harzl stepped back; they could work out their drama without him. The train waited patiently while he and the kid got Snori inside. Spencer and Jana helped each other get on behind them.

>—<—<

Snori watched the Chicago Line come into the station. It had been one month since Snori had broken his leg.

"Arrival, one passenger, the station inspector," Chicago Line announced.

"Thank you, Chicago Line," Harzl answered as he put away his tiny TV. He had been catching up on his shows but didn't enjoy them very much anymore. He had to leave Snori at home with Alazavier watching over him until his buddy mended. The vet bills were enormous, and he was going to be in debt for a long time. No more Cheshire Chocolate Chews or Carnivore Jerky Treats for either one of them.

Gwyn Ivershae disembarked. He hadn't seen or spoken to her since everything had happened. All of their communication had been by fax and had concerned fixing the station and cleaning up the mess. She had let him know that both Nancy and Cortney were well and free from the vampires. She hadn't asked about Snori, and he didn't say anything about the barghest. He was worried he was about to be fired for keeping Snori at the station.

Jana had stopped by two days ago to return Harzl's freshly laundered hoodie. She apologized for her role in subduing him, and explained that Spencer Beaumont had been a lawyer working for a powerful wizard family but had run afoul of them and been sold to the vampires. As if they had a right. They had said they would free him if he brought back Nancy and the gargoyle. Jana helped him out because she owed him for something he had done for her last year. They seemed to have a thing for each other, but Harzl didn't care about that, it wasn't any of his business. Drama was only fun when it was on the television.

"Harzl Hellirverja, it's good to see you again," the banshee greeted him.

Harzl came out from behind the counter. "Pleased to see you as well, Gwyn Ivershae."

She looked the same as she had that day, long gray dress and coat, long white hair.

"Are you here to inspect the new construction?" Harzl asked when she didn't say anything more.

"I am, but I'm also here to find out how Snori and the gargoyle child are doing. And don't worry, you have my word that they have been, and will be, left out of any report I make. I know you have your obligations."

Harzl relaxed for the first time in a month. "Thank you, Gwyn Ivershae."

"I'm sorry I didn't say so earlier; I can see this has weighed heavily on you."

"Do not worry about me. Snori is resting from his injuries, and the boy is tending to him."

"He's staying with you?"

"Yes, his people are aligned with mine."

"Of course. And what will become of him once Snori is healed?"

"I'll be taking them both to my father's clan."

"Oh? I thought the barghest was your pet?"

"He is, but I can't let him stay at home all day by himself, and I know I can't bring him here anymore."

"Are you coming back?"

"I am, but only until I can pay off Snori's vet bills, and then I will have to resign."

"What if I said I would like to offer you the station manager position?"

"I would say thank you, but I have to think about my options."

"What if I said you could keep Snori with you as the official rat catcher? The trains are fond of both of you."

"Then I would say yes."

"Excellent, the trains will be pleased."

Harzl felt a gladness in his soul. He could have the job he liked and keep his little buddy. His father would take care of the gargoyle boy, and it would give him a good excuse to go home during the holidays. Something he hadn't done in years, because he'd always felt like the odd sibling. Now he had something to look forward to other than the next season of *British Bakery*.

THE RETURN OF THE MAGE

by Charlaine Harris

"It's a rescue?" Batanya said. The signal had come through to the mechs very early in the morning. It had been erratic, weak. But it was a rescue signal.

"No one from the Collective has gone to Coturigo in twenty years." Clovache, Batanya's Second Officer, had come to fetch Batanya from a meeting. It had been a welcome interruption. Batanya had been balancing her knife on her fingertip to pass the time.

Since Clovache was on duty, her light hair was plaited and tucked appropriately under a net, and her helmet was in her hand. Batanya's short black hair was smooth on her head and uncovered. Both wore their liquid armor, which was not liquid at all but a thin and stretchy fabric that repelled most blades and bullets. It was fabulously expensive, and each mercenary of the Britlingen Collective spent the first years of service saving for the purchase.

When the two women arrived at the hub of the Collective, a wide lobby with doors to the entrance to the mercenaries' wing, the Hall of Contracts, and the Sending Halls, they found a short man waiting. He was a mage, from his long hair and long robe. Like Batanya, the mage looked like a native of the surrounding area: dark hair, slight build, brown eyes.

"You're Vandler?" Clovache said. The mages and the mercenaries did not mix, as a rule. "This is my First, Batanya." Batanya was in charge of a klader, three teams of ten mercenaries apiece.

The man nodded. "We received the signal thirty minutes ago. Is one of your teams ready to go?"

"Of course." Since Batanya's klaven was on duty, one of the three teams was ready to go, around the clock. "And here they are," Batanya said, as Geit's team trotted into the Hall. When you were on the active team, you ran, at a pace you'd been taught in training.

Teams had a contract for missions, and even though this was a team planning to investigate a recovery signal for one of its own, the form had to be followed. Batanya filled in the blanks herself, Clovache signed too, and two minutes later the doors to the Hall of Sending swung open. Vandler, the sending mage, went in with Geit and the other nine mercs. Geit blew Clovache a kiss as he mounted the platform.

That was not regulation. Batanya sighed. She was going to have to recommend that one or the other be transferred to another klaven, and Clovache had been her friend and comrade for years.

There were several grubby mechanics in coveralls around the platform, twiddling with the machinery, going about their mysterious business. Vandler had begun chanting a safe distance away. Geit's team, armed and ready, stood on the platform.

The mages, the mercs, and the mechs. All the parts of the most expensive, efficient, and well-known bodyguard, mercenary, and extraction teams in the known worlds.

The doors closed and from within came a trickle of sound as the team went to their mysterious destination.

There was no telling when they'd return, so Clovache returned to her duty station while Batanya went for a run. The sprawling Britlingen enclave topped a large hill, and going up and down was Batanya's favorite exercise. She peeled her liquid armor down to her waist for the downhill run. Her modest bra was not going to shock anyone on this mountain. Going down was fun and dangerous, and Batanya concentrated with her formidable focus. All her klaven would laugh themselves sick if she broke a leg.

At the bottom, Batanya ran in place for a count of thirty, then started back up, bouncing from high spot to high spot, short black hair fluttering. It was a cool day but her sweat dried almost as soon as it appeared.

Batanya glanced up to see that Clovache was waiting for her at the archway on the top of the hill. She knew immediately the news was bad. When she reached the archway, she stopped, and had to exercise a lot of restraint so she wouldn't lean over with her hands on her knees to pant.

"Speak," Batanya said.

"Klader Leader Batanya," Clovache said formally.

So the news was very bad. Batanya gave a short nod. "Second Clovache."

"Geit's team is dead, almost all of it."

Clovache was using as much restraint at Batanya. Geit was Clovache's lover, had been—off and on—for years.

"Who has returned to tell us so?"

"Therryl. Some of the bodies came back with him. Not Geit or Simone."

A double disaster for Clovache and Batanya, both personal and professional. "What does Therryl say?"

"He is waiting for you. He is dying."

The two began to run in the ground-eating trot that all mercs knew like their own heartbeat. In tandem the two women entered the building. "Clear way!" Clovache shouted a couple of times, and those mercs in the hall ahead of them picked up the call.

There was a small crowd at the infirmary doors: friends of the team members, mercs from the other two teams in the klader. They were silent as Batanya and Clovache passed through the doors.

Inside the infirmary, bodies sprawled on gurneys pushed about the room. Bits of armor and clothing littered the floor when they'd been ripped from the bodies to see if the mercs could be saved. Wounds gaped and had quit bleeding. None of them would make the trip into the hospital beyond the next set of doors.

There was activity around one gurney. Therryl's.

The orderly who turned to face them had a smear of blood on his arm and held his hands in the air as a reminder not to touch anything. "The mage is working on Therryl, but it doesn't look good." The orderly stepped aside.

The mage was Vandler, who had sent the team to its destination. He was pushing magic into Therryl's wound and working so hard he didn't react when Clovache and Batanya appeared at his side.

Therryl himself would not have noticed if a hundred people had entered the room. The mercenary was ridden by pain, his eyes shut, his muscles tense, tears running down his cheeks. Therryl's bloodstained hands gripped the sheets so hard Batanya was surprised the fabric didn't shred.

The wound in Therryl's side was the kind you didn't survive. It must have been delivered from very close, since the power of the thrust had penetrated the liquid armor. Batanya was sure it was a spear thrust, though she had seldom seen one.

"Therryl," Batanya said. "I'm here. Report."

"They didn't want us to see the man," Therryl said. He spoke in a burst, between deep breaths. "They fought us back . . . with spears . . . I got everyone close to me . . . best I could . . . to bring back."

"Who were they?" Batanya kept her voice as calm as she could.

"Coturigans," Therryl said. "Can I go?"

"Die with honor," Batanya granted.

Therryl died with a final gasp of relief.

Clovache began the ritual of farewell immediately. The others heard the familiar words from beyond the closed door and a chorus of voices joined in the lament. They bid Therryl farewell, prayed his bones would lie in peace, praised him for having fought, congratulated him on having no more battles to fight.

The mage, looking almost as bad as some of the corpses, leaned against the wall, his eyes shut, listening.

When the ritual was finished, the two women looked at each other, and Batanya nodded. Her armor had been peeled down all this time, and now she pulled herself back together. "This time you come with us," she said.

The mage opened his eyes. "Me?" Vandler said. "Mages don't go on combat missions." He was indignant and more than a little anxious.

"You will. You sent my team to die. Now you'll go with Batanya and me to retrieve our dead."

Vandler was gaping at them, his lips curving up in an incredulous half smile. "I won't be any help at all."

"You can die with us," Clovache said. "Geit and Simone are still missing. And we're going to get them now."

"Get two injections from the infirmary," Batanya said. Searching the faces of the onlookers, she said, "Marcus, give me some protection." She hadn't been armed for her run, but she needed something now. The burly mercenary tossed Batanya a paraton, not her favorite weapon. It looked like a flashlight and was held like one. Instead of a light, the paraton issued a burning ray. It would do.

Clovache had already trotted off.

"Injections? What for?" Vandler asked.

"In case Geit or Simone is in as bad a shape as Therryl was," Batanya said.

"I'm not going," Vandler said, his jaw stuck out.

"Then I'll give *you* one of the injections, take you with us, and leave you there unconscious."

Vandler glowered at her. Mages weren't used to being given ultimatums. "I have done my job," he said.

Clovache was back, stuffing two injectors into her belt. She exchanged a look with Batanya. They each grabbed one of Vandler's arms and dragged him into the hall of sending. The mercs around them opened the doors so they could enter without letting go.

The doors fell shut, and they were in a quiet space. The mechs in the room stared.

"We need to return to the same coordinates," Batanya told them, her voice as smooth and calm as if she were ordering a drink. "Vandler has agreed to show us where the signal came from."

The mechs, a man and an old woman, looked confused and glanced from Batanya to Vandler, who was so outraged he wasn't able to speak. But the mechs started about their preparations. Probably because of the smooth-barreled gun Clovache had drawn.

The two mercs hauled Vandler up on the platform. "Send," Batanya bellowed, and the mechs obeyed. Since Vandler had done the necessary chanting so shortly before, the sending worked.

Batanya, Clovache, and Vandler arrived on a small island of solid ground in the middle of a swamp. Short trees were all around but glimpses of light blue sky could be seen between the fronds.

Birds called and something splashed into the mud-colored water on their left. Vandler fell to his knees. The sending was hard the first few times.

She and Clovache were back to back, Vandler between them, anticipating an immediate attack. Batanya held the paraton in defense position, her forefinger having already pressed the tiny lever that would prime the weapon, her thumb on the firing button.

"Look," said Clovache. There was a body a few feet away.

"Simone." The long light hair was a vital clue. Whatever had slithered into the water had been eating on the body, and much of it was missing.

"Not Geit," Clovache said, choking on the words.

Batanya knelt by the body. "Go in peace to the fields of plenty, Simone," she said. It was an abbreviated version of the death chant and all she could manage at this moment. She gave the clearing a comprehensive look, reading the evidence as clearly as if she'd been present.

"Their dead are gone, and Geit is not here," Batanya said. "His team must have done some damage. I see drag marks."

Clovache followed the torn mud and grass. "This way," she said, pointing.

"What is this place, Coturigo?" Batanya asked Vandler, who had finally gotten to his feet.

His jaw was rigid with his anger but he replied. "It's a primitive place. A jungle planet. But possibly with rich lodes of three rare minerals underneath, which is why the previous party was sent here all those years ago. There was a mage with them, and he had a beacon. They did not have amulets back then."

Batanya's hand went to the one around her neck. They called it an amulet, but it was really a tiny machine with a plain veneer. If she pressed the little button on the side, the mechs at home would know she needed extraction immediately, and they would know exactly where she was.

"How this beacon got activated so many years later that we received the rescue signal this morning, I don't know." Vandler shook his head. He had gotten his anger under control. "We need to look for your team leader and get out of here. We can send a properly armed team later to follow this mysterious beacon."

Batanya nodded understanding. Clovache was waiting impatiently for them to move off the patch of dry land and onto the narrow neck of dirt marked with blood and the passage of many feet. Batanya passed her, paraton at the ready; Vandler came behind her, and then Clovache fell into place guarding the rear.

Batanya was sweating as they ran. If the memory of Therryl's gaping wound hadn't been so fresh, she might have been tempted to peel her suit down again. On the other hand, she was not getting scratched by the violent plant life and bitten by insects as Vandler was, going by his curses.

"Be quiet. We have to listen," Clovache hissed. After that, the mage was silent.

Batanya was focused on the ground. Most of the prints were of bare feet or sandals. The drag marks were almost certainly from Geit's boots.

Glancing up and ahead, Batanya froze and dropped down. She could see Geit through a clump of tall reeds. He was moving, but his stance was odd. Something was very wrong.

"Clovache," Batanya said, in as quiet and level a voice as she could command. "I see Geit, but he's suspended in the air and moving . . . not by his own power."

Clovache crouched down by Batanya. "What is he doing? How is he . . . ?"

"Some kind of an invisible stake moving with magic," Vandler answered from behind them.

"Stay here." Batanya crept forward. If Geit had been conscious he would have heard them by now, even with the swamp noise. He was an experienced warrior in all kinds of terrain, including swampland. For him to be exposed and displayed . . . this was clearly a crude ambush, with Geit as bait.

Batanya worked her way closer. She lifted the paraton and looked through the tiny scope mounted on top. Geit's eyes opened and closed. He was still alive. His chest looked oddly blurry. Batanya figured that some sort of invisible noose was passed around him under his arms. That was what was holding the man upright. Blood soaked the material of his liquid armor, chiefly on his left arm. Batanya winced when she saw tears running down Geit's weathered face. Just like Therryl's.

"Geit," she said urgently.

The merc's eyes flickered. He began to struggle, suspended in the air. It was horrible to see.

But they couldn't go charging in. For one thing, he might be rotating on top of water.

"Who would have set off an old beacon?" Vandler muttered. "Who would have called a team here to be killed?" The mage could not seem to think to himself. Batanya wondered if all mages talked this much.

Clovache was creeping closer to Geit, inch by inch. The sun finally made its way through the trees of the swamp. A ray glinted off something in the air around Geit.

"Freeze where you are," Batanya commanded. For the first time in ten years, she wasn't sure Clovache would obey.

But she did, at least for this moment.

"There's a trap right in front of you," Batanya said. "It shines when the light hits it."

"I see it now," Clovache said, after a long moment of silence.

"Throw a rock through," Vandler suggested. "Or a stick. Anything."

"Try it," Batanya said, after mulling it over.

Clovache reached down to pull a branch from the sticky earth. With some caution, she scooted forward a bit and held her arm directly in front of the circle of the trap. In one quick move, she tossed the stick through and snatched her arm back. There was a clear, but small, popping sound.

Instead of falling back to the ground, the stick was suspended in midair, rotating along with Geit.

"Crap," Clovache said. The trap was sprung.

Batanya heard the slightest noise in the brush behind her and knew they'd been diverted for too long.

"Ready!" she said. Though Vandler was puzzled for a moment, Clovache wheeled, her back to the oblivious Geit. Clovache drew her gun in one hand and a knife in the other. Batanya leaped into the tiny clearing, glad to discover it was solid, and turned to face the other side.

Vandler came with them. He caught on instantly and raised his hands, popping a shell around them.

The first volley of weapons bounced off the shell. Those were the fierce spears that had wreaked such havoc with the first team. Vandler's shield held for the blast, but shivered. "Won't hold them for much more of that," he said.

"Thanks," Batanya said. It might be the last thing she ever said to Vandler. Since he'd stopped bitching and started helping, it was the least she could do.

Clovache screamed, not a shriek of pain or fear, but an attack alert. She fired, her Salton gun making the soft *tat, tat* known through many worlds. Two of the attackers fell before they had a chance to retrieve their spears.

There was one of those odd pauses that can happen in the middle of a fight. None of the attackers were quite within range, and it seemed they were not going to throw more spears.

Into this pause ran a young man, maybe seventeen, his copper hair streaming behind him. He wore only a loincloth and was waving his arms while yelling.

Batanya couldn't understand him, but she was pretty sure he was saying, "Stop! Stop!"

The war party came out of their concealment. They appeared to be led by a tall woman with golden skin and long copper hair, tied back.

The boy deliberately stepped between the war party and the Britlingens and began to deliver a long harangue, his hands gesturing wildly.

Batanya took advantage of the moment to examine the Coturigans. They were definitely golden, taller than the Britlingens, and they were robust. In this tropical climate, all the locals were dressed in some kind of covering between the waist and the knees, but otherwise they were a clothing-optional crowd. A few of them carried spears, but those had been thrown, except for the tall woman's weapon. A few carried bows and arrows, machetes, and slings. The rest were armed with knives and clubs.

Batanya could reach two spears that had been stopped by Vandler's shield. She crouched to pull them under Vandler's protective spell. She herself might not be skilled in spear throwing, but at least the hostiles would not have them.

Then she watched the result of the young man's oratory.

It was clear the attack team was dismayed.

"Maybe they were lucky with the first crew?" Clovache said.

"I think the boy has magical training," Vandler said. He was so full of curiosity he sounded like a different man. "He's very young. But some of his hand movements look familiar."

"He's the one keeping Geit up in the air?" Batanya said.

Vandler shook his head. "No, that's a crude and almost made-up spell. If I had to guess, I'd say it was the woman. I think she's his mother."

"Huh. Can you talk to him?"

"I can try." Vandler straightened from the crouch he'd fallen into at the first hint of danger. "You, magician," he said, loud and clear.

The boy, whose coppery hair was mostly plaited and decorated with feathers and bones, stared at Vandler. "Yes, mage?" he said, in accented though understandable Britlingen.

"He can speak our language," Clovache said. That was significant and strange. Normally, only the people who hired Britlingens could speak with them, another piece of mage-work.

"I can speak your language. So can she." The young man pointed at the tall woman. "My father taught me," the boy said, haltingly. "My mother didn't know . . ." He hesitated for a long moment. Clearly, he was about to lie to someone. "She believes you have come to steal him."

There was a lot to chew over in that sentence. The safest answer was "Maybe," but Batanya didn't think anyone would be satisfied with that.

"We don't know who we were to see here," she said, which was the most diplomatic answer she could think of. There followed ten seconds of everyone wanting to stand down but no one wanting to be the first. Just in case.

"Let us talk," the tall woman said. Her accent was much heavier than her son's. "I promise your safety. On my son's head." She re-peated herself in her own tongue, turning to look at the war party.

The war party looked relieved.

"I'm lowering the shield," Vandler said. "If you believe her? I do."

"Me, too," Batanya said.

Vandler lowered his hands with a sigh of relief. He was bleed-ing from his left arm, Batanya noticed. Grazed by a spear before he got the shield up, looked like.

"Why have you come here?" asked the tall woman. The young man was very anxious to hear the answer to this, Batanya noted.

"We sent a team here to answer a distress beacon," Batanya said. "As soon as they arrived, they were set upon and killed or injured. Their bodies came back to us since one of them had enough energy to press his amulet, which brought them back to the Britlingen Collective. We three came to retrieve the last two. One of them is dead. The other hangs in the air behind us." She didn't turn to look, but she knew Geit was still turning in the air.

"You are invaders, out to abduct our mage and take him away," the woman said.

"Then who set off the beacon? Of course we assumed whoever was here was ready to come home," Vandler said rather crossly. He was not even looking at the woman, because he was intent on healing the gash. The sleeve of his robe was blood-soaked.

Vandler didn't realize, but Batanya did, that everyone in the war party was staring at him. After a couple of minutes, during which time the gash disappeared, the silence penetrated his spell-casting, and he raised his head to look around him inquiringly.

The tall woman said, "You are a mage who can heal wounds?" She was staring at Vandler with hungry eyes. "You are a Britlin-gen, though?"

Vandler, surprised, said, "Yes, all that."

Things were moving well, Batanya thought, but Clovache had had all she could stand. She was looking back at Geit and her face was stripped down to basic emotion. She decided to hurry things along, since Clovache would not be able to remain calm for much longer. "Lady, I am Batanya, a leader of the Britlingens who fight. This is Clovache, a fighter too. The mage is Vandler. He is a great healer. If you will let Geit go, we would like to get him down."

The woman glanced down at her son, who nodded mutely.

"My name is Perro." The boy inclined his head toward the tall woman. "Marla, my mother."

Exchanging names seemed to seal the deal on Coturigo. Marla twisted her fingers curiously and Geit dropped abruptly to the ground. Clovache sprang to him and crouched down.

"How is he?" Batanya asked, turning her head slightly to be sure Clovache heard her. The woman might have made a promise, but she wanted to keep her own eyes on the situation.

"Far from well," Clovache said, a savage edge to her voice. "We need to avenge Geit and leave this place." She sounded angry.

"The woman released Geit from the magic," Batanya said. "Willingly."

"Yes, First." Clovache didn't say that with any enthusiasm or regret, but she said it.

Vandler stepped back from the boy, who had come close to Vandler to stare at his non-existent wound. "Like it was never there," Perro said to Vandler, admiringly.

"Yes." Vandler sounded calm, assured, but he looked exhausted.

"Vandler, evaluate Geit," Batanya said. "Sit beside him."

Vandler gave her a grateful look before doing his best to walk briskly to Geit's side. He sank down on the grass to examine the mercenary carefully. Combat and healing had taken their toll on the mage, but he was doing his best to conceal that. Batanya approved highly.

"A superficial knife wound to the ribs, which has stopped bleeding. His armor did a good job there," Vandler called. "It's the blow to the head that is serious. Geit needs to return to the Collective."

Perro and Marla looked at each other.

"If you will agree, my second here will accompany the wounded man and the body of our comrade back to our base," Batanya said. She felt Clovache's muscles jump in protest. Clovache would not feel right leaving her here.

"No," Perro said, for his mother. "The other woman warrior must stay, but you can . . . send . . . the body of the dead woman and this soldier."

"I agree," said Clovache before Batanya could ask her. "Let me get Geit and Simone home, and I will stay with my leader."

Marla nodded. "Then you three must return to our village to meet our chief, Hannuman."

"Hannuman?" Vandler was clearly astounded. "Really?"

He turned his back on the tribesmen to tell Batanya, "Hannuman is the only mage who has simply vanished. Quite a legend in our world."

Only among the mages, apparently.

Batanya made a *come on* gesture with her fingers.

"He was the nastiest son of a bitch who ever walked the halls of the Collective, and then one day he vanished when he'd been detailed to come here with a mining party from Sentra. Hannuman was a metals mage. The Sentrans didn't want to pay for a rescue attempt, and Hannuman's beacon did not start sending. No one heard from him again. That's what the older mages tell us."

"Presumably it was he who set off the beacon?" Batanya was

helping Clovache raise Geit to his feet. Geit barely knew where he was, though he recognized Clovache and leaned against her. He was having trouble making his muscles obey his will. The blow to his head had been serious.

What if Perro and Marla changed their minds? Geit would die. "I'm going to help my soldier get this man back to the body of our sister," Batanya said, loud enough that the attackers' party could hear her. "I will return as soon as they are gone."

"No," Marla said instantly. "If you two leave with your wounded, what's to stop your people from sending even more soldiers here?"

A very good point, since that was exactly what Batanya would have done if Vandler hadn't been with them.

"I will send Geit and the body of our sister back to the base," Clovache called. "Batanya and the mage will stay here. I'll return. You have my word."

"This man will go with you to make sure you comply," Perro called. The boy and not his mother, Batanya noticed with interest, waved a big man with a club forward. "He doesn't speak your language, so don't think you can talk him into anything else."

That's a boy who's used to being deceived, Batanya thought.

"I accept," Clovache called. "Let's get moving."

Marla gave the big man an order in their language. He dropped his club and came forward. These people were not trained or dedicated warriors. The big man seemed so eager to help that Batanya immediately knew he was the one who'd hit Geit in the head.

Between them, the Coturigan and Clovache managed to steer Geit in the right direction. Geit made an effort to help, but he had no control over his body.

Just in case Marla had said in Coturigan, "Big Guy, kill them when you're out of sight," Batanya waited on the alert, a spear in one hand and the paraton in the other. Vandler seemed unconcerned, and he and Perro looked at each other with unabashed curiosity.

In less than four minutes, Clovache and the big man returned. Clovache said, "Done, First."

Batanya felt a wave of relief. Geit's survival was out of her hands now. She spared a moment to wonder what was being made of the return of an injured merc and a dead merc, with no sign of the three who had gone to look for them.

Any response from the Collective would take longer since she and Clovache had acted so hastily in forcing Vandler to bring them here.

Marla talked to the war party in their own language for a minute. As a result, the largest men stayed to carry the bodies, while the wounded gathered behind the Britlingens.

Marla looked at Batanya and said, "Come."

The Britlingens walked for a while in silence, careful to follow in the footsteps of the people before them. Something large thrashed around in the boggy water just out of sight. Marla said something to Perro and smiled at him, but the boy kept his grim face on. "We hardly knew how to use magic before Hannuman taught us," Marla said to Batanya, looking back at her.

"Hmmm." Batanya didn't think this was idle history. "And you learned our language from Hannuman." She sped up a little, hoping for a conversation.

"Yes. He was sure the Keechobish would return for him."

"What does that mean?" Vandler said, just as neutrally as Batanya. The mage was surprising her again.

"Alien People with Weapons."

That pretty much said it all, Batanya thought. "So Hannuman taught you some mage craft?" Batanya asked, since it was her turn.

"Oh, yes, that was why he was given me as wife," Marla said.

She spoke calmly, but her expression said that some of the teaching had not been pleasant. "It helped us so much, having a mage. He could do things for the village that we didn't know how to do."

From the corner of her eye, Batanya saw Vandler's hands curl into fists. The mage did not like that tidbit at all. "So Perro is your son with Hannuman." Vandler managed to sound no more than mildly curious.

"Our middle son. We have three." For the first time, Marla smiled.

Batanya could not feel sure how the local woman felt about Hannuman, but she could read loud and clear that Marla loved her sons.

The edge of the village was within sight by now. It had been built on the largest area of solid land Batanya had seen, possibly the edge of a major land mass.

First were outhouses . . . no trouble recognizing those. Then there were huts scattered at random in the cleared area. *It must be a constant battle to keep the forest at bay*, Batanya thought.

As they progressed into the heart of the village, there were pens of animals, some Batanya couldn't identify, with children guarding them. She saw a well, a large communal cooking pit, and what might have been a village oven. Most of the people looked well-nourished and able, and there were plenty of children.

"Not many old people," Clovache said quietly.

"No signs of any mining," Batanya said. She would have liked to look longer, but Marla and Perro had picked up the pace.

An anxious group waited in the center of the village. The wounded were surrounded and taken off to a small hut. Perro peeled away to stand with two other young men, one golden-skinned but blond, one lighter but copper-haired. *His brothers*, Batanya figured. The three began to whisper to each other, but she could not interpret their expressions.

Now most of the villagers held back in a cluster. Only two sturdy Coturigan men and Marla led the newcomers forward. Marla's sons followed close behind, looking grim.

There was one man waiting for them, under a sort of primitive pavilion.

The floor was beaten dirt and the posts holding up the roof were painted in bright colors. There were seats under its shelter, not the stools Batanya would have predicted, but real chairs with backs and arms and cushions to soften the wooden seats.

The largest chair, the only one occupied, held an old man who must be Hannuman. His hair was white and streamed over his bare shoulders in true mage style. His skin, after twenty years under the Coturigan sun, was brown and freckled, not the attractive gold of the local people.

"A mage, all right," Clovache said with a grunt.

Hannuman had disdainful pride draped on his shoulders like a cloak.

Batanya, Clovache, and Vandler watched the old man for what seemed like a long time. Though he wasn't looking back at them, at least not directly, Batanya was sure he was giving them a thorough examination. It appeared the old mage was not going to welcome them or acknowledge them first. But then, he'd been king in this swamp for two decades. It was a humble kingdom, but his own.

"Are we expected to bow?" Clovache whispered.

Damned if I will, Batanya thought. But she thought again, and inclined her head at the same moment Vandler did.

And Batanya noticed that despite his aloof air, Hannuman was gripping the arms of his chair so fiercely his hands were white.

Marla went to one knee in front of her husband and began to talk to him in their language. While Hannuman appeared to be listening, his head inclined, his eyes were actually on Vandler.

Batanya did not like the old man's expression. *Not* good. Why wasn't Hannuman delighted at the arrival of another mage? Surely he was all excited about taking his family back to the Collective— or at the very least, he'd be full of the chance to tell his own story at last.

After all, he'd set off the beacon.

When Marla fell silent, Hannuman raised his hand. The few conversations among the people behind them stopped.

Batanya had to clamp her lips together to repress a sigh. Someone had a god complex.

"After all these years you have finally returned to get me," Hannuman said coldly. "At least, I presume that the warriors my wife has told me of came from home?"

So this was Hannuman's reaction. He was angry at them. Batanya remembered the bodies of her team strewn around the infirmary, and she shuddered. "Our people have died, and some of yours, too," she said. "Why did you tell your people to attack when you had activated your beacon?"

"What?" Hannuman was shocked. It was genuine, if Batanya was reading him right. "The beacon worked after all these years? How can that be?"

Out of the corner of her eye, Batanya caught the two brothers rounding on Perro, their eyes wide. "Yes," she said loudly, to keep Hannuman's attention. "We sent a rescue squad immediately. They are almost all dead because they answered the summons of your beacon. We three came to find the remaining bodies."

Hannuman glared at her. "The hell you say!"

"I do."

"Who are you?" Hannuman asked Vandler directly. Apparently, he was done talking to Batanya.

Batanya didn't dare look at Clovache.

"I'm Vandler, a healer and destination mage from the Collective."

Hannuman could not have looked blanker if Vandler had declared he was a monkey. "I am one of the great mages of my age," Hannuman told them with calm certainty.

Vandler didn't speak. He might have been struck wordless by the claim.

"Do they not still talk of me?" Hannuman said.

"From time to time," Vandler answered carefully. "It's been twenty years."

Marla had backed away from her husband, but she was still on one knee. She was listening intently.

"Twenty years," Hannuman said slowly. "That long. I lost track."

All three of the sons had had birthdays, which surely they observed somehow or another. That should have marked the time clearly enough.

"I had long given up working on the beacon. Who repaired it and activated it?" Hannuman said, as if the Britlingens were sure to know.

Vandler shrugged. "There is no way to tell. The signal came in quite faintly. It took the techs some time to be sure they'd tracked it to the right location."

The old man's eyes swiveled to the three young men and he fixed his sons with a terrible glare. "Was it you, Bertol? Or you, Ronoldo? Or . . . *Perro*?" And Hannuman's voice snapped on the last name.

It was a frightening glare if you were a kid with an overbearing and conceited father. Marla cringed, too.

Batanya hated bullies.

"Does it make any difference?" Batanya demanded. She wanted to skip this family drama and begin their exit from this place, with or without Hannuman. She had to accept that her team had died for an asshole. There was so much to do at the Collective. Relatives, if the mercs had any, had to be told. Bodies had to be committed to the fire. "We are here to take you back. Are you ready to go? What about your family?"

"My *family*?" Hannuman looked as if he couldn't understand the connection.

There was an appalled silence as they all realized that Hannuman had not even considered taking his wife and sons with him.

Marla went from cringing to furious. It was great. She was on her feet, eyes flashing, her plait of copper hair swinging. Her spear was in her hand in a throwing position.

"No, no, stop, please stop," said Clovache in a monotone.

Batanya had to bite her lips to hide a smile.

In one violent motion, Marla broke her spear over her knee and tossed down the two pieces. "I divorce you!" she said in Britlingen, and then repeated it in Coturigan.

Her sons were frozen with astonishment. Suddenly, Perro grinned.

"Excuse me," Vandler said loudly. "Hannuman, what is your intention? Will you stay here with these good people, your wife, your sons? Or do you intend to return to the Collective with us? And when you have answered that, maybe you will impress us with the story of how you came to be the only survivor of the mining company party."

Hannuman skipped the hard questions for the easy one. "Because I popped on a shield to cover myself at the first sign of an attack. Everyone else was killed within minutes. But the local people saw what I had done, and that made them curious about me. They kept me alive to learn from me. Gradually they understood what I could do for them. I became their king."

Vandler had popped a shield over *all* of them when they'd been attacked.

"And you will come with us?" Batanya was anxious to get this settled.

Not to Batanya's surprise in any way, the boy Perro stepped forward. "We will let you take him without further struggle," he said, imagining he sounded scary and noble. "But you must leave behind the mage you brought with you. We have not learned enough. Our father knows about finding minerals, and he knows about protecting ourselves, and he knows about punishment. But you, Vandler, you know other things. Things we need."

This was another conversation stopper. Marla flushed. Maybe she was wondering if she'd have to have children with Vandler, too. Maybe she was delighted she might get rid of Hannuman. Maybe she was humiliated that her husband might walk away from her and their children without a second glance.

"No one's arguing that they have to keep him," Clovache whispered. That hadn't escaped Batanya's notice.

Hannuman shrugged. It was obviously okay with him if someone else sacrificed his freedom for Hannuman's.

Batanya and Clovache formed a little huddle with Vandler, who was clearly stunned.

"Can you make our conversation private?" Batanya said.

Vandler made some gestures in the air and chanted a little. Batanya watched a chickenlike bird raise its head and crow perhaps five feet away, but she heard no sound.

"That worked," she said.

"Of course it did." Vandler gave her a wry smile.

"Hannuman's return won't be any asset to the Collective. If you want, we'll just walk out of here and leave him to face the music for showing them how little he cares," Batanya said.

"He's a rare shit," Clovache said.

"He's a rare shit who can order everyone in this village to attack us. The odds look good that they'll obey him, maybe excluding his immediate family," Batanya said.

"They'll obey," Vandler said. "You see that framework over there?" He pointed.

A sort of bamboo grid, about the size of a man, was set upright into the ground on one side of the clearing. There were strips of gleaming metal running through the lattice structure.

"That's a punishment device," Vandler said. "It looks like nothing. But you don't want to know how painful it is when it's powered by a strong mineral mage."

"And yet Hannuman can't heal," Batanya said. "That's what's impressed Perro. Thanks, Vandler." She met his eyes.

Vandler sighed. "Here's what I think . . ." he began.

Three minutes later he removed the quieting spell and Batanya wheeled around to face Hannuman, whose face was twitching with impatience.

"Hannuman will return to the Collective with us, as he wants. Vandler will stay for a year," Batanya said. "He will teach whoever can learn. Then he must have the right to return to the Collective. In peace. If I don't see his face a year from now when I get to this spot, a larger force of us will come and you will be annihilated. I swear to this, as a Britlingen."

She turned slowly so she could look each villager in the eyes. She wanted to be sure they knew how sincere she was.

They appeared to believe her. A few flinched.

"Then we are agreed," Hannuman said regally, standing.

Vandler stood straighter. "We are agreed. I will see my rescue party in a year," he said to Batanya. "Don't forget to make sure they come for me." He tried to smile.

"You make sure they don't attack us when we get here. This coward has already cost enough lives." Batanya said that very clearly.

Hannuman snarled but didn't say anything. What was there to say? He'd made his choices and they added up to cowardice and betrayal.

Perro admitted to repairing the beacon. "I didn't know my mother's hunting party would be close enough to attack. I am sorry for all the loss."

It was like he'd read her mind.

Well, that would make Vandler's time here even more interesting. Batanya gave Vandler the Britlingen salute, raising her right fist to her upper left chest. Clovache followed. And to Batanya's surprise, Vandler duplicated the movement.

"You're much better than I thought," Batanya said, and Vandler laughed.

She smiled at him.

"Better go before I have time to rethink this," Vandler said. "Or he does." He tilted his head toward Hannuman; the older man was frowning with impatience, the narrow lips turned down in an expression that must be habitual since the wrinkles were so deep. He didn't seem to want to say goodbye to anyone or take anything with him.

The two mercenaries beckoned to the mage and he came to join them, not even glancing at his wife and his children. Marla had gone to her sons and put her arms around them. She stood with her back to her former husband.

Batanya gave Vandler a quick nod, and she and Clovache set off with Hannuman in tow. They did not speak but followed the path back to the clearing where Geit had been, then across the narrow strip of land leading to the spot where the first party had arrived. It would be easiest to return from that point.

"You know, I did much for those savages," Hannuman said, looking straight ahead of him.

"Sure you did," Batanya said.

"I could tell they loved you," Clovache said, deadpan. They stood on either side of Hannuman, and each gripped a stringy arm. Clovache pulled out her knife with her free hand, and the next instant it was at Hannuman's throat. With his hands held, he could not attack them with magic.

"What say I cut his throat and we toss him into the swamp?" Clovache said.

"He'd be eaten up in no time," Batanya agreed.

"And certainly no loss."

Hannuman's furious and frightened old eyes latched on to Batanya. He did not dare speak, not with the knife so close.

"Better not," Batanya said. "It would be satisfying, though. Maybe Geit would like the privilege."

Clovache shrugged. "All right, then." She slid her knife back into its sheath with one smooth movement.

Batanya activated her amulet at the same moment Clovache did.

In the second before they reappeared on the platform where they'd been two hours before, safe in heart of the Collective, Batanya made a mental note to tell the mechs that she wanted to be sure she was the one sent to fetch Vandler.

In one year.

THE VAMPIRES KARAMAZOV

by Nancy Holder

In another life, it would be time to chant the morning prayers: *Having risen from sleep, we fall down before thee.*

But Alexei and his family had risen from sleep with the setting of the sun, and would go back to sleep with the dawn. A midsummer's night was ending in New York City: hot, dirty, unpredictable. Alexei sat on a roll-around chair and faced a bank of camera monitors, the latest generation of tech. When the Karamazovs had first moved to New York in 1866, their home security system consisted of a chair and a rifle. As far as they knew, they were still the only living vampires in New York. No one had contacted them. No one had come after them. Still, they watched.

Alexei was on duty. Braced. He was always on duty, but his brothers didn't know it. In their previous lives, he had taken holy orders as a monk, and as he could minister to no one else, his violent, graceless family was his flock. They were in ceaseless need: his father and brothers were like children, aggressive and violent. He was different, but then, he had always been different. No one else in the family would have dreamed of giving himself to the Church. But then again, no one in the family would have dreamed of becoming a vampire.

He caught the whirr of the elevator down the hall, the thunder of Pavel's boots. His blissful solitude was about to end, and he consigned himself to the ensuing chaos as his father and brothers returned from their night revels, as inevitable as the sunrise. Drinking, whoring, feeding. The anonymity of modern life in New York eliminated accountability. Back in Victorian-age Russia, your neighbors saw you. If you committed a sin, your priest heard about it. Now there was no shame, only boasting, showing off how outrageous you could be, how many likes you could accumulate for bad behavior. Maybe it was foolish to hold vampires accountable for wrongdoing as had been defined for human beings. But the laws of the true God existed, and had endured for two thousand years, or else the world held no meaning.

But what about his existence? If he spent his time contemplating Christ, but couldn't touch a cross, and was afraid to pray for fear of sullying the Lord's name—what led him to the conclusion that he could turn anyone from the path of darkness to that of the light, least of all himself?

He had murdered his first victim. He had not known how to stop. The blood, flowing; his adrenaline pumping. The sheer lust. He had given in to it. And for that he was damned. He couldn't confess, couldn't receive absolution, couldn't become clean again because he was cut off from the Holy One forever. God didn't know of his struggles to repent. He didn't know there was a sorrowful demon in vain pursuit of his own lost soul.

Then why not sin? asked the devil on Alexei's shoulder.

He watched the monitors as the lumbering boots sounded, remembering the shifting hues in the stained-glass windows of the monastery, how the light would play over the huge mosaic icon and make the sad Madonna smile. The soft tolling of bells.

Then Pavel burst in, slammed the apartment door so hard the picture frames rattled, and flopped against it as if he had just outrun a band of marauding Cossacks. He was dressed like a Russian mobster in black leather pants, a black bomber jacket, black boots, and shades. His dark hair was close-cropped, his head almost shaved. He looked like someone you should avoid.

"Hi, Lex," he said.

Alexei gritted his teeth. He hated the nickname.

Vodka fumes and the succulent aroma of blood billowed around Pavel as he staggered across their living room with its garish red velvet couches and Turkish rugs and plopped down into the empty chair beside Alexei. He'd drained some homeless person or maybe a beautiful rich girl, and no doubt efficiently disposed of the body. No doubt at all. No corpses, no questions. It was how they had lasted so long. Alexei's secret vow never to take another human life endangered the family. For him, it was the lesser of two evils.

Pavel said, "I saw a car accident. Bad one." He burped, which should be scientifically impossible. But being a vampire should also be scientifically impossible.

Alexei knew a confession when he heard one. "Were you careful?"

"Of course." Pavel shrugged. "No one saw."

It still unnerved Alexei that Pavel no longer answered his questions with sarcasm or scorn. Papa's oldest, illegitimate son had been filled with poisonous jealousy all his human life, a crafty, manipulative imp who had goaded their half brother Dmitri into murdering Papa back in St. Petersburg. During the court trial, Pavel freely recounted his last conversation with Dmitri before

Dmitri decided to act: good and evil were nothing but useless concepts. Morality was a fiction that promoted oppression of the masses. There was nothing sacred about human life. Breaking two of the commandments—dishonoring your father, killing him—was perfectly acceptable, especially if your father withheld your financial birthright and slept with the woman you loved.

Of course the judge was appalled. Alexei believed that the court had found Dmitri guilty despite flimsy evidence and the lack of witnesses because the Karamazovs as a family were so debased—with the exception of the youngest, Alexei, who had become a monk.

One had to consider that Pavel had been born of a sinful union, in a time when shame existed and a birth outside of wedlock was a scandal. It was a lot to overcome when you knew that people whispered about you behind your back, rolled their eyes, murmured, "What do you expect? Look at his mother." People didn't think like that anymore.

We are not people.

Another whirr of the elevator was like a growling dog, punctuated by yips of wild laughter. More Karamazovs coming in before the blazing dawn. Ivan had nearly burned to death the first morning after their rising. Lesson learned: Direct sunlight caused vampires to burst into flame.

"Oh yeah, yeah, uh-huh, uh-huh, uh-huh! I am so *into* you!" Out in the hallway, Papa bellowed some vaguely familiar song at the top of his lungs. There were no other tenants on their floor, or the floor above them or below—that was where most of their money went, renting so many apartments—but *still*, it was so careless. They didn't need complaints—or drawing attention to themselves by dressing like thugs, for that matter.

The door crashed open. Dmitri, taller than Papa, stared at

Alexei as he half carried, half dragged their drunken father across the threshold. Both of them wore black trousers and black T-shirts. Dmitri also had on a linen blazer, which classed him up. Dmitri was the tallest and the sexiest of the Karamazov brothers. Also, the most powerful of the four brothers now that he was Papa's favorite. The murder had been a blessing, as far as Fyodor Karamazov was concerned.

"Oh, boys, boys, you shoulda come!" Papa shouted. He started singing again.

Dmitri was not smiling. His forehead was furrowed. Alexei went on alert: something was up.

"Let me get you into bed, old man." Dmitri leaned over to gather Fyodor in his arms.

"*Old? Man?*" Papa flailed at Dmitri. "I'm the fucking *king* of the vam—"

The front door opened again and now Ivan stood in the doorway in board shorts, a T-shirt, and flip-flops. His gaze was riveted on his father. The shock on his face reminded Alexei of when they had risen from their graves for the first time. When Alexei tried to catch his eye, Ivan shook his head and wiped his face with trembling hands.

Oblivious to all the undercurrents, Pavel got up and stumbled into the kitchen. "Let's keep the party going. Who wants vodka?" he called.

Ivan walked over to Alexei, his back to Papa and Dmitri. He stared at Alexei as if he didn't know who he was.

"How was your evening, Ivan?" Alexei asked quietly. Ivan remained silent.

"I want vodka! I want to drink with my sons! My boys!" Papa bellowed. "I love you all! And all your mothers! And vodka!"

"You've had enough." Dmitri flung his arm around their father's shoulders and walked him into the hall, toward their bedrooms. Ivan took a step in their direction, then fell into the chair that Pavel had vacated.

"Alexei," he murmured, "someone saw Papa."

Alexei stayed neutral, because he himself had most likely left witnesses, since his victims survived his feedings. Besides, each of the Karamazovs had slipped up at least once in all the decades. When Ivan didn't continue, he braced himself. It was more than that. Something had gone very wrong.

"And . . . Dmitri dispatched the witness," Ivan finally said.

Pavel returned with a bottle of vodka and four shot glasses, set them all down on Alexei's desk with a clatter, and said, "Jesus, the old man is really out of it tonight."

Ivan looked down at his hands. When Pavel began pouring out the shots, Ivan grabbed one and threw it back without waiting for the others. Pavel refilled the shot glass and the three clinked in a toast. The vodka was good, cold.

"Ivan, what happened?" Alexei prompted.

"There was a-a child," Ivan whispered.

"No." Dmitri loomed behind Ivan, stone-faced, rigid. He had returned from putting Papa to bed. "It was not a child. It was a baby."

"What was a baby?" Pavel poured another round.

Dmitri said, "Papa tried to attack a baby."

Shocked senseless, Alexei crossed himself. The other three recoiled from his gesture. Pavel's cocky attitude evaporated and he stared in the direction of his father's bedroom, lips parted, eyes wide.

Dmitri leaned forward and grabbed the vodka bottle. He chugged half of it down, then clutched it against his chest and said, "Family meeting. Let's go out on the balcony."

Ivan led the way, opening the sliding glass door, and Alexei was swept along outside with the others. Their balcony was sheltered by an awning that Pavel and Ivan had tied securely in place a few months ago. It stretched above their heads like a ceiling, and the family replaced it every couple of years. Below, the filthy alley that separated their dirty brick skyscraper from the dirty brick skyscraper opposite was bathed in pink and gold from the rising sun. Rays touched the graffiti that coated the bottom floor, the trash that was piled like snowdrifts.

"He was going to go after the baby," Dmitri said. "I stopped him. But the mother . . . the mother was there and saw him . . ." He took another swig of vodka. The other three brothers traded unguarded looks of horror.

"What about the baby?" Pavel asked.

"I left it in the stroller. Someone will find it." Dmitri gazed down into the alley. Alexei followed his line of sight. Spray-paint explosions of graffiti promised violence, retribution, revolution. "No one will find the mother."

There was silence. They did not kill children. That rule was ironclad. But to kill a young mother, to leave the child alone . . .

"Afterward, Fyodor Pavlovich said I was mistaken, that he only wanted to look at the baby," Dmitri said. "It was a lie."

"Yes," Ivan said. "I saw the whole thing." Pavel threw him a questioning look, and Ivan said, "I saw them on my way home. Of course I ran into them. It was my usual route."

Dmitri nodded as if to confirm Ivan's statement. He and Ivan moved closer together, a unified front. A tick of suspicion—or maybe simply false hope—tugged at Alexei.

"He wouldn't do that," Alexei said.

Ivan shook his head. "You weren't there, Alexei. You didn't see."

Alexei tried again. "He *didn't* do that. The sin was not committed."

"'Not committed.' *Not committed.*" Pavel laughed. "Is that what it says in God's ledger book? 'Fyodor Pavlovich Karamazov: Sin number two hundred thousand and seventy-five. Not committed because someone stopped him. Skip to sin number two hundred thousand and seventy-six.' When no one *could* stop him."

"We have free will. All of us," Alexei said. Except . . . he had been unable to stop himself. The police officer, his first victim. The one he had drained until her heart had given out . . .

Pavel snorted. "We're *vampires.* And you're a balalaika. You're a dusty lacquer jewelry box with a little fairy-tale princess on the lid. You're not a monk anymore, little brother. We humor you when you make your little faces and tsk-tsk-tsk at us. But everyone here is a black sheep."

"Wolf," Ivan corrected.

Silence. No one came to Alexei's defense. Angry, frightened, he focused on the graffiti. The wall was a mess, so profane and ugly. Such a display would have been unthinkable back in their days in St. Petersburg. Offenders would have been whipped for vandalism. Or worse. Life had been cruel, and often unjust, but there had been far more respect.

Fyodor Karamazov was their father.

Their father who had turned them into vampires without warning. Without asking. How, he had never said. Nor why.

"He cursed us. He rules us. He treats us like serfs." Pavel rapped his knuckles on the balcony railing. "Do you have any money of your own? A life of your own?"

"You're trying to do it again," Alexei said.

"What?" Pavel raised his eyebrows in feigned innocence.

"Make a case for murdering him." Alexei lifted his chin. "And I will not discuss it."

"Lex, Lexi-boy, so stern and sure," Pavel taunted, cocking his head and pretending to strum a balalaika. "Don't you think your god would be happy to have one less of us Karamazovs on this earth? Listen to Dmitri. Your father the precious tsar of your life was going to slaughter an innocent."

There was silence. Finally, Dmitri said, "Alexei, Pavel has a point."

"Which you both can make so easily, since you're the two who killed him in the first place," Alexei snapped. "You're a devil, Pavel. And you *are* a sheep, Dmitri."

He left them there and stomped into his room. Locked the door just to make his case and stared at the ceiling. Papa was snoring, not a care in the world.

"Oh, my Father," Alexei blurted, then clamped his mouth shut. He must not pray.

After a time, he got back up and walked into the living room. Ivan should be stationed at the bank of monitors; he wasn't there. Though the sun was out, Alexei went onto the balcony and watched the people walking through the alley. Guys in jeans and T-shirts, the occasional suit. Women in sleeveless tops and dresses. Kids. A black-and-white dog.

His eyes watered from the indirect sunlight. His skin puckered as he kept vigil. *I want to love* you, he thought. *I want to hunt you down and kill you.*

>×<

"Alyosha," a voice said, using his real nickname, "how long have you been out here?"

Alexei stirred. Then his eyes flew open as he realized Dmitri was squatting on his haunches and leaning over him. He could barely see him. There was so much *light*.

"Out here?" Alexei repeated, muzzy. "What time is it?" He

tried to sit up fast, but Dmitri put a hand on his chest. The sky glowed blue, yellow.

"Easy. It's three in the afternoon. I thought you were in your room."

Of all the brothers, Dmitri looked the most Slavic. A man blessed by the motherland, a country that tried and tried again to be just, and to be good, and sinned and failed and yet believed in hope. In the old days, in the old country, Dmitri had been closest with Alexei. With their father so often drunk or off chasing women, Dmitri had practically raised Alexei, the youngest brother. But once Alexei had joined the Church, Dmitri had wandered off, his job done. When Papa had refused to give Dmitri his birthright and allow him to set up his own household, he had rebelled in all the worst ways, drinking, brawling, whoring . . . and bashing their father's head in with a fireplace stanchion.

"It's dangerous out here," Dmitri said.

As if Alexei didn't know that. He had no idea why he had fallen asleep on the balcony in broad daylight. He slowly got to his feet and smoothed back his damp hair. He was sweating.

"Back home, when I studied with Father Zosima, do you remember?" Alexei said. "Everyone believed he was a saint. But when he died, he rotted, and everyone was stunned. They thought his body would stay pure."

"I remember," Dmitri said. He grinned. "It caused quite a scene. And a stench. Speaking of which, you could use a shower."

"Will our bodies rot, if we die?" Alexei ran a hand along the railing. "I wanted to serve and glorify God. And now . . . I have no idea if God wants anything to do with me. Or if I should leap off this balcony so as not to cause further offense."

"Alexei Fyodorovich, don't torment yourself. You're not like Papa," Dmitri said. "You're your own man."

"I'm not a man anymore." Alexei began to sob. He'd had no warning that he was going to, but he wept with every cell of his monstrous body. Every shred of his possibly nonexistent soul. "Don't look at me, Dmitri. I beg of you. Please, go inside and don't witness this."

"Never be ashamed of longing," Dmitri replied. His voice was gentle, as when Alexei had been a little boy.

"I long for oblivion," he said.

"No. I think you long for heaven."

"I don't think we can ever go there."

Dmitri shook his head. "You can't know that. And if your faith sustains you . . ." He frowned. "I had no idea you wrestled with such misery. We used to be so close. I thought once the Church got hold of you . . ."

Alexei swallowed hard. "If I had one moment where I could forget what we—what I am, that I am not an accursed monster—"

"No, no, not *you*, little cherub. I—"

The balcony door slid open. "There you are!" their father cried, sticking out his head. He had a bottle of vodka in his grip and he reeked of alcohol. "I was afraid you'd run away from home, Alyosha! What the hell are you doing out here? You'll go blind! He's out here, boys!" he slurred over his shoulder. He drank straight from the bottle, swaying, grabbing hold of one of the nylon poles that supported the awning. Alexei darted forward and took his arm, steadying him.

"Easy, Papa," he said, surveying the awning. Intact. Safe.

"Look at all those people." Papa made a show of smacking his lips. "Too bad we can't fly. We can't turn into bats."

"Or wolves," Dmitri said archly.

"We *are* wolves," their father retorted. He puffed out his chest. He had stopped aging at around sixty. No one knew exactly how old he had been.

After about a minute, Pavel and Ivan shuffled out in sunglasses and sun hats. They should all be wearing them. Alexei had to squint. The skin on his face was taut and itchy. Pavel and Ivan stood together awkwardly, as if wondering why they were all risking a fiery death instead of going back inside.

"Oh, look at that," Papa said.

A woman with dark brown skin and a bouncy black ponytail was jogging down the center of the alley. She looked like a runner in her pink T-shirt and gray leggings, and she had the body for it. She moved as if life was good and no one would jump her or murder her.

"Look at that ass," Papa crooned.

Something passed between Pavel and Ivan. Something decisive and solid. In unison, they moved closer to their father, Pavel ambling around to flank his father on his left side. Ivan was on his right. He stood between them now, leering at the woman, calling to her, trying to get her to look at him. His bottle of vodka sloshed in his hand as he wobbled on rubbery legs.

"Beautiful! Beautiful girl! Hey!" he called, waving. She ignored him.

"Look at that neck, Papa," Pavel said, digging him in the ribs with his elbow.

Papa snorted and leaned forward. In his sunglasses, Pavel turned his head in Alexei and Dmitri's direction. Dmitri sauntered behind Papa.

"Hey, baby!" Papa shouted. Drunk on his ass, leaning over the balcony, waving with both hands. Whistling at her.

Ivan and Pavel did the same, hooting, whistling. The woman didn't react. She must have been used to this kind of treatment.

Papa leaned farther over. Ivan and Pavel crowded him in. And in that moment, Alexei finally understood what was happening.

"No, no, don't," Alexei said, rushing toward him. "Papa, step back. Step back now!"

Dmitri half turned, pushed Alexei hard against the wall, and mouthed, *Stay back.* Ivan and Pavel moved in closer, like advancing jackals.

Alexei lurched forward, trying to push Dmitri aside. Dmitri blocked his way. "Please, Papa. Get away from them!"

Pavel shouted, "Now!"

The vampires Karamazov started moving at once. Alexei lurched forward and found himself pushed against the railing as his three older brothers grabbed their father and started to hoist him up. A troika of murderers. Papa flailed and fought for purchase, but he had already leaned over too far. He was bowed outward, forward from the waist up, nearly clear of the protection of the awning.

"You bastards! Bastards!" he shrieked. "Help! Hey, help!"

A couple people looked up. A short man in a Jets T-shirt started tapping on his phone. A woman in a short denim skirt shouted, "Hey!" and began running toward the building and waved her arms. "Hey, someone call the cops!"

Alexei grappled with Dmitri, punching his shoulder with both fists. Dmitri shoved him hard; Alexei tumbled onto his backside and smacked the back of his head on the concrete. For a few seconds the bright world spun around, and his vision faded to gray with yellow dots.

Papa was yelling at the top of his lungs. Ivan was screaming, too: "You idiot! You selfish bastard! Die!"

Ears ringing, vision clouded, Alexei lunged at Dmitri's legs. Dmitri kicked backward at him, shaking his head, bellowing, "Go inside! Get out of here!"

"Alyosha, save me!" his father shrieked. "Save me!"

All the rays of the sun gathered around Papa's head like a halo.

Or maybe his hair was catching on fire. The top of his head was less than an inch from the edge of the awning. One second, two, and it would be too late.

"God damn you all!" Papa shouted.

"Go inside, Lex! Pack our shit!" Pavel bellowed. "Get ready to run!"

"Oh, Lord Jesus Christ!" Alexei cried, flinging himself at his brothers, hitting, yanking at them. "Oh, God, my Father!" pummeling their backs and shoulders as they held Papa farther out and made ready to pitch him into the street. Was he burning? Was his face turning black? "Saint Sergius, on my soul!" He reached for Fyodor. "Papa! Papa!"

"Stop them!" Papa cried.

Then through all the yelling he heard a voice inside his head: *Will you die for him?* Oh, was it Christ who spoke? Was it the Lord?

"Yes," Alexei said.

That drunken lout, the one who damned you—

"Yes!"

The demon who separated you from me?

"Yes! I will! I will die, I will die!" he yelled, raining fists down on Dmitri's back. "Save him!"

Amen, said the voice.

The brilliant sunlight changed to washes of pink, light blue, lavender, swirls of soft color. The shouting faded and low church bells tolled. Images shifted, altered: his father stood out in bold relief, arms extended, but his brothers became cloudy, insubstantial. Alexei stretched his hands toward Fyodor Pavlovich. A strange pressure built in his shoulder blades, followed by a sharp release.

Alexei had wings. They were feathery and huge, extending on either side of his body.

He had no time for astonishment as somehow they lifted him upward, forward, floating—flying?—over the heads of his brothers. He grabbed his father around the waist, fully expecting it to be a useless action, but he wrestled Papa from the grip of his brothers and swooped upward. Surely he would not be able to hold him, or they would plummet into the alley below if he did.

His father shrieked and struggled. Papa began to burn, his skin to sizzle. Alexei folded the tips of his wings in a shield against the sunshine. Papa clung to him, panting, weeping. His brothers gaped up at the two of them. The crowd in the alley yelled, pointed, running to keep pace as he flew higher, and higher; the pastel washes around him deepened to crimson, indigo, emerald green: stained glass. The soft tolling became a chant he and his brother monks sang at Easter, the Resurrection:

Let my prayer arise. Lord, I have called to thee . . .

For an instant, he was in the monastery, in the stillness and joy, and it was before. All was right with his soul.

"With my soul," he said aloud. He moved his wings, and they flew higher.

"Alyosha, Alyosha," his father murmured, clinging to him. "What is happening? Where are we going?"

His father began to glow, and then to burn, flames dancing in his hair, over his face. But he didn't seem to feel it. The tips of Alexei's wings caught fire. Orange flames, blue, the purest white.

"Fear not," Alexei said. In Holy Scripture, the first words angels said to those who saw them.

Having risen from sleep, we fall down before thee.

He flew higher still, and everything that was not of God was left behind. Blazing like a comet toward the golden sun, the smile in the whirlwind, the gates of heaven.

THE NECESSITY OF PRAGMATIC MAGIC

by Jennifer Brozek

Maureen stood near the museum's front door. As the only paid docent for the Stewart Historic Museum, she was part greeter, part information desk, and part receptionist. Today, she waited for the postwoman. Her first tour didn't start for an hour and that was if anyone showed up on a Monday morning. Not likely, but she always put on a good face for the museum.

Kulwinder, the small Indian mail carrier who worked the downtown area of Kendrick, walked up with an armful of boxes. Maureen hurried to open the door for her, dragging a small cart behind.

"Thank you. Thank you," Kulwinder said as she settled the stack of boxes onto the surface provided.

"What happened to your pushcart?"

"Wheel fell off. Wouldn't you know it? I have to fix it later. How come . . . ?" The postwoman gestured to the museum cart.

Maureen's eyes wrinkled as she smiled. "Had a hunch and I've learned to listen to them after all these years."

"Good woman's intuition." Kulwinder gestured with her chin. "One of those packages is from Egypt. Marked 'Important.'" She hesitated. "Feels funny."

Tilting her head, Maureen asked, "Funny-haha or funny-bad?"

The postwoman realized what she'd said and shook her head. "Don't mind me. Just an odd day." She hurried away with a backward wave of the hand.

Maureen watched her go, then considered the cart of mail. People who said things "felt funny" were usually right. That, coupled with this morning's intuition, meant that the "important" package needed a bit more attention than usual and she would have to keep an eye on it. She wheeled the cart to the main curator's office. Raven, the curator's secretary, wasn't at her desk, but the curator's office door was open and Mr. Harold Sperling was in. As usual, Harold was knee-deep in the unending museum paperwork.

She knocked on his doorjamb. "Mail's here. Something interesting." The distracted man looked up. He had the impatient look her son often had on his face just before he moved out. Maureen smiled. "It's from Egypt." She pointed at the brown, well-taped box. "But if you'd rather I just put it in your mail slot . . . ?"

He sighed and wiped his face with a hand. "No. I need a break anyway. Bring it here." He gave her a wry smile as she wheeled the cart over. "Got one of your feelings?"

Maureen shrugged. She kept her opinions to herself. Harold was open-minded—one had to be when living in a special city like Kendrick—but it was best to keep some things to herself.

Harold picked up the "important" package and peered at the return label. "Hmm. No name, but Egypt. I'm not familiar with the area. I wonder if this was supposed to go to the Kendrick Museum of Art and Science. No harm taking a look. Then I'll give

Susan a call." He shrugged, picked up a box cutter, and began to cut open the tape with careful, tiny movements. It took a full minute for him to cut enough of the package tape to open the box. As he put down the box cutter with one hand, he grabbed a pair of well-used cotton gloves with the other, putting them on as a force of habit.

Inside the box was a paper-wrapped object, surrounded by straw. The object, heavier than it appeared, thumped to the table. Harold paused, tilting his head as he frowned at it.

"What is it?" Maureen leaned forward to see it.

"Oh, you're still here. Well then . . ." Harold shook his head as if clearing it. He untied the string, letting the paper fall away. Inside was a worn stone tablet the size of a large book. Covering most of it were whorls and swirls of decoration. They seemed to come from the bottom right corner of the tablet, where the rough figure of a man appeared to play a pipe.

Maureen shifted to get a better look. Something about the image struck her as familiar but she couldn't place it. "What is it? A music player?"

"Perhaps. It would seem to be a celebration of music, considering how much of the tablet is taken up by these swirls. Assuming that's what they represent. You can't make assumptions." Harold spoke in an offhand, lecturing way that faded as he looked closer at the artifact. "See here, while there's the musician, the pipe does seem to be what it appears to be, there's this bold line here, separating the musician from the . . . music? Maybe. I'm not certain."

Maureen gazed at the engraved line Harold indicated. It did seem to separate the musician and the music. Almost like a barrier. She wondered if the piper was keeping something at bay. Again, the nagging sense of familiarity came to the forefront. She almost had it. "Is there anything on the back?"

Harold shook himself again. "Don't you have other duties, Mrs. Burton?"

She took a step back. "I do. I'm sorry for rushing you. Would you like the rest of your mail here or . . . ?"

"Put it in my box. You've given me enough work to deal with for one morning." He didn't look at her as he turned back to the package the stone tablet had been wrapped in. "Egypt," he muttered, already lost in thought once more.

Maureen glanced at the tablet, then wheeled the mail cart out. She didn't like it. She couldn't put her finger on why, but she knew she did not like it at all.

>——<

Maureen sat in the greeter's chair reading a book. Monday afternoons were slow. She often alternated between the information desk and the greeter's chair to keep things interesting. Today, she wanted to be near the exits of the building. She didn't know why, she just knew it was how she felt, and at her age of seventy-one, she'd learned to follow her instincts and urges.

Closing the book, Maureen sighed. She looked at the cover. It was a British murder mystery by one of her favorite authors, but she couldn't remember what it was about. She couldn't concentrate. "It's a strange day," she murmured.

A scream ripped the air from the direction of the administrative offices. Maureen dropped the book into her chair and was already hurrying that way before she identified the source of the short, sharp scream: Raven, Harold's secretary.

Maureen was the second person to reach her. Ethan, the barista from the small museum café, was there, hovering about the woman with red and blue hair. They both looked frightened.

". . . nightmare. Daymare. I don't know. I dreamed that I was trapped in a cave and there were spiders all around me. I could hear them in the dark. Moving. Whispering." Raven shuddered.

Ethan, barely eighteen, shoved his hands in his pockets. "Want some coffee? I mean, if you're tired?" He looked way out of his depth and implored Maureen to save him with a frantic look.

Raven turned to Maureen. "I wasn't asleep. Not really. It was like I was daydreaming, but I couldn't wake up. I've never . . . This has never happened to me before."

Maureen nodded, touching Raven's shoulder with a soothing hand. "Of course not." She meant the words. In the six years Maureen had worked here—two part time, four full time—Raven had never dropped off for a nap while she was on duty. "I'm sure some peppermint tea will do the trick. Plenty of sugar and milk, if that's the way you like it."

Peppermint was one of those herbs that held a natural kind of magic that lent itself to the spell she'd augment it with as soon as she got to the café. Cleansing, happiness, healing, love, protection. All of these things were needed. Perhaps more.

Both Ethan and Raven nodded. They relaxed as Maureen took charge of the situation. "I can get it for you," Ethan said.

Something niggled against her mind and she spurred the two of them onward with a gentle command. "Please, get one for me, too, if you wouldn't mind. And Raven, go splash some cold water on your face."

Raven stood as if snapping to attention. "Yes. Yes. I must look a mess."

Maureen watched both of them go in opposite directions, then headed deeper into the administrative side of things down the back hallway. Just as she reached the break room—that was next to the mail room and one of the filing rooms—a man down the hall gave a muffled shout. Maureen abandoned her previous thought and took off in a hurry toward the voice. Jack, the museum's maintenance man, if she wasn't mistaken.

Jack burst out of one of the storage rooms and sprinted to the back door. He slammed it open without a pause and stopped when he made it to a shaft of sunlight. He turned his face to the sun and spread his arms wide as if bathing in it.

"Jack?"

He shook himself, then gave her a sheepish smile, but didn't move from the sunbeam. "Bad dream. I don't usually nap at work, but . . ." He stopped. "It wasn't a nap. I wasn't asleep, but I wasn't awake. I was daydreaming."

"Daydream nightmare?"

He nodded. "I was in darkness and suffocating. It was like the darkness itself had weight." He shook himself again, a full-body gesture almost like a shudder. "Just needed to see the sun."

After a couple minutes of silence, Jack glancing between her and the sky, Maureen beckoned him back into the museum. "Come on in and get some peppermint tea from the café. It's a good time for it. I'm getting some myself." As Jack did, Maureen knew something very strange was happening to the denizens of the museum. Right now, peppermint tea was what would help everyone, but she needed a better answer. There was only one person she could turn to.

>–<

Felicia opened the door before Maureen knocked. "What?"

"A pleasure to see you too, dear."

The other older woman stepped back, letting Maureen into her tidy cottage. "It's not Wednesday for tea. I could feel you coming miles away—all the way from the museum. Something's wrong. What?"

Maureen clasped her hands together. "You *do* care."

"I care about my solitude, my games, and my time. The sooner I help you with whatever it is, the sooner I get back to my routine." Felicia paused and peered at Maureen's face, glanced at the clock, and scowled some more. "Shall I put tea on?"

"Please."

Maureen waited until Felicia returned with a tea tray. She smiled as she noted that her cranky friend had added finger sandwiches, fruit, and cheese wedges to the usual small tea cakes and cookies. "Something's up at the museum. I think it has to do with a package that just arrived from Egypt."

"But you don't know?"

"No."

"All right, tell me."

Maureen told the tale from beginning to end, starting with Kulwinder's arrival and ending with the mini tea party in the museum café. "Everyone huddled together like they needed protection. I didn't feel any of the bad vibes. I don't know why not. But the most interesting thing is the fact that Mr. Sperling didn't poke his head out of his office, even though Raven screamed right outside it. Nor did he answer my knock."

"What did you wear today?" Felicia took a sip of her tea.

"What I'm wearing now. I came . . ."

She stopped as Felicia shook her head impatiently and asked again, "What did you *wear* today?"

"Oh. Yes. Well, my usual protections and wards against that which would harm me."

Felicia gestured her cup at Maureen. "Clearly they worked. That's why you're fine. Now. What do you want from me? Why aren't you going to the Wilson girl to solve this problem?"

"Karen Wilson?"

"She's the only Master of the City representative I know of. She's the one who deals with things like this." Felicia took a vicious bite of a finger sandwich.

Ignoring the implied threat, Maureen shook her head. "We all like the Wilson girl . . ."

"Speak for yourself."

". . . but she doesn't have any actual magical power. She's mundane but she's got allies and she did get adopted by a baby gargoyle which links her into that set. Still, it's not like she could do anything about this herself."

"Then her allies could take care of it."

Maureen sipped her tea, watching Felicia over the rim of the teacup. "The Stewart Historic Museum may be the smallest regional museum in Kendrick, but it's *my* museum and I am asking you for help. I don't want my little museum to come to the attention of the Wilson girl, her allies, or the Master of the City. That's borrowing trouble when I don't need it. At least, not until we've solved the problem. Please?"

Scowling all the more, Felicia took another bite of her sandwich, then gestured it at Maureen to continue.

Satisfied that she was going to get her way, Maureen pursed her lips, thinking. "The stone tablet. There's something about it. Something I don't recognize, but *you* might."

"Me?"

"Well, you have a different way to your magic than I do. You might . . . you know?"

Felicia clunked her teacup down. "I'm not a black witch. I simply do not suffer fools. At all. I am a *pragmatic* witch. If someone gets hurt in the process, they deserve what they get."

Maureen let out a slow breath through her nose. "Like I said, you have a different way about you and your magic than I do. You may have come across this in your . . . pragmatic way. Will you help?"

"Will it get you to leave me alone quicker?"

"Yes."

"Fine. What do you want to do?"

"Come to the museum tomorrow and help me figure it out."

Felicia shook her head. "No."

Maureen tilted her head in a question.

"No," Felicia repeated. "If I'm going to do this, we go now, to-night, and nip this thing in the bud before it has time to grow."

"But the museum isn't open right now."

"Do you really want the public around when I use my 'pragmatic magic' to fight something from a stone tablet? Do you?"

It was Maureen's turn to frown. "No. Not really."

Felicia stood. "Fine. Let's get ready. Do you need anything from your house?"

"No . . ." she said, looking Felicia up and down. "I have my satchel with me. But there is one thing . . ."

>—>—<

"I hate you so much," Felicia growled, her arms crossed. "I do *not* want to wear that ugly thing." She glared at the blue canvas vest with "Docent" emblazoned on its front and back in white.

Maureen's face remained passive, pleasant, and uncompromising. "All docents need to wear these. It's the only way you'll be allowed in the back hallways. Please?"

Felicia snatched the vest with a scowl and put it on. "You owe me for this."

"I know." Maureen gave her a once-over and nodded her approval. They both wore comfortable black pants and black shirts along with the docent vests. They also had identical satchels over their shoulders—embroidered with colorful symbols, patterns, and swirls. Felicia's curly gray hair had been pulled back into a low ponytail. "You look respectable."

"I'll teach you about respect . . ."

"More to the point, you look like you belong. A docent-in-training if the night guard catches us doing something we shouldn't." Maureen kept her voice light and unconcerned.

"We're standing in the darkened parking lot of the closed museum. Of course we're doing something we shouldn't."

"Now, now. No one knows whether I bring prospective docents in after hours for training. It's a plausible enough story. Besides, you were the one who said we need to do this now."

Felicia waved a hand. "Fine. Let's get on with it."

The two of them walked up to the back entrance to the museum. Maureen stopped and looked at the cars parked next to the building. "Looks like Harold's car and Joseph's car."

"And they are . . . ?"

"Harold Sperling, the curator. He's usually gone home by now." Maureen flipped through a ring of keys. "Joe's the night security guard. There's two of them. One works three nights a week. The other, Adam, works four nights a week."

"Didn't ask for their life stories." Felicia made a gesture with two fingers and a small glowing glyph hung in the air for a couple of seconds before fading away. "Also, the last fifteen minutes of video surveillance is gone along with the next two hours."

"Felicia!" Maureen paused as she opened the door.

"What? Do you want to be on camera? Also, do you think we're going to do this without any damage?"

The other woman grimaced. "All right. But let's keep the damage to a minimum. Please?"

"I'm the 'pragmatic' one, remember? I'll do what I have to do."

Felicia nodded ahead and down the hall as she closed the door behind them. "You're up."

Joseph Lolen, the night guard, hurried down the hallway toward them. "Maureen? You're not supposed to be here. Did you forget something?" He looked around, nervous and unhappy. "Who's this?"

"This is Felicia. I'm taking her on a tour of the museum before she starts formal docent training." Maureen pointed at Felicia's blue vest.

Joe rubbed the side of his head, his body jerking in small, uncomfortable twitches. "I don't think that's a good idea. That's not standard procedure. There's something wrong here tonight. You two need to go."

Maureen muttered, "Oh, bother." Then she looked Joe in the eye. "It's time for you to take your lunch. You've decided to go to that twenty-four-hour diner on Central Way. You're hungry. You've got the time. I'll be here."

Joe's eyes got a faraway glassy look. "Crystal Creek Café. Right. You'll be here." He drifted past them to the back entrance. "I'm hungry." Without looking left or right, he exited.

As the security guard left, Felicia snorted. "I'm not the only pragmatic witch around here. Even I don't cloud the mind like that on a whim."

Maureen peered down her nose at her companion. "Not a whim. I needed him away from here. He wasn't acting like his normal friendly self. You can feel something coming from that way, can't you?" She gestured down the hallway toward the back offices.

"Yes. Something we need to deal with." Felicia narrowed her eyes before she nodded for Maureen to lead the way.

The two of them moved through the dimly lit hallway until it opened up into the vestibule where Raven usually sat outside the curator's office, the office filing and printer room, and the small break room for the staff. They stopped next to the secretary's desk and gazed at the curator's office door.

"He's still inside. I can feel him."

"I can feel whatever he's doing and it's not good." Felicia stepped forward and touched the doorknob. "Locked." A twist of her ring later, she gestured to the door. "No longer locked. After you."

Maureen gave her a look. "Thank you."

The moment the door was open, Maureen knew that everything that was happening to the museum workers was the fault of the stone tablet and Harold. His usually messy office was even more of a disaster with most of the furniture pushed to the walls, clearing a spot in the middle where Harold Sperling sat cross-legged in the center of a drawn circle. Before him was the stone tablet and a couple of things collected from around the museum. A knife from the 1700s, a small woven basket from the Makah Indian tribe, and several large crystals from the geology exhibit. None of them should've been out of their cases.

Maureen and Felicia stared at the scene for a long minute, taking it in. Felicia clapped her hands a couple of times. Harold did not stir. He seemed to be asleep with his eyes open.

"Well, I've always wanted to knock him upside the head," Maureen said as she reached for a small but heavy statue sitting on a pedestal just outside the doorway.

"Hold your horses." Felicia shook her head. "One, you have no idea what kind of magical barrier is around him. Two, if I'm not mistaken, that's actually a valuable piece of artwork. Three, we know where the entity is. You have no idea where it would go next. Into you? Into me? Use your head, woman."

Glancing down at the statue in her hand, she knew it was just a reproduction of *Sleeping Muse* by Constantin Brâncuşi. The father of modern sculpture, his work was technically perfect, but not especially pretty. She returned it to the pedestal and stared back into the office, taking the scene in again.

They stood that way, side by side, shoulder to shoulder, for a few silent moments.

"I've seen enough," Felicia said as she reached out to the open door and pulled it closed.

"What is it? It's familiar, but . . ." Maureen shook her head. "I can't grasp hold of it."

"Whispers in the dark."

"Meaning?"

Felicia looked troubled. "Just what I said. This is bad. Very bad. I don't know the exact ritual he's doing but we've got to stop him before he finishes it."

"So you know what it is?"

"I've seen . . . *heard* . . . something about it. I thought it was rumors. Legends." Felicia shook her head. "If he finishes, I think all of us will be having nightmares for a long time to come. In any case, all of it is bad news on burnt toast."

"I can see that. Do you know what to do about it?"

The other woman thought for a long moment. She started to speak, then stopped herself several times before she finally asked, "Can you play a musical instrument?"

Maureen blew out a breath. "Ah . . . yes. Badly."

"Can you follow a simple tune and keep it up while all hell breaks loose?"

She saw how serious Felicia was and turned her flippant answer into a short "Yes."

"Good. The first thing we need to do is make sure everyone is out of the museum. The second is that we're going to need a few things." Felicia waved a hand at Maureen. "Go do your mind-clouding thing if there's anyone else in the building."

"There shouldn't be."

"Go check. *Now*. Then we'll get to work."

Maureen was partway down the hall when she stopped. "What are you going to do?"

"Pray." The word fell from Felicia's lips like a heavy stone hitting the ground.

>—<

Much to Maureen's surprise, Raven was still in the museum. She stood in the women's bathroom, staring at her face in the mirror. Her eyes were large, pupils dilated. She didn't react to Maureen entering the lavatory.

"Raven?"

At first, it seemed like Raven hadn't heard Maureen. Then the short woman turned, her multicolored hair fluttering in an unfelt wind. "The music will not hold Him. It failed before. It will fail now."

Goose bumps broke out all over Maureen's body. The voice coming from Raven's mouth did not belong to the secretary. It was deeper. Older. So old. So ancient. What could one do against something so powerful? She gave her head a violent shake, making her fluffy white hair fly. "That's enough of that."

Pulling a bundle of herbs from her satchel, she lit it with an arcane word. When the bundle burned enough to smoke, she blew the flame out, leaving the fragrant herbs to smolder. Maureen blew the smoke into Raven's face.

Raven took an involuntary breath and began to cough. When

she looked up, her eyes got wide with confusion and terror. "Maureen? What?" She looked around. "Why am I here?"

"You're dreaming." Maureen blew more smoke into Raven's face, making her flinch back. She cupped the younger woman under the chin and forced her face up. When their eyes met, she said, "You're dreaming. It was scary but it's fine now. You're going to go home. You're going to leave now. You're not going to stop, though you'll obey all traffic laws. When you get home, you're going to sit in your car and wake up. You were exhausted. Do you understand?"

Raven nodded as Maureen forced the compulsion deep. She hated doing things like this. But, like it or not, sometimes Felicia's pragmatic ways were necessary. Right now, it was more important to get the innocents out of the building than to be gentle about it. They'd never know what danger they'd narrowly avoided.

Though, Maureen considered, as she closed and locked the rear entrance behind Raven, she would have to watch everyone on staff for remnants of whatever it was they were about to expel from her museum.

With Raven escorted out, and a final check that the building was actually empty, Maureen returned to Felicia. The other witch had been busy. She sat outside Harold's office with her colorful satchel at her side. From it, she'd taken some of her personal implements—her ritual knife; incense that was burning; several small bags of salt, now open but still full. There was more, but Felicia struggled to her feet. "Good. I need you to find a wind instrument. A pipe. A flute. Something that you can play."

"Are you going to tell me what we're doing?"

"As soon as I figure it out. And that starts with you getting yourself something you can blow."

"All right. All right." Maureen thought about it. "There's an exhibit of modern-day Pacific Northwest Native American instruments . . ."

"Maureen?"

She focused on Felicia.

"I don't care. Just get it. Things are getting worse, if you hadn't noticed."

Now that she mentioned it, Maureen could feel the tightness of a headache at her temples. "Right." She hurried away. The museum felt abandoned and desolate, even though the evening lights were on. Things seemed to watch her from the shadows as her steps echoed against the tile floor. Yes, things were getting worse. Strong enough to get through her wards.

Fortunately, the specific exhibit she was thinking of was only behind a rope barrier and not behind glass. Maureen didn't want to think what would've happened otherwise. The museum was scraping by as it was. A damaged exhibit could be the end of things. She shook her head. "Don't borrow trouble. You have enough to deal with already."

As Maureen moved through the dim hallways she felt watched. She stopped and listened, trying to find the source of her disquiet. Something whispered in her ear, words too low to understand. She whirled around. Nothing but shadows. Again something whispered in her ear. This time she heard it.

Weak.

She turned to catch sight of movement in shadow.

Invisible old woman.

"No." Maureen shook her head. "Not that." She turned again as a shadow hand stripped her of her satchel.

Useless, unwanted, unloved.

The shadows grew all around her until she could see nothing of the exhibit she'd been headed toward. She stepped backward but the shadows were solid behind her. They closed in, muttering, covering, smothering her.

Weak, old, worthless. Wicked, unwanted, hated. Nothing to this world.

Maureen pushed against the whispers as much as she did the slowly constricting shadows. Her breath came in pants as she felt squeezed physically and mentally. Everything disappeared.

Hag. Hated. Witch. You will die alone and unremarked.

Anger flared at those last words. Maureen forced herself to calm. She knew the whispers were using her own fears against her. The fears of an old woman in a society that does not love or revere the wisdom of age as it once did. The hatred of a society that prized youth above all. The fear of a child rejected by a father who did not want her to follow in her mother's footsteps, who had followed the path of the women in her family for generations.

"Hag, you say? Weak, old, useless? I will show you what this witch can do."

Maureen closed her eyes, blocking the shadows from sight. Tilting her face upward, she found the light within that burned inside all of the women of her family and cupped her hands before her. She felt the warmth of her inner light before she sensed it glowing from her palms. Harnessing her anger and fear, she funneled it through that light and let it be transformed. Peace descended and she opened her eyes.

The shadows were still there but they'd drawn back from her.

"It's time for you to go. I have work to do." She released the transformed power in a single burst of light that banished the shadows that had sought to stop her. Without looking, she reached out a hand and found the satchel that had been pulled from her shoulder. The object of her need before her, Maureen completed her task.

>—><—<

Flute in hand, she walked at a good clip back to where Felicia was waiting. This time, it looked like her peer was ready. She waved the flute at Felicia. "I have it."

"Good. Here's the tune." She hummed a five-note tune. "Got it?"

Maureen twirled her hand for Felicia to repeat the tune. "D . . . E . . . C . . . C . . . G. Okay." She gave an experimental whirl on the flute, taking a couple of times to find the correct notes. She fingered the flute until Felicia nodded.

"That's right. Hold the fourth and fifth notes a touch longer."

Maureen did as she was told. She repeated the musical phrase four times and stopped. "Just keep repeating this?"

"Yes. Don't stop. No matter what happens. Just play the music. Steady and consistent."

"Inside or outside the room?"

Felicia grimaced. "Inside. As soon as I close the door, start. Ready?"

"Ready."

Felicia opened the door and all was set as it was before: Harold in the middle of the room within a ritual circle with the implements and the stone tablet. Though, this time, he, and all the things within the circle, were floating.

Maureen began playing at Felicia's nod. She moved to one side of the room as Felicia walked around the ritual circle, prodding it with a sensibly shod toe. With a grunt, Felicia poured one pouch of salt in a haphazard line on top of one quarter of the circle. She looked over her shoulder, gimlet eyes hard. "Keep playing. It's about to get messy."

Maureen nodded her upper body, not missing a note.

With a breath, Felicia steeled herself and heaved a mighty kick at the quarter of the circle covered in salt. Her foot rebounded against air and she yelped at the pain. "Bastard," she muttered, then reset herself and heaved a second kick at the circle. Again it rebounded. "Third time swings true." On her third kick, Felicia also thrust her ritual knife before her as if stabbing leather.

The sound of tearing fabric ripped through the air.

Maureen shifted to keep Felicia in sight and to blow her musical attack toward Harold through the tear in the ritual circle. Wind buffeted them both as Felicia forced her way into whatever ritual spell Harold was part of. At this point, she was sure that Harold had no idea what he was doing—if it was him in his body at all.

Felicia held out her exposed forearm and slashed it with her knife. Her cries of pain, if there were any, were lost to the howling wind. She chopped the air with her injured arm in the four cardinal directions; blood flew from her wounds to splatter against the basket, knife, and crystals floating in the air. As the crimson droplets struck true, the implements crashed to the ground.

When Felicia's blood struck Harold and the stone tablet, he wobbled but remained in the air and Felicia's blood was sucked into the tablet.

Felicia slashed her already injured arm again before she dropped her knife and grabbed the tablet, pressing her bloody arm to the stone. Harold let out an unearthly shriek.

Maureen bobbled the tune as the sound raked over her mind. It took her a precious moment to regain her fingering. In that one moment, Harold backhanded Felicia hard.

Felicia stumbled back a step but didn't let go of the stone tablet. With her own horrifying shriek, she wrenched herself away from Harold, twisting the cursed thing from him. Still shrieking—this time in the tune that Maureen played—she raised the tablet above her head, then slammed it to the ground with as much adrenaline-fueled anger as she could summon.

The stone tablet broke into pieces and all sound stopped except for Maureen's playing. Harold collapsed to the carpet. Felicia picked up the biggest unbroken piece and looked at it. "You can stop now."

Maureen broke off in midtune. "Are you all right?"

Felicia shook her head. "I've been better. But I'll be fine soon enough."

"Oh, dear. What a mess." Maureen looked around the room. "We need to fix this."

"I'm going to leave that to you." Felicia put the piece of stone into the docent vest pouch pocket. "Keeping this to study. Best if it's not put back together again."

"Yes." Maureen gazed at Harold's unmoving form. "I have an idea. You rest."

><><

"Mr. Sperling? Harold? Are you all right?" Maureen shook Harold's shoulder.

Harold blinked owlish eyes at Maureen. "What? What happened?"

"You hit your head on the desk after you dropped the artifact."

"What? I dropped the artifact?" He looked between Maureen and Felicia.

The two of them nodded and said "Yes" at the same time. Without consulting each other, they both pushed the compulsion deeper into his mind until he could see himself dropping the stone tablet. Maureen eased off as his eyes got wide with the "memory" of what happened.

"I'm so sorry, sir. You were showing it to me." Felicia didn't look a bit sorry. "I guess it was heavier than you thought."

Harold pushed Maureen's hands away and struggled to his feet. "What?" he repeated. "What happened?"

Maureen handed him a paper cup of water. "When you dropped the stone tablet, you dived for it but hit your head. You were bleeding."

He looked at the room and the shards of stone on the floor. "I'm bleeding? Why is my furniture like this?"

"I don't know. It was like that when we entered. I just came to introduce Felicia to you. She's trying out to be a docent like me."

Felicia chimed in, "It seems like a good job for an older woman like me. Good pay, too."

Harold shook his head too vigorously and staggered. Maureen steadied him before steering him to lean against his desk. "No. I'm sorry. Docent isn't a paid position." He glanced at Maureen. "Usually. I still don't know why we pay you. Then again, you do more than docent duties. Always have." He shook his head again, more carefully, holding it with one hand. "I'm afraid the Stewart Museum doesn't even have room for another unpaid docent."

"Are you sure?" Felicia asked, trying and failing to keep the smile off her face.

"I'm sure." He pulled himself together. "Now, if you two would leave me. I need to make sense of this mess." He turned to his desk and frowned. "Why would I move . . . ?"

"Have a good evening, Harold. I'll lock up." Maureen took Felicia by the arm and led her from Harold's office, closing the door behind her.

Felicia made a sound that was half laughter, half snort. "Just wait until he figures out what time it is."

"Are you sure you're going to be fine with that thing?" Maureen nodded to the docent vest pouch pocket.

"Oh, yes. I'm sure it's fine now."

The two of them walked in silence until they got to the museum's back door. Maureen grimaced. "I suppose we ought to let the Wilson girl know about this now."

Felicia scoffed. "Why? We dealt with it."

"Because you were right. She's the Master of the City representative and because we *did* deal with it. This is the sort of thing she'd like to know about. Also, I'm sure one of her allies is going to tell her about the power flare we sent up tonight."

"Point. I could feel you across the museum. What did you have to fight?"

Maureen shook her head. "Nothing too bad. So, you'll do it? The report?"

"That's up to you. Write whatever you want. I'll sign it afterward." Felicia eyed Maureen. "What? Why are you looking at me like that?"

"Docents don't get paid? Weren't you the one to tell me about this job? Paycheck and all?"

Felicia looked away, her nose in the air. "I don't remember."

Maureen put her hand on her hip. "Felicia Care, what did you do?"

The other woman rolled her eyes. "Fine. You won't let it go until I tell you. I convinced some people with more money than sense that this little museum would be the perfect pet project. They pay for you and a little bit more every year and the museum prospers."

"You didn't."

Felicia scoffed. "I did. It got you out of my hair. You wanted company and something to do. I wanted my privacy and solitude. I have my own duties to attend to. It was practical. Besides, you really do a lot more than just docent duties here, don't you? And your museum is thriving just enough, isn't it?"

"I guess it is."

The two of them stood at the museum's back entrance, Felicia looking elsewhere and Maureen smiling at her until Felicia grumbled, "Aren't you going to let me out? That door isn't going to unlock itself."

"Oh, yes." She unlocked and opened the door. "Tea on Wednesday?"

"Don't we always have tea on Wednesday?" Felicia swept out the door and down the stairs. She waited at the edge of the parking lot with an expectant look on her face.

"I'll bring my report with me. You might have one or two things to add to it." Maureen smiled and shook her head before relocking the museum door. She patted the door's metal frame, then joined Felicia, and they both walked to the car with a satisfied step.

DATING TERRORS

by Patricia Briggs

December 1

Ruby woke up drenched in sweat, the essence of magic in her nose and mouth. She'd been dreaming again—for the last month or more, and that usually meant that a change was coming.

Her dreams were prophetic—which usually meant that *after* something horrible happened she could figure out what the vague pictures she'd gleaned from her night terrors had been trying to tell her. This time she had an impression of dark fur and golden eyes.

The terrible thing about this dream had nothing to do with its contents. Her unconscious use of magic had undone all the good that living in the middle of Seattle had done. The protection provided by the buildings of steel and cold iron could not keep her magic from reaching out if she used it in the way the dream had made her use it. The tattoo on her wrist, both a sign of ownership and a tracking sigil, burned.

He was coming.

December 10

To Asil@marrok.com

Goodness, our gift to you has certainly yielded unexpected results, hasn't it? What fun we are all having!

For your information, we have decided your last date was a success for you. Congratulations! Our discussion grew heated at times, but eventually we came to an agreement. During the required two hours of your date, no one ran screaming into the night. All deaths happened after the required time, so we feel they were irrelevant. Good for you! Three down, two to go.

Your next date is scheduled for Tuesday in Seattle. Please note the attached emails between *you* and your date from the Internet site HauntedLove.com, which, they advertise, is a site for ghost hunters who want to hunt with like-minded people who are still breathing. She is worried about meeting a strange man alone, so your date will begin with a ghost hunting session with her whole team: afterward, should you both choose to do so, you can take her out to dinner. Try not to kill all of them—at least not until your two-hour goal is achieved. They may come back to haunt you, and ironic twists generally should be avoided.

We are very happy you have emerged from your hermitlike existence and feel the credit should be given to us and our gift to you this holiday season.

Merry Christmas,
Your Concerned Friends

To ConcernedFriends@marrok.com

Irrelevant. That is an interesting word for the results of the last
date you arranged for me.
 Inshallah.
 I accept your gift which keeps on giving—though I feel it *is*
relevant to remind you, again, that I am not a Christian. Giving
me a Christmas gift seems inappropriate for this enlightened and
woke era.

Asil

————

To Asil@marrok.com

The gift honors the giver. And what, exactly, do you mean by "woke"?

>—>—<—<

A few wet snowflakes dropped onto Asil's windshield, making up
in mass what they lacked in frequency. Wiper squeaking, Asil
drove up the narrow mountain that led nowhere but the house of
the Alpha of the Emerald City pack in the wilds outside Seattle.

 The log mansion sprawled half-hidden in a canopy of trees, a
fair blend of practicality and beauty. He pulled in next to the only
other occupant of the fair-sized parking lot, a battered Ford Bronco.
The dented rust-red hood sported a layer of snow, indicating that
it had been parked for a few hours but not all night.

 Asil got out of his car and took a deep breath of the frigid air,
testing the smells of the woods of the Cascades against the woods
of his home. Against the woods of his *current* home.

This forest smelled, not unpleasantly, of moist and rotting organic matter, even under its white coating. In Montana, fifteen below zero did not allow for much moisture in the air no matter how much snow was on the ground. He judged the current local temperature somewhere in the high twenties because the snow was what his young friend Kara liked to call "fighting ready" because it would be easily gathered into balls to pelt others with.

One moment he was thinking of a snowball fight Kara had initiated that had eventually enveloped most of the pack, the next he was ambushed by the scent of another wood, the unique smell of his home, his real home. A scent that now existed nowhere in the world.

His breath caught and he closed his eyes, imagining himself . . . home.

For a moment he almost had it. The warmth of the sun, the rich scent of flowers and fruits—his mate's cooking filling the air. Ah, Sarai. He could feel the stone path under his feet, see the warm glow that leaked out of windows, knew that all he had to do was walk into the house and he would see her.

But part of him understood that the house that had been his home and the fields and groves surrounding it had been gone for centuries. Understood that his mate, his Sarai, was dead.

It seemed like he would be caught forever in that long-ago moment, stuck betwixt and between, unable to walk forward into the home he had shared with his mate or return fully to the present. It was a subjective eon, but only a few seconds in real time before the reliving passed as they all had so far, and he stood, once again, on a mountainside next to his car.

He missed his dead mate so much that his lungs refused to move and his heart forgot how to beat. If he could only turn back centuries and exist in a time where his Sarai lived. He stood beside the open door of his car, put his head down, and fought to breathe through the pain.

He had not been able to figure out if such moments signaled an attack by the wolf who shared his battered, worn-out soul, or if it was some trick of the half of his brain that was human. But he had not had such a strong remembrance since his stepdaughter had died, at last, a few short years ago.

He had hoped he was done with them.

The brisk mountain air cleared his head, but he wondered if he was fit to take a woman on a date today. He needed to go back to the Marrok's pack where there was someone strong enough to stop him if he lost control of his wolf. Someone merciful enough to end him if he did not emerge from one of those relivings. He would call and cancel this foolishness.

In response to that thought—and he was certain that it was absolutely in response to that thought—a sudden cool shiver traveled through him from head to toe. For that single moment he felt as though something, someone, turned their attention to him. And then the moment was gone.

"Inshallah," he said, momentarily shaken. Then, a fierce grin, his wolf's grin, stretched the cold skin of his face. It appeared that he was going on a date.

The door to the big house opened and a man walked out. Unlike Asil, he did not bother with a coat—werewolves don't feel the cold the way humans do and this wolf had no need to blend in. But he wore boots designed to handle the treacherous ground of winter.

He was bigger than Asil—not an unusual thing as Asil was not a tall man. The stranger's face was scarred—it looked like the marks of a knife. He carried authority on his shoulders with the unconscious grace of someone who was used to being in charge and getting things done, a mantle worn by people who know what it was to kill in order to protect their own.

What he was not was the Alpha of the Emerald City pack.

The world brightened and the shadows lost their power as Asil's beast, restless from the last few minutes, rose in affront at the insult. The Moor was not a lesser foe, someone to be handed off to lackeys. Maybe, a small part of him observed, it wasn't only the wolf who was unsettled.

The big man stopped where he was and his irises glinted with secret gold. He closed his eyes and fought to hold his beast in check when Asil's wolf's call had stirred it to violence.

"My Alpha's apologies," said the man, keeping his eyes closed. He bit out those first three words as though every syllable caused his tongue to bleed. But he regained control of his voice and muted it to more courteous tones. "He had intended to be here, but one of our pack had a run-in with the police and he had to go negotiate that wolf's release."

And he had been deemed the lesser threat? Asil half lidded his eyes to better disguise his next course of action, deliberately keeping his muscles loose so the other wolf would not know when the attack would come.

"My Alpha said," continued Not-the-Alpha, "if the Moor wishes us to die, we will die. He does not need me to give him leave to come to my city, it is a courtesy that he comes to us. Tell him that he is at all times a welcomed guest to me and mine, a thing freely given that we acknowledge the Moor could have taken if he chose."

It was truth couched in terms of flattery. Asil relaxed and half smiled in appreciation of the clever wording that had been de-signed to hold him in chains of courtesy. That the word "guest" bound not only the Emerald City pack but also Asil to an ancient and unwritten set of laws that this pup was probably too young to understand, though his Alpha, a cunning and vicious chess player, well knew how Asil would hear them.

Asil's wolf was touchy and inclined to violence at the best of times—and after a brush with old memories, the beast very much wanted to put this wolf before them on his knees, presenting his throat.

Asil reminded his wolf they were guests—and moreover that they had things to do. He had that date, one of a set that had somehow altered from challenges to missions. If he'd had any doubt about that at all, it had been banished by the moment where Allah had turned His attention to Asil.

This was not the first time in his long life that it had been given to him to be the hand of Allah. It was merely the first time it had been so clearly indicated. It was wiser, he had found, not to balk at tasks so set.

He contained his wolf after a struggle that was more difficult than he liked. Once that was done, for the moment at least, he considered the words he'd been given.

The Emerald City pack had just offered him a key to their territory, and such things could bite back. He did not intend to do anything this day that should reflect badly upon the pack. And by the nature of guesting laws, if that changed, all he would have to do would be to notify Angus, Alpha of the pack, directly before all hell broke loose. For this short time period, the hospitality offered should pose no trouble.

"I accept those terms," Asil said.

The other wolf looked at him, his eyes still wolf and wild. Asil's wolf told him that, though strong of will and power, this one had not yet seen half a century as moon called. He was thus vulnerable to the wild turbulence of Asil's wolf, especially as unsettled as this other wolf was, a dominant having given a message of submissive to a strange wolf.

It was not Asil's purpose today to abuse his just-accepted status as guest by forcing this perfectly fine and trusted member of Angus Hopper's pack to attack him so Asil's wolf could taste his blood. He had assumed that the brief moment of epiphany, of purpose, had brought his wolf back from instability. But his eagerness to taste this young strong wolf's blood was proof that Asil's self-assessment of how well he was controlling his wolf was demonstratively wrong.

If not for his understanding that this mission was important, he would have driven back to Montana. The Marrok was too far away to help him. The Omega wolf Anna was too far away to help him. It was such moments that reminded Asil just why he had given up his Alpha status in Spain to travel all of the way to the backwoods of Montana.

He had only himself here. He pulled that old wolf back and tucked him deeper into his mind, trapping him in the steel of his will. And that will, the will of the Moor, was enough—as it had always proved to be enough. But Allah knew, as did Asil, some time, not too far from this, even Asil would be overmatched against the great old beast who owned his soul.

As soon as Asil battened down his wolf, the other man turned, putting his back to Asil. "Sorry," he said. "I'm sorry. Give me a minute." And quietly he muttered, "I didn't expect . . . well." He shut up.

He had good control for one so young. Asil felt the drop in tension as if it had been a balloon pierced by a nail. When the other turned around, his eyes were human blue and they met his own frankly before dropping in deference to Asil's dominance.

"I'm Tom Franklin," he said, "Angus's second. In the name of my pack, I bid you welcome to Seattle."

>—≺

Ruby sat on the front porch of the huge old Victorian mansion that was the subject of their current ghost hunt while winter rain pounded the roof overhead and rushed merrily out of aged, but mostly intact gutters. Normally she'd have been helping to place the team's cameras and various bits and pieces of electronic gadgetry, but not today.

She should have been traveling in a bus headed for some anonymous city where she could lose herself again. Instead she sat on the railing surrounding the Victorian's extensive covered porch, her back against one of the square posts facing Alan, who was similarly situated at the opposite post.

They waited for her Internet date to show up so they could use him to kill a monster.

"It's perfect," Alan's wife, Miranda, had said enthusiastically.

Miranda had caught Ruby packing to run. Her very pregnant downstairs neighbor and best friend was a force to be reckoned with. Ruby found herself making tea and telling Miranda the whole story—something she had sworn never to do again. Miranda had summoned Alan—who had come up with a solution: a blind date.

"Perfect?" Ruby had said, repeating Miranda's words incredulously. "Take some poor werewolf who is already being pranked with blind dates from Internet dating sites—and throw him into a battle to the death?"

Miranda shrugged. "You don't know these kinds of werewolves the way I do. Those old ones, the powerful ones, they deserve everything they get."

Both Alan and Ruby had known that Miranda was talking about Alan's Alpha.

Alan had laughed. "This will be fine. I called up an old friend who knows this wolf. Unless your captor is one of the fae's Gray Lords—" He paused with a little question in his voice and Ruby shook her head. He wasn't that, she was sure. She'd seen him bow and scrape before other fae. A Gray Lord wouldn't do that.

"Then this Asil Moreno can handle him. My contact was pretty sure he wouldn't even be upset about it. He has something of a hero complex." Alan frowned a little. "Unusual first name. I feel like I should know something about that name."

"He's old," said Miranda briskly. "You've probably run into someone who told you a story about him or something."

Ruby thought, *I bet he won't be so quick to use a dating site after we get through with him.* And felt horridly guilty.

"Moreno comes here," Miranda pronounced blithely. "You be nice to him long enough that he likes you."

"Sort of like a hooker," muttered Ruby. Being nice to people wasn't her best thing.

Miranda smacked her hand lightly. "And then you use magic. Your tormenter, called by your magic, appears to take you. And this werewolf kills him. Easy."

Even Alan had given Miranda a thoughtful look at that. "Easy," he murmured. "Hmm."

And that was why Ruby was watching the rain pour down instead of being miles away. She had her earbuds in, listening to music, because music calmed her down and Alan had warned her that she didn't want to be in a full-blown panic when her date appeared.

She didn't hear Alan's phone ring, but she saw him put it to his ear. After a moment, his head tilted just a little away from her as if he was watching the rain fall on the mostly quiet road. If she hadn't known him so well, she probably wouldn't have known he was making sure she couldn't read his lips.

It was a moot gesture, because half a second later, quiet, sweet Alan said something in Mandarin in tones that made the words a universal curse.

Her noise-canceling earphones were not designed to quiet raised voices. She pulled them off as soon as he disconnected. He grimaced. "Stevie Nicks? Really?" Alan liked his music modern and raucous or classical, and nothing in between.

"Stuck in the eighties," she said without apology. "Do you need to go? Family emergency?" More quietly, "Miranda?"

She didn't think it would be Miranda. If something had gone wrong there, he wouldn't be hanging around with that look on his face—he'd have been off the porch and running for his car. But Alan's family owned an herbal shop and Alan should have been there helping out. He'd taken the day off for her sake.

"No," he said. "That was Tom."

Tom was Alan's packmate, second only to Angus Hopper in the pack that ruled Seattle.

"What did Tom have to say?" she asked. "Pack business?"

Alan sighed. "I wish. Sort of. Your date—"

"The werewolf with the hero complex and the kind of friends who set him up on blind dates for their own entertainment?" she inquired.

Alan was upset enough he didn't snark back. Instead he said, "You know when werewolves enter another pack's territory they have to check in with the Alpha."

She nodded. He'd already told her that was going to happen.

"Angus was tied up and he had Tom do the welcome." Alan said. "Tom just got through talking with him. We might have to rethink this whole thing."

"He's not strong enough?" Ruby asked.

"Tom said Moreno is scary as hell." Alan's voice was neutral.

"Which is what I need," Ruby said slowly, wondering not for the first time why she'd let Miranda talk her into this. "Scary as hell" did not sound at all reassuring.

Alan nodded. "Yes. But maybe not this scary. I think I'll call my packmate, the one who let me know about the way Asil Moreno was set up with these dates. He's met this wolf. He's the one who told me Moreno could run off anything bad we were likely to run into. Let me grill him a bit. If I don't like his answers, we'll call the whole thing off."

"Can we?" she asked. Alan was a submissive wolf—low in the pack power structure. She was pretty sure that her blind date wasn't a submissive wolf.

Alan dropped his chin and looked away. "Maybe. Probably. Go back and listen to some Air Supply and I'll figure something out."

She'd met Alan and Miranda a half dozen years ago. He shouldn't have belonged to the small group of lesser magically enhanced people, including Miranda and Ruby, who had clustered together for mutual protection. As a werewolf, Alan was much more capable of defending himself than any of them were, and he also had a pack of stronger wolves to back him up.

But a couple of the witches in Ruby's group of friends bought herbs from his shop and brought him with them to one of their meetings. His soft, unthreatening manner had quickly led them all—Ruby included and she was as wary as a beetle in a henhouse— to consider him one of theirs. He'd married Miranda, the only one of their group with enough magic to mix anything stronger than sleeping draughts, a couple of years ago. There was no question that Alan made their little group of mostly powerless misfits safer than they'd ever been.

Alan never complained about playing guardian, but he'd also never claimed to be a power in his own right. The werewolf part was enough to keep most of the other predators at bay, though. Larger predators walked warily in Seattle because his pack was diligent about removing anyone who made trouble on that scale.

She worried someday they'd ask Alan to help them—and he'd get hurt or die trying to keep one of them safe. She hoped it wasn't today.

She should have left Seattle already. She was going to get someone killed. Again.

Ruby hadn't stayed alive and free as long as she had by playing long shots. She'd agreed to this ridiculous scheme because Miranda had been frighteningly adamant—and there wasn't much Ruby wouldn't do for her. And because the only bit of her prophetic dream, the one that had cost her so much, that Ruby remembered was the dark fur and golden eyes of a werewolf—and that werewolf had not been Alan Choo.

She rubbed her wrist, feeling guilty, scared, and unhappy. Well, the guilty she might be able to do something about. Alan seemed pretty sure Moreno would help if asked. She just wouldn't ask him.

This wasn't the first time she'd escaped—though this was the longest her escape had lasted. She wondered, bleakly, if she shouldn't stop trying to get away. He would, eventually, kill her. The first time he'd caught her, she'd had people who tried to help her—they had all died. She hadn't tried to find help again. Until now.

She rubbed her wrist where the tattoo burned.

"This is wrong," she told Alan. "I can't bring someone else into my trouble. And this poor man doesn't even know what he's getting into. He thinks we're going to explore a haunted house and eat dinner."

"Ruby," said Alan in the tone of a man called upon to use more patience than he had.

"He's a werewolf. Not someone who uses magic as a weapon," she said, as she had when this had first been proposed. She hoped Alan would be more reasonable than his wife had been. "That's like wielding a club at a submachine gun."

"Hold up," Alan said. "I understand you are having second thoughts—I might be too, if for a different reason. I need to make a call before we have the wolf, himself, at our door."

Moreno was supposed to be here in a half hour.

Alan met her eyes. "Ruby, I have been assured this wolf can help. He apparently is a most efficacious club. But I need to make sure you will be safe with him." His eyes narrowed and he brought out the big guns. "Afterward feel free to explain to me why you aren't going to try everything we can come up with in order to be here for Miranda when the baby's born."

She gave a huff of frustration. "All right," she said, because her common sense was no match for Alan's ploy. They both loved Miranda.

He nodded. "Okay. I can't have you overhearing our secrets, Ruby. Not even you. Put your earbuds in and let me make a call."

She did as he asked—though not Air Supply. Twisted Sister seemed more appropriate somehow. She closed her eyes because she didn't want to betray Alan by reading his lips—because he was right, she could do that.

But not even "Hot Love" could keep her from hearing Alan say, "What do you mean Asil Moreno is *the Moor*. You had me arrange a date for Ruby with *the Moor*?"

Ruby pulled out her earphones and met Alan's horrified gaze.

Problem? she mouthed.

He nodded, looking wild-eyed. He concluded his call but kept his phone in hand. "I'm canceling this," he said. "Dangerous is one thing. Messing around with the Moor is out-of-the-fire-into-the-frying-pan business."

Unfortunately, before he could make a call—or explain to Ruby who the Moor was and why that had changed Alan's mind, the Subaru with Montana plates they'd been told to look for splashed through the temporary stream where pavement met sidewalk and stopped. Her date was here. Twenty minutes early.

Alan gave a frustrated growl and said hurriedly, just before the engine stopped, "Treat him like you would Angus, if Angus were both crazy and ten times as dangerous as he is."

The Subaru's door opened. Alan shut his mouth and visibly tried to get control of himself.

Out of the mud-spattered car, the most beautiful man she had ever seen emerged. He glanced at them, then walked around the front of his car. He strode through the downpour with no more notice than if he'd been walking through dry sunshine as his shirt darkened and clung to every cut inch of him. It was an effect she'd have expected in a men's cologne commercial or one of those racy Calvin Klein ads. She'd never seen anything like it in real life.

He stepped across the torrent of water without visible effort or a break in stride. His movement made her mouth dry and her pulse speed up—not a reaction she welcomed just now.

His skin was dark and his features were Arabic—"the Moor" might be as much a description as an epithet, she thought. As he got closer, she could see his eyes; the color made her think of liquid bitter chocolate. It made her nervous that her mind was giving her edible similes to describe him. This wasn't really a date.

The photo on his profile had been a rose. She'd thought, casually, that it might be to conceal a blemish. She hadn't considered that it might be to keep him from getting millions of queries and unsolicited offers of modeling contracts.

He was no more than average height, maybe less. His hair was short, as dark as his eyes, and it curled just slightly in the rain. There were no age lines on his face, but she knew better than to expect that with a werewolf.

He didn't look crazy. Or even particularly dangerous—or at least not dangerous in any way that didn't have to do with sex.

>×<

The address Asil had been given belonged to a grand old Victorian that reigned supreme on a quiet street of lesser houses. The light snow in the mountains had given way to a heavy, cold rain and he was soaked to the skin before he had even shut the car door.

His date sat on the wall of the porch, safe and dry. A man with Asian features stood near her. The man was a werewolf. Even the rain could not hide his scent from Asil.

He considered how that changed the game he was playing as he made the wet journey onto the porch. The werewolf kept his gaze on Asil's shoes—but the woman had no trouble meeting his gaze; her own carried a challenge and, he thought, a reluctant interest. The werewolf, on the other hand, smelled terrified—but Asil was used to dealing with such a reaction.

Ruby Kowalczyk looked a lot like her photograph—which people didn't always. She wore tight pants that followed the muscled curves of her body until they—the pants and the curves both—disappeared into the loose flowing blouse hanging halfway down her leg. The feminine blouse was balanced by black combat boots.

Her red-brown hair was in a neat braid, revealing her strong jaw and straight nose without precisely flattering her. Her ice-blue eyes were framed in dark lashes sparkling with glittery mascara. She looked, maybe, nineteen.

But Asil's wolf knew better. The air carried her scent to him through the winter rain—something magical and old—though not anywhere as old as he was. Fae, he thought, or half-fae. Enough blood to give her long life and the power that roiled and coiled about her but was oddly contained. Trapped. He didn't know how his wolf knew all of that, but he'd long since ceased doubting anything the old beast told him with such surety.

Her profile had said she was around thirty, a bookstore clerk and amateur but experienced ghost hunter. His had listed his age as thirty-five, a financier with a yen for adventure. Ghost hunting experience: interested novice.

He was pretty sure she had only lied about her age—which was a woman's prerogative, after all—and the mealy word "around" could be stretched to gossamer to prevent a lie. In his experience half-fae could lie—but most of them tended not to. His own profile had been a lie from start to finish, but then, he wasn't fae and he hadn't written the cursed thing anyway.

Asil ascended the stairs and when he'd reached the dry boards under the porch roof, the other werewolf held out his hand, his gaze never rising above Asil's shoulder.

"Hello," the wolf said. "I'm Alan Choo."

His fingers shook only a little, but his breathing was ragged and Asil could feel the other wolf's tension rocketing to the sky at Asil's touch when he took the offered hand.

Which was unacceptable to Asil and his wolf. The submissive wolves were the heart of the pack, to be protected above all others.

Asil let go of Alan's hand, then reached up to touch his throat with light fingers.

"You are in no danger from me," Asil told him—a little surprised to know he meant it.

It had been a long time since he'd been able to make such a promise to someone who was not an Omega wolf. Alan must be very submissive for Asil's wolf to be so certain—especially after his almost disastrous meeting with Angus's second. But his wolf's determination resonated in a way that Asil had almost forgotten, as if his wolf were stable and sane once more—as it had been a century or two . . . no, four. Four hundred years since he'd felt like this. Calm, centered, certain.

Interesting.

Hearing the truth in Asil's words, Choo took a deep breath and straightened, his body still obviously wrung with adrenaline but settling into calmness, which said good things about how well Angus watched over his wolves.

"Mr. Moreno," said Ruby briskly, dismounting the porch rail and starting toward the door of the house without pausing to actually greet him. "The others are working on setting up our cameras and sound equipment. How about you come with me and I tell you what we are doing and why?"

Gone was the reluctant interest, the nervousness . . . the fear he'd seen in her. She might have been a real estate agent—or a tour guide—surface friendliness used as a barrier to prevent any real interaction. Any intimacy.

It was so forcefully done that Asil felt an involuntary smile spread across his face. Alan Choo made a small, defeated sound, as if he expected a disaster.

"Wait, Miss Kowalczyk." The command in Asil's voice was enough to pull her to a reluctant halt. "We need to discuss a few things first, I think. No?"

>—×—<

Ruby didn't know why she stopped in her tracks. It wasn't because he said her name correctly despite his faint Spanish accent. Spanish was about as far from Polish as it was possible to get.

No. There had been something about the way his voice hit her nervous system that caused her to do what he said without thinking about it. Power with a capital *P*. Fear had her spinning around to face him, unable to let him stand at her back even with Alan there.

He watched her face, the beautiful dark man, frowning a little. For all of Alan's reaction and Moreno's obvious ability to command her movement, she couldn't feel anything odd about him. She could tell when someone had supernatural abilities: witch, werewolf, or fae. She couldn't always tell what someone was, but she could tell they were something. In this moment, he seemed no more than human.

She tried to remember if she'd felt his wolf when she'd first seen him—the way she'd understood Alan was a werewolf before he told her. Because she couldn't feel any of the wildness that usually surrounded werewolves, and that was one of her few talents, even if it worked best on dead people.

She waited for him to do something else to her, but he just watched her with liquid dark eyes. She met his eyes, knowing it was a foolish challenge to a dominant werewolf. For a moment nothing happened—and then she felt as if a veil he held around himself opened to her in a way she wasn't used to with living beings.

Instead of the usual jumble of emotions and thoughts, she received only one overwhelming impression: age. Years and time so deep it caused a resonance in her bones and sent her magic humming—and her wrist burned as if the tattoo caught fire.

She froze, suddenly not at all concerned with the danger in front of her, or the reaction that her instant obedience to his voice had caused in her belly. Because her magic had moved, flexing against the binding, and she felt *him*. Not Moreno, but her monster.

This was not the faint touch of the beginning of a hunt—as she'd felt two weeks ago. He was somewhere near—and he was so hungry. The tattoo on her wrist flared with brutal intensity and she broke into a light sweat as her stomach roiled in terror.

"Ruby?" asked Alan, reading her reaction.

But Moreno just waited. Asil Moreno, who was now her only option for freedom because she'd left running until too late. She looked at the beautiful intruder she'd invited into the one positive thing she managed to do in the world and wondered if she should drag him into her own personal hell.

His lip, she noticed absently as she examined him, was starting to tighten along the edge, hiding a smile—or anger. It was hard to say. But she thought his eyes warmed a bit—though not, she thought, deeply. He held out his hands and, moving his feet minimally like a model, he spun in place until he was facing her again.

Apparently, her examination had been too obvious.

"Ruby," said Alan again—and she heard the alarm in his voice.

"My apologies," she told Moreno. "I—"

He shook his head and raised a hand. "Obviously there is more going on here than a blind date, Miss Kowalczyk. You know who and what I am—" He waved at Alan, indicating without words that she wouldn't have had Alan, the werewolf, with her if she hadn't been expecting a werewolf. "And I know you are of fae lineage." He tapped his nose with one elegant finger as a wash of gold spiderwebbed across his eyes and faded, leaving the original inky brown behind.

She'd never seen anyone's eyes do that; that was not how werewolf eyes turned to wolf. She became aware that Moreno was patiently waiting for her response—so she nodded slowly.

"Really," he said, his voice resigned, "I no longer expect these things to even feel like dates." He considered her, glanced at Alan, and said, "I presume you need my help."

Alan nodded.

"No," she said—responding to his taking her choice away from her. It was irrational to be angry with him for that—he had driven all the way here from somewhere in *Montana* thinking he was going to go ghost hunting and have a nice dinner. And when he figured out they'd had different plans—he'd jumped right in with graciousness she should be grateful for.

She was aware of Alan's mute dismay as she continued, "I don't think my problem has a solution, Mr. Moreno. It is unfair to bring you, a stranger, into my private battle. How about I show you something of what my team can accomplish—let you finish this date without incident as I'm informed there is a betting pool of some sort? Then you can return home in time for your next dating adventure."

She smiled at him, inviting him to accept her word on the matter. "I've had this—" Her tongue stumbled as she tried to find a way to word it so it would not feel like a challenge to him. And it had to be the truth because werewolves could smell a lie. "—*problem* for a long time, and it is unlikely to kill me." No matter how much death would be preferable to the endless cat-and-mouse game.

"*You* do not know who I am," he said slowly.

"The Moor, right?" Ruby said, hoping—after she said it—that it wasn't really an epithet.

But he didn't appear offended. He looked at Alan and, evidently seeing something she didn't in her friend's face, Moreno shook his head and changed whatever he'd been going to say.

He gave her a charming smile, which made him even more beautiful—and she was sure he was secretly laughing at her.

"By all means," he said. "Let's go hunt ghosts."

Behind him, Alan's eyes widened in surprise at Moreno's response. She wondered what Alan had expected the other werewolf to do.

>—<

Asil decided not to argue with her determination to push him away from whatever she'd originally wanted from him. His experience in the past three dates indicated he did not need to force matters—disaster would come in its own time. He braced himself for the rebellion of his wolf at his decision to be patient—and it did not come.

The wolf agreed with his assessment. And he'd scared her once already when she'd instinctively obeyed his command. His wolf was unhappy about that. Asil was intrigued by the strangeness of sharing his skin with a reasonable being.

Today's date was only minutes long, and already it was shaping into something at least as interesting as his last three dates had been.

He followed Ruby and Alan into the mansion and found himself in a large, lightly furnished room awash in colored light filtering down from two gigantic Tiffany stained-glass windows. The effect was modified somewhat by the sound of someone in the heights of the building swearing like a sailor.

Alan and Ruby exchanged a look. Alan said, "Someone needs to keep Terry from killing Peg. If you two will excuse me?" He didn't wait for a reply before running lightly up the stairs.

Ruby watched Alan leave as if he were a life buoy sliding out of her reach. Asil's wolf wanted to go grab Alan and stand him back beside Ruby so she wouldn't be unhappy—but, and this was the amazing part, did not make any move to make that happen.

When Alan disappeared above them, Ruby swallowed. Then she turned to Asil with a bright-fake smile. "Okay, Mr. Moreno—"

"Asil," he told her silkily. "Please."

"Asil," she said without dropping her smile a single watt or making it a degree more real. "Every ghost hunting team I've ever spoken to has a routine they follow when they are looking for hauntings. We start with a walk-through—"

"For psychic impressions," Asil said, not quite interrupting her, but disturbing her rhythm, pushing at her in a way not quite flirtatious. But not quite not flirtatious, either.

She gave him a wary look. "Yes." At least the plastic had gone out of her expression.

"I'm not a psychic," he told her.

"No," she agreed dryly, "it wasn't on your profile."

He almost grinned at the bite in her voice. *There* she was— the real person beneath the mask and the roil of fear and uncertainty.

"I cannot apologize for the profile," he said, a purr in his voice that caused a flush of something she almost controlled. "I didn't write it."

Arousal, his wolf assured him. *The binding spell she wears sometimes hides things from our sense of smell, but look at the darkening of her eyes and the warmth of her skin.*

If the ground had rolled under his feet, he would not have

been more startled than he was at hearing his wolf speak to him. He hadn't spoken to his wolf this way since his wife had last walked beside him. The only other werewolf he knew who spoke to his wolf like this was Charles—one of the myriad of things that made Asil dislike Charles. He was not above admitting to jealousy.

Ruby drew in a deep breath. "Alan's wife and I did a walk-through on this place a couple of weeks ago when the owners first asked us for help."

She paused as if she were waiting for him to throw her off her game again. But he was too busy trying to regroup. He let her pro-ceed unhindered, even though it irritated him when she dropped back behind the safety of her tour-guide mask again.

"We aren't proper psychics. I'm not even sure what makes a 'proper psychic' anyway," she said. "Though I wouldn't admit that in front of another ghost hunting group on pain of death. Miranda is a witch—a white witch, but powerful enough for her kind."

She didn't, he noticed—though he was still half-distracted—say what she brought to the table. The fae were a varied group—and the half-fae were even more so. That her powers were wrapped up so tight meant all she'd have to work with was what managed to escape.

"We also come prepared with the history of the house," she continued briskly. "Some of that we get from the owners, but we do record searches, too. Mostly we don't find anything too useful that isn't already well-known to the owners. A complete history with names and dates isn't necessary to help the spirits anyway."

"Help them?" he asked.

"That's what we do," she said. "Help trapped spirits."

Because you can't free yourself, he thought with sudden under-standing as to why she would feel driven to take up such a hobby. But he didn't say that aloud.

She waited expectantly, but when he kept silent she shrugged and led him into a smaller room off of the entry room.

"This house was built in 1898 and was restored in the eighties by the grandmother of the current owner. There are plans to turn it into a bed-and-breakfast, but those plans are on hold until they can deal with a restless spirit or two. This is the reception room— where the original owner, one Eben Mercanter Benson, welcomed important guests."

Asil looked around the octagonal room. It was a fine example of its type—a room designed to impress guests with the wealth and power of the homeowner. He counted six kinds of wood in the ornate floor, and the oak fireplace mantel made seven. Arching high ceilings were adorned with painted Italianate scenes. The fireplace had been converted to gas sometime in the fairly distant past but still had the original surround.

He touched a sparrow carved into the corner of the mantelpiece with a little smile—it was a charming creature.

Our kind of space, said his wolf. *Beautiful and skillfully wrought— as we are.*

Asil thought a question at his wolf—a wordless, infinite question encompassing the utter strangeness of speaking to each other once again, the change from broken beast to coherent thought. What had changed?

I don't know, the wolf answered. *But it has something to do with her.*

Asil realized abruptly that Ruby had quit talking and turned his gaze from the sparrow. She was watching him with an odd look in her eyes. He gathered together the things she had been saying and came up with a cogent question.

"Are not ghosts an asset in the world of bed-and-breakfasts?" he asked. "Were you asked here to prove it is haunted? And if you free the trapped spirits here, won't you be making their enterprise less successful?"

She smiled and relaxed a little.

Appreciating that we are letting her keep her distance, observed his wolf. *But we are patient hunters.*

Yes, agreed Asil, not at all certain he wanted to take this hunt the same place his wolf did. But he wasn't certain he didn't either.

This *was* a date, no? He was careful not to smile at Ruby just then; she might notice his sharp white teeth.

"Well-behaved ghosts are welcome," Ruby told him. "But apparitions who won't allow guests to sleep are more problematical—and this house has a troublesome poltergeist, a spirit who throws things. My team and I aren't here to provide proof of ghosts, we look specifically for trapped spirits and we find a way to let them rest."

"So why the cameras and microphones if you don't intend to prove anything?" He nodded toward the camera in the corner of the room.

"Ghosts aren't like a mouse infestation," she told him. "They aren't always present. We're going to try to contact something today, but we'll also leave the cameras in here for a couple of days. If we find a particularly active spot, we'll come back for a second try. We are looking, in this case, for a spirit who sobs brokenly or screams in the middle of the night. And whatever likes to throw sharp things like scissors, kitchen knives, and apparently, once, a hammer."

She continued to educate him about what she and her team did as they strolled through the old, empty house, visiting formal and informal dining rooms, bathrooms, a billiard room and a modern kitchen, a laundry and an old-fashioned butler's pantry. Not much of it was unknown to him. He disliked being ignorant and had spent several days researching ghost hunting, watching several television shows because apparently this was a thriving industry.

But while she told him about this thing she loved to do, her body relaxed, her voice softened, and she forgot to keep him at a distance. And she forgot to be afraid of whatever it was Alan Choo had gone to great effort to save her from.

While she talked of EVP (electronic voice phenomenon), EMF detectors, and other alphabet soup devices, he took in details of the house. He'd always had a fondness for Victorian architecture— it was as excessively gorgeous as he. This particular house was a grand example of its kind. Every room, including the bathrooms, had a transom panel over the top of the door filled with etched amber glass. Plaster walls were worked into patterns covered with bronze leaf. Ceilings were painted or frescoed. Everywhere one looked, there was attention to detail.

"Our team has a ghost box," she was saying, as they started up the narrow servant stairs in the back of the kitchen. "But we don't use it much. We have better luck with dowsing rods and EVP. And all the static hurts Alan's ears."

She looked at him and then away as if mention of Alan reminded her that he was a werewolf.

On the first floor . . . ah, he was in America . . . on the *second* floor, the excesses of the lavish ground floor gave way to common sense. There were two more bathrooms, one modern, one charmingly original with an odd spiral-shaped pipe that created a surround shower with rudimentary shower heads placed more or less at random all over the pipe. A person showering in such a contraption would find themselves uncomfortably deluged by water. It was a ridiculous thing—something he'd never encountered—for all he'd lived through the years when it had been built. Perhaps it had been invented for this house. The thought pleased him.

They returned to the hall and entered the library. The room was well-lit and lined with fumed oak, leaded glass-fronted bookcases. A Persian rug covered the red oak floors nearly wall to wall. A few comfortable-looking chairs provided places for visitors to read.

Ruby took a step into the room and paused. As she did so, Asil's nose was flooded with rose perfume, of a variety he hadn't smelled for years—ambergris perfumes were no longer common. Ruby's face relaxed into a real smile and she reached out to touch something he could not see, though his wolf told him there was something . . . someone there.

"Well, hello, you," Ruby said, her voice darker than it had been. Asil's wolf wanted to roll in that voice. "We aren't here to bother you and we should be out of your way soon."

She glanced at Asil, who nodded. Yes, he knew there was someone here, too.

"Housekeeper, I think," she told him. "She feels like someone who takes care of the house. She might be a maid, but she carries an aura of authority I don't think a low servant would. Miranda and I have met her before."

"Do they speak to you?" he asked.

She shook her head, her attention still mostly on the spirit who was starting to fade—if the perfume scent was anything to judge it by.

"There are people who can speak to them," she said. "Peg can—you'll meet her in a few minutes. But I'm not one of them. I get . . . a feeling. Emotions and stray memories mostly. Psychic impressions. I have a little psychometry, too. Just a touch, but it can be—" She paused. "Gone." She turned her attention to Asil again and the softness he'd seen in her retreated as she completed her last statement. "Psychometry can be useful in some circumstances."

She led the way out to the hall and opened a door to the master suite, which was, as most of the house had been, furnished in period furniture, though, as he recalled that era, the house lacked the authentic overcrowded feel.

Here, all the luxury of the ground floor had been allowed back in. There were etched ruby glass transoms over the doors, these tilted open to allow for better air flow. In the sitting room and bedroom the walls above oak wainscoting were covered in gold-embossed leather. The ceilings were frescoed nature scenes in the sitting room and bathroom. But in the bedroom there were naked nymphs and fawns dancing through the imaginary forests in a most un-Victorian manner.

"That is unusual," observed Asil.

Ruby laughed. "I loved the Victorian period. All very proper in public, but hidden depths where no one could see."

It might have been a crude remark—the Victorian era was famous for the pornography it produced. As if all the sexual repression needed an escape valve. But that was not what was in her face.

She loves the hidden things, his wolf told him.

"Like beautiful mahogany tabletops buried under runners, vases, figurines, and bric-a-brac?" he observed dryly.

She laughed. "All the clutter." She smiled at him—and it was a real smile, mischievous and glorious. It made him understand exactly why Alan Choo, submissive werewolf, had snuck behind his Alpha's back to pull the second most dangerous werewolf in the world to save this woman.

"I don't miss corsets either," she told him.

"I wouldn't think so," he said, his revulsion immediate. He loved the shape of women as Allah had intended—all shapes of women. Strapping them into the distorting cages of the late nineteenth century had been disgusting. But . . . "They weren't so bad when they started out, though—when they enhanced the female form rather than twisting it into something grotesque. I loved the court fashions of the Renaissance—that was an era for glorious clothing. I had this coat . . ." He hummed happily.

Her smile faded and she stared at him, her mouth falling open a little. She cleared her throat and said carefully, in the formal tones of an earlier, more mannerly era, "I'm afraid you have the advantage of me."

"Ah," he said. "With your power, it is difficult for me to tell how old you are. The fae have interbred with humans since long before my birth, but since the Guerra de Brujas—" she looked bewildered so he translated "War of the Witches," which did not seem to help. "Inquisition?" he tried, and that seemed to be something familiar to her. "Since the time of the Spanish Inquisition, the fae banned interbreeding until quite recently." He paused. "Though there is some debate about whether either the Guerra de Brujas or the Inquisition had anything to do with it, or if it was something entirely internal to the fae."

He shrugged. "At any rate, my point is that you are an outlier. I can tell from the feel of your power that you are older than thirty—"

She grimaced apologetically.

"Well," he said, "your profile was better than the pack of lies that my profile is." He was pleased when she laughed.

"And you have too much power to be less than half fae—and that fae could not be one of the goblins or lesser folk who sometimes ignored the edicts of the more powerful fae. Therefore someone like you should have been born no later than the fifteenth century or less than thirty years ago. Maybe forty—I don't keep time in decades much anymore."

She stared blankly at him, as if she didn't understand what he was saying.

"I have never met a half-fae of anywhere near your power born between the fifteenth century and the twentieth century," he clarified. "And I have met a lot of half-fae."

"What," she said slowly, "do you mean about my power? I have a half-assed touch of empathy and an even lesser touch of psychometry. And sometimes I get prophetic dreams that I only remember in bits and pieces—mostly about nothing important." There was a certain grim acceptance on her face. "If I had power I wouldn't have—" She stopped talking. Not because she didn't want to talk to him, he thought.

Because there were no words for how different her life would be if she had power, his wolf growled.

She didn't know.

"I am no magic worker," Asil told her apologetically, spreading his arms to indicate his unworthiness. "But I can tell you are powerful, though trapped behind some dark weaving."

She wrapped her arms around herself—one hand clasping the leather-bracelet-covered wrist. She turned to look through the window at the sheets of water pouring from the skies. Her breath was a little shaky and Asil could not tell what her reaction was because the scent of acrid foreign magic filled his nose.

Not her magic, the wolf said, agreeing.

With that in mind, Asil gathered power. It was true he could not work spells, but this was werewolf magic, a hunter's beguilement—there was no finer hunter in the world than he.

"Who bound your gifts?" he asked her.

>→←<

She'd kept Alan's warning in the back of her head, but Moreno just didn't feel dangerous. He asked good questions, laughed when she wanted him to laugh—and made her forget that oddness at first where he seemed to be challenging her—maybe flirting with her. He meant her to be at her ease—and he put her there.

It only just this moment occurred to her that his ability to do that might be part of his danger.

And then he . . . he lied to her? She knew she had no power. *Knew* it.

Her wrist had been burning but it eased enough that she could rub it. Asil's question wrapped around her somehow, but she couldn't quite remember what he'd asked.

"It doesn't matter," she said . . . she lied—though she hadn't meant it to be a lie. She rocked a little on her feet, like a child waiting to be called in for punishment.

Asil watched her, his brown and gold eyes mesmerizing. Her wrist still hurt, but she was able to stop swaying.

"There are people in this city who are good with magic," he suggested, and she had the feeling he was being careful. "Angus uses a witch named Moira, I believe."

Her throat tightened and the tattoo around her wrist flared. "I can't do that," she whispered in a voice she hardly recognized as her own. "I have to stay away from powerful creatures. They will hurt me."

"Yes," Asil agreed, and for some reason that agreement made the pressure that had shrouded her head, without her noticing, ease just a little. His voice was very soft when he asked, "Why did you agree to meet with me today? Alan knows what I am."

She blinked at him. "But you're a werewolf. You aren't an Alpha."

His eyes narrowed—briefly displeased, she thought. But then he tilted his head. "Who have you been told not to approach? What geas was put upon you, Ruby Kowalczyk?"

There was a thread of enchantment in his voice—not like that shove of power on the porch. This was an invitation, a rope thrown over a steep embankment, something to grab as she overcame an imposed inability to discuss certain things.

She clung to his gold-washed eyes for the resolution she needed to give him her list. "I need to stay away from powerful magic users who are witches, vampires, fae, and werewolf Alphas," she told him. It was a safer thing to talk about. Sometimes she woke up whispering that list to herself.

"I see," he said, as if he did. "I imagine you want to talk about something else."

"Oh yes," she agreed wholeheartedly, feeling a rush of relief. "Please."

"Were we going to meet your team?" he asked.

She blinked at him, having lost track of their conversation somewhere. "I'm sorry," she said, not quite sure why she was apologizing.

"There is nothing to be sorry for, surely," he murmured.

His eyes were very dark, and they seemed to hold safety in their depths.

And she wasn't supposed to stare into his eyes—he was a dominant werewolf and they viewed such things as a challenge. She dropped his gaze and swallowed. "Uhm. The team. Right."

The ornate staircase was less ornate as it rose from the second to the third floor, where servant rooms had been remodeled into a kitchenette and two bathrooms marked with "Ladies" and "Gentlemen" signs. Most of the floor was a grand ballroom. The family had been renting it out for events for years.

Her team was gathered here.

Alan looked up and waved from the floor before turning his attention back to untangling The Beast, a carrying bag with eight one-hundred-foot electrical cords that liked to turn into one large Cthulhu-like monster. That they hadn't even managed to get the cords untangled meant they were experiencing technical difficulties.

The others were huddled around the newest of their cameras, its innards spread out across one of the folding tables. They'd bought it used, and when it decided to run, it took really terrific video. But it was huge and cranky. Miranda was the only one who didn't have trouble with it, but she was working today.

"Hey," Ruby called, and they all looked up, their faces reflecting various states of frustration, except for Becky's. Becky never got ruffled. "Everyone, this is Asil, my date today. Asil, the grumpy old guy in the Seahawks shirt is Terry."

Terry held out a hand and Asil shook it, smiling. "Good to meet you," Asil murmured. "Sorry to interrupt."

Terry grunted. "Glad to meet you, too. 'Bout time Ruby caught some luck. Probably good to have an interruption before someone tossed that old thing into the nearest wall."

"And Max," said Ruby.

Max had huffed a laugh at Terry's words and held out a hand. "Good to meet you."

Asil shook his hand, too. Ruby watched Max's face—sometimes Max caught things when he touched people. But nothing but casual pleasure showed on his face. At least he hadn't run screaming, which he'd done on one memorable occasion. They never did figure out what was wrong with that guy, but they hadn't let him join their team either.

"And last but not least, our computer guru, Peg."

Peg did not reach out to shake hands. She didn't touch people unless she had to. In her case it wasn't any psychic sensitivities but shyness. Asil won points by giving her a simple bow that smoothed over any awkwardness caused by her mumbled welcome.

"It is my pleasure," he said, and it felt as if it might be the truth.

Ruby took a step toward the camera—not that she knew as much as Peg or Terry—but the compulsion to try to fix something other people were struggling with was an inborn condition she was afflicted with as much as anyone else.

"Aren't you going to introduce him?" Asil asked in tones of mild puzzlement, his eyes focused just beyond Peg.

Peg said with sudden animation, "That's my twin brother, Dusty. Most people can't see him."

Ruby was the only one of the team besides Peg who caught more than occasional glimpses of Dusty, who'd died in a car accident when he and Peg had been thirteen. In fact just now, Ruby couldn't see him herself. When she and a couple of friends had started ghost hunting, Peg had been their first client. Asil gave Dusty the same shallow bow he'd given Peg. "Pleased to meet you, too, Dusty," he said.

A notebook fell off the table where it had been sitting next to the dissected camera. Peg giggled as though she were still thirteen instead of fiftysomething. Sometimes Ruby's teammates were the creepiest thing they ran into during ghost hunting.

Terry cleared his throat. "So?" he asked with a raised eyebrow.

Ruby shook her head. "He hasn't asked."

Alan gave a soft laugh. "Pay up."

Max collected from everyone—Ruby included—and Alan was four bucks richer.

"Dare I ask?"

Ruby looked at Asil. "Everyone asks why we're here hunting ghosts in the daylight."

"Daylight doesn't affect ghosts," said Asil, sounding taken aback. "The dark just makes it easier to scare people."

"And trip downstairs," agreed Max heartily as Alan folded the bills he'd collected with great ceremony and put them in his wallet.

"Ah," said Asil. "That sounds painful indeed."

And over the next half hour Ruby watched from the sidelines as her Internet date charmed his way effortlessly into her team's good graces. Even Peg—who generally had no liking for any member of the opposite sex—opened up to him shyly as they bonded over a dislike of Max's favorite coffee brand.

He was gentle with her friends—and she finally admitted she was glad Miranda had talked her into this date. But there was no way she would ever let this sweet and beautiful man meet her nemesis.

She shivered and worried at the steady burn on her wrist.

>─><─<

Asil could have been of help fixing the camera—modern gadgetry was one of his many talents—but his prey was not the ghosts who lived in this house.

He gave half a thought to his still-damp pants, which would doubtless pick up every speck of dirt on the ballroom floor. Ah, well. He sat down beside Alan and started with a plug and began to work backward in the tangle, moving as quickly and efficiently as he could without tearing the cord in half. Apparently they all needed to be separated and then strung throughout the house—and Asil had decided that was how he was going to get Alan alone.

"There are better ways to store extension cords," Asil observed to Alan in the nonthreatening voice he'd been using since he'd entered the ballroom.

"Dusty likes to tangle them," Alan explained. "Or so I'm told. I've actually never seen him—caught a whiff now and then. But my wife says he tangles the cords, so I believe he tangles the cords."

"And thus you stay married," murmured Asil.

He knew his voice was light and his body language was neutral, but Alan angled his head to expose his throat without even being aware he was doing it.

Watching the geas work on Ruby and getting an inkling of how she'd been living since she'd . . . escaped? The situation had that feel—of an interrupted hunt with wounded prey. Then meeting Ruby's team—her collection of broken people—had just about been the cherry on top of his gathering rage. And Alan had sensed the edge of Asil's anger.

It was a good thing Asil's wolf had decided to revert to the partner he'd not been for the last few hundred years. If he were still dealing with the rabid fiend, even his amazing control might be strained.

Ruby had gathered together a band of misfits and given them a mission, an odd mission of rescuing miserable spirits. Still, no one who spoke to any of them for longer than half a minute could doubt their dedication. Caring for others, even if those others were dead, when they could hardly care for themselves—it touched Asil's heart.

Peg was a white witch who used up all of her meager power feeding the shadow of her brother. Terry was a white witch too, and he had less than half the power of even Peg. Normally he did not like witches, but not even his wolf could find anything threatening about those two. Max had some sort of lesser fae somewhere in the family tree. With Ruby's power straightjacketed, the lot of them had about enough magic to light a witch lantern.

Allah in His infinite wisdom knew that a little magic was so much worse than no magic. There were dozens of types of creatures out hunting for victims with just a little magic.

He no longer wondered why Alan had been the one waiting for him on the porch with Ruby. In this group, the submissive werewolf had been the most powerful guardian they owned. Without Alan, this lot were bait looking for a big bad shark to eat them.

"You are going to help," said Alan, very softly. If Asil had not been sitting next to him, he would not have heard him.

"I am," Asil said. He had two of the cords untangled—and reached for the next to see that the rest of them lay in neat bundles. He stilled for a moment, unhappy to have had such a thing happen without his notice.

He looked into the face of the shadowy boy and said, "Thank you."

You are going to help, the boy said, though his still mouth never moved.

To that spirit, Asil said, "Inshallah."

"And that's not weird," muttered Alan, staring at the tidy cords.

Asil stood up and gathered cords. "Come, my friend. You and I can lay these while the others work on that poor camera, no?"

For all that it was gently said, Alan heard the demand in it. He nodded, grabbed the two cords Asil had not, and followed him out of the door and down the stairs.

"I don't actually know where these cords go," Alan said.

"It does not matter," Asil said. They were far enough away from the ballroom that their voices would not carry if they were quiet. "We need to talk and this is an excuse. You need to tell me what Ruby's troubles are."

"No." Alan stumbled—not from clumsiness; he was not clumsy. He was a werewolf. But he was torn between loyalty to Ruby and the demands of a dominant wolf. The power gap was so large between a submissive wolf and Asil that Alan's resistance was impressive.

His refusal could not last, but Asil decided to wait until they were off the stairway before he forced the issue. If Alan fell all the way down the stairs he'd make enough noise to summon the others. He would try persuasion first.

"I can help," Asil assured him instead, knowing Alan would hear the truth in his words. "I understand you wish your Ruby—"

Our Ruby, growled his wolf. And it was far too soon for that.

"—would tell me everything herself," he told Alan as they came to the ground floor. For lack of another goal, he continued into the reception room and dropped the cords to the ground. "But I do not think we are going to have so much time."

Alan shook his head, hunching his shoulders as he dropped his cords onto the ground on top of Asil's. "It isn't my place—"

Asil could make him—they both knew it.

"You must," Asil said, his voice gentle.

But he backed off again because the pressure he was putting on the submissive wolf was bothering his own wolf—submissives were to be cared for.

He said, "There are few others in history who have been as strong, as capable as I."

It was not his habit to affect false modesty. That others were unused to meeting someone of his abilities—of his beauty—was not his problem. That did not mean he didn't understand how his statements of truth affected people.

He expected to amuse Alan, to soften the atmosphere so they could better converse.

"I know," said Alan.

Pleased, Asil continued, "It is my place to protect the innocent because they cannot protect themselves." He tipped Alan's face up to meet Asil's eyes, knowing that his wolf peered out, too. It was not a threat—and it was something he had not dared do since before this city was built on a swamp—to allow his wolf such freedom. "That is your job, too. Protect your people, Alan Choo. Tell me what you know."

Alan's lips parted—and closed again as they both heard Ruby running down the stairs.

>—<

Ruby held a wire for Max and privately came to the conclusion that by the time they were through fixing the camera, not even Miranda would be able to get it to work again. Something tugged at her shirt.

She looked over her shoulder to see Dusty, his face expressionless as always, pointing to where Alan and Asil had just been.

He is questioning our wolf. Though Dusty's face was several feet from her, his voice whispered directly into her ear and let puffs of air brush past her cheek. From long practice she didn't jump. Dusty was harmless. Mostly.

She let the wire go and ignored Max's indignant exclamation. "Peg," she said. "Take over here. Terry, don't let Max kill Peg or vice versa. I have to go hunt down my date."

She thought Dusty might come with her—he tended to follow drama—but she was alone as she ran down the stairs. Charming and sweet he might be, but Asil was more dominant—and in her limited experience, dominant wolves didn't even know when they were being overbearing.

She heard Asil say, his voice warm and soft, "Tell me what you know."

Ruby found them in the reception room and took in the body language with something approaching fury. "Are you bullying Alan?" she asked—though it wasn't a question.

"No." To her surprise, when Alan turned to her there was a smile on his face. His smile widened and his voice was peaceful when he approached her. He kissed her cheek. "No, he isn't. You need to tell him about your problem. He's promised to help. I'm going upstairs to keep everyone in the ballroom until you're finished."

And he left her alone with her date.

Asil raised an eyebrow at her. "What do you have to lose?" he said. "Whoever has you bound is coming, no?"

"I can run," she told him.

His liquid eyes grew sad. "No, *querida mía*. You are tired of running. This is why you have summoned me."

She stared at him, feeling tears gathering in her eyes, and she did not know why, except she wanted—oh, how she wanted to give him her trouble. And it had nothing to do with him—and everything to do with the burning sensation radiating from her tattoo.

"He is nearly here," she told him, whispering it. "He isn't supposed to come yet."

"Tell me," he said, his eyes the color of Medici gold—old, violent, and compelling. His voice was rich with invitation, coaxing her to trust him.

"He told me he was my father," she said, her voice and body stiff. She didn't know why she started there when the story could be boiled down to the few sentences she'd told Miranda. She looked away from Asil's exquisite face because there was no beauty in this story. "I don't know. I don't think he is. But I don't remember anyone else. All I remember of being a child is him—and being sick all of the time."

Impulsively she struggled with the laces on her wrist covering, but they wouldn't cooperate with her tear-blinded eyes and the shaking clumsiness of her fingers. Asil's graceful, well-kept hands closed over hers, stilling them. Then he made a single, elegant gesture and the leather separated and fell away from her wrist, revealing the ugly black lines of symbols on her skin.

"He did this after the first time I ran away. I was still a child." She tapped one of the dark lines. "This is his blood. He told me I could never escape him with these. Then he quit locking the door." She didn't want Asil to think her weak—though of course she was. "I tried removing the skin—but the marks go all the way to the bone." She paused. "I could cut the whole thing off." She had thought about it more than once.

Except for when he'd broken her wristband, Asil had not released her hands, though his grip was soft and she knew she could pull away if she wanted to. But somehow, she had the feeling that as long as he touched her, nothing could harm her.

"A possibility," he murmured, but there was a velvet growl in his tone. "But not a good one. No need to be hasty just yet. What does he want from you, Ruby? Why does he bind your magic and try to keep you close?"

But that wasn't the question she wanted to answer. "Do you think I haven't had people who tried to help me before?" She turned away, pulling her hands free and rubbing at her eyes. "Good people who were hurt—killed—because of me."

He didn't ask why, if she was reluctant to put anyone else in harm's way, she had agreed to arranging this date. She answered him anyway.

"If it weren't for Miranda, I'd never have agreed to asking you to come," she said. "You'd have to meet her. She's about four and a half feet tall with a temper like a wet cat. When she's really mad, she screams at you in Mandarin." Ruby heaved a sigh. "And she's six months pregnant with a baby who isn't sure he wants to hang in for the finish. I didn't want to upset her."

He was so quiet that she wondered if he was still there. She turned around finally to see him standing patiently, exactly where he had been when she pulled free.

"I was supposed to beguile you with my wiles," she told him. "So that you would want to help me. Then I would do magic, any magic, and he would come. Hopefully while you were still here and willing to fight for me." She swallowed. "It was not fair. I wasn't going to let it happen." She wanted him to know that. "He wasn't supposed to come unless I did magic. A lot of it."

"Inshallah," said Asil with a graceful shrug. He didn't look at all upset. "Who is he?"

She bowed her head. "A monster," she told the werewolf, and was rewarded with a smile that displayed very white teeth. And she gave in. "I don't know what he is, other than fae." She paused, and then whispered, "He feeds from me."

Asil tilted his head so she knew he was listening. He didn't say anything—probably because he judged she was more likely to tell him more that way.

"He lets me escape sometimes," she told him, knowing that it was true. "I think it's because if he didn't, I would have died a long time ago. It is hard to live without hope." And didn't that sound pathetic and helpless. She grimaced at herself.

"Fed how? Like a vampire?" he asked.

She shook her head. "It isn't . . . isn't usually physical—though he does that sometimes, too. Drinks my blood, eats my flesh."

The lines around her wrist suddenly lit from within, as if they had been inked with blue neon instead of blood. Her world stopped.

Did she really hear the creak of wood? Or did her imagination supply the sound of his feet on the front porch?

"He is here," she told Asil.

She'd locked the main door of the house, but it didn't surprise her when she heard the door open and shut. She couldn't move, couldn't look around. She heard and felt him walk into the reception room. Her eyes held Asil's as hands closed over her shoulders.

"Ruby, my Ruby," her captor said. She'd always thought his voice beautiful, but compared to Asil's, it was thin and a little harsh. "I named her so because her price is above rubies," he said conversationally. "Ruby, don't be rude. Introduce me to your werewolf friend. Is this Alan?"

>—✕—<

Wendigo, said Asil's wolf. *Wechuge. Jikininki. Preta. A hungry ghost.*

None of those terms was precisely correct, Asil thought, but they weren't wrong either.

The one who held Ruby was taller than Asil, but not a big man. His face was chiseled and masculine—and looked to Asil's cynical eye as if he'd tried a little too hard to resemble an old-time movie star. There was a little too much Cary Grant in his jaw and Montgomery Clift in the mouth. He wasn't as beautiful as Asil, even while using magic.

But Asil was old and he didn't need any fairy ointment or special magic to see through a fae glamour to the real creature beneath.

Addictions were terrible things, and immortal creatures were not immune. Ruby's enemy had once been some kind of goblin, Asil thought, or maybe another lesser fae type. He could not be sure because there was not much of the original creature left.

Some of the greater fae could feed upon others with no harm done to themselves—and perhaps if this one had stuck to feeding upon those lesser than he, he would have been safe. But though Ruby had been young and vulnerable when this creature had found her (because there were no blood ties between them), her power was far greater than his.

And it had eaten away at him until there was not much of the original fae left. As soon as the creature had touched Ruby's skin, he had begun to feed, filling himself with Ruby's magic to fill the gaps his feeding had caused. There were other bits of foreign power that clung to the fae's inner being—but Asil could sense the deeper, older scraps of Ruby's power.

Asil was pretty sure he could kill the fae—as long as he did it before the creature absorbed very much of Ruby's magic, though fae could be terrible foes.

But.

He flexed his hands lightly and consulted his wolf. This morning at Angus's house, where he had so nearly lost control, so nearly slayed Angus's second, he would never have considered this path. But in Ruby's presence, his wolf had been healed, and with an able partner . . .

Yes, agreed the wolf.

"He's not Alan," said Ruby, answering her captor's question, her voice taut, her eyes wild—though she did not struggle against the hold the fae had on her. "It doesn't matter who he is. I will go with you if you leave him—leave them be."

She was trying to protect him. His wolf all but purred—though he liked the idea of the fae touching Ruby no better than Asil did.

"No, I'm not Alan," said Asil in pleasant tones that would have sent anyone who knew him running for cover. "You may call me Mr. Moreno."

His last name was not well known because he had used it for less than a century. His prey would not know he was the Moor— would not fear him properly.

Montgomery Clift's famous lips smiled. "You may call me Mr. Smith, then."

>—><—<

"His name is Ivory Jim," Ruby told Asil, and winced as the fae clamped his fingers down with punishing strength.

She didn't know why she'd bothered correcting him. Asil was neither fae nor a magic user who might be able to use a true name to lend more power to his spells. Maybe it was because Ivory Jim was here—and saying or thinking his name would not call his attention to her more than it already was.

"Ivory Jim," purred Asil, smiling with white teeth. "I am so happy to meet you."

And then he moved.

Everything happened so fast she never could remember exactly what Asil did. She wasn't sure she even caught anything with her eyes—it was like living through a stop-motion scene. One instant she was trapped beneath Ivory Jim's hands. She heard a great booming sound. Then she was free, still in the entryway of the reception room, but facing the opposite direction she had been, as if she had simply turned around, though she had done nothing of the sort. In front of her was the entry hall, large enough to hold several dozen guests at once, but now holding only Asil and Ivory Jim.

Ivory Jim was scrambling to his feet, having apparently been flung into the sturdy front door—possibly the source of the sound she had heard. Asil waited for him, his back to the doorway of the formal dining room. His eyes shone bright gold in the complex light of the stained-glass windows—for that moment, the uncanny beauty of his face looked almost savage.

"Watch out, Asil," called Alan from the stairs, where all of her people gathered on the landing halfway between the second floor and the first. "Magic attack."

And at Alan's warning, she realized why Asil's pose worried her. His only chance was to keep this physical—and he had given Ivory Jim time to gather magic. Asil covered his eyes before the invisible blow struck him—and then the magic became visible as his body jerked taut. For the length of a lightning strike, Asil glowed with a brilliant blue light.

She could smell burnt flesh and ozone as Asil's body dropped to the ground—a smoking, blackened heap that still, unbelievably, moved. With a crunch of skin or fabric, Asil lifted his head and looked toward the stairway.

"Alan Choo," he said out of a mouth that was blistered and bleeding, his voice a rough sandpaper roar, "keep those people back and safe."

Ruby looked at the stairs, too. Asil's words had caught Alan as he leaped off the landing. The impact of the command looked almost as if Alan'd been hit in midair by a baseball bat. He was already spinning around as his feet hit the ground and he rebounded back up to the landing like a gymnast on a springboard.

The distraction gave Ivory Jim time to hit Asil with a second blast. Her nemesis strode forward, a smile growing on his face as he closed in on Asil. Ruby caught a flicker of movement—and then Dusty threw himself at Ivory Jim's feet. The fae stumbled, his magic faltering and dying with the distraction. Dusty disappeared from the floor and his cold presence resonated from just behind Ruby—as if he'd taken refuge.

Ivory Jim snarled and reached one hand out toward Ruby—and she felt the razor-pain as he stole her magic wholesale. Stole it to kill Asil. The beautiful man whom she had helped lure here—because he helped those weaker than himself.

She stared at Asil's scorched body—naked now with clothing burned away and blistered skin still bubbling in reaction to the last strike of magic. Impossibly, his eyes opened and met hers. She was sure there was some message in them, but she could not read it.

Ivory Jim had come again. Had captured her again. He was going to use her magic to kill a man who had done nothing except offer to help her.

She would not, could not let that happen.

>><<

Asil prepared to defend himself. He would give Ruby one more strike—and then he would do what he had to do. But as he met her eyes, he saw his intervention might not be necessary.

It began in the pupil of her eye. The black expanded and then reshaped itself until it was slitted like a cat's eye. Then the ice blue of her iris darkened to deep velvet gray. The color did not stop there, rolling over her skin and hair and clothing as if an ocean wave had drenched her with gray rather than water—though he could smell water in the room now, as if his thoughts had brought it to life.

There was a *whoomp* in the room, the sound of her magic freeing itself from its bindings. It made his chest tight as if a heavy weather system had just made itself felt in the room—like a forming tornado.

Asil, not one to forget his enemy, glanced at Ivory Jim. A flicker caught his eye—and thirteen steel knives apparated in front of the fae before flashing into motion and burying themselves in the fae's body. Blood burst from the wounds as Ivory Jim looked down at himself in surprise. Stainless steel was as fatal to the fae as cold iron, and the fae's knees buckled.

Asil moved, rolling off the floor, crossing the room and grabbing the dying fae without wasting any effort on gentleness. He tossed the body onto a carpet—one he was fairly sure was a reproduction of an antique.

The floor in the entryway was parquet—if blood spilled on the wood, it might ruin it. The craftsmanship of the people who'd fitted that floor made it as much a piece of art as anything in the Victorian mansion, and he would not let it be damaged if he could help it.

Asil's burnt skin cracked as he moved, but he was not concerned. He was powerful, he had been hurt worse before—he would heal. He looked at the floor—there were a few drops of blood, but not so much it would soak into the wood through the finish.

"Asil!" Alan's voice cracked a sharp warning.

Asil caught the knife out of the air before it could strike him and looked to Ruby.

She stood where he had left her, in the wide doorless entry of the reception room. Her brilliant eyes were black with power and her hair moved as if she stood in a wind. Dusty curled around her left leg. They weren't the same color—Dusty's skin was a few shades darker and a hair less blue.

Her power didn't smell of death and the dying; he rather thought it had more to do with water of some kind. But she'd spent a long time with the dead and she knew how to communicate with them. It made sense that she had instinctively called upon them for aid.

Asil had dealt with a few poltergeists in his time, though they hadn't been so named. There was a limit to the harm such a spirit could do at any given time—Asil had been attacked with one knife, not a baker's dozen like the fae who was even now breathing his last.

Alert to it, Asil could feel the amassing of power—so much less than what surrounded Ruby—but it still made the room smell of ozone. He thought it would take a few seconds—maybe a minute—before the creature could manifest another weapon.

Asil strode across the floor to Ruby, put his hands on her icy cheeks, and kissed her.

There were other things he could have done to pull her back to herself. He could have shouted her name with his power to back it—the same way he'd driven Alan back to protect Ruby's people. But he wanted to kiss her.

It was a chaste kiss, a brush of lips, no more. She was in no condition to give consent. But the contact allowed him to wrap her in his power, in the warmth of his wolf, to make her feel safe.

"Asil?" she said, blinking at him with eyes that were once again blue, almost human.

He stepped back—and slapped aside a flying pair of knitting needles with the knife he still held.

"Stop it," she said. He wasn't sure it had quite dawned on her yet that the poltergeist—and Dusty—were acting on her behalf. But her words were nonetheless effective.

The vase that had been flying toward him dropped like a stone. He caught it before it hit the ground and moved away from her to set the vase on the mantel. After a moment's thought, he set the knife beside it. He didn't think the poltergeist would throw it at him again. He left the knitting needles on the floor where they had fallen.

Ruby stared at Asil, breathing hard, glorious in her power. If he had been more presentable, he'd have preened a bit under her gaze. But he wouldn't be beautiful again until he sloughed off the burnt bits.

"You did that on purpose," she said, her voice hoarse.

He smiled at her. "Of course. It is a lovely vase. There was no sense in letting it break."

She shook her head. "You could have killed him in the first attack, couldn't you? You moved so fast."

"My mission was not to kill him," he told her peacefully.

Ours, said his wolf. *Our mission. Our Ruby. She makes us whole.*

"You offered to help me," she said.

The ache of the burns was fading already.

"I did," he agreed.

"If you had killed him it would have freed me—and you wouldn't have been hurt."

"I offered to help you," he said again. "I didn't offer to kill the monster for you. Though I would have, of course, had it been necessary."

"Thank you," she told him—and he could see from her expression she was a little shell-shocked. Understandable, he thought. A lot had happened in a very short period of time—much of it would change her life forever.

Us, said his wolf joyfully. *We will change her life.*

Alan quit stopping them, so Ruby's people trampled down the stairs. Asil stepped back so they had room to surround her. They needed to be sure she was safe too.

"I will leave you now," he told her. "The threat is gone and you need time to process what it means to your life." Asil looked at Alan. "You should stay with them. I will dispose of the body." Angus had acreage in the mountains for more than one reason.

Alan gave him a nod of thanks.

Asil rolled the dead fae in the carpet—noting that he'd been right about it being a reproduction. Using a carpet to carry a body was a cliché, and he didn't enjoy resorting to clichés. But carpets were useful in soaking up blood as well as masking the body, though this one was not big enough to swallow the fae whole—Ivory Jim's polished dress shoes hung out of one end of the roll.

But Asil's scorched and naked body was going to need disguising every bit as much as the dead creature he carried away with him. He began the look-away magic—it was a little reluctant to come to his call until Alan joined in the casting. The submissive wolf had a fine touch with magic. Maybe it was because his wife was a witch.

Outside, the rain soothed Asil's burns as it washed away soot and the last vestige of Ivory Jim's magic. Alan accompanied Asil to his car and opened the hatch for him.

Body safely stored, Asil faced Ruby, who had trailed out after them. The rain fell slower against her than it should have, clinging to her cheeks and neck in heavy droplets as if it loved the touch of her skin, too.

"I owe you dinner," she said, her voice ragged. "Not tonight. I couldn't . . . not tonight."

He smiled, took her hand in one of his, and kissed it. "Not tonight," he agreed. "But if you are willing, I would love a second date."

Ours, said his wolf fiercely.

Patience, he counseled.

She stepped closer to him and leaned forward and kissed him. An exact match to the kiss he'd given her—except for the cool rush of her power flowing over him like a waterfall in the rain, mending the few burns which were not mended already.

On the porch he heard Peg giggle. "Naked. He's naked out there and she's kissing him."

He did not mind being naked. He liked clothing, but he was beautiful when he was naked as well, especially since the blisters were no longer distorting his features.

Ruby pulled back, raised her chin, and said, "What are you doing on Saturday?"

><—<

To Asil@marrok.com

Congratulations! One more date to go!

———

To ConcernedFriends@marrok.com

No.

ABOUT THE AUTHORS AND EDITORS

Kelley Armstrong is the author of the Rockton thriller series and the Royal Guide to Monster Slaying middle-grade fantasy series. Past works include the Otherworld urban fantasy series, the Cainsville gothic mystery series, the Nadia Stafford thriller trilogy, the Darkest Powers & Darkness Rising teen paranormal series, and the Age of Legends teen fantasy series. The story in this volume is from Darkest Powers, about teen necromancer Chloe Saunders.

Annie Bellet is the *USA Today* bestselling author of the Twenty-Sided Sorceress, Six-Gun Shifters, and the Gryphonpike Chronicles series. An Alfie Award winner and former Hugo Finalist, she holds a BA in English and a BA in medieval studies and thus can speak a smattering of useful languages such as Anglo-Saxon and medieval Welsh. Her interests include rock climbing, reading, horseback riding, video games, comic books, tabletop RPGs, and many other nerdy pursuits. She lives in the Netherlands with her husband.

Anne Bishop lives with unicorns, dragons, and two shy parakeets. She is a *New York Times* bestselling author and the winner of multiple awards, including the RT Book Reviews 2013 Career Achievement Award for her fantasy fiction, the RT Book Reviews 2017 Career Achievement Award for her urban fantasy fiction, and the William L. Crawford Memorial Fantasy Award for the Black Jewels Trilogy. Her most recent novel is *Crowbones*, a cozy thriller set in the world of the Others. When she's not writing, Anne enjoys gardening, reading, and music . . . and pondering how to get her imaginary friends into more trouble.

Patricia Briggs is the #1 *New York Times* bestselling author of the Mercy Thompson series and the Alpha and Omega series. She lives in the dry part of Washington state with her family and a small herd of horses.

Jennifer Brozek is an award-winning author, editor, and tie-in writer. *A Secret Guide to Fighting Elder Gods*, *Never Let Me Sleep*, and *The Last Days of Salton Academy* were finalists for the Bram Stoker Award. She was awarded the Scribe Award for best tie-in Young Adult novel for *BattleTech: The Nellus Academy Incident*. Her editing work has earned her nominations for the British Fantasy Award, the Bram Stoker Award, and the Hugo Award. "The Necessity of Pragmatic Magic" is Jennifer's first return to Kendrick since *The Karen Wilson Chronicles*. Visit Jennifer's worlds at jenniferbrozek.com.

Jim Butcher is the author of the Dresden Files, the Codex Alera, and a steampunk series, the Cinder Spires. His résumé includes a laundry list of skills that were useful a couple of centuries ago, and he plays guitar quite badly. An avid gamer, he plays tabletop games in varying systems, a variety of video games on PC and console, and LARPs whenever he can make time for it. Jim currently resides mostly inside his own head, but his head can generally be found in the Rocky Mountains of Colorado.

Charlaine Harris is a true daughter of the South. Born in Mississippi, she has lived in Tennessee, South Carolina, Arkansas, and Texas. Her career as a novelist began in 1981 with her first book, a conventional mystery. Since then, she's written urban fantasy, science fiction, and horror. In addition to over thirty full-length books, she has written numerous short stories and three graphic novels in collaboration with Christopher Golden. She has featured on bestseller lists many times, and her works have been adapted for three (soon to be five) television shows. Charlaine now lives at the top of a cliff on the Brazos River with her husband and two rescue dogs. She has three children and two grandchildren.

Kevin Hearne is the *New York Times* bestselling author of the Iron Druid Chronicles, Ink & Sigil, and the Seven Kennings trilogy, and co-author of the Tales of Pell with Delilah S. Dawson. He likes dogs, fountain pens, and tacos, and will occasionally pretend to know something about hockey.

Nancy Holder is a *New York Times* award-winning author of over ninety novels and two hundred short stories, essays, and articles. She is the writer on Mary Shelley Presents, a comic book/graphic novel series from Kymera Press, an all-woman-owned-and-staffed comic book company. *Mary Shelley Presents: Tales of the Supernatural* has been nominated for Superior Achievement in a Graphic Novel by the Horror Writers Association. She is a Baker Street Irregular ("Beryl Garcia"). Her most recent publication is *Sherlock Holmes of Baking Street* (not a cookbook!), co-edited with Margie

Deck. Find her @nancyholder on Twitter, on Facebook, and at nancyholder.com.

Kerrie L. Hughes is a paranormal girl in a way too normal world. She's primarily known as an anthologist and short story writer but has recently ventured into novels. Cauldron: Tales from the Great Lakes Grimoire is her first series, featuring witches, wizards, shifters, dragons, spirits, and of course, the Fae. In her spare time she researches art, history, and psychology. She has been known to cast spells, read fortunes, and meet ghosts. She may even know a vampire or two.

Chloe Neill is the *New York Times* and *USA Today* bestselling author of the Captain Kit Brightling, Heirs of Chicagoland, Chicagoland Vampires, Devil's Isle, and Dark Elite novels. She was born and raised in the South but now makes her home in the Midwest, where she lives with her gamer husband and their bosses/dogs, Baxter and Scout. Chloe is a voracious reader and obsessive Maker of Things; the crafting rotation currently involves baking and quilting. She believes she is exceedingly witty; her husband has been known to disagree.

R.R. Virdi is a two-time Dragon Award finalist and a Nebula Award finalist. He is the author of two urban fantasy series, the Grave Report and the Books of Winter. He has worked in the automotive industry as a mechanic and holds a deep love for American classics. As of August 2021, one of his short stories will be taken to the moon on the Peregrine Lunar Lander. The hardest challenge for him up to this point has been fooling most of society into believing he's a completely sane member of the general public. He currently resides in Northern Virginia, where he wanders local hills in the dead of night while issuing challenges to fistfight the moon.

Ready to find
your next great read?

Let us help.

Visit prh.com/nextread

Penguin
Random
House